Praise for *Doesn't She Look Natural?*

. . a lighthearted read that is simply to die for."

—Sandra Byrd, author of *Let Them Eat Cake* and other novels

Doesn't She Look Natural? proves the point that Angela Hunt is one of ıe most versatile authors writing today. . . . I loved this book."

—BJ Hoff, author of the Mountain Song Legacy series, the American Anthem series, and the Emerald Ballad series

Not only did this story entertain and pull me into the lives of a mily in the midst of a huge season of testing and trial—it also ıallenged me spiritually and twisted my heart."

—Novel Reviews

. . a top-notch inspirational plot that maintains a lighthearted touch."

—*Library Journal*

ngela writes with humor, tenderness, and creates such emotional nsion that I had to remind myself to take a breath! I can't wait to see ıere Angela takes her Fairlawn series—*Doesn't She Look Natural?* is ghly recommended."

—CBD reader

oesn't She Look Natural? is an entertaining and thoughtful read and romising beginning to a new series."

—Faithful Reader

She's in a Better Place

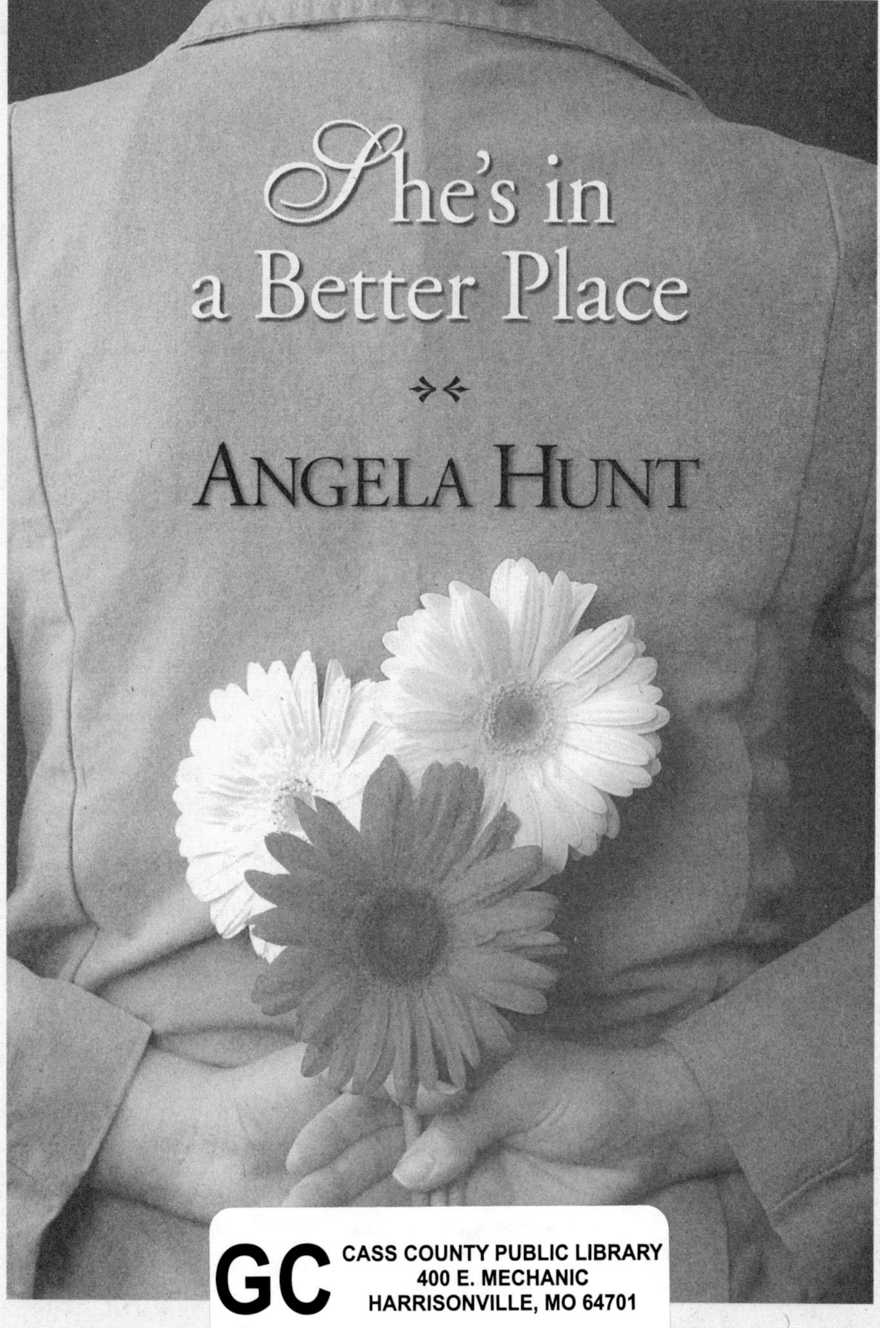

She's in a Better Place

Angela Hunt

TYNDALE HOUSE PUBLISHERS, INC.
CAROL STREAM, ILLINOIS

Visit Tyndale's exciting Web site at www.tyndale.com

Visit Angela Hunt's Web site at www.angelahuntbooks.com

TYNDALE and Tyndale's quill logo are registered trademarks of Tyndale House Publishers, Inc.

She's in a Better Place

Designed by Beth Sparkman

Library of Congress Cataloging-in-Publication Data

Hunt, Angela Elwell, date.
She's in a better place / Angela Hunt.
p. cm. — (Fairlawn series ; # 3)
The third book of the Fairlawn series.
ISBN-13: 978-1-4143-1171-5 (pbk. : alk. paper)
ISBN-10: 1-4143-1171-0 (pbk. : alk. paper)
1. Graham, Jennifer (Fictitious character)—Fiction. 2. Divorced mothers—Fiction.
3. Mentoring—Fiction. 4. Terminally ill—Fiction. 5. Funeral homes—Fiction. I. Title.
PS3558.U46747S54 2008
813′.54—dc22 2008028169

Printed in the United States of America

15 14 13 12 11 10 09
7 6 5 4 3 2 1

Life is pleasant. Death is peaceful.
It's the transition that's troublesome.

—Isaac Asimov

Corpses should be better behaved.

Mr. Lyle Kourtis, aged ninety-three years, has been resting on my embalming table for less than an hour, but he's already belched four times. I wouldn't mind so much—the dead do burp and even shift occasionally—but the hour is late, darkness is pressing at the windows, and I'm alone in the chilly prep room.

Gerald had run to the drugstore for cotton balls, so I've been left to bathe Mr. Kourtis. The job won't be difficult—the old man is as thin as a bird, and rigor is not so pronounced that he's resisting my efforts. The arterial embalming is well under way, the Porti-Boy rhythmically clicking as it sends embalming fluid through a plastic tube and into our client's carotid artery. A bath will help the solution move through the arteries in the gentleman's limbs.

I pick up the hose, turn on the water, and test the temperature by spraying a stream over my wrist, the same place I used to test bottles of formula when Clay and Bugs were babies. The water doesn't have to be warm, of course—Mr. Kourtis certainly won't care if it's cool—but Gerald has ingrained in me such a respect for the dead that I can no more imagine giving my client a cold shower than I could perform an embalming without a hand towel draped over the body's most private organs.

My professors in the mortuary program thought my methods quaint, but they are Gerald's methods, born out of love for others.

As the Porti-Boy clicks and hums, I spray the few strands of white hair on Mr. K.'s head and smooth the deeply scored lines from his forehead. This man came to us from the Pleasant Valley Nursing Home, where he had been a resident for nine years. According to the file we found waiting on the zippered body bag, he outlived two of his sons. A daughter, Felicia, lives in Winter Haven, while a granddaughter lives here in Mt. Dora.

Fortunately, we didn't have to consult Felicia before beginning our work. Mr. Kourtis was wise enough to preplan his funeral, so Gerald and I have proceeded according to his wishes. The administrator at Pleasant Valley informed Felicia Kourtis Josten of her father's death, so I followed up with a call and left a message asking if she had any preference as to the time of the funeral service.

I suspect that it may be attended by few family members. The daughter may be in her seventies, and though Winter Haven is only an hour's drive away, miles of teeming tourist traffic lie between our funeral home and Felicia Josten. I don't know many older folks who like driving at breakneck highway speeds . . . which is probably how they survived to be older folks.

I squirt a dime-size glob of shampoo into my wet palm and work it into Mr. Kourtis's thin hair. "I hope your daughter can make it," I tell him. "But if she doesn't, don't you worry about having a crowd. People in Mt. Dora love a good funeral."

The back door opens, followed by Gerald's laugh and a rush of cool April air. "Congratulations," he says, stamping mud from his shoes. "Though you won't find it written in any book, one of the surest ways to know you're ready to be a full-time funeral director is when you start talking to the clients."

I grin as I pick up the spray nozzle. "They don't seem to mind a little conversation."

"They don't. But do let me know if they start talking back." Gerald tosses a bag of cotton balls onto the counter and lumbers to the sink where body fluids and clotted blood are draining from the trough in the side of the prep table. "Everything okay?"

"Everything's fine," I say, rinsing Mr. K.'s hair and sending a stream of soapy water into the trough as well. "No plumbing problems tonight."

"Good." He reaches for a pair of latex gloves. "You want me to shave him?"

"Already finished. His cheeks are clean and prickle-free."

"I wish everything about this case were prickle-free."

I glance up. "Is there a problem I don't know about?"

"Maybe not . . . but at the time Mr. Kourtis signed his preneed papers, his daughter and his second wife had a falling-out. They flew out of here like a pair of hornets, buzzing at each other the entire way."

"There's no mention of a wife in the file. The daughter is listed as next of kin."

"That's because the woman divorced Lyle right after she put him in the home. If the ex-wife and the daughter meet at the funeral, we might see a few fireworks."

I smile as I spray Mr. K.'s shoulders with an antibacterial solution. "That contract was signed a long time ago. Surely you don't think those women are still feuding."

"Women have an awful long memory about such things."

"So do some men."

"Point taken. But I'm wondering if we shouldn't do something to keep those gals apart in the chapel."

I rub soap into Mr. Kourtis's skin, massaging his upper arm and working the pink arterial fluid through his capillaries. "I don't think you need to worry. If both women show up, surely they'll come together in their grief. They'll have to realize that they both loved this man."

Gerald gives me a narrowed glance. "Funerals don't always bring out the best in people, missy."

"Just leave it to me." I reach for the spray nozzle again. "If they both show up, I'll have a talk with them before the service. If they still have hard feelings toward one another, I'll do what I can to bring them together . . . or seat them on opposite sides of the chapel."

"Sounds good." He leans one hand on the table and surveys the room. "Okay, what else do you need?"

I glance at him, noticing that his voice sounds more gravelly than usual. Dark circles lie under his eyes, and his color seems . . . off. "You look exhausted." I shut off the water. "Why don't you go on up to bed?"

Gerald gestures to the man on the table. "I oughta help you."

"It's okay; I don't think I'm going to have any problems. In a couple of hours I'll be done and headed upstairs to tuck the boys into bed."

He looks around as if searching for something to do, but I sidestep and catch his eye. "Thanks for the cotton balls. You go on up, and I'll call you if I run into a problem. We'll get Mr. K. casketed tomorrow."

Gerald sighs and turns toward the door that leads to the staircase.

I watch him go and shake my head when the door finally clicks behind him. I don't know why he's so worried about Mr. Kourtis's survivors. In all Gerald's years at Fairlawn, I know he's noticed how funerals often bring people together. The power of a meaningful, reverent memorial service is one of the reasons I'm proud to say I'm an apprentice funeral director.

Morticians fix things. We repair broken bodies and restore ruptured relationships. When death comes, we minister to the deceased and help the living continue with their lives. We act as the hands of Jesus in caring for the dead and ministering to the grief-stricken family.

Gerald stepped into my life and helped me put its frayed elements back together. If not for him, I don't know where my boys and I would be.

I startle when another soft burp escapes Mr. K.'s lips. "Don't you worry," I tell my client, reaching for a towel. "I'm going to make sure your family members enjoy a dignified funeral service. You'll be proud of them."

I smile as I wipe glistening water droplets from the old man's face. After two years of living in Mt. Dora, I think I understand why God brought my boys and me to the Fairlawn Funeral Home.

Leticia Gansky lowers the phone and reaches for her husband. "Pop-pop's passed on," she says, squeezing Charley's shoulder. She blinks at the sting of sudden tears. "He died this afternoon."

Charley turns his attention from the blaring TV tucked beneath the kitchen cabinet. "Huh?"

"My grandfather died." She returns to her chair at the kitchen table. "Mom said he died after lunch. Right after a big plate of beef Stroganoff."

Her husband stops chewing. "The old geezer was done in by a plate of pasta?"

Leticia struggles to swallow her irritation. Men can be so dense. "Don't think so. After lunch he went to his room, lay down for a nap, and didn't wake up."

Charley snorts. "When you're old, that's a good way to go. What was he, two hundred and six?"

"Ninety-three." Leticia drops her chin into her palm. "Ninety-three and he still had all his marbles. Mom said the last time she went to see him he was complaining about politics. Said the commercials cut into his soap operas."

Her husband looks back to the television, where overpaid athletes are playing a baseball game in some faraway city.

Leticia picks up her fork. "Imagine being ninety-three and still following your favorite soap operas."

Charley stabs a Tater Tot and pops it into his mouth, then grins at the TV, where a runner is sliding across home plate.

After taking a bite of chicken, Leticia chews slowly and wonders if she should feel sad. She loved the old man, but for the last few years the family has been expecting him to die at any moment. Even though Pleasant Valley Nursing Home is only ten minutes away, she hasn't visited Pop-pop in months. Charley keeps her busy answering the phones for his air-conditioning business, and she has her daughters and grandchildren to think of. Between their needs and Charley's, Leticia doesn't have time to go trotting down to the old folks' home every time she feels a twinge of guilt.

But she will make time for the funeral. Pop-pop was smart enough to take care of everything beforehand, so she'll send a nice spray of flowers, make sure to sign the girls' names to the card, and show up early for a front-row seat.

Maybe she'll be asked to say something during the service. After she clears the dishes, she ought to sit down with a pen and paper to see if she can come up with something sweet and amusing to say. Pop-pop was such a great guy—in his day, he was so popular, folks always said he should run for mayor.

A shame he had to outlive most of his friends.

"You know—" Leticia swallows a bite of chicken—"it's too bad we don't hold funerals while people are around to enjoy them. Might be nice to tell about the good things folks have done while they're still able to appreciate the comments."

Charley grins as another baseball player scores; then he winks at her. "Whatever you say, hon." He picks up his iced tea glass and tips it until it chinks against hers. "I couldn't have said it better myself."

The man has just toasted a comment about *death*. Was he even *listening*?

She lifts her own iced tea glass and swirls it until the sweetener in the bottom disappears. Charley might miss having a hot meal waiting when he finally comes in from work, and he might miss clean laundry after a week or two. But if she died, would he miss *her*?

Would anyone?

Ninety-five minutes after pulling on my rubber gloves, I turn off the Porti-Boy, disconnect the trocar, and drop the instrument and the tubing into the sink. I'm getting better at the cavity embalming . . . and much faster.

I insert the trocar plugs, then take a wet washcloth and check the body, searching for any spots of dried blood or fluid. When I'm convinced that I've missed nothing, I replace the towel over Mr. K.'s midsection. I'll dress him in the morning.

I have already completed most of the procedures necessary for an open-casket viewing—including the closing and sealing of the eyes and mouth—but a couple of final steps remain. I turn Mr. K.'s face fifteen degrees to the right so his features will be visible as people approach the casket, and I pack the nostrils with cotton so no seepage will occur during the funeral. The cotton is not visible, yet something else is—nose hairs, which will be even more noticeable when Ryan applies face powder tomorrow morning.

I use a cotton swab to rub Nair into Mr. K.'s nostrils. While the depilatory does its work, I massage moisturizing cream into the skin at the man's neck, face, and hands to prevent them from drying out in the chilly air-conditioning. Finally, with a cotton ball gripped in a pair of forceps, I take a swipe of the interior of the nostrils to remove the lotion and any unsightly nose hairs.

When I'm satisfied that Gerald could not have done any better, I cover the body with a crisp, clean sheet, checking to be sure the fabric isn't touching the tip of the nose. I don't want to come downstairs tomorrow and discover that Mr. Kourtis's proboscis has been flattened by the weight of a linen sheet.

I clean up my workstation, tossing cotton balls into the trash and wet towels into the hamper, then remove my apron and turn off the light.

Nine o'clock, and I'm afraid I'll find a sink full of dirty dishes when I climb the stairs. We ate pizza tonight, and even though a delivered dinner is easy on the cook, I'm always amazed at the mess that can result from two young boys and a pizza box.

At the top of the stairs I glance to the left. Light streams from Bugs's and Clay's rooms.

I check on my youngest son first. "Hey, bud." I find Bugs in bed, hunched over a video game. "Shouldn't this lamp be out?"

He grins, displaying an adorable gap where his front teeth should be. "I was waiting on you to kiss me good night."

"Sure you were." I set the video game on the nightstand and sit on the edge of the mattress. "Anything special you want to pray about?"

Bugs presses his lips together as if in deep thought, then shakes his head. "Nothin'."

"Okay. You want to pray, or shall I?"

He closes his eyes. "Dear God, please bless Mr. Gerald and Lydia and Aunt McLane and Uncle Jeff and my teacher and the preacher. Bless Skeeter and Grandma, too. Help us not to catch the measles. In Jesus' name, amen."

My seven-year-old's generous nature never fails to touch a soft spot within my heart. Though we haven't seen my sister, McLane, and her husband in almost a year, Bugs never fails to remember them in prayer.

I pull the covers up to his chin as he snuggles beneath the quilt. "Someone at school have the measles?"

"Maybe. Ashley had bumps. Miss Dickson didn't know what they were, but she said they might be measles."

"I doubt it. I'm pretty sure your friends have all been vaccinated."

"Have I been fascinated?"

"*Vaccinated.* Yes, you've had shots to protect you from measles and lots of other serious diseases." I kiss his forehead—letting my lips linger a moment to be sure his skin feels normal, not fevered—and turn out the lamp. I leave the door open because Bugs likes the hallway light left on until he falls asleep.

My next stop is fourteen-year-old Clay's room, and though he doesn't have to go to bed at nine, by this hour I like to know he's heading in that direction. I find him sprawled on the carpet with an open book on the floor and a notebook under his hand.

I tilt my head and study the textbook. "Algebra?"

"I hate it."

"You understand it?"

"Mostly."

"That's more than I did. But your father was a whiz, so I don't think you can use genetics as an excuse."

Clay sighs, but he doesn't complain when I stoop to tousle his hair. "Finish up soon, okay? I'll stop in to pray with you in about half an hour."

"'Kay."

I step into the hall in time to see Skeeter, our Jack Russell terrier, trot into Bugs's room. He'll sleep with Bugs tonight. Though my mother doesn't think pets belong in human beds, I can't see the harm in it. Skeeter doesn't have fleas or anything . . . at least not yet.

In the living area I turn off the television, scoop up a couple of pillows, and toss them back onto the faded couch. Apparently the boys watched TV with Gerald while I worked downstairs. Now everyone has headed to bed, and I will follow them as soon as I've tied on my Wonder Woman cape and cleaned up.

After collecting several scattered LEGO bricks and dumping them into an empty vase, I gather the ruffled newspaper and tuck it under my arm. When the living room looks a little more presentable, I strengthen my resolve, bracing myself for the approach to the heart of the house.

The kitchen is not as bad as I feared. Four plates are stacked by the sink, the top dish filled with gnawed pizza crusts that have hardened to the consistency of bones. The big, square box won't fit in the trash can, so someone has thoughtfully propped it against the wall. Four plastic cups remain scattered over the table, along with a couple of crumpled napkins, a joker from a pack of playing cards, and a whistle tied onto a shoelace.

All in all, not so big a mess. At least there's no sauce on the walls or strings of cheese petrifying on the Formica tabletop.

I move to the dishwasher and pause to peek through the doorway that leads to Gerald's room. The door is open, unusual for this time of night, and Gerald is not in bed. In the shadows I see him standing by his desk, one hand on the back of the chair, the other on his hip. His head and shoulders are curled forward, as if he is taking a moment to catch his breath.

I know that posture—my father died a painful death at home, and my mother nursed him in his final weeks. I often saw him in this same position after he'd suffered an agonizing spasm and withdrawn inside himself to gather his strength. Something in me quivers in a surge of unpleasant premonition.

"Gerald?" I leave the dishes and step toward him. "Are you okay?"

His gaze darts toward me, but he doesn't answer. I'm not sure if he won't . . . or if he can't.

Panic spurs the uneven beat of my heart. "Gerald—" I keep my voice low to avoid alarming the boys—"do you need help? Do I need to call 911?"

"Don't make a fuss." His voice comes out hoarse, but at least he's talking.

"But you're not okay. Can you lie down? Do you want some water?"

I pry his hand from the chair. His arm is less pliable than some corpses' I've handled, but he allows me to lead him to the bed. He stretches out and folds his hands across his chest, his movements stiff and awkward.

I stand beside him feeling useless. "Let me help you. I can call your doctor—"

"I'm fine."

"You don't look fine."

The corner of his mouth quirks. "I've . . . never looked *fine*, but . . . Evelyn must have seen something . . . she liked."

I resist the urge to roll my eyes. Soon he'll be asking his late wife to look down from heaven and witness his landlady's senseless cruelties. "Be serious. Do you want a blanket? Do you want me to help you take off your sweater and shirt?" I feel slightly embarrassed about offering this sort of personal assistance to a man who has always respected my privacy, but if this is a true emergency . . .

"Stop fussing, missy. I'll be . . . all right. Just . . . give me a moment to . . . catch my breath."

I move back, willing to let him take care of himself, but Gerald doesn't appear to be in any hurry. Yet what will it matter if he decides to sleep in his work clothes? Still, I'm not going to let him lie here uncovered on a chilly night. I pick up the blanket at the foot of the bed, shake it out, and drape it over him.

"Tomorrow," I say, employing my firmest voice, "you are going to see a doctor. I'll drive you."

"I don't want . . . you to fuss."

"I won't be fussing. I need you, so you need to get well. It's a matter of practicality."

"You have to . . . take care of your boys."

"After I take the boys to school, I'll drive you to your doctor or the walk-in clinic. You don't look good, and I want you to get checked out. So promise me you'll come along and not give me any trouble."

When Gerald closes his eyes and sighs, I take that response as acquiescence.

"Good night." I tuck the blanket around his bare feet before heading toward the doorway. "I'm leaving the door open, so call out if you need me." I say this as if he's merely going to bed with a headache or a sore throat, while inwardly I'm wondering if he has the strength to call for help. Even if he does, can I hear him from the opposite end of the house? Maybe I should find a bell or something he can ring.

For a moment he doesn't answer; then a weary reply reaches my ears: "Yes, warden."

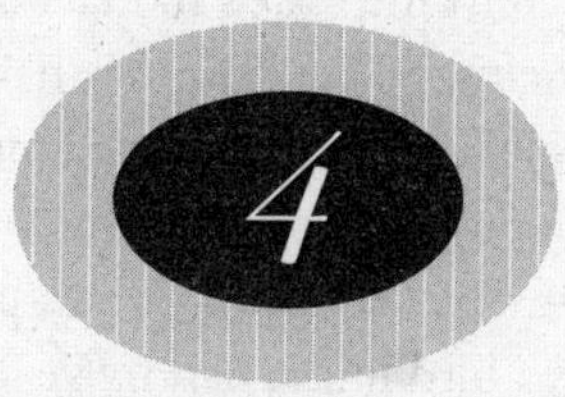

At the end of the gleaming conference table, Ross Alexander pulls his iPhone from his pocket and quietly taps the e-mail icon. When the whirling daisy stops spinning, he sees five new e-mails from friends and associates.

No e-mails or text messages from Marianne, but he hadn't really expected to hear from her so soon. She said she and her mother might spend all day at the bridal shop, so he shouldn't worry.

Easy for her to say. With expenses piling up and the wedding still four months away, he can't help but wonder how he and his future father-in-law are going to pay for what Marianne's mother lightly refers to as "Fulton County's Wedding of the Year."

He can only hope she's joking.

"Ross?"

He drops the iPhone into his lap as sharp-faced Greta Tomassi, CEO of Aldridge Elms, Inc., stares in his direction, her eyes as sharp as pinpricks. "Yes?"

"Suppose you tell us what your approach will be in the next quarter. The southeast region has some serious catching up to do if we're going to meet our growth goals."

Ross leans forward in his chair and forces a smile. "We do have plans to catch up, and our prospects might be the brightest of all. As you know, a large number of retirees live in Florida and Georgia, and more from that demographic move to the area every day. Furthermore, most of the region's independent funeral homes are dying—sorry, no pun intended. The mom-and-pops can't compete with the chains, and most of their directors aren't interested in mass-marketing or the latest technological developments. So we definitely have an edge—"

"I didn't ask for a regional review," Greta interrupts. "I asked how you planned to reach our acquisition goals for your region."

Ross clears his throat. "It, uh, shouldn't be a problem. First, any funeral home for sale is a bird in the hand. I've always found my best leads in the trade magazines."

The faces around the table register nothing but apathy. He's not giving these people anything new.

"My, um, next strategy involves writing my states' licensing boards for a list of people who have recently applied for embalmers or funeral directors licenses. New graduates who are going into the business might know of other directors who are in a state of transition. And people in transition are likely to be amenable to the idea of selling."

Greta tilts her head. "Dealing with bureaucracy takes time, and you have only three months to bring your region back in line with our targeted goals. Aldridge Elms aims to be *the* largest death care company, not the second-largest, and to achieve that end we need to own and operate three hundred funeral homes by the end of this fiscal year. Nothing less than three hundred will do, ladies and gentlemen, so you must meet or exceed your regional quotas. No excuses accepted."

When she raps the table with her bony knuckles, Ross feels the sound slam against his spinal column. Last quarter he was charged with acquiring six funeral homes for the southeast region, and so far he's managed to sign only three. By the end of June he needs to acquire three more in order to keep his job, a job he desperately needs in order to pay for the rehearsal dinner, the honeymoon, and a gorgeous wife with champagne tastes.

But he can do it. He's been a bit distracted of late, but acquiring three mortuaries in three months for Aldridge Elms . . . For a man with a golden tongue, how hard could that be?

Now, if he can only convince Marianne that twenty bridesmaids are too many.

Lydia Windsor, my closest neighbor, and I are sipping sweetened iced tea and rocking in the shade of my front porch. If we were wearing hoop skirts and a couple of wide-brimmed hats, we could be a postcard for lazy afternoons in the old South.

Lydia runs the bottom half of her glass along her forehead. "Quiet here today."

"Too quiet," I answer. "Things have been slow lately. I've got a client settling in the prep room, but he's the first we've had in a week."

"Are y'all doing okay? I mean, is the wolf at the door?" Her tone is light, but I see real concern in her eyes.

"The wolf's at least a couple of blocks away. Gerald's been a good manager, so we're not about to go under. Not yet, anyway."

"Speaking of the G-man, I've been meaning to ask him about my crepe myrtles. Is he in there with your dead guy?"

"The G-man is at the hospital. I went with him to see his doctor first thing this morning, but he didn't have an appointment, so we had to wait. When he finally got in, Dr. Harding decided to send him to the hospital for some tests. Gerald wasn't happy about that, but I convinced him to go."

Lydia's brow furrows. "How sick is he? Sick enough to stay at the hospital overnight?"

"He keeps saying he's fine, and I don't think they could hold him if they tried. We still have to casket Mr. Kourtis, and I'll need Gerald to help me with that. Until I get my license, he's supposed to supervise my work."

Lydia snorts. "I keep forgetting you're not legal yet. Seems like you finished school months ago."

"Yeah, but Florida requires a year of supervised apprenticeship after school. After that I have to pass my national board exams, and *then* I can get my license. Still have a few hoops to jump through."

We rock silently for a while; then Lydia sighs. "Seems like just yesterday you and the boys drove up to this place."

I chuckle. "In some ways it does."

In other ways, I feel as though Clay, Bugs, and I have passed a dozen years at Fairlawn. On the drive from Virginia to Mt. Dora we ended one life, our new life beginning the minute we stepped out into this wide, green lawn. Our time at Fairlawn has been good . . . if a bit odd.

Trouble is, I'm not sure we're going to be able to survive financially. Gerald keeps assuring me that slow spells are to be expected in the death care industry, but I haven't been able to ignore the fact that we held fewer funerals last month than any other on record. A new mortuary has opened in Tavares, only a short drive away, and I'm afraid some of our Mt. Dora folks have been going over there.

"I'd love to drum up more business for you," Lydia says, her eyes closing in the midday heat. "But that'd mean encouraging people to die. I'm sure you see the problem."

"We don't need more bodies," I answer, dabbing at my damp temples with a wadded napkin. "The death rate around here is steady enough to support a couple of mortuaries. What we need is for people to think of Fairlawn when they need funeral services. When Uncle Ned went into the nursing home and shut down the business—well, that hiatus hurt us. People started going to the homes in Eustis and Tavares, so Fairlawn fell under the radar."

Lydia's eyes widen. "I know just what you need."

"I need to be better at selling preneed packages. But I'm a lousy saleswoman."

"Not what I was thinking."

"So you're saying we need a natural disaster?"

"No. Coupons! When I was at the grocery store yesterday, the woman in front of me got a cartload of free groceries because she had so many coupons."

"What would the coupon say? 'Buy one, bury one free'?" I stop rocking and wince. "I can't afford to give a discount that deep. Oh, and the puns! Can you imagine the jokes we'd be hearing?"

Lydia laughs. "Okay, so no deep discounts. How about 20 percent off?"

"Won't work. People who come in for preneed contracts already eat into our profit margins. They pay for tomorrow's funeral with today's dollars, so we take a financial hit the minute they sign the contract."

"So why do you offer those things?"

I shrug. "It's a service. It works only because we put 70 percent of that income in conservative, interest-bearing accounts. Theoretically, it should benefit everyone involved."

Lydia waves my explanation away. "Then don't give the discount on preneed contracts. People could clip the coupon and keep it for when they need it. Twenty percent off one of those fancy caskets—you can't tell me you'd lose money. I know those things have a *huge* markup."

"The markup is more than 20 percent," I admit, "but I don't think a coupon is going to encourage people to think of Fairlawn as dignified and respectful. And that's what people want when a family member passes. Most people don't set money as their first priority—they care more about doing right by their loved ones."

Lydia looks down the road toward Twice Loved Treasures, the shop where she sells gifts made from other people's castoffs. "I used to think we had a lot in common, but dignity is the last thing on people's minds when they visit my place."

I smile, thinking about the gift she helped Bugs make the other day. From sliced up CDs, a Styrofoam sphere, and hot glue, they created a funky and functional mirror ball, which Bugs insisted on hanging in the upstairs bathroom. The boy now bathes in a blaze of spinning stars.

"That's okay," I assure her. "When people show up at my door, they really aren't thinking about recycling."

She stops rocking and smiles at me. "I've got it. The definitive answer to your conundrum."

"I don't think billboards are the way to go."

"Not a billboard, a slogan. Lots of funeral homes have them."

I stare at the simple sign in our front yard, adorned only with the name of our mortuary. "That's not bad. We could paint a slogan on the sign and include it in our yellow pages ad."

"But you're not going to write it. Not that you and Gerald wouldn't come up with something perfectly nice, but the wittiest slogan in the world isn't going to get people buzzing about your place. What you need is a slogan *contest.* Let the townspeople submit their entries; then you and Gerald choose the one you like best. All you have to do is come up with a clever and original prize for the winner—like 50 percent off a fancy oak casket."

Lydia's grinning, so I know she's kidding about the casket, but the contest is a brilliant idea. If we advertise in the local paper, we'll get lots of interest . . . maybe from people all over Lake County.

I swivel to face my friend. "That's an idea. If we ran the contest long enough, word would spread throughout the county."

"You don't want to run a contest *too* long. A couple of months, tops, or people forget about it and you lose your word-of-mouth buzz."

I'm way ahead of her. "If we ran an ad in the *Daily Commercial*, the newspaper might even consider a feature article."

"I'll bet that nice reporter who wrote about you inheriting this place would do a follow-up piece. She'll be on the story like freckles on a redhead."

Maybe I've been setting my sights too low. Instead of trying to reach the people of Mt. Dora, maybe I should be aiming for the citizens of Leesburg, Tavares, and Eustis as well. After all, the funeral directors in those towns have been more than happy to accept clients from my area.

"We'd be the talk of the county. Especially if we offered a free casket—maybe even a free funeral as a prize."

"Get serious, girlfriend. If you want people to get excited about your contest, offer something that makes them think about living."

"What . . . like a free colonoscopy?"

"Like a Caribbean cruise!"

"Are you kidding?"

"I'll bet you could find a five-day cruise out of Tampa or Port Canaveral for less than a thousand bucks. You offer *that*, and I guarantee the slogans will start pouring in."

I smile as the notion spins in my head like a colorful carousel. I'm not sure what Gerald will think about this idea, but I'm not going to dismiss it. I'd stand on my head to win a free cruise, and writing a simple slogan won't be too difficult for anyone. We'll probably get a lot of duds, but who knows? We might find a real gem in the flood of submissions.

"You know—" I give Lydia a broad smile—"I think you might be on to something."

While a rerun of *Pimp My Ride* rumbles from the television, Ross finishes his bag of Doritos, then drops into a kitchen chair. His laptop waits, ready to work, but first he needs to get the orange Dorito dust off his fingers.

No more of this, probably, after he's married. Marianne would faint if she walked into the kitchen and saw him licking his fingers instead of washing his hands at the sink.

He wads the empty chip bag and pitches it toward the trash bin at the end of the table. He's put off his search long enough; time to chart a course, make some deals, and keep the corporate dragon lady happy. And time to assure his fiancée that everything is proceeding as planned.

After opening the *Mortuary Management* Web site, Ross scrolls through the list of funeral homes for sale. He skims the ads, searching for locations in Florida, Georgia, and Alabama. Several homes are available in Mississippi and Arkansas, but he needs prospects in his region, particularly those in the Sunshine State. Florida and funeral homes go together like doughnuts and coffee, and any home he procures there is bound to be successful.

He exhales through his teeth when he spots three new listings—one in Savannah, one in Tuscaloosa, and one in Birmingham. All are close enough for him to drive over for a personal interview with the respective owners. After Ross presents his pitch over a nice hot lunch, the owners will almost certainly agree to sign on the dotted line. Few funeral directors have been able to resist Ross's offer while a For Sale sign swings in front of their establishments.

He jots down the names of the mortuaries and scans the listings for details. With any luck, he'll be able to avoid involving any real estate agents—he can make a better offer if the firm doesn't have to pay a sales commission. He'll also be able to deliver a smoother pitch if he's not constantly interrupted by some bulldog agent who insists on looking out for the client's best interests.

A quick sale could benefit everyone concerned—an outdated funeral home will become another property for Aldridge Elms, and the previous owners will receive a fair price for their property. Once the assets have been evaluated and the terms settled, the former owners will be handed a fat check to enjoy in retirement while renovators from Aldridge Elms descend to redesign the facilities so they offer all the conveniences of the modern funeral industry.

While none of the Aldridge Elms homes are identical, most offer the same features: one slumber room, done in restful beige and blue; one casket display wall, lit with soft lighting; one reception area, stocked with silk flowers and boxes of tissues. At the back of the building the new manager will find one preparation room, one refrigerated space, one storage area, and one small office. Outside, one white minivan for pickups, two sleek funeral coaches, and three black Lincoln sedans for grieving family members to rent at the prime hourly rate.

No living quarters will exist on the remodeled premises, because Aldridge Elms funeral directors and embalmers do not live "above the shop." They live in ordinary homes and carry their own mortgages. The only concession Aldridge Elms corporate heads make to acknowledge the round-the-clock nature of the funeral business is providing a closet and a cot in the preparation area.

After searching the Internet yellow pages, Ross finds the names and phone numbers of all three prospective businesses. He takes down the information, then leans back and chews on the edge of his thumb. Three good prospects are the minimum he needs to reach his goal by the end of the quarter. His job depends upon his success, and the Hawaiian honeymoon he promised Marianne depends on his commission. So if he's to have a happy honeymoon, he'd be wise to acquire at least one additional funeral home. A spare.

Since he has exhausted his leads at *Mortuary Management*, he needs to dig a little deeper. He can always sniff around when he talks to the morticians in Alabama and Georgia, and there *have* to be prospects in Florida, where the National Funeral Directors Association is holding its annual convention in early May.

Flushed with the prospect of a fresh opportunity, Ross logs on to the NFDA Web page and searches for information about the upcoming convention. Though the meeting will attract funeral directors from all over the nation, the gathering is certain to be well populated with business owners from the Southeast. They'll know which establishments are in danger of going under, and with a little encouragement, they'll point Ross toward someone whose property is ripe for the plucking. He'll approach with a compassionate smile, and after a few hours at the hotel bar, he's sure to win the confidence of a weary funeral director who'll confide that his mortuary isn't doing so well.

Then Ross will pat him on the shoulder and assure his new friend that all is not lost. Sometimes opportunity knocks in disguise.

I jerk upright when I hear the slam of the back door. After looking out the window to be sure Gerald's car is in the driveway, I leave my desk and hurry to the prep room.

It's nearly three o'clock, and Gerald has been gone most of the day. Each passing hour tightened my nerves, and though I tried to tell myself he stopped to see an old friend or to enjoy a nice lunch, I'm terrified to think he spent all day at the hospital.

I find him perched on his stool in front of the embalming table, where Mr. Kourtis still waits under a sheet. Gerald's skin appears slightly yellow under the glow of the fluorescents, and his eyes are surrounded by circles of bluish darkness. His forearms rest on his legs, and those capable hands are trembling.

The sight of his trembling fingers alarms me more than anything.

I approach quietly, wading through an atmosphere of uncertainty. "Gerald?"

He blinks at the table, then turns toward me. "Are you ready to casket Mr. Kourtis?"

"Mr. K. can wait." I pull up a stool. "What did the doctor say?"

Gerald makes a slight chuffing sound. "What do doctors know? They poked me and ran machines over me and scratched their chins and looked thoughtful. Didn't tell me a thing I didn't already know."

"So you're . . . okay?"

"I keep tellin' you I'm fine." He wipes his palms on his slacks. "Anything going on around here?"

I glance at the legal pad I scribbled with my notes and left on the counter. "After our walk this morning, Lydia and I talked about how to drum up additional business. She gave me an idea—an idea I like a lot."

The corner of Gerald's mouth twists. "I hope she's not offering to sell her recycled stuff on our front porch—"

"She said we should run a contest and offer a Caribbean cruise as the prize."

His jaw drops. "Land sakes, where are we supposed to get the money for a thing like that?"

"We could dip into our savings. Or maybe we could charge an entry fee with each submission."

"I don't like that—too much like gambling. And those savings are reserved for a rainy day."

"Have you looked out the window lately? I hate to be negative, but I think there's a storm looming on the horizon."

"You haven't seen anything yet, missy. In the summer of '97, Ned and I went six weeks without a single burial. I was beginning to think folks around here had discovered some kind of miracle elixir for long life."

I might have argued the point, but something in the set of his jaw tells me I'd lose. So I try a different approach. "There's no denying that sometimes you have to spend money to make money. If the contest results in just two extra funerals, we could break even. And there'd be another benefit."

"I'm all ears."

"We'll ask our entrants to come up with a slogan for Fairlawn. Who knows? We might get a really good one—something that would make Fairlawn the first name to pop into people's heads during a time of crisis."

Gerald scowls. "We might get a boatload of rubbish."

"True, but we don't *have* to use one of the entries as our official slogan. If we don't like any of them, we can come up with our own motto. But for the few weeks that our contest is running, people all over Lake County will be thinking of Fairlawn. That can't be bad for business."

He sucks at the inside of his cheeks and finally nods. "As long as the procedure is respectful," he says, pointing at me. "If things get silly, this contest could hurt us."

"It won't get silly. I promise."

"Yeah, well, I hope you can keep that promise." Gerald crosses his arms. "By the way, that doctor made me take another appointment in the morning."

The hair on the back of my neck rises. "Is this another examination or more tests?"

He shrugs. "I don't think it's any big deal, but the doctor says she'll have my test results by then. She said I should come in so we can talk. The stubborn woman didn't want to wait until later in the day."

"I'll take Bugs to school." I speak in a flat voice as a whisper of terror murmurs in my ear. Gerald has been so convinced that nothing is wrong, and I've wanted so desperately to believe him. . . .

I touch his arm. "You want some company? I could swing by the office after I drop Bugs at the school—"

"I won't hear of it." Gerald pats my hand, but a shadow lingers in his eyes. "I'll be back soon enough. Don't forget; we have the Kourtis funeral at three."

I stand and push my stool under the table. "I'm going upstairs to check on Clay and Bugs. You coming up?"

"In a bit. I'm going to unpack the Kourtis casket and get things arranged. You come down when you're ready, and we'll get him in the box."

"Okay." I'm sure everything's fine, but maybe Gerald needs some time alone. With reluctance, I leave him to go upstairs and check on my sons.

By the time nine o'clock rolls around, the boys are in their rooms, I'm in my pajamas, and Mr. Kourtis is resting in his casket. Gerald and I placed him inside just before dinner; then I ran upstairs to heat up a can of soup and make sandwiches while Gerald adjusted the pillow and placed the man's shoes near his feet.

Now I'm sitting cross-legged on my bed, my legal pad on one knee, jotting down details about our slogan contest. We'll accept entries through the end of May, and the winner will receive a Caribbean cruise . . . for one. I know that sounds cheap, but I don't think we can afford to send two people much farther than the Tampa coastline. I hope there are some clever people out there who like to travel alone.

Now . . . how do I find the words to make our contest irresistible?

Should the ad be lighthearted? *"Wanna take a sea cruise?"*

Or should we attempt a more dignified approach? *"Fairlawn Funeral Home seeks a consoling message. . . ."*

Maybe there's a way to combine the two styles: *"Fairlawn Funeral Home offers an opportunity for which you might be eternally grateful."*

Stymied by my choices, I glance toward the doorway and wonder if Gerald is still awake. I heard him come up the stairs about twenty minutes ago, so by now he's definitely in bed, either asleep or trying to get that way.

Father, strengthen him and make him well. The prayer rises from my heart as naturally as a sigh. *I can't afford for Gerald to be sick, not while I depend on him to help me run this business. I know this is a selfish prayer, but I can't imagine any good time for you to knock Gerald off his feet.*

I startle when the phone on my nightstand rings. I glance at the clock, afraid it might be a pickup call, but it's so early the odds favor my mother or Daniel Sladen, the lavishly tressed local lawyer who's become a good friend. Of the family.

I lift the receiver. "Hello?"

"What's wrong?" The voice is my mother's.

I draw the phone into my nest of pillows and curl up among them. "Nothing's wrong; not really."

"Don't pretend with me—I hear worry in your voice. Are the boys okay?"

"They're fine."

"The dog?"

"Great."

"Daniel?"

I smile as my thoughts drift toward the man who is attractive enough to quicken the pulse of every woman in town. "Last time I saw him, he looked as fine as ever."

"Gerald?"

I nestle lower into my pillows. "I'm a little worried about him. He hasn't been feeling well, so I made him go to the doctor."

"What did the doctor say?"

"She sent Gerald to the hospital, where they ran some tests, but they won't know anything until tomorrow. He keeps trying to blow everything off, but I can tell he's worried."

"But what are his *symptoms*?"

I should have known she'd ask. Mom subscribes to the *Mayo Clinic Health Letter* and reads *Prevention* magazine with religious fervor. When we lived with her right after my divorce, she spent every night watching the Discovery Health channel.

Come to think of it, she might be able to diagnose Gerald's problem faster than the medical professionals.

"It's hard to put my finger on it," I tell her. "Sometimes I catch Gerald holding his stomach or his back, and every once in a while he complains of indigestion."

Mother snorts. "Show me a seventy-year-old man who doesn't do those things."

"Yeah, but you know Gerald—he doesn't like to complain, so I think he may be hiding things from me. This afternoon, though, when I saw him downstairs, I thought he looked kind of jaundiced."

She draws in an audible breath. "That sounds like a gallstone. The bile ducts get blocked, and bang! Suddenly you're as yellow as canned corn."

"He wasn't *that* yellow," I answer, but I feel a smile creep across my face. Gallstones are not serious. They're nearly as common as ulcers. "What do they do for gallstones?"

"Sometimes nothing," Mom answers. "Sometimes they take out the gallbladder, but that's not a big deal. Just don't feed him too many fried foods. And don't worry—I'm sure Gerald is going to be fine."

Because I so desperately want to believe her, I do.

Gerald stares at the brown spot on the back of his hand. Funny, as often as he handles chemicals, he always thought some variety of skin cancer would get him. Now it appears that something on the *inside* of his body has turned traitorous.

"So if you'll step outside and speak to my nurse," Dr. Harding says, "she'll get you set up for a liver function test, additional blood work, and an ultrasound."

Gerald grunts. "I don't know, Doc. You drew enough blood yesterday to satisfy Dracula. I don't have all day to sit at the hospital—"

"Mr. Huffman—" Dr. Harding sinks onto the little rolling stool and stares up at him—"these tests will take only a few minutes, but I can't make a conclusive diagnosis without them. Don't you want to know what the problem is?"

"You said you'd know today."

"The blood work didn't give us complete answers. You need more tests."

"Then maybe it's better not to know."

The woman eyes him with a calculating expression. "You don't really believe that, do you?"

Gerald runs his fingertips over the edge of his unbuttoned shirt. "I've lived a long time. Maybe I'm better off not knowing what's going on under the hood."

"If your car developed a rattle, you'd take it to a mechanic to be fixed, wouldn't you? Once we know what's causing your problems, we'll be better equipped to repair the situation."

Gerald draws a slow breath and studies the back of the exam room door. Doctors love to talk about fixing things, but in his time he's seen way too many people who simply can't be fixed. He meets the doctor's determined gaze. "All right, I'll talk to your nurse. But I don't want to spend all day sitting in some hallway."

"They'll get you right in and out. I promise." Dr. Harding stops to write something on the chart in her hand, then flips the cover closed. "Come on out when you're dressed, and my receptionist will take good care of you."

Sure, she will.

Gerald slips from the examination table and finishes buttoning his shirt. The nurse took his blood pressure again today, the doctor did more poking and prodding, but no one told him anything about why he hasn't been feeling up to snuff. The doctor keeps talking about tests, and all of them probably cost an arm and a leg. He and Jen have health insurance, but the deductibles are high to keep the premiums low. He'll probably end up emptying his savings account just because his stomach has decided it can't handle jalapeño peppers anymore.

When he has buttoned and tucked in his shirt, he steps into the hall and looks toward the curved counter they call the nurses' station. Two women are working there, and one of them looks up as he approaches. "Mr. Kauffman?"

"Huffman."

"Oh yes, that's right. I called the imaging center at the hospital, and they can get you in this morning. You can drive straight there if you like, and you should only have to wait a few minutes."

Good grief, has the whole world heard that Gerald Huffman is an old grump who hates to wait? Not exactly the image he wants to project.

The medical assistant hands him a slip of paper with a time and phone number on it. He thanks her and heads to the counter where another woman will take his insurance card and his credit card. He might as well empty his pockets on that desk.

He has just signed his name to the charge slip when the exit door opens. "He's right in here," a nurse says.

A twinge of unease nips at the back of his knees when he spies Jen standing in the waiting room. "What's wrong?"

"N-nothing," she stammers, glancing from him to the nurse. "I thought I'd come down and see if you need help."

"You shouldn't have come all the way out here."

"I was running errands, and this office was on the way."

Jen's lying, and they both know it. Furthermore, she's left Fairlawn unattended. And they have a funeral this afternoon.

"You need to get back to the house. I'll be tied up a little while."

Her eyes widen. "Why?"

"A few more tests, the doctor says. Pictures and blood work and labs. But you go on home, and I'll be along directly."

"It's not . . . gallstones?"

"It's a national secret is what it is. No one will tell me anything."

Her eyes remain worried, but she smiles and hooks her purse on her shoulder. "You call me if something comes up. Or if you start feeling woozy."

"Why would I feel woozy?"

One of the nurses forces a laugh. "Go on to the hospital, Mr. Huffman." Then to Jen: "We're trying our best to get rid of him."

The young woman probably means her comment as a joke, but Gerald doesn't feel much like laughing as he follows Jen through the reception area and into the main lobby.

"I mean it," she says, slipping her arm through his. "Are you sure you don't want me to go with you? I have plenty of time before the Kourtis funeral."

"You need to get back to Fairlawn. The flowers will be arriving soon."

"Lydia promised to keep an eye out for any deliveries. And I left a note on the door—anyone who gets by Lydia can leave the arrangements on the porch, and I'll bring them in later." Her gaze rises, sweeping over his face in gentle accusation. "Why don't you stop being so stubborn and let me drive you to the hospital?"

"I appreciate the offer, but I'm fine." He stops outside the elevator as she presses the call button. "You go on back. If you get bored, you should do some studying. You have to take that national board exam next week."

"I have ten days. Plenty of time." Jen smiles again, then releases his arm. "I'll see you at home for lunch, right?"

"I'll be there," he promises, sliding his hands into his pockets.

Lord willing, he will.

Leticia smiles as the strains of "How Great Thou Art" rise to the ceiling of the small chapel. Ruby Masters is playing her heart out on the organ, and the mourners in the pews are dabbing at their eyes. Around the casket, sprays of daisies and carnations stand in lovely wreath arrangements, one of them featuring a glittering Bible with a red satin bookmark.

Pop-pop would have loved the service. The First Baptist minister brought a brief message, and two men from Pleasant Valley Nursing Home delivered eulogies. They clattered forward on their walkers and talked about how kind and selfless her grandfather had been. "A true gentleman," the last fellow said, his voice rasping into the microphone. "A pleasure to have at the home and not at all the sort who would steal your girlfriend or your chocolates."

Leticia hasn't heard about rampant thievery at the nursing home, but it is nice to know her grandfather wasn't suspected of any crime. A pity, really, that he can't hear the kind words offered by his friends. A pity, too, that he doesn't have more friends present, but he has outlived so many of his peers.

She can't help but notice several empty chairs. This service is well attended, she supposes, considering that it's a weekday and the fact that Pop-pop hasn't left the nursing home in years. Yes, a lovely service, but she would have enjoyed seeing more people with sincere sniffles.

She glances at the end of the row, where her mother sits with her hands folded, purse on her lap. She's nodding in her wheelchair, so she and Mildred, the friend who drove her from Winter Haven, must have talked nonstop on the drive—probably about Pop-pop's greedy ex-wife who, fortunately, has had the good sense not to show up.

Leticia makes a mental note to ask Jennifer Graham if the gold digger sent flowers or a card. She probably snagged an even richer man and moved back up north.

Leticia stiffens when her mother's head bobs forward, almost smacking the purse on her lap. She nudges Mildred, who elbows Mother, who lifts her head and dabs at her eyes as if she had fully *intended* to nod off in the middle of "I Won't Have to Cross Jordan Alone," sung by an outstanding baritone from the First Baptist men's choir.

Leticia draws a deep breath and leans back in her chair. In light of her genetic inheritance, she'll probably live well into her nineties, too—outlasting her mother and all her friends. By the time she passes, her children will be in assisted-living facilities, her grandchildren will have moved away, and her cousins will have been absorbed into their grandchildren's families. The Kourtises come from good stock, so they're far more likely to lose their hair than their health.

When the last note of the song dies away, six young men enlisted by the minister stride forward to act as pallbearers. Four of them are in their shirtsleeves, and it's highly unlikely that any of them knew Pop-pop.

Leticia feels the corners of her mouth droop. All of her family members will probably have small funerals like this one. The pallbearers will be young men who don't own proper suits, and the people who bring eulogies will struggle to show up and trudge to the front of the chapel. And the mourners? They'll be doing well to remain awake through the service.

Long life may be a blessing, but what's the sense in living long and being blessed if no one knows you've done it?

She turns toward her husband, who is breathing deeply and evenly at her left side. "I'm not having a funeral like this," she murmurs.

Charley lifts his head. "Is it over?"

"Shh! My funeral's going to be better—and standing room only. Everyone in town will come to see me off."

He crosses his arms and lowers his chin. "Humph."

Charley doesn't believe her. He never takes her seriously unless she's talking about dinner or church gossip. But he'll soon realize just how serious she can be.

Yessiree, when Leticia Gansky makes a resolution, she keeps it.

I wake to the sound of a steady downpour. For a disconcerting moment I can't remember what day it is. I'd give anything if it were a Saturday, with nowhere to go and nothing to do. But then I remember that yesterday we buried Mr. Kourtis, which means today is Thursday, a school day, and staying in bed is not an option.

I toss off the covers and pad down the hallway to Clay's room, shake him awake, and repeat the procedure with Bugs. When I'm sure my youngest is lurching toward the bathroom, I wander to the kitchen and put on the teakettle.

I have just dropped a tea bag in my steaming cup when the phone rings. I jump to answer it, hoping to let Gerald sleep a bit longer, and am surprised to hear Daniel Sladen's voice in my ear.

"Good morning, beautiful. Hope I didn't wake you."

"No, I'm already in the kitchen. Is something wrong?"

"Polly Prose died about an hour ago. Her daughter didn't want to call so early, so I volunteered to contact the funeral home—provided, of course, that she choose Fairlawn as the mortuary."

I prop my elbow on the counter as I dunk my tea bag. "Why did Polly Prose's daughter call you?"

"She's an old friend of the family, and I drew up Polly's will a couple of years ago. She named me the executor of her estate, so when she died—"

"—her daughter naturally thought of you." I smile, inexplicably relieved. "Thanks, then, for the referral. And you'd better be careful. People are going to think we're silent partners or something."

"In *collusion*," he says, supplying the word, "and I doubt anyone would say that. Will Gerald be making the pickup?"

I glance toward Gerald's room, where a thin, dark line still marks the bottom of the door. "I don't think he's awake yet. He hasn't been feeling well, so if he's not up by the time I get the boys ready for school, I'm thinking I should let him sleep."

A dark image hovers at the edge of my mind—Gerald laid out on his bed, still dressed in his trousers, shirt, and favorite red cardigan, but as cold as a marble slab.

"You'd better check on him," Daniel says, apparently reading my mind.

"I will. If he's feeling under the weather, I'm going to make him stay in bed. So if you'll give me Mrs. Prose's address . . ."

I jot the information on a piece of notebook paper, then hang up and pop two slices of bread into the toaster. As the elements glow with heat, I walk to the bedroom door and rap gently. "Gerald?"

I nearly melt in relief when the door opens. Though he hasn't turned on a single light, he's up and dressed, his hair combed. His face is still lined with weariness, but he's wearing his suspenders and the special string tie he favors for pickups. His trousers, I notice, look baggier than usual. Is the man losing weight?

"I heard," Gerald says, adjusting his tie. "Polly Prose, is it?"

"Yes, but you don't have to go right this minute. Daniel's at the house and—"

"I'll go so you can get the boys off to school. You have a busy day ahead with your studying and all."

"I told you not to worry about my exam. And you need some breakfast. Let me at least make you some toast and put the coffee on."

He shakes his silvered head. "I'd better bring Polly over right away. Her daughter will want to get the house picked up for the folks that'll be dropping by. She might have quite a crowd, on account of her station in the community."

I halt midstride. "Who *is* Mrs. Prose's daughter?"

"Jacqueline Prose. You've met her, haven't you? She runs the library."

I dip my head in a small nod, remembering the dark-haired woman who was anything but friendly the first time I dropped by the local library. I'd barely arrived in town, but the woman seemed to disapprove of me from the beginning.

My inner eye imagines the scene at her house—Polly lying in a back bedroom while Jacqueline pours coffee for Daniel at a cozy kitchen table. She might have called him in the middle of the night, and like the gentleman he is, he got out of bed and went to the house before sunrise. Maybe Jacqueline's eyes are red from weeping and Daniel is feeling compelled to slip a comforting arm around her shoulder or reach across the table to pat her hand. . . .

Why does that image bother me so much?

"You're right," I tell Gerald. "The sooner we get started on the embalming, the easier our work will be. You go on over to the Proses', but let Daniel help you with the lifting. I'll take the boys to school and meet you back here."

Gerald smooths his tie. "I'll bring the body in."

"No, you wait until I can help you."

"Polly's not a big woman. She's built like her daughter, tall and willowy."

For no discernible reason, my temper spikes. "You can wait for me, Gerald Huffman. I'll help you get her into the prep room and on the table; then you're going to sit and observe like a good mentor. I don't want you wearing yourself out. After we get Polly on the pump, we'll call the doctor's office to see about your test results."

He pulls a piece of toast from the toaster. "There's no rush. Not when we have work to do."

"Nothing—not even work—is more important than your health. If you won't call the doctor for your peace of mind, do it for mine."

"Everything's more important than my aches and pains." Gerald pats me on the shoulder. "Let me head over to the Prose place before Jacqueline works herself into a tizzy."

"Does the woman fall to pieces in a crisis?"

A half smile lifts his mouth as he stops to smear butter on his toast. "The woman falls to pieces whenever Daniel's around. She's had a crush on him for years."

I stare at Gerald, stunned beyond words. I couldn't have been more surprised if he'd announced that the man was secretly engaged to a European princess. "Does Daniel know about this crush?"

Gerald twinkles at me as he snatches a bite of toast. "Mrngiufh," he says, heading toward the stairs.

❦ ❦ ❦

I hate to admit it, but Gerald is right about my busy schedule. The rain forces me to drive both boys to school, which means I have to take Bugs to Round Lake Elementary, come back to the house, hurry Clay along, drive him to the high school, and return home. To make matters worse, Clay's at the age where he doesn't *like* being dropped off by his mother. He slouches against the door the entire time we're on the road, then flees the vehicle as if I were a gun-wielding carjacker who coerced him to ride in a soccer mom minivan.

When I finally make it back to Fairlawn, I notice that Gerald's pickup wagon is parked next to the back porch . . . with no body in sight. The stubborn old man has gone ahead and moved Polly Prose himself, though I warned him not to.

I park in my usual spot, run into the house, and pop into the prep room. As I suspected, Gerald already has our client hooked up to the Porti-Boy.

I glare at him. "You were supposed to wait."

He shrugs. "She's as light as dandelion fluff."

"Yeah, and I'm Miss America. Let me help, Gerald."

He slips off a rubber glove and smiles. "We're holding steady here. Why don't you go on upstairs and, you know, put on your face?"

My hand rises to my cheek as I realize what he means—the unusual events of the day have thrown me out of my usual routine, so I've been running around town without even a dab of makeup. I'm one of those unfortunate women who doesn't look like herself without mascara and at least a smear of lip color. No wonder the school crossing guard gave me a strange look.

"I'll be back," I promise, turning toward the stairs.

After a quick shower and some sorely needed personal care, I skip back down the steps. I'm eager to help Gerald, so I'm a little dismayed to discover a client in the chapel.

"I'm so sorry," I say, hesitating in the doorway. "Have you—are you waiting for me?"

"Gerald said to have a seat," the woman says, standing. She's middle-aged with bleached blonde hair, and she looks vaguely familiar.

"I'm sorry to keep you waiting. I'm Jennifer Graham."

"Leticia Gansky." She steps toward me with an outstretched hand. "I don't know if you'll remember me from the funeral, but I'm Lyle Kourtis's granddaughter."

"Mrs. Gansky." I shake her hand and smile. "I thought you looked familiar. And haven't I seen your name on a few invoices?"

She laughs and waves her hand. "Oh, that. Yes, my husband operates Gansky's Get Great Air. I think he did your air-conditioning."

"He saved us from melting; that's what he did." I gesture to the sofa. "Please make yourself comfortable. How can I help you?"

She thanks me and sits on the couch in a relaxed pose, though one hand keeps fingering the strap of her leather purse. I've come to expect jittery nerves from prospective clients. Few people are comfortable with talking about death, and even fewer are eager to plan their funerals.

But Leticia is here because of her grandfather. I only hope she hasn't come to complain.

"I wanted to stop by," she begins, "and tell you how much my family and I enjoyed Pop-pop's service. In fact, you've got me thinking that it's time I planned my own funeral. Seems like such a waste to put it off. I mean, my grandfather had a nice tribute, but he'd have enjoyed it ever so much more if he'd had a direct hand in the planning. So that's what I'd like to do—plan it, enjoy it while I can."

I blink, not sure of what she's trying to say. "Your grandfather did preplan his funeral," I point out.

"Yes, but he didn't enjoy it, did he?"

"He might have enjoyed the planning. Most people do, once they put their minds to it."

"Perhaps that's so, but he didn't enjoy the *funeral.* How could he, being dead and all?"

I press the palms of my hands together and remind myself to be patient. "Let me make sure I understand. You're here because you want to preplan your funeral."

She beams. "Exactly."

Now she's speaking a language I can understand. A preplanned funeral involves a contract, which requires a financial payment, which guarantees a regular income for our faltering budget. Though 70 percent of a preneed payment goes into a secured investment account, the other 30 percent helps immeasurably with cash flow.

I glance out the window, where the sun is beginning to peek out from behind the clouds. I'd rather be embalming someone than selling, but this is also a necessary part of the business. "Mrs. Gansky, you're making a wise decision. Before we begin, can I get you something—a cup of coffee? tea, perhaps?"

"No, thank you." She tightens her grip on her purse. "Charley would kill me if he knew I was here; he thinks the idea is silly. But I told him I am set on knowing exactly what will be said and done at my funeral. After all, nobody plans to fail; they only fail to plan. Isn't that what they say?"

"That's what I've heard." When I reach for the materials on the shelf beneath the coffee table, I'm distracted by the sound of footsteps in the hallway. Gerald passes through the foyer, closes the front door, and crosses the front porch. He must be on his way to the doctor's office, and everything in me wants to go with him.

"Ms. Graham?" Leticia lowers her head and gives me a doubtful look. "Is this a bad time?"

I'm tempted to tell her I need to handle a family emergency, but Gerald wouldn't approve of my turning a client away. He'd say I was being foolish if I insisted on going with him, especially since I have a potential paying customer on the sofa across from me.

"It's a fine time." I draw the folder into my lap. "We have a specialized questionnaire for our clients, so I hope you don't mind taking a moment to fill this out. While you're doing that, I'll see if I can find the latest catalog."

I slip a fresh questionnaire into a clipboard and hand it to Leticia. While she fumbles in her purse and murmurs something about reading glasses, I go into the office, pull out a new brochure from the casket distributor, and stop in the prep room to peek at Mrs. Prose. The Porti-Boy is percolating with assuring regularity, and she hasn't puffed in any unusual places. All is well.

When I return to the chapel, Leticia has nearly finished the questionnaire.

"So much to think about," she says, tapping the tip of her pen against the clipboard. "But this is a good start. I'd like to stipulate a few other details, though."

"We'll do everything we can to fulfill specific requests." I take the clipboard and scan her notes. "I see you've chosen burial over cremation. That's an excellent choice."

Leticia laughs. "I do *not* want to end up collecting dust on somebody's mantel."

"But, um . . . you don't want to be embalmed?"

She grimaces. "It's not strictly necessary, is it?"

"No, not unless you're going to have a viewing. Unless a viewing is held within twenty-four hours of death, I would strongly urge you to consider embalming. Otherwise . . . well, the body begins to disintegrate, and most people aren't particularly comforted by signs of decay in their loved ones."

Leticia clutches her purse with both hands. "Naturally, I don't need it."

I'm about to ask why, but I stop myself. My job is not to pry or pressure but to present the available options calmly and rationally. Mrs. Gansky might be afraid of needles, or perhaps she's an environmentalist who would prefer a "green" burial. After all, people carry their opinions to their graves. I can only hope that if I'm around when this woman expires, I'll be able to persuade her survivors to keep the casket closed.

I glance at the next item on the preneed form. "As to the location, you want to have the funeral here instead of at a church?"

"Isn't that all right?"

"Absolutely. But many people prefer to have the memorial at their church, particularly if they're expecting a crowd—"

"I would hope to have a crowd, but my pastor probably wouldn't approve of me having this kind of service in the sanctuary. I don't think anything like this has ever been held at our church."

At this point, I break every rule and frown. I don't know what church this woman attends, but I can't imagine *any* church that's never been used for a funeral. What kind of service could she be imagining?

Then again, maybe Mrs. Gansky is off her meds. Or adjusting to new ones.

I try to focus on her questionnaire. "You've listed six songs you want played or sung. That's fine, but don't you think six might be too many? That's a solid half hour of music."

The woman's eyes glow with confidence. "I want the songs to be sung while the guests are filing in. I don't want them gossiping while they wait, so I thought I'd fill the chapel with music. I want them to sit and listen. To really be in the mood."

In the mood for *mourning*? I draw a deep breath and skip to the next question on the list. "You want a blond resting vessel?"

"Right." Leticia strokes the short hair at the nape of her neck. "I'd like to find one in a shade that matches my hair."

I slide the casket brochure toward her. "We have several lovely models in golden oak or ivory. You can take this home and give it some thought, and we also have an album with other pictures. . . ."

When she narrows her eyes at the page, I press on. "I see you want your minister to give a sermon—"

"It'll be the reverend from First Baptist. He's always brief and to the point."

"Assuming, of course, that he's still pastoring there when the time comes." I frown at the next notation. "After the sermon, you want an open mic?"

Leticia laughs. "I didn't know what else to call it. But when the preacher's finished, I want to invite anyone who's willing to come up and say a few words. As many people as want to speak. For as long as they want to talk."

Her eyes take on a soft, distracted look. "That was the only thing I regretted about Pop-pop's funeral. He was beloved in his time, but when he died, not many people were around to say so. Just a handful of acquaintances, really, when he had once been one of the most respected men in town. I thought it a shame more people weren't here to see him off." She gives me a quavering smile. "I suppose that's an unavoidable problem when you outlive your peers."

I'm tempted to point out that most people would consider ninety-three years a more than adequate trade-off for a few eulogies. But I'm not here to argue with this woman. I'm here to help her face death with peace of mind.

"Some would say," I begin, "that life is about earning accolades from God, not men. They'd say that we'll get eternal rewards in heaven."

"Oh, I know all that. But sometimes heaven can seem awfully far away. Then again, some days it feels like I've already got a foot through the door." Leticia dashes a trace of wetness from her lower lashes. "I'm only fifty-five, and do you know I've already begun to lose friends? My best friend from high school died last year—leukemia. Another friend died in a highway accident. And two years ago an old boyfriend of mine jumped from a bridge down in St. Petersburg. My friends are dropping like flies, and we're barely into middle age."

I fold her questionnaire. No one likes to consider his own mortality, but often it's when we're forced to confront it that we realize death is nothing to be feared.

"Death is simply an end to mortal life," I say, softening my voice. "I've come to think of it as a doorway. Now that you've taken the first step in preparing for it, you can spend the rest of your days knowing you've taken a lot of pressure off your family."

"I know all that, too." She drops her pen onto the coffee table. "And I suppose now you want to talk about finances, but whatever payment plan you want to set up is fine with me. I can either make payments or send you a check for everything. Whichever you'd prefer."

Again, I'm startled by her direct approach. Most people squirm and get a little defensive the moment we approach the discussion of paying for the funeral. Too many books, magazines, and movies have portrayed morticians as vultures eager to flay the bereaved in their most vulnerable moments. Obviously, Leticia Gansky isn't like most people.

I take a deep breath. "I'll need you to look through the brochure and select a suitable casket. Once you've decided, I can add up the totals for the services you've requested. I'm sure we can settle on a reasonable payment plan if that'd be preferable to a lump sum—"

Leticia leans forward, cutting me off. "What we really need to settle is the *date*. I have to get it on my calendar and make sure my family's schedule is clear."

I tilt my head. "Settle the date . . . to sign the contract?"

"The date for the funeral." Her brow furrows. "Maybe next month, if you can get the casket here on time. The weather should still be nice, and if we have it on a Saturday, my grandchildren will be out of school."

My thoughts spin in a slow whirl. Is the woman confused? or planning to commit suicide? I close my eyes and wish Gerald were here. "Mrs. Gansky . . ."

"Hmm?"

"Are you planning to die within the month?"

I open my eyes and find Leticia gaping at me. "Why would you think that?"

"Because you're setting the date for your funeral."

She tips back her head and laughs. "Did you think . . . Oh my! I thought I explained, but maybe I only *thought* I did. I'm always doing that: charging ahead like I've already explained myself when the people around me don't have the faintest idea—"

"Maybe we'd better start at the beginning." I set her questionnaire on the coffee table and clasp my hands. "You came here today because you want to plan a funeral. Your own. Am I right so far?"

Leticia nods, her eyes bright and blue. "I told you I thought it was a shame to wait until someone is as old as Pop-pop before they have a funeral. So I want to have a *living* service. I want it to look like an ordinary funeral, except I don't plan to be dead. I suppose I *could* be, but if I am, you can bet it was a surprise."

"Where, exactly, do you plan to be during this service?"

"Well, I suppose I'll sit next to the casket, if that's all right."

I exhale as several nerve endings in my head throb in protestation. Either they're planning a mutiny, or I have a migraine coming on. "Mrs. Gansky—" I meet her determined gaze—"I can appreciate the sentiment behind your plan, but a living funeral might not be a good idea. First of all, people are going to know you're not dead—they will see you sitting by the casket. Don't you think that will affect what they say and do during the service?"

Leticia tucks her chin like a turtle retreating into its shell. "I hadn't really thought about that."

"For another thing, a living funeral—it's a contradiction in terms, isn't it?"

Her lower lip begins to tremble. "Why shouldn't I gather my loved ones around so they can tell me how much they love me?"

"You *can* do that," I remind her. "On your birthday or on Mother's Day, tell Charley to throw you a party."

"Where's the fun in a party you've been *told* to have?"

"Then ask him to throw you a surprise party. I'm sure you know how to drop a hint or two."

Leticia gives me a look of disbelief and frustration. "I've dropped so many hints over the years it's a wonder we can walk through the house without tripping. No one hears me. No one even pays attention."

Not knowing what else to say, I spread my hands. I'm beginning to feel like I've wandered onto the set of the *Dr. Phil* show. "I'm sorry." I slide the questionnaire over the table. "You should take this home and give the matter some more consideration. If you want to preplan your funeral, we'd love to help you. But if you want to hear how much your family loves you, maybe you should talk to them. I don't think a funeral's what you really want, and I don't think your loved ones would like the idea."

She stares at the folded paper on the table. "Could we arrange a surprise funeral, maybe with cake and punch at the end?"

"That's not a good idea. People won't like it if you get them all upset for no real reason."

Leticia exhales heavily and pulls the questionnaire toward her. "Perhaps you're right. But I will take this home because I do need to plan my funeral, and so does Charley."

I'm a little reluctant to encourage her, but this is Charley Gansky's wife, and we love Charley Gansky. During our first summer at Fairlawn, when we walked around in a sweat and tied wet bandannas around our necks just to get through the day, we'd have done anything for the man who gave us air-conditioning.

I slide the casket brochure toward her as well. "I'll talk to Mr. Huffman and see what he says about setting up a preneed plan for you and Charley. With adjoining plots, maybe we can arrange a discount."

"We'd appreciate that." She drops the questionnaire and brochure into her purse and stands, but as we walk toward the foyer, I can't help noticing that the sparkle has gone out of her smile.

"Don't be disappointed," I say as I open the front door. "It's an interesting idea, but we like to keep our customers breathing and aboveground for as long as possible. I would be honored to handle your funeral, but I don't want to handle it next week or even next month. In fact, I'm sure you have many wonderful years ahead of you."

"Sweet of you to say so." Leticia pats my hand as she passes through the doorway, then turns around on the front porch. "Are you *sure* there's no such thing as a living funeral?"

"Maybe there is," I answer, "but I believe they're called retirement dinners. Or surprise parties. And there are no caskets involved."

Gerald runs his hand over the cold enamel at the side of the embalming table and imagines his own body lying where Polly Prose now rests. He will lie here, hands limp and useless at his sides, while Jen systematically plunges the hollow trocar through his abdomen and into his internal organs, allowing the pump to siphon out all the elements of decay. She will pierce heart, lungs, stomach, pancreas. . . .

What good is a pancreas, anyway, and why has his decided to call it quits? His heart and liver are still committed to the long haul, and his gallbladder hasn't caused any problems since he gave up fried foods and diet sodas. His kidneys are a little overactive these days, but they haven't given notice yet. Maybe he shouldn't have taken his pancreas for granted all these years. Who knew that the flat slab responsible for secreting enzymes could cause an entire body to fail?

He closes his eyes to visualize the ten-inch organ that sits between the stomach and the intestines. In anatomy class he learned that the pancreas has four regions: the head, neck, body, and tail. Now it seems fitting that the pancreas should be described like an animal. After seventy-three years, his has decided to bare its teeth and snarl at him.

The stomach pain that stabs at him after a heavy meal—he assumed it was indigestion. He blamed his itching on dry skin and his weight loss on his avoidance of fried foods and other dishes that give him stomach trouble.

Gerald straightens and fills his lungs with air, lifting his gaze to the lace curtains at the window. He's spent more than twenty years in this house, most of those hours in this room. On this table he has prepared tiny babies and aged men; he has tucked all of them into beautiful boxes and laid them down to rest until the Lord's return.

Soon Jen will do the same thing for him.

A sob rises from someplace far below the pancreas. How can death sneak up on a *mortician*? He shouldn't be surprised to discover that his mortal body has weakened. He ought to be grateful he's lived so long and so well. He's had a relatively easy go of things—no serious arthritis, no broken bones, no prostate problems like so many of his friends.

Yet he has an adenocarcinoma, Dr. Harding told him in her office. A common type of pancreatic cancer, caused by malfunctioning DNA. By some chemical quirk, a few rebellious cells were encouraged to grow into a greedy tumor that has spread to his lungs and liver.

Metastatic. A word that sounds a bit like *fantastic* but isn't.

And treatment? "Too late for surgery," Dr. Harding said, her voice softening. That's the trouble with the pancreas—the little beast doesn't raise much of a fuss until things have spiraled out of control. So the best she could offer was palliative care, otherwise known as keeping the patient comfortable until it's time for him to go.

Gerald listened without speaking, overcome by the odd feeling that the doctor was talking about someone he barely knew, an old friend with whom he'd lost touch. While he was grateful that his unfortunate friend wouldn't have to undergo the rigors of radiation or chemotherapy, the poor old fellow was still going to die.

"Palliative procedures," Dr. Harding continued, glancing at her notes as if reluctant to meet his eye, "include a possible surgical bypass so the tumor won't block the bile duct. Or we could insert a stent. Of course I'll prescribe drugs, particularly morphine, which will help ease any discomfort. We could even cut some of the nerves so you're unable to feel pain."

"No cutting." Gerald surprised himself with this pronouncement, but her sudden use of the word *you're* brought the situation into sharp focus. *He* had cancer; *he* was dying. Not some distant friend.

He looked into the doctor's wide brown eyes. "I don't want to be cut—I don't want the boys to see me with bandages and such. If there's nothing to be done, then I don't want to be a pincushion. I'll take your pills, do whatever you think best, but I don't want surgery."

Dr. Harding made another note on her chart. "We'll be giving you enzyme tablets. They'll help your body absorb the nutrients you need and cut down on your weight loss."

Gerald almost laughed aloud. For twenty years he'd been hoping to lose the spare tire around his middle, and now that cushion seemed to be a precious hedge against death. He ran his hand over his chest, then patted his belly. "Anything else I need to know?"

The doctor made one more note before tucking the chart beneath her arm. "I'm going to send a registered dietitian to your home. She'll write out menus for you, and I think you'll find that eating several small meals a day will be easier to handle than two or three large ones. If you're feeling queasy, eat soup, plain rice, or a baked potato. Take the vitamin supplements I'll be sending with you, and if you feel the urge to snack, go ahead and indulge yourself—fresh fruit, nonfat yogurt, and crunchy vegetables are all good choices. And drink plenty of fluids."

She reached into her pocket and withdrew a notepad, then scrawled out a name. "A support group for terminal patients meets every week at the Methodist church on Fifth Avenue. Not everyone feels the need for counseling, but if you do, these are good people."

Gerald gave the doctor a wavering smile. "Are any of them around long enough for you to know what sort of people they are?"

The doctor patted Gerald's hand, sending the scent of peach soap toward his nostrils. "I won't sugarcoat this, Mr. Huffman—barring a miracle, I don't think you have longer than three or four months. While you don't have the luxury of denial, you do have the blessing of foresight. If you need to tie up loose ends, now would be a good time to do it."

From a different pocket, she took out a card and handed it to him. *Hospice*, it said, and beneath the word Gerald saw another name and phone number.

"These are good people, too," the doctor said. "They'll help your friends and family care for you. You may have to visit the hospital occasionally, but most patients are much happier at home."

With that she patted Gerald's shoulder and walked out of the exam room, leaving him sitting on the edge of the table in a column of light and swirling dust motes.

Just like that. Read a diagnosis from a chart and you're on your way; pull a card from a pocket and you're done. If only he could walk away from his diagnosis as easily.

Now Gerald takes the hospice card from his pocket. He'd give anything to toss it in the trash and carry on as if nothing has happened. He could force himself to eat and take Advil for the discomfort. He could retreat to his room when the pain gets too bad. When he can't stand the agony, he could drive to the hospital for some heavy-duty drugs. When his strength is finally gone, he could lie down, close his eyes, and let his spirit fly to heaven. But Jen knows too much. She'd be furious if she discovered he'd hidden the truth from her, and he can't leave this life on bad terms with Jen and her boys.

And about the children . . . Gerald presses his hand against his belly as an unfamiliar pain grips his gut. He's going to have to give Clay and Bugs some kind of explanation. It's not as if they're unfamiliar with mortality. They look death in the face two or three times a week, and they've lost a father, but they've never watched someone waste away before their eyes. He'll have to explain that his pancreas has quit on him; the little critter is plumb worn-out. Not that he was ever aware of it, because the pancreas is a quiet worker, unlike the melodramatic heart or the demanding lungs.

Yet when the pancreas quits, it's over. No respite. No transplant. The end of the road.

At his age, he shouldn't be surprised to find himself facing the end. As a Christian, he's not worried about the afterlife. He knows heaven exists, and he's sure of his reservation.

But he will miss his new life with Jen, Bugs, and Clay. He will miss them more than words can say.

After my bizarre meeting with Leticia Gansky, I grab my purse and drive to the grocery store, then head to the elementary school to pick up Bugs. Gerald might be home by now and I want to talk to him, but I don't want to barge in and demand answers. When the time is right, he'll tell me what he wants me to know.

Bugs and I have time to kill before Clay gets out of school, so we go to McDonald's for an ice cream cone before pulling into the high school parking lot to wait. Clay could walk home, of course, but since he doesn't have his bike, I thought he might appreciate a ride. Besides, I want to take advantage of this opportunity to talk to both boys.

The high school doesn't have a carpool line, and I'm pretty sure Clay will flame out in embarrassment if he sees us parked at the front curb. So Bugs and I slide low in our seats and try to see who can do the best job of lick-sculpting the soft ice cream until it resembles the pointed turret at Fairlawn.

When the school bell finally rings, swarms of gangly adolescents spill out of the double doors. Many climb into Jeeps, sports cars, and SUVs, while others stream over the sidewalks, dividing into groups of two and three for the walk home. I crane my neck and peek out the passenger window, hoping for a glimpse of Clay. I finally spot him walking alone, head down, backpack slung over one shoulder. He didn't know I was coming, so he hasn't looked for us in the parking lot.

I tap the steering wheel as Bugs hangs out the window. "Clay Graham!"

My oldest son's head jerks up. He turns toward us and hesitates, torn between running away and acknowledging our existence. Since the latter option will save him a long walk, he finally rushes toward us, eager to be away before someone recognizes us as his relatives.

I start the van as he dives into the backseat and slams the door. For a moment he slouches in an adolescent pout; then he spies the McDonald's bag by my side. "Did you get me something?"

I slide the bag through the opening between the seats. "French fries. Probably not very hot but still edible."

He opens the bag and scoops a handful of stringy fried potatoes into his mouth.

Beside me, Bugs fastens his seat belt and gives me a look. "He didn't say thanks."

"I'm sure he meant to," I answer, easing into the traffic, "but his mouth's full of food."

"You should always say thanks before you eat," Bugs insists. "Or you might barf."

Clay kicks the back of his brother's seat.

"That's enough of that," I say, glancing at Clay. "And you're welcome."

I wait until both boys are quiet before mentioning the topic that's uppermost in my mind. We're on East Fifth Avenue when I begin the conversation I've been dreading. "Guys, we need to talk about something serious."

Clay catches my eye in the rearview mirror. "Is Grandma coming to visit?"

"Not that I know of—not soon, anyway. No, it's Gerald. He hasn't been feeling well, and I think he may be really sick."

Bugs faces me. "Didn't he get fascinated?"

"It's not the measles, Son."

"Then what's wrong with him?"

"I don't know, but he had to go to the hospital to have some tests. I think he knows what's wrong, but I haven't had a chance to talk to him yet. Whatever it is, we need to be sensitive. You guys might need to tone down the noise level when he's not feeling well. Go easy on Gerald, especially if he's trying to rest."

Bugs sits up straighter and stares out the front window. "Is Mr. Gerald gonna die?"

"Everyone dies, Bugs."

"I don't want him to die."

"None of us wants to lose him. We want him to stay with us for a long time." As much as I'd like to, I've learned not to make promises on God's behalf. Last year, when we agonized over my sister's unborn baby, I pretty much told my sons that since God had promised to answer our prayers, the baby would be okay.

God *did* answer our prayers, but not in the way we expected. So though I am longing to give my children reassurances, I've learned not to second-guess the Lord.

Clay says nothing, but when I glance back at him, he's looking out the window, not eating, not moving. He's deep in thought, and that's when I realize that my news may have hit him the hardest.

❧ ❧ ❧

Gerald is rocking on the front porch when we turn up the driveway, so I herd the boys into the house and shoo them toward the stairs before they have a chance to pepper him with questions. Bugs turns on the steps to shoot me a wide-eyed look, but I put my finger across my lips and march him up the staircase.

"Move it," Clay grumbles. "She'll tell us more later."

I touch Clay's shoulder. "Keep Bugs occupied, will you? I'll come back inside in a little while."

He nods, a shadow hovering in his blue eyes, and I am again reminded of how much sorrow my eldest son has endured in the last several years. He's been through a divorce, plus he's buried his father, his cousin, and a close friend. He's had to adjust to a new middle school and a new high school. Though moving to Mt. Dora hasn't been easy for Clay, staying in Virginia wouldn't have been a picnic, either.

Sometimes the road is rocky no matter which way you travel.

I squeeze his shoulder and send him upstairs; then I turn and step back onto the porch. Gerald is still rocking, his chair creaking in a regular rhythm as he stares at the long line of pine trees between our property and the lake.

I take the chair next to him. For a while we sit and rock together, two souls resting in the quiet conclusion of a spring day.

Finally, I gather my courage. "You saw Dr. Harding this morning?"

"Yep."

"She gave you your test results?"

"It's the pancreas."

I wait, but Gerald isn't feeling verbose. "And?"

"Three or four months," he says, his voice flat. "The doctor doesn't think I'll be around to celebrate the Fourth of July."

From out of nowhere, a random realization pierces me like a sniper's bullet: I'll have to buy the fireworks this year . . . because Gerald won't be here.

I gasp at the impact. "Why, that's impossible. No disease works that fast or comes on that quickly—" *Except pancreatic cancer.*

"You're gonna be fine," he says, slowing the pace of his rocker. "You'll finish your year of apprenticeship next month, and I'll sign off on any paperwork you need before your board exam."

"Gerald, that's not important now."

"Yes, it is."

"I mean, you shouldn't be thinking about me. We need a second opinion; we need to research and learn about treatment options."

"All my bills are paid," he continues, shifting his gaze to the trees, "and my will is tucked in a little box inside my dresser drawer. Daniel has a copy. My funeral's been preplanned for so long I've plumb forgot what I wrote down, but my tastes haven't changed so much."

I stare at him, my eyes welling with tears.

Gerald tries to smile at me, but the corners of his mouth wobble with the effort. "I want you to know that I'm going to see Daniel about leaving a little something for the boys' college fund—"

"Please stop." My hand catches his. "Don't talk about those things now."

He tilts his head toward me, but he doesn't meet my eyes. When he speaks again, his voice contains an uncommon quaver. "What else would you suggest we talk about?"

I want to talk about seeing another doctor, visiting another hospital, maybe flying up to the Mayo Clinic. This man is precious to me and my boys, and I'd move heaven and earth to save him. But I loved my father, too, and not even the finest physicians at Walter Reed could halt the progress of his disease.

I've learned that some truths are unpalatable, but still we must swallow them, digest them, and allow them to seep into the bloodstream of our lives. The truths of suffering may taste bitter, but they nourish the soul with strength that cannot be found in more pleasant experiences.

Like a vaccination.

Gerald is no fool; he has no death wish. If he thought a treatment would help, he would pursue it. So if he wants to accept his diagnosis without heroics, I need to respect him enough to honor his decision.

I lift my gaze to the sky, where the sun has begun to descend in the west, creating a vivid panorama of gold-streaked blue and crimson. "Maybe we shouldn't talk," I finally whisper. "Maybe we should sit here, watch the sky, and rock awhile."

So while tears stream silently down my cheeks—and, I suspect, Gerald's too—that's exactly what we do.

When Gerald leaves the porch and slips into the prep room—his way, I think, of avoiding Clay and Bugs because he's not able to face them without breaking down—I go upstairs to my bedroom, close the door, and call my mother. I manage to hold myself together while she says hello and asks about the boys, but when she inquires about Gerald, a lump the size of Boston moves into my throat.

"Jen? You still there?"

An anguished cry slips out of my mouth, a howl that sends her into full-on protective mother mode. "Good grief, what's wrong?"

"G-Gerald."

"Did he have a heart attack? I always knew he shouldn't be doing so much heavy lifting—"

"It's not his heart, Mom. It's his pancreas."

She snorts in my ear. "What doctor made that diagnosis? They're always blaming the pancreas, but what does it do, anyway? Does anyone really know?"

"Dr. Harding knows. She did all kinds of tests and told Gerald that he won't be with us more than three or four months."

"Three or four . . . Oh, honey, I'm so sorry. I was fond of that old man."

In typical fashion, my mother swings rapidly from denial to anger to sad acceptance. Her final swing, however, is always toward helpfulness, though usually I call it *meddling*.

"So when do you want me to come?"

"What?"

I honestly hadn't thought about Mom flying down to help, but maybe I shouldn't dismiss her offer. After all, I have no idea how Gerald's illness is going to affect us. Is he going to be bedridden at the end? Is he going to need a nurse? How much will I be able to do for him while I'm running the business and caring for my kids?

My gaze falls on the nightstand, where last night I left my legal pad after faxing the final copy for our newspaper ad. How can I oversee a stupid slogan contest while Gerald is fighting for his life? How can I do anything without him?

I want to support Gerald as much as I can, but I am well aware of my limitations. He wouldn't want me to shut down the funeral home, and we can't afford to close our doors, not even temporarily. If we take three months off, I'm afraid we'll go under.

Like it or not, I'm going to need help.

"Thanks for the offer," I tell Mom. "Don't feel like you have to rush down here, but I could really use you. I don't know a thing about nursing someone who's sick."

Her responding sigh ends in a cascade of weariness that reminds me of how haggard she looked when she took care of my dying father. I wasn't living with my parents during those months, but I know his illness drained my mother. Still, she kept him at home and cared for him there until he drew his last breath.

"Give me a couple of days," Mom says. "Let me close up the house, hand over my Red Hatter sash, and get my last load of donations to the church thrift store. Then I'll fly down, and we'll get through this together."

13

Joella checks her to-do list one final time, stuffs it in her purse, and hands her boarding pass to the airline employee.

"Fifteen C," the attendant says, returning the slip of paper.

Joella grips her carry-on bag and strides down the Jetway, feeling altogether too much like a cow in a cattle chute. She's flown a lot since Jen and the boys moved to Florida, and the experience hasn't grown any more pleasant. Seems like today's airlines are intent on moving thousands of people in as little time and space as possible.

She finds her seat—on the aisle, thank goodness—and drops into it, then feels an unexpected lump under her rear. Frowning, she leans to the side and conducts a rather inelegant search before snagging a paperback. She waves the book before the eyes of the young woman in the middle seat. "This yours?"

"Sorry," the girl says, grabbing the book.

Joella fumbles for the belt and latches herself into place. After safely stashing her bag and purse beneath the seat in front of her, she crosses her arms and closes her eyes, praying that the world will leave her alone for a few precious moments.

How awful that this thing with Gerald should happen right when Jen seems to be getting a handle on her muddle of a life. This is going to be a turning point for Jen, no doubt about it. One of those unexpected situations after which everything changes. One minute you're planning to do thus and so; the next moment your plan is shattered to smithereens by a disaster that darts into your path.

Joella smiles when she hears the flight attendant close the cabin door. Finally they can be on their way.

What will Jen do when Gerald has passed? There's no possibility she can run the funeral home single-handedly. Not even Gerald could manage it as a one-man shop; some jobs simply require two pairs of hands—and hauling dead bodies requires more brawn than Jen has ever had. That hairdresser, Ryan, often helps out, but he's so thin a strong wind could snap him in two. Besides, he has a salon to run, so he's not going to be available if Jen needs someone during regular business hours. When Jen has to haul a 280-pound corpse on a Wednesday afternoon, who's going to help her?

"If you'll direct your attention to the flight attendants for our safety instructions . . ."

Joella keeps her eyes closed, certain that if the plane goes down, she won't have time to duck and cover or whatever they want her to do. Some situations—like a jet falling out of the sky—are simply hopeless.

But Jen . . . surely there's hope for her. She could take on an assistant. She could look for an apprentice, but nobody in his right mind is going to want to be *her* apprentice, not when the ink on her diploma is barely dry. If she's lucky enough to find an experienced assistant, that person will be so much more knowledgeable he'll probably be bossing Jen around within a week.

Joella sighs, reluctantly convinced that Jen will have to sell the funeral home. The house is certainly in better shape than when she first inherited it, but she's invested thousands of dollars she might as well kiss good-bye. She'll be lucky if she can sell it as a business and even luckier if she can sell it as a residential property. Nobody wanted to buy Fairlawn a couple of years ago, and nobody's going to want to buy it now.

If Jen *could* sell it, maybe she'd come home to Virginia. Maybe she could find a place near Joella so the boys could be close to their grandma again. It's a shame those fatherless boys have to live so far away, especially when their mother works twenty-four hours a day to keep family and business together.

She opens one eye a slit as the flight attendant holds up a laminated card and gestures toward the emergency exits. The girl to her left pops her bubble gum while lazily turning a page of her book. Across the aisle, a man coughs noisily into his hand, undoubtedly spraying germs throughout a six-foot circle of contagion.

Joella squeezes her eyes shut and tries not to think about the bacteria oozing all over this plane. She'll be inhaling the sharp scents of disinfectant soon enough, because they'll have to be careful around Gerald. In his weakened condition he can't be exposed to germs, so they'll have to keep him away from strangers and remind the boys to wash their hands.

She smooths her damp palms on her slacks as the plane taxis down the runway. Her chest rises and falls in a deep breath; then she freezes—is that sudden stitch beneath her left rib a spasm or a pain? She tries to inhale again and feels a repeat of the sharp stab.

It's nothing, surely . . . but what are the symptoms of a heart attack? Men say they feel as if an elephant is sitting on their chests, but women say it's more like an aching arm or pain in the jaw or something. . . .

A stab in the chest?

She leans into the aisle and studies the upper storage bins at the front of the cabin. If the plane has defibrillators, up front is where they'll be. If in another minute or two she can't breathe, she can press the flight attendant call button. Or yell for a doctor. Or gasp a call for help to Miss Bubble Gum. Out of the two hundred plus people on this jet, surely one of them knows how to zap a heart back to life. She's seen it so many times on TV, she could almost do it herself.

The stitch in her chest eases as the plane levels out and the engine noise subsides to a steady roar. Beside her, the girl pops another bubble and turns another page. The man across the aisle coughs again, then runs his hand over his armrest.

Joella deliberately lifts her arms and stares at the locking mechanism on the tray table in front of her. That little plastic latch must be swarming with viruses, all of them intent on wreaking havoc in a human host. How many people have sneezed and coughed and popped bubble gum bubbles in its vicinity?

She's not going to touch it, not once during this flight. If she can help it, she's not going to touch *anything* that might contaminate her with germs she'd end up delivering to Fairlawn . . . and Gerald.

14

"Congratulations, Mr. and Mrs. O'Donnell." Ross lifts his frosted root beer mug and clacks it against his clients'. "May you enjoy your retirement, and may the Heavenly Rest Funeral Home continue to serve the needs of Tuscaloosa."

Ross has celebrated contract signings in far swankier places than this Cracker Barrel, but Sean and Mary O'Donnell seem to prefer a down-home ambience. Sean ordered the chicken and dumplings; Mary splurged on fried okra, grits, and ham. To maintain a spirit of camaraderie, Ross ordered vegetable soup and corn bread, but he'd eat a bowl of bug-infested mud if doing so would result in another deal for the Aldridge Elms bean counters.

The Heavenly Rest Funeral Home isn't much to look at, but it has assets of over three million in the bank. Not trusting in mutual funds or regulated annuities, Sean O'Donnell preferred to keep his investment funds close at hand. His mortuary's preneed deposits are liquid, ready to be drained off by the purchaser. That will upset several parties—592, to be exact—when they realize their preneed contracts have been invalidated, but Aldridge Elms does not have to honor contracts made with another party.

"I must admit—" Sean sets his mug on the table—"that what you said makes perfect sense."

"It's the perfect time to liquidate," Ross answers, picking up his spoon. "And franchises are *the* effective model for today. Corporate firms can operate so much more effectively than independent shops, and the larger the firm, the better the deals they can cut with wholesalers. These savings, of course, can be passed on to the consumer—savings that will always undercut the mom-and-pop shops, no offense intended."

"None taken," Sean says, grinning. "Mary and I have known this was coming—we just never thought we'd be able to take advantage of it. To be sure, we never imagined a big firm like the Elms would be interested in our wee operation."

"Aldridge Elms wants to be the best, the brightest, and the biggest." Ross stirs his soup and gives Mary a smile. "In fact, if you know of any other morticians who might be considering a change or facing retirement, I'd love to have their names."

Sean scratches his neck and stares at the ceiling, but Mary elbows him. "There's that one fellow we met a couple of years ago at the convention. Remember him?"

"Who?"

"The man from Florida. He had a partner, remember, but the partner died. The home was going to get passed to some distant relative, but the guy said he didn't know if the heir would have the courage to stick it out."

Sean's eyes grow thoughtful. "Yeah, Gerry. Where was he from? Mt. Pleasant? No, Mt. Dora."

"That's right. The home had a real pretty name—Fairhill or Fairlawn. That's it—the Fairlawn Funeral Home." Mary twirls a finger in her red hair. "Seems to me it was a little home in a real nice town. Gerald—the guy Sean talked to—was real disappointed that the home might soon be up for sale."

"Have you heard anything from this man lately?" Ross sips his drink, trying to conceal his eagerness. A consummated sale is a bit like a wedding. It's not polite to rush off and court someone else before you've finished toasting the newest bride.

"We skipped the convention last year," Sean says, glancing at Mary. "But you can always call him and ask. His name's Huffman. Gerald Huffman."

Ross taps a note to himself on his iPhone. "And his mortuary is in Mt. Dora, Florida?"

"Picturesque little town," Mary says. "Famous for antiques and such. But a real sweet funeral parlor. The old-fashioned kind, where the director lives above the shop."

Ross saves the note, slips the phone back into his pocket, and lifts his mug again. "I might give him a call one of these days. But right now, let's celebrate your new lives together. Here's to a bright future for Sean and Mary O'Donnell!"

A birthday should be celebrated, but Leticia's has barely been noticed.

Leticia sits jammed between her husband and son-in-law at the corner of her dining room table and watches her family feast on a birthday luncheon she worked hard to prepare. Her daughters, grandsons, son-in-law, and husband are stuffing themselves with her pot roast, garlic mashed potatoes, perfectly smooth gravy, biscuits, congealed strawberry salad, and lattice-topped apple pie. Everyone's talking a mile a minute, but no one's talking about her. Or even *to* her.

Is this any way to celebrate her life? Jennifer Graham said she should throw herself a party, but that woman has never seen the Gansky clan in action. How would a party look any different from the scene before Leticia's eyes? If she strung crepe paper around the room, no one would care. If she taped balloons to the china hutch, the girls would have assumed they were left over from the women's missionary union meeting. She could have put a pointed paper hat on her head and worn a Happy Birthday sash over her chest—Charley would have shrugged and chalked it up to his wife's foolishness.

At the far end of the table—in the chair Leticia usually occupies—fourteen-year-old Brandon reaches for a second helping of mashed potatoes and gets his hand tapped by his mother. "Watch your manners," Stephanie snaps, glancing at Jason, her husband of less than two years. "Say 'Please pass the potatoes.'"

Brandon scowls at his mom, then drops his hands into his lap. "Wasn't hungry, anyway."

"Eat. You need to eat," Emily says, glancing with approval at her own son's brimming plate. Austin appears to have been overindulging at every meal lately, but Emily says his round cheeks and puffy belly are only a phase. A fatherless boy has to find something to fill his life, and with Emily working until five every day, what can the boy do after school but watch TV, play video games, and snack?

Stephanie smiles across the table at her sister. "Dillard's is having a sale. Want to go over there after lunch?"

Emily stops chewing and swallows hard. "How can we leave Mom with the dishes?"

"We'll go after we help clean up. The ad says 75 percent off in the juniors' and misses' departments. You couldn't find a better deal on eBay."

Emily glances at her son. "I guess I could go. It'd give the boys some time together, wouldn't it?"

Leticia bites her tongue. So . . . even on her birthday, her girls want to run off to the mall and leave her to babysit their children. They won't see it that way, of course, because Charley and Jason are here, too, but soon the men will park themselves in front of the TV, turn on ESPN, and remain glued to the sofa until suppertime.

Stephanie gives her sister a dimpled smile—the same smile that caught Jason's attention and Brandon's father's—and squeezes her husband's arm. "That okay with you?"

Jason grins and reaches for another biscuit. "You girls go out and have big fun. Just don't spend big money."

Stephanie giggles and waves for Leticia's attention. "Okay with you, Mom?"

Leticia chokes back a sob. Just once, she wouldn't mind being invited to go out with her daughters. But she doesn't shop in the juniors' or misses' departments, and she can't remember the last time she found shopping more appealing than having a free hour to relax and take a load off her feet. "Fine," she says, her voice sounding strangled in her ears.

"Great." Stephanie stands and lifts her plate, then pauses to speak to her son. "When you're finished, make sure you take your dishes to the sink so Grandma can put them in the dishwasher, okay?"

Brandon mumbles in response as Leticia lowers her head to hide the tears stinging her eyes. It's her birthday, but no one has thanked her for the dinner. Three days ago she buried her grandfather, but no one has asked about Pop-pop's funeral or wondered if she's missing him.

Her heart stirs with new sympathy for Pop-pop. Dying tucked away in that nursing home . . . it's almost as if he never lived. As if he ceased to matter once his children grew up and moved into lives of their own.

Leticia looks around the table—at Charley, round and full everywhere but on the top of his head; pretty Emily; Austin and Brandon; newlyweds Stephanie and Jason. If she disappeared in the very next minute, would anyone at this table even notice?

Not unless someone asked her to pass the pie and grew tired of waiting for it.

She places her fingertips on the edge of the table and grits her teeth. She has invested her *life* in this family, and all she wants is a little gratitude, a little recognition. Maybe a hug now and then. Is that too much to ask?

An hour ago she set this table with high hopes. She imagined this as a warm and loving dinner, filled with laughter and appreciation and maybe even a compliment or two. After a few minutes Charley would remind everyone that it was her birthday, and the girls would raise their glasses in her honor and the grandsons would look at her with bright eyes and beaming smiles. . . .

Then the family trooped in, one of the boys burped, and the illusion vanished.

They need to be taught a lesson. They need to realize how much she does to make their lives more comfortable, but short of dying or taking an extended vacation, she's not sure how to drive the lesson home.

Leticia looks up and blinks tears away, regarding her loved ones with a rueful smile. She's not giving up. She'll teach them to appreciate her if it's the last thing she does.

Which it may very well be.

Just before lunchtime on Saturday, I send Clay and Bugs down to Lydia's house on the pretext of borrowing a cup of sugar. A true friend in a time of need, she has graciously volunteered to keep my boys occupied while Gerald and I sort through the difficult emotions and details involved in his prognosis.

The boys know the entire truth. Last night the four of us sat around the dinner table, and I told the boys Gerald is sicker than we had thought at first. He would be leaving us in a few months, but until then, we were going to do everything we could to help him carry on as usual. When we could no longer do that, we would do our best to make him feel comfortable and loved.

"We don't have to worry about Gerald," I told Clay and Bugs, "because we know we'll see him again in heaven, but we want to be sure his last months are peaceful and happy. It will probably be a while before we're with him."

Gerald didn't say a word the entire time I spoke. When I finished, Bugs slipped out of his chair and threw his arms around the old man's neck. Gerald's silvery head bent over Bugs's shoulder, and my eyes filled with tears.

When I could see clearly again, Clay stood next to Gerald, too, his face buried in Gerald's neck and his arm stretched across the man's shoulders as if he would accept some of the burden if he could.

My precious little men. Gerald has come to mean so much to them.

I dash away another tear and watch the boys until they enter Lydia's front gate. Then I go back in the house, brush my hair, and pick up my purse. I'll have to leave for the airport in a bit, but before I go, Gerald and I need to talk about some important personal matters.

I find him waiting on the front porch, sitting in his favorite rocker. My feet feel as heavy as lead as I clump across the wooden porch to join him.

"You need to have those steps painted and checked every year," Gerald says, gesturing toward the stairs that lead down to the sidewalk. "Sometimes the nail heads work their way up through the wood. You don't want somebody tripping down the stairs at a funeral."

"I'll make a note of it." I drag one of the rockers over and turn it so I'm facing Gerald when I sit. "This still a good time for you to talk?" I speak gently in an attempt to plumb his mood, but from the flash of resolve in his eye, I can see that he is done with melancholy.

"No time like the present, missy. I've put in a call to Daniel, and I'm hoping he can see me this afternoon. I want you to know I have a little money saved—not a lot, but I want it to go into the business. I've poured my heart into this place, so why not pour my earthly treasure into it, too?"

I catch his hand. "You don't have to leave us your money. You have a daughter and a granddaughter, right? They're your family."

A woebegone smile flits across his features. "They won't want to hear from me."

I shake my head, unwilling to believe that anyone wouldn't want to hear from this sweet man. "How do you know? Shouldn't you call them and . . . well, let them know your news? Some people who've been estranged have a change of heart when they realize they have very little time to reconcile. If you call your daughter, surely she'll want to make things right."

Gerald grimaces and tugs at his ear. "My door has always been open. Kirsten knows where I live; she's known for years."

Kirsten. . . . I don't think I've ever heard him use her name. "How do you know how she'll react?"

"I know her. I raised her. And she broke my heart." He gives me a smile brimming with a great deal of sadness. "Truth is, you've been more like a daughter to me than Kirsten ever has, and you've invested everything into this mortuary. I want to help you; I'd like to be sure that the ministry of Fairlawn will continue after I'm gone. So I'm going to ask Daniel to make a few changes in my will."

"Gerald, please don't do this. You don't understand what's been happening in your daughter's life. Maybe she's at a place where she's willing to reconcile. Maybe she's realized that her daughter needs to meet her grandfather . . . while she still can."

Gerald's eyes soften. "Her name's Katie, I hear."

"Your granddaughter? It's a pretty name."

"If she looks like her mama, I imagine she's a very pretty girl. I would like to see her before I check out."

I squeeze his arm. "Do you want me to call Kirsten? ask her to bring Katie for a visit?"

He blinks slowly, but I feel a subterranean quiver go through him at the suggestion. I can't comprehend what he's feeling, but obviously he is torn between desire and something else. "No," he says, his voice ragged. "Let's not torment ourselves."

I don't understand what he means, but when he leans forward as if to stand, I catch his hand again. "Please promise me this: don't completely disinherit your daughter. I don't mean to tell you what to do with your money, but I don't want to look your daughter in the eye at the funeral and have her think I stole what was rightfully hers. Please don't cut her out of your will. It wouldn't be right."

Gerald studies me in silence; then he nods. "You may be right. For your sake, I'll not forget her in the will. But I'd be surprised if you see her at the funeral. I'll be surprised if we see Kirsten at all."

❧ ❧ ❧

I slant into the right lane on the turnpike as a determined roadster beeps from somewhere in the vicinity of my rear bumper.

"What is *with* the drivers down here?" Mom clutches at the shoulder strap of her seat belt and turns to glare at the offending bumper beeper. "Always in a hurry. I thought people came to Florida to retire and relax."

"Not everyone down here is retired," I remind her, watching as the offending driver blasts by me in a blur of metallic red paint and gray hair. "And even fewer are relaxed. The young people are trying to make a living, and the older folks are enjoying their second adolescence."

When Mom straightens and stares straight ahead, I remember why she's come—Gerald. That precious man will not enjoy any golden retirement years.

"Exactly how old is he?" Mom asks, obviously tracking with my train of thought.

I concentrate on remembering Gerald's last birthday. We ordered a double-layer chocolate cake, and Gerald made a big deal out of Bugs's helping him blow out all those candles. "He was born in January '35," I tell her. "So that makes him—"

"Seventy-three," she answers, a note of satisfaction in her voice. "That's a nice long life. The Bible says anything over threescore and ten is gravy."

I snort softly. "Is that from the collected proverbs of Rachael Ray?"

"I'm saying he's had a long life, longer than a lot of people. I'm as sorry as you are to see him go, but it's not like he's dying before he's even had a chance to live. He's had a family, friends, a career—"

"Two careers, actually. Did you know Gerald was a minister before he came to Fairlawn?"

Her brows arch. "Where did he pastor?"

"Somewhere in Georgia, I think. He left his church not long after his wife died. He's never said so, but I suspect he was emotionally burned out. He came to Mt. Dora, Uncle Ned took him in, and he learned the embalming trade. He's been here ever since."

"That explains a lot." Mom laces her fingers. "How he's so at ease with people and all. He's really good at comforting the bereaved."

"I'm going to miss him something awful." The confession rises from some place deep inside me, along with a sob that breaks from my throat in an undignified hiccup.

Mom smiles at me with compassion in her eyes, then rubs my shoulder. "Of course you will, but you're going to do fine. Gerald's taught you everything you need to know, and he's been your right-hand man."

"He's been more than that," I correct her. "He's been like a father to the boys. Even before Thomas died, he was an incredible example for Clay and Bugs. I used to worry about how not having a dad would affect them, but Gerald has been everything they've needed."

"The Lord will take care of those boys." Mom squeezes my shoulder. "He didn't bring you down here to abandon you, Jen."

"I e-mailed McLane and Jeff with the news," I add, reminding my mother of my half sister and brother-in-law who are stationed in Europe. "They were crushed. They love Gerald, too."

Mom dips her head in an abrupt nod. "Everyone loves that old man. We should all be so lucky when it's our time to go."

"They love him because he loves *them*. And . . . I'm going to miss him something terrible. . . ." I stop talking because we've covered this ground before. Yet I know we'll cover it again, probably several times in the days ahead.

What is it about human nature that makes us need constant reassuring? I know God is faithful and I know he is true, but the moment an unexpected development crowns the horizon, my heart does a double beat and my stomach falls to the tips of my toes.

God is good to me, though, and he's sent my mother. I know she'll stay as long as it takes to see Gerald through this illness, so with her help, I'll survive.

If we don't drive each other crazy first.

"Do you have any of that antibacterial lotion?" She reaches for my purse. "The man across the aisle coughed like a TB patient through the entire flight."

"Center zippered pocket," I say, knowing that she'll go through all the sections of my bag no matter which compartment I tell her to search. What better way to take stock of my life than riffling through my stuff?

Mothers and daughters, I've decided, are a lot like oil and water.

Both are liquid, both are precious, and both are determined to maintain their boundaries. I feel like an absolute porcupine when Mom shows up, but I don't remember ever feeling prickly around my father. Fathers and daughters must operate under a different dynamic.

"Gerald has a daughter," I say, glancing at the fields of scrubby grass and palmetto beyond the highway. "I asked if I should call and give her the news, but Gerald said no. Don't you think that's odd?"

Mother responds with an emphatic nod. "I do . . . unless he wanted to call her himself."

"That wasn't it. I don't think they talk at all. The only thing I know about Kirsten is that she lives outside Atlanta and has a daughter Gerald has never seen."

"Must have had a huge falling-out if they're not even speaking."

"Maybe, but the thing is, I think Gerald really wants to hear from her, and I know he wants to see his granddaughter. So I wondered if I should secretly call her and invite her for a visit."

Mom stares out the window, then tucks a piece of hair neatly behind her ear. "I think you should. Even if they're estranged, a daughter needs to know what's happening with her father. Maybe it'll take something tragic to fix whatever problem's come between them."

"What if it was a really big problem?"

"God can sort it out. When we're faced with a problem, he will always do what we are unable to do. But he will never do what we can do ourselves."

"So I should call her?"

"I vote yes. The sooner the better."

❧ ❧ ❧

After getting my mother settled in the guest room, I lead her downstairs, where we find Gerald cleaning out old files in the office. His face lights up when he sees Mom, and after they share an embrace, he pulls away and gives her a wink.

"I need to go to town," he says, speaking to Mom, "and I'm not supposed to drive since I've been taking this medication that might make me drowsy. I have to see Daniel Sladen at his office, but after that, could I interest you in a hamburger and maybe some ice cream?"

Mom tilts her head and smiles, though I can see hesitation in her eyes. I'm sure she'd rather relax upstairs until the boys come back from Lydia's, but she has flown all this way to help us. "I'd like that." She places her hand on Gerald's arm. "Did you want to go soon?"

He checks his watch. "My appointment with Daniel is in half an hour. Shouldn't take but a few minutes—I don't have much patience with paperwork."

She faces me. "Looks like I'm pulling taxi duty for your tenant. Will you give the boys a hug from me and tell them I'll see them later? And no rummaging through my suitcase for their surprises." When I nod, she turns back to Gerald. "I'll meet you on the porch in a few minutes. Let me freshen up a bit, and then I'll be ready to go."

I would have stayed to help Gerald clean up the files, but Mom grips the back of my neck and almost pushes me out the door. When we reach the foyer, well beyond the range of Gerald's hearing, she whispers in my ear, "This is your chance—call the daughter."

I blink. "I don't even know her last name."

"You're a bright woman. Do what all those people do these days to find things on the Internet."

I crinkle my nose. "What people? And what do they do?"

"You know, they doodle them."

"They *google* them, Mom."

"Right. And if that doesn't work, snoop." She leaves me on the landing and climbs the stairs, humming a careless little tune as she goes.

Twenty minutes later, Mom and Gerald come out of the house and walk toward his old Plymouth. He makes a few wisecracks as he ambles toward the car, even asking me if he should strap on Bugs's bicycle helmet before getting in a vehicle with my mother.

"Hush up and get in, old man," Mom calls, giving him a look that could melt ice. "Be nice or I'll leave you in town and make you walk home."

Something in me cringes to hear her speak so sharply to a sick man, but the sight of Gerald's grin assures me that he doesn't want us to treat him as if he were made of spider silk. Mom is doing her best to behave normally, and perhaps that's what Gerald needs right now.

Mom slides behind the wheel, and Gerald gets into the passenger seat, hanging one elbow out the open window and drumming his fingers against the roof.

I wave good-bye and hope the excursion will be pleasant for both of them.

When they have gone, I go into the office and turn on the computer. I type *Kirsten Huffman Atlanta* in the box on the Google search page, and the screen fills with dozens of entries. Trouble is, I have no idea if any of these people are related to Gerald, and it'd take me weeks to call them all.

I go to one of those people finder Web sites and try the same name. Again, several entries, but no way to determine if any of them are Gerald's daughter. Most of the entries have approximate ages listed, but I don't have a clue how old the woman is. The computer needs more information, and I don't have it. So it looks like I'll have to resort to more old-fashioned means of information gathering.

I scoot up the stairs and am overwhelmed almost immediately by a cloud of guilt. Mom agrees that Gerald's daughter should be told about his illness, but in order to do that, I'm going to have to violate his privacy. Except for the time I went through my husband's dresser drawers in search of proof that he was having an affair—a search that resulted in a devastating affirmation—I've never snooped in anyone's room, and I *hate* the thought of prowling through the belongings of a man I genuinely respect. But don't desperate times call for desperate measures?

The door to Gerald's bedroom stands open, exposing the almost Spartan furnishings—a double bed, a dresser, a desk, a bench with a small television on it, a trunk. A closet has been cut into the corner, and next to it is a tiny bathroom. Not the most palatial living quarters, but Gerald has never complained.

I hesitate on the threshold, then reach behind me for the dish towel next to the kitchen sink. Maybe I can go in his room on the pretext of dusting. If I happen to spy an address book or something, that's not really an invasion of privacy, is it?

I fold the dry dish towel and run it over the top of Gerald's dresser. Not much clutters the surface—only a lamp, a worn Bible, a clock, a mason jar filled with pocket change, and a framed photograph of a woman and a little girl.

I pick up the photo and wipe the surface, but Gerald hasn't allowed any dust to accumulate here. The woman is lovely, probably in her early thirties, and the little girl looks to be about five or six. In summer sundresses, they squint into the camera as they stand in front of a small house. Their smiles speak of a lovely morning and good times.

If Gerald snapped this picture, they were smiling for him. Perhaps he took them to the beach that afternoon or to an amusement park. Maybe it was a birthday or some other special occasion.

My blood thickens with guilt as I turn the picture over and slide the protective backing out of the frame. I drop the stabilizing cardboard onto the bed and study the back of the photograph. Fortunately, someone in Gerald's family took the time to record details; a feminine hand labeled the picture, "Evelyn and Kirsten, summer 1977."

I reassemble the photograph, rub my fingerprints from the sterling silver frame, and replace it on the dresser at exactly the same angle and location. Now . . . what happened to Kirsten after she grew up?

I tiptoe through the bedroom, peek into the closet, and pause at the bathroom door, feeling more intrusive than ever. I probably shouldn't feel so uncomfortable—after all, I am the landlady and I own this house—but a person's bathroom is the repository for their most intimate secrets. I don't really expect to find any clues about Kirsten in here, but for the sake of thoroughness, I take in Gerald's life with one swift glance.

A row of pill bottles stands between the sink and the wall, their labels covered with fine print and red-stickered warnings. Gerald's toothbrush hangs aslant from the ceramic holder cemented into the wall, its bristles splayed. His comb lies on the vanity, positioned directly beneath the light switch, and a silver hair curls from between the dark plastic teeth. A handheld device lies on the other side of the sink—a nose hair trimmer?—and a cloudy juice glass waits by the faucet.

I lift my gaze to the mirror, where a yellowed note card hangs by a stretch of transparent tape. Typewriter print reveals a faded message:

> O God, I beg two favors from you; let me have them before I die. First, help me never to tell a lie. Second, give me neither poverty nor riches! Give me just enough to satisfy my needs. For if I grow rich, I may deny you and say, "Who is the Lord?" And if I am too poor, I may steal and thus insult God's holy name.

I recognize the verses from Proverbs, and it certainly sounds like Gerald.

I back out of the room without making a sound. As repulsive as the idea is, I'm going to have to dig a little deeper.

I step toward the bedroom window and peer outside. No one stirs on the lawn, so the boys are probably either still at Lydia's or at the park. I hear nothing but the slight whisper of the wind and the caw of a crow in the pine trees. Gerald and Mom have probably reached Daniel's office by now, so they're not likely to return anytime soon.

I grit my teeth and move to the dresser, then open the top drawer. Inside I find underwear and socks, neatly folded and stacked, nothing else. I poke a tentative finger between the piles of clothing, hoping to find something useful, but apparently Gerald isn't the sort of man who hides his worldly treasures among his boxer shorts.

I open the second drawer—shorts, undershirts, and T-shirts, most of which are still stiff with fabric sizing. Gerald's not really a T-shirt guy, and the only time I've seen him wear shorts is when he washes the hearse.

The third drawer contains three cardigans, a couple of file folders, and a single pair of long underwear, yellowed with age. I flip through the file folders, but they're filled with personal income tax returns—pages I have no need to read.

Fortunately, I strike pay dirt in the bottom drawer. Among dusty photograph albums, a college yearbook, and several old church directories, I discover an address book. I turn to the *H*s and find Kirsten's name. Several names, actually, cascading down the page like a waterfall of short-lived commitments:

~~Kirsten Huffman~~
~~Kirsten Bishop (Steve)~~
~~Kirsten Lovett (J.J.)~~
~~Kirsten Skinner (Lloyd)~~
~~Kirsten Phillips (Tommy)~~
Kirsten Phillips (Hawkeye Jones)

The last listing is followed by a telephone number, no address, so I walk into the kitchen for a pen and copy the string of digits on the inside of my palm.

Just to be sure I haven't missed anything important, I flip through the pages of the book. A note card falls out, and on it I see my name written in block letters:

JEN—

IN CASE OF AN EMERGENCY, YOU'LL PROBABLY WANT TO CALL KIRSTEN PHILLIPS IN ALPHARETTA, GEORGIA. 770-555-3857.

I lean against the dresser. Obviously, Gerald meant for me to find this. But did he mean for me to find it now or later? Did he slip this card into his book last week or after we first met?

I shake my head. What does it matter? Gerald knew I'd have to contact his daughter eventually, so he did what he could to make things easy for me. Maybe he was subconsciously hoping I'd do exactly what I'm doing now. Beneath his denials, perhaps he's hoping I'll call Kirsten before he dies. Surely he's hoping she'll come to see him and bring his granddaughter.

After slipping the note card back into the address book, I change my mind. I fold the card and put it in my pocket, then return the book to Gerald's bottom drawer. If he checks his addresses again, he'll know I found the card. And that's okay.

I close the drawer and idly run my dish towel over the surface of the handles. Something in me insists it's ridiculous to feel so guilty; I'm only doing what's best for Gerald and his daughter. Surely in time they'll both realize I was right to go snooping.

But despite Gerald's reassuring note, right now I feel as guilty as Eve.

Gerald rubs the soft leather of Daniel Sladen's wing chair and wonders how the material stays so clean. With so many sweaty-palmed clients sitting in this seat and considering the end of their lives, you'd think the leather would be stained with perspiration.

"I hope you know," Daniel says, his eyes dark with concern, "that as much as I'm delighted to serve you, I'm very sorry to hear the news that has brought you to my office."

Gerald rubs the armrest again. "I appreciate you meeting me on a Saturday. I should have come sooner. I should have done a lot of things sooner, like getting to the doctor in the first place."

Daniel clears his throat as he sifts through a stack of folders. "Well, I'm going to do everything I can to make sure you have nothing to worry about except taking care of yourself."

"You don't have to fret about me. Joella's in town now, so Jen will have some help. We'll be fine."

Daniel removes a sheet of paper from the first folder and drops it onto the desk. "Obviously, a man in your situation has many things on his mind, so these documents are designed to make sure your wishes are followed even if you reach a point where you are unable to express your desires. You already have a will on file; in a few minutes we'll go over those terms to see if you want to make any changes. Other than your will, the two documents I recommend are a medical power of attorney, also known as a living will, and a durable power of attorney."

Gerald can't remember ever having heard so much legal jargon in a single breath—and that can't be good. "Do I really need to fuss with all that?"

Daniel folds his hands. "The living will gives someone else the authority to make medical decisions for you if you are unable to do so—for instance, if you've slipped into a coma. The durable power of attorney has more to do with matters *outside* the hospital—the agent you appoint in that form will have the authority to pay your bills and sign legal documents in your stead. Bottom line, this person will act as your legal representative until the day you revoke the power of attorney or . . . you pass away."

Gerald scratches the itchy spot on the back of his left hand. "Does my representative have to be a family member?"

"Absolutely not. But I would urge you to choose someone you find totally trustworthy. You'll be giving them complete control over your affairs."

"So—" Gerald grins—"they could steal me blind if they'd a mind to?"

"Indeed they could. I'd advise you to take some time and carefully consider your choice."

"I've no need to think about it." Gerald strokes his chin. "I'd like you to be the executor of my estate, since you know my will and all. As to my legal representative, there's only one person in my life who fits the bill, and I think you know who that is."

Daniel shifts in his chair. "Something tells me I ought to refrain from making any comment at this point. The decision should be yours, completely yours. But if you want to ask—"

"I'd like Joella Norris to be my agent," Gerald interrupts. "She's right out in the waiting room, if you need to ask her approval before we square things away."

The lawyer's left brow rises. "You want Jen's mother?"

"She's a woman of a certain age. As much as I love Jen, I don't want to put extra pressure on her. But Joella . . . she'll do the job, and she'll stick around until everything's settled. She's a tough bird, and I think she can handle anything the good Lord sends our way."

Daniel braces his hands on his chair and pushes away from the desk. "All right, then. If you'll wait here, I'll ask Mrs. Norris to come in."

"Hold on." Gerald puts out a hand. "I've been wanting to ask you something in private, and lately I've been reminded that there's no time like the present."

Daniel studies him thoughtfully. "Yes?"

"As you know, Jen's become like a daughter to me."

"I know you two are close."

"And seein' as I'm the man who's been like her father for the last couple of years, I'd like to know your intentions regarding her. Because if they're not honorable—"

Daniel cuts him off. "I assure you, Gerald, the last thing in the world I want to do is hurt Jen."

"You're not toying with her affections, are you? She can take care of herself, but I've got to consider those precious boys. They've gone through a lot in the last few years. They've lost their dad and they're going to lose me—" his voice breaks, but he pushes on—"and I don't want them to lose anyone else."

Daniel stands and comes around to the front of the desk. "I appreciate what you've said, and I think you know I care for Jen a great deal. It's because I know she's been through a lot that I've tried to take things slow. She's needed time to work through her feelings, get the business on its feet, and get through school."

"She's finished with all that. As soon as she passes the national board exam, she can apply for her license."

"I'm proud of her . . . and grateful to you for helping her get this far. But I've wanted to give her all the time she needs before I take our relationship to the next level. Trust me, waiting hasn't been easy."

"Take it from me, son—" Gerald leans back in his chair as he crosses his legs at the ankle—"patience is a virtue, but life is brief. You don't want to wait too long."

I'm filling out our quarterly payroll forms when Mom and Gerald come home. I hear the murmur of conversation as they pass through the foyer, followed by the sound of heavy footsteps going up the stairs. Gerald's steps.

A moment later, Mom slips into the office and sits in the chair across from my desk. She smiles, her eyes shiny with a secret. "Well, that was certainly interesting."

I'm only too happy to look up from the Florida Employer's Quarterly Report form. "Did Gerald get everything squared away?"

"I don't know *all* the details," she says, "but I know who'll be calling the shots in his last days. He appointed someone you know as his agent for his living will."

I pull the copy of my federal 941 from the printer. "Daniel?"

Mom shakes her head. "Guess again."

"Um . . . our pastor?"

"Come on, Jen. Think."

A hollow feeling settles in the pit of my stomach. "He didn't choose *me*, did he?"

"You're off the hook."

"Then who?"

"Me."

For an instant I can only blink in bafflement. Over the years, I have witnessed encounters in which Mom and Gerald bickered like feuding neighbors. So why did he choose her and not me?

"Apparently," she says, studying her nails with a critical eye, "he trusts me with his life. So either he really thinks a lot of me—"

"Or the man hasn't another friend in the world," I finish, my tone dry. "He trusts me with his life, too. So what in the world possessed him to choose you?"

Mom gives me a don't-be-difficult look. "Why are you so surprised? Maybe Gerald trusts me to do what's best for him. Or maybe he has figured out that I'm experienced in . . . this sort of thing."

Or maybe he doesn't want to burden me. The truth hangs between us, unspoken, intangible, but undeniably real. Gerald and I have come to depend on and trust each other with every aspect of the funeral home business. I know he would have trusted me with his ultimate welfare, but he won't want to make things more difficult for me at the end. Even approaching death, the man is a consummate gentleman.

So I can be hurt that he didn't choose me, or I can support my mother.

I give her a reassuring nod. "I'm glad he chose you. I know you'll take good care of him. He knows that, too."

She smooths her slacks. "And where are my darling grandsons?"

"Playing by the lake. They'll be back soon for supper."

"Good. I've missed them." Mom glances at my paperwork. "How about you? Were you able to contact Gerald's daughter?"

"Well . . ." I hold up the note card I found in the address book. "I hated to do it, but I went on a fishing expedition and found this. Trouble is, I can't bring myself to dial the number. I don't know if Gerald meant for me to find this now or . . . after."

She reads the card, then meets my gaze. "As the agent of his living will, I'd recommend that you call this woman as soon as possible. A daughter has the right to know her father is dying."

"Even if he . . . ?"

"Sometimes people say things because they don't want to be hurt. Call her, and I'll bet she comes. What daughter wouldn't?"

"I still don't know if I'm doing the right thing." I turn the card and read the message again. Gerald knows that in an emergency, I'd contact his daughter. Isn't this a kind of emergency?

"Why are you hesitating?" My mother looks at me. "It's like you're *afraid* of this woman or something."

I bite my lip, unwilling to admit that Mom might be right. It's not that I'm afraid of Gerald's daughter, exactly, but the way he speaks of her . . . I'm afraid I'll invite her and something will go horribly wrong. What if she drives down here in a panic and has a wreck? What if the little granddaughter is killed? Maybe I'm letting my imagination run away with me, but I see accident victims every month, and I know that death can occur anytime, anywhere. And that's not all that can go wrong. Gerald's daughter might hate me, and she might bring more pain than pleasure into his final days.

"Are you sure it's the right thing to do?" I lock my gaze on Mother's. "Can you promise me that everything's going to be okay?"

"I can't promise anything," she says, exasperation in her voice. "But anyone with the slightest trace of familial devotion would come if you called to tell them a parent was dying. So pick up the phone and dial the woman's number."

Emboldened by the fire in my mother's eye, I obey. After three long rings, a machine answers.

My pulse flutters when I have to leave a message at the beep. "Um—" desperate for help, I glance at Mom—"my name is Jennifer Graham from the Fairlawn Funeral Home. Your father is very ill—in fact, he's terminal—and I thought you ought to know. Please give me a call as soon as possible." After leaving our number, I exhale in a rush, drop the phone into the cradle, and wipe my damp hands on my jeans. "Mission accomplished. Now the ball's in her court."

"Don't worry," Mom says. "She'll call back. Any daughter would."

During dinner, I can't help noticing that Gerald looks completely wrung out. I don't say anything in front of the boys, but when they have finished eating and gone outside with Mom for a last chance to run before bedtime, I keep Gerald at the table and meet his gaze head-on.

"I know you," I tell him, "and I know you're going to push yourself too hard in an effort to spare me some work. You don't have to do that, Gerald—not anymore. You've given me so much; now it's my turn to take care of you."

A blush rises from his collar as he fumbles with his string tie. "I don't need anybody waitin' on me."

"Yes, you do. You're going to need care in the coming weeks, and I want to help you. Mom wants to help, too, and together we're going to do whatever we can to make sure you're comfortable and . . . well, we want you to feel as good as you can feel. We'll cross whatever bridges we have to cross when we get to them, but we're going to do it together—understand? I don't want you putting on that stoic face of yours. If you're tired or hurting, tell us. You're going to have to speak up so we'll know what you need."

I know he doesn't want to hear these things, but to his credit, he swallows hard and looks at me from beneath his craggy brows. "I don't want to be mollycoddled."

"I wouldn't know how to coddle a molly if you handed me one with printed directions," I answer, "but I think I'll know how to take care of you. What I don't know, I'll learn. But you're not allowed to suffer in silence. I want to know what you're thinking and feeling. You can tell me anything."

Gerald's face contorts in a quick grimace, and his lower lip trembles. His mouth draws into a little rosette, then unpuckers as his hand creeps across the table and grasps mine. "What—whatever did I do to deserve a friend like you, Jennifer?"

The way he says my name tears at my heart. He rarely calls me Jennifer. It's usually missy or Jen. But he's not kidding around with me now; he's speaking with gut-level honesty.

"I'm probably the Lord's way of keeping you humble," I say, keeping my voice light as I squeeze his sandpapery fingers. "I'm your thorn in the flesh. But you have a deal. I won't mollycoddle you if you promise not to suffer in silence. We have to be honest with each other."

He presses his lips together and nods. He might have added a word or two, but I don't think he can trust his voice.

So we shake on it instead.

❦ ❦ ❦

I don't know how he does it, but Gerald gets out of bed as usual and goes to church with us on Sunday morning. I'm actually glad, not only because it's good for him to be with people who love him, but because I don't want him to be home alone when his daughter calls.

At least I don't *think* I do.

We grab a quick dinner from KFC and come home to picnic at the house. Gerald loves eating outside, though we rarely do it because it seems like so much trouble to drag chairs around the table tucked into the corner of our porch. How logical is that?

Mom sets the bags of food on the table and has the boys gather the chairs while I run upstairs to grab glasses and a pitcher of lemonade. Before running up the steps, however, I check the phone to see if anyone has called to leave a message. No blinking red light.

Skeeter dances between our feet as we sit on the porch and eat chicken, biscuits, and mashed potatoes dripping in gravy. Mom eats with the newspaper open in her lap, and I am chomping corn on the cob when she startles me with a loud belly laugh. "A *cruise*?"

She's seen the contest ad. I grimace and lower my corncob. "No comments, please."

She turns toward me with an incredulous smile on her face. "You're giving away a Caribbean cruise? Where do I sign up?"

I reach for my napkin as Gerald grins. "No freebies," he says. "You have to give us a winning slogan."

Mom ignores him, reserving her judgment for me. "How can you afford to sponsor a contest like this?"

"The cruise won't be that expensive," I tell her. "I think we can get a good deal—four days on a ship out of Tampa isn't that pricey. I have a travel agent looking into it."

"We could send them in the dead of winter," Gerald adds, his eyes crinkling at the corners. "So go on, Jo. Sign up."

Mom opens her mouth, probably about to challenge him to do the same thing; then her jaws abruptly clamp shut.

After a second, I realize why. Gerald won't be here next winter.

When he stands to stretch his legs and throw Skeeter's ball, I lean close enough to whisper in Mom's ear, "I wouldn't be running the contest if I'd known about Gerald's prognosis. By the time I found out, I'd already called in the ad."

Mom blows out her cheeks and sets the paper aside. "I hope you know what you're doing."

She's not the only one.

When we have finished eating, I smile at the sun-spangled lawn and realize that stockpiling memories like this isn't a bad idea. Gerald is rocking contentedly, one hand on his stomach, the other shading his eyes as he watches Bugs throw Skeeter's favorite red ball. Skeeter bounds after it, then brings it back to Bugs, but feints at the last minute and dashes toward Clay.

If only I could freeze these moments so that nothing would ever change. I wish I could etch this afternoon into Bugs's memory so he will never forget Gerald. As Clay steps into that period of life where friends matter more than family, I hope he recalls the love that binds us on this lovely afternoon.

If I ruled the universe, I'd let my boys grow up—slowly—but I'd keep my mentor and my mother just as they are.

As Mom and Gerald chuckle at the antics on the lawn, my heart swells to about three times its normal size. In a minute or two it might burst from an overflow of emotion.

"If we're going to get to the drugstore," Gerald says, "we'd better get moving. I know you like your after-church nap."

"It's not *me* snoring up a storm on the couch every Sunday afternoon," Mom answers, fussing at a spot on her dress with a wet napkin. "But you go on down to the car and let me get my purse."

After Mom and Gerald climb into the Plymouth for another trip into town, I clear the porch, go into the office, close the door, and redial Kirsten Phillips's number. The phone rings twice before a tiny voice answers. "Hello?"

My pulse skips a beat as I close my eyes and try to picture Gerald's granddaughter. "Hello? Is your mother named Kirsten?"

"Uh-huh."

"Is she home?"

"She's asleep."

"Well, it's really important that I speak to her. Would you wake her up and tell her I need to talk to her?"

"Just a minute." The phone clunks on a hard surface; then I hear nothing.

After three long minutes, during which I find myself wishing for Muzak, an older and decidedly irritated voice scrapes over the line. "Yes?"

"Kirsten?"

"Who wants to know?"

"My name is Jennifer Graham. We've never met, but I left a message on your answering machine yesterday." I pause, waiting for some response—yes, she got my message; yes, she's been meaning to call—but all I hear is dead air. "Anyway," I continue, nonplussed by her silence, "your dad and I work together at the Fairlawn Funeral Home—maybe you know about it."

"Yeah, he sent me a Christmas card."

Again I wait for some elaboration, but she doesn't seem inclined to engage in conversation. Maybe she's still half-asleep.

I rush on, "I'm sorry to be the bearer of bad news, but your father has been diagnosed with pancreatic cancer, and the doctors are giving him only about three more months. I thought . . . I thought you ought to know."

When she doesn't respond in any audible way, I hold the phone away from my ear and make an exasperated face at the receiver. What is *wrong* with this woman?

"Well," she finally says, "I guess we all have to go sometime."

I resist the urge to sputter. Is that *it*? Cruella De Vil would be more sympathetic.

"I'm sure this is a shock," I say, trying to give her the benefit of the doubt, "but if you'd like to come for a visit, my boys would be happy to bunk together for a couple of nights so you could stay with us. If you want to stay longer, I'm sure there's an apartment you could rent by the week. Everyone here adores your father, so I know the entire town would welcome you."

I expect hesitation this time—a rustling as she flips the pages of her calendar, an absent clearing of the throat as she struggles to wade through the thick shock of bad news—but her answer is immediate. "I can't get away," she says, her voice sharp and exact, "and I can't take my daughter out of school."

"I've found that school officials can be very understanding about family emergencies."

"I have a job. I work on commission, so I can't take a day off anytime I want to. If I don't work, I don't get paid. We don't *eat*."

I'm finding it hard to believe that the little girl in the photo on Gerald's dresser has grown into such a sharp-tongued woman. I'm also wondering if this phone call was a terrible, tragic mistake.

I close my eyes and try again. "Believe it or not, I understand. I know how precarious life can seem when money is tight and you're worried about keeping a roof over your family's head. But if you come, we'll do what we can to help you."

"Why would you do that?"

"Because your father loves you, and he'd love to see Katie."

"No, he wouldn't."

Now we're approaching an area where I can help. Eager to untangle whatever misunderstanding has arisen between Gerald and his daughter, I press on. "I lost my father a few years ago, and I know how it feels to realize it's too late to say things that should have been said. I asked your father if he'd like you to come, and he said his door would always be open to you. So if you can get away for even a couple of days . . ."

"Thank you for calling, but it's not going to work out."

"Please. Kirsten." I draw a deep breath and reach for the last of my persuasive tactics. If kindness, duty, and earnestness won't sway her, perhaps the prospect of an inheritance will. "I don't mean to tell you how to run your life, but I think you should know that your father has been thinking about changing his will. I don't know what his plans are, but if you'd like to talk to him—"

"Lady, are you hard of hearing? I said I don't want to see him. Now if you'll excuse me, I was out late last night."

Before I can stammer out a response, the phone clicks. I stare at the cold object in my hand, then lower it back to the desk.

I don't believe it, I don't understand it, and I don't want to accept it. But I have to admit one thing: Gerald certainly knows his daughter.

And right at this moment, I think I hate her.

Kirsten drops the phone onto the kitchen counter and props a hand on her hip. Two thirty in the afternoon, and Katie's cereal bowl is still on the counter, the box of Corn Pops open by the sink. On the bar between the kitchen and living room, a dried film of congealed milk looks like someone's after-party puke.

And Hawkeye, worthless slug that he is, is sleeping on the couch while he's *supposed* to be at work.

Barely bridled fury heats Kirsten's face as she marches into the living room. "Hey." She nudges Hawk's bony elbow with her knee. "Wake up."

He rolls onto his back and lifts his hand, shading his eyes from the light coming through the window. The strong odors of cigarette smoke and stale beer rise from his clothes. "What?"

"You were supposed to work today. Didn't Joe say he had a job for you at that house?"

Hawkeye groans and turns back onto his side, closing his eyes as he dangles an arm over the edge of the couch. "He called. Said they found another trim carpenter."

"I didn't hear the phone ring."

He moistens his lips with his tongue. "You were asleep."

"I *always* hear the phone ring, and it didn't ring until just a few minutes ago. You're lying."

"I wouldn't lie to you, babe." Like a cockroach seeking the darkness, Hawkeye burrows his head under the stained sofa pillow.

Kirsten clenches her fist, wondering if she dares risk letting him know just how ticked she is, but then Katie comes in from the hallway, her mouth rimmed with something dark. "Kate! What have you been eating?"

The girl pulls on a strand of her long hair. "It's only a candy bar."

"Where'd you find it?"

Katie points to the kitchen. "Under the sink."

Kirsten exhales heavily, then strides into the kitchen. Sure enough, someone—undoubtedly Hawkeye—has stashed a bag of chocolate bars under the sink. Her heart rises to her throat as she removes the bag and checks the contents. It's not a Ziploc but the original manufacturer's wrapping, and the candy bars appear untouched. So these aren't some recreational concoction manufactured by one of Hawkeye's chemically dependent pals.

But why did Hawk stash these with the cleaning supplies? Either he put them here in a drunken fog, or he was saving the chocolate for one of his more creative friends.

She holds the bag before Katie's blue eyes. "You should never eat anything you find under the sink—do you understand?"

"But they're candy bars."

"Kids shouldn't snoop around in the kitchen. If you're hungry, get something out of the pantry."

Katie nods, but that look—that *wall*—comes down behind her eyes. It's a look Kirsten has seen on the faces of four ex-husbands, but she's always startled to see her nine-year-old daughter wearing it.

Kirsten pulls her thin robe around her and tightens the fabric belt at her waist. "You hungry now?"

"Already had cereal for breakfast."

"I see that. So do you want some lunch?"

"Like what?"

"Beefaroni? Soup?"

Katie clambers onto a barstool and sits at the counter, her feet kicking the cabinet as Kirsten rummages through the nearly empty pantry.

She bought three cans of soup last week, but they're gone. So are the boxes of macaroni and cheese. She opens the refrigerator and scans the shelves filled with Styrofoam containers and beer cans. She grabs a take-out box and sniffs at a handful of cold chicken wings. Probably not more than two or three days old. "You want chicken wings?"

"They're gross."

"Sorry, but there's not much else in here. You're gonna have to eat leftovers until I can get to the grocery store."

"Can I go with you?"

Kirsten glances at Hawkeye, who's still zonked on the couch. She had high hopes for their relationship, but the man has proven himself worthless as a roommate, a partner, and a babysitter. Like it or not, she'll have to take Katie to the store today.

"I guess so." She closes the refrigerator and pauses by the sink as a memory passes over her, pebbling her skin like the breath of a ghost.

Her father had loved to tell the story of the Prodigal Son in his sermons. His eyes would fill with tears as he spoke of the troubled younger brother who ran away from home and spent his inheritance in "riotous living," whatever that was in toga days. When he'd spent all his money on wine, drunken friends, and camel-robed women, he found himself longing to eat from the pigs' slop buckets.

She stares at the chicken wings, one of which is covered in a gelatinous goo. A pig would probably feel right at home in her refrigerator, but she is not going back to the old man. She can't.

Kirsten slides the foam container into the microwave, hits the power button, and leaves the oven to do its work while she sinks onto an empty barstool and lets her head fall to the laminated countertop.

Katie reaches out, her slender fingers tugging at the straggly bangs in Kirsten's face. "You okay, Mom?"

"I'm fine. Just tired."

"Oh." Katie rests her chin in her hand. "So are we going to the grocery store?"

"Later. After I get my shower." She closes her eyes. "Did I ever tell you about the magic refrigerator we had when I was growing up?"

"There's no such thing." A skeptical note enters Katie's voice. "You're lying."

"Shows how much you know. When I was a kid, we'd take something out of the refrigerator, and the next day there'd be another full dish in its place. Good food, too, and cakes." Kirsten sighs in remembered bliss. "You wouldn't believe the cakes. Red velvet and carrot cake and German chocolate, all made from scratch. Once my dad had to go to the hospital. Not a big deal—his tonsils or gallbladder, maybe—but that refrigerator churned out food for weeks. Soups and stews, congealed salads, and enough baked goods to end starvation in Africa. Whatever you wanted, sooner or later it would show up in our kitchen." She opens her eyes.

Katie's gaze drifts to the avocado green fridge in the corner. "Did you have pies?"

"Sometimes."

"Cherry pie?"

Kirsten extends her hand and pushes Katie's overgrown bangs out of her face. "That was my favorite, too."

She bites her lip as another memory brushes the edges of her mind: when she was about Katie's age, she and her father sat at a counter like this one, sharing a warm cherry pie and a bowl of whipped cream. He bet her two hugs and three kisses that she couldn't eat half a pie by herself, so she set out to prove him wrong.

How can the beloved Gerald Huffman be *dying*? He had always been invincible. People called Pastor Gerald whenever they had trouble, so he never had time for problems of his own.

Yet her mother was the main reason their refrigerator magically filled with food. For five years she struggled against breast cancer, and finally the disease won. During those difficult months, her father had been a pillar of strength—preaching every Sunday morning, Sunday night, and Wednesday night; visiting the hospitals on Monday mornings; preparing his sermons on weekday afternoons. When he wasn't preaching, visiting, or studying, he was at Mom's side, laughing with her on good days, holding her hand on days that were not so good.

When Mom felt up to it, they went out to breakfast at the local

Village Inn; on bad days Dad had Kirsten eat in her bedroom because even the aroma of food made Mom nauseous. He arranged for a neighbor to take Kirsten to school and asked his secretary to be sure she had a ride home.

He'd been everything a sick woman could need in those days . . . and everyone loved him for it.

Her father did his best to remain available to his church members no matter what was happening at home, and he worked hard to find an answer to every parishioner's question. People turned to him when they wanted a strong dose of God's truth, but though Kirsten listened to every word her father said from the pulpit, she never heard answers to the questions she was asking: *"If God loves me, why is my mother sick? If he hears our prayers, why hasn't he answered them?"*

By the time her mother died, Kirsten stopped listening to her father's sermons. She stood by his side, a bewildered sixteen-year-old, as the funeral director lowered the casket into the open grave. Behind her, she heard the mourners murmuring that her father was a brave man, a wonderful man, a holy man of God.

Apparently, everyone adored Gerald Huffman—superman, super pastor, super saint. Everyone except his daughter, who learned that God was a fake and her father a big fat liar.

Like an athlete who unconsciously favors his sprained ankle, our family quietly adjusts to the reality of Gerald's illness. We try not to call attention to our efforts, but the boys lower their voices in the house, and Clay takes out the trash without being reminded. Bugs sits shoulder to shoulder with Gerald on the sofa as they watch *American Idol*, and Mom's gibes lose a bit of their sharp edge.

By Tuesday morning I've heard nothing from Gerald's daughter, and now I know better than to expect a call. I feel awful about Gerald not being able to meet his only granddaughter, but I feel worse for Kirsten, who for some reason has cut a precious man out of her life. She will be the poorer for it.

A dietitian came to the house yesterday, armed with a list of suggested foods to eat and other foods to avoid. Mom sat at the kitchen counter with the woman and made out a shopping list while Gerald grumbled from his bedroom doorway.

"If I'm on my way out," he told me later, "I'm going to go out happy. So I'll avoid the foods that are likely to give me a bellyache, but I'm not following that no-fat, no-carb, no-flavor routine."

On Tuesday night, over a dinner of tuna fish sandwiches, lima beans, and potato chips, the boys watch as Gerald and I open the first batch of entries for our slogan contest. Apparently Lydia was right—

when you're trolling for public interest, a Caribbean cruise makes great bait.

I open the first envelope and stare at the card inside. Our ad clearly stated that entries should include a slogan for the Fairlawn Funeral Home, but the card in my hand has a name, address, and one line: "Put me down for the cruise!"

"I hope they're not all like this." I pass the note to Mother and open another envelope. This one is a repeat of the first but with a different name and address.

Mom hands Gerald the card. "I hardly think 'Put me down' is an appropriate slogan for a mortuary," he says, grinning as he passes the entry to Clay. "Surely there's something better in these other letters."

I open another enter-me-in-the-contest note and toss it into the space between the bowl of lima beans and the bag of potato chips. "Honestly—" I reach for another piece of mail—"do people not read directions anymore?"

"Here's another one." Mom flings a mostly blank note card onto the pile. "No slogan, but she really wants to win."

"Here we go, ladies—looks like a bona fide entry." Gerald unfolds a page as the corners of his mouth twitch. "'Fairlawn: where you'll look better dead than alive.'" He smiles. "Ryan would be flattered."

"He *does* do good work. A couple of weeks ago, I heard a woman tell her friend that Ryan is better than Botox." I pull another page from an envelope and read: "'Fairlawn: where people are dying to get in.'"

"I have the feeling that will be your most popular entry," Mom says, shaking her head. "But here's a unique one: 'Remains to be seen.'" She blinks. "I don't get it."

Across the table, Clay looks at Bugs and chortles. "I think it's funny."

"I don't think a slogan is supposed to be humorous," Mom says. "It should be comforting."

By this time, I'm giggling myself. "Remains to be seen" isn't comforting or respectful, but it *is* clever. "Let's keep that one," I tell Mom. "Maybe we could send that guy a memorial calendar or something."

"Here's one." Gerald draws a breath to speak, then coughs. As he bends sideways to avoid coughing over the table, I listen to the hacking sounds and study his profile.

Last night I thought about canceling the contest, but when I mentioned the idea to Gerald, he urged me to continue with my plans. Though at first he wasn't exactly enthusiastic about this slogan campaign, I think the experience will be good for him. Anything that takes his mind off dying is a good thing.

He finishes coughing, takes a deep breath, and reaches for his glass of water. While he drinks, Bugs looks at me with worry in his eyes.

I give him an understanding smile. *We're going to be okay.*

"'Come for the lodging,'" Gerald finally reads, "'stay for the view.'"

I turn to Mother. "Sounds more like an ad for a cemetery—don't you think?"

"They must think you own the graveyard." She frowns. "They don't understand that a mortuary isn't a boardinghouse for stiffs."

For some reason, Clay thinks Mother's comment is funny—either that or he and Bugs have been dropping lima beans into their laps and flicking them at each other under the table again. If I find little green piles of squashed beans on the floor after dinner . . .

Gerald braces his elbows on the table and looks at me. "Do you really think we'll find a winner among entries like these?"

"This is only the first batch," I say, shrugging. "And these people obviously didn't think very hard about what they wrote. When we begin to hear from entrants who actually put some thought into it, we'll get some good slogans."

Gerald riffles through the letters and cards in the center of the table. "These people sure do want a cruise, but I haven't heard a motto that even comes close to something we can use. It makes me wonder—do people even know what a funeral home does?"

"I didn't, not before I buried Nolan," Mom confesses. She picks up a potato chip and waves it at us. "To tell you the truth, I didn't want to even *think* about what funeral homes do. Way out of my comfort zone."

"But you've changed your perspective," I point out. "Now you understand, right?"

She smiles at me. "Honey, if ten years ago someone had told me I'd be proud to have a daughter in the funeral home business, I'd have called for the wacky wagons. Now I'm beginning to think there's no better business in the world for you . . . or even my grandsons."

Clay and Bugs as morticians? I hadn't really thought about either of the boys taking over this place, but that might not be a bad idea. They're used to funerals now, and they're no longer squeamish about dead bodies lying downstairs. Maybe, like me, they can learn to see this work as a real ministry.

"This one has possibilities." Gerald rattles a slip of paper from an envelope. "'The Fairlawn Funeral Home: Always fair and always there.'"

Always there. The latter phrase resonates with me, because lately I've been conscious of a sincere desire to keep things just as they are. We've been through so much struggle and sorrow in the last two years, I'd give anything if we could freeze this moment in time and forevermore resist change.

I hold up my index finger. "Finally, an entry with potential."

Kirsten slams the car door, takes two running steps, and yelps when her foot slides off her three-inch heel in the parking lot. She mutters a soft curse and leans on the side of the car as she rubs her twisted ankle—what a picture of grace she must be, out here in front of a dozen wide windows. When she's sure she can walk, she resettles herself on her shoes and ignores the stabbing pain in her right foot as she limps toward the sales office of Alpharetta's Park Towers.

She grimaces as she struggles to open the heavy door, but once inside the office, she smooths her face and limps toward her desk. High on the wall, the automatic air freshener sends out a spray of lilac scent to mask the odors of stale coffee and confined humans.

Unfortunately, John Sergeant pops out of his wormhole and cuts her off. "Ms. Phillips, may I see you in my office?"

She points to her desk. "Sure. Let me drop my purse and grab a cup of—"

"Now, please."

Kirsten glances at her coworkers, both of whom are hunched over their desks and pretending to be busy. If Mr. Sergeant weren't here, they'd be loitering by the coffee machine and swapping can-you-believe-it? stories about fussy customers and their granite countertops, coffered ceilings, and walk-in closets large enough to house a family of four.

She lets her purse slip from her shoulder to her wrist and trudges into Sergeant's office. He's already behind the desk, so she sits in the guest chair and glances out the window overlooking the sales area.

One of her coworkers catches Kirsten's eye and makes a face that clearly says, "Good luck, kid."

"I know—" Sergeant folds his hands—"you're aware that mornings are critically important to our sales effort. People who want luxury housing are early birds; they know what they want and they come early to get it."

"I know, and I'm sorry I'm late. I had car trouble this morning—"

"This is the third time, Ms. Phillips."

"And every time I've had a good—no, a *great* excuse. First my car broke down, and then there was that accident on the interstate. You *know* how terrible traffic is around here."

"Mornings are prime time in our business. We need our people in the office promptly at nine."

Kirsten glances at her watch. "It's only nine fifteen."

"That's a quarter of an hour."

"But . . . there are no customers here." She gestures to the window, which opens to a view of her coworkers and a detailed tabletop model of the Park Towers complex. Dozens of little fake trees surround the towering cardboard edifice, and someone has even found tiny white swans to float on the kidney-shaped blue blob that's supposed to be described as a luxurious man-made lake but is actually a retention pond necessary to prevent flooding.

Sergeant glares at her, his thin mustache quivering atop his upper lip. "Whether or not we have customers in the office is irrelevant. What matters is a dependable sales team. You were hired to work in this office from nine until five on weekdays, and you've been late on three separate occasions. I'm sorry, Ms. Phillips, but I have to let you go."

Kirsten closes her eyes long before he gets to the final stabbing sentence. Why is this happening? She's actually done well in this position, having sold four units in three months. She isn't a top salesman, but the job has enabled her to keep groceries on the table and pay a couple of months' rent. "Wait." She opens her eyes and holds up her hand. "I know I'm not perfect, but you could do a lot worse than me."

"I could also find someone who knows how to get to work on time."

"Come on, John." Kirsten gives him the smile that first drew Hawkeye's attention from across a crowded room. "Cut me a little slack, okay? Surely we can work something out."

Instead of being charmed, the boss eyes her as if she were a bad smell. "I think not. I need you to get your personal items from your desk and vacate the premises."

"I have a little girl." She meets the boss's gaze head-on. "My boyfriend is a deadbeat, and my daughter—well, her father's not around, so she needs me to provide for her."

"Maybe she needs you to be more dependable." Sergeant stands and tugs at a button on his sports coat. "I think we're settled up, aren't we?"

"You don't owe me any money, if that's what you mean. Though a little common decency would have been nice."

Sergeant expands his chest. "All right, then." He has the nerve to hold out his hand. "Best of luck in your new position."

Suddenly Kirsten is eighteen and standing in the parsonage foyer, feeling the wind on her face as her father opens the front door. "I'll always love you," he says again, "but if you're going to make bad choices, you can make them on your own. It hurts too much to watch you rebel against everything your mother and I have taught you."

Without a word, she picks up her suitcases and sets them out on the front steps, then goes back for the cardboard box stuffed with coats and shoes. Dad does not bend to help but stands in the rays of the setting sun, his eyes as dark and full as the sea, his chin quivering with some emotion she does not want to explore.

Now Kirsten rises, ignoring Sergeant's outstretched arm. "I've been meaning to tell you," she says, hoisting her purse to her shoulder. "That mustache looks like something my daughter might have painted on with a felt-tip pen."

Without waiting to observe the effect of her barb, she limps out of the room, not stopping even to say good-bye to her coworkers, who are peeking over the tops of their computer monitors like terrified rabbits.

"See ya, suckers," she calls, yanking on the heavy door handle.

❧ ❧ ❧

An accident on the interstate slows traffic to a near standstill, and Kirsten's temper is boiling by the time she gets back to the apartment. After pulling into her parking space and shoving the car in gear, she freezes with her hands on the wheel. A young girl is sitting alone in the playground. The hair is long and blonde, exactly like Katie's. . . .

But that can't be Katie because Katie should be at school. Hawkeye was supposed to drop her off before he went to the unemployment office.

Kirsten climbs out of the car and hurries toward the gated playground, one of the few amenities for apartment residents. The girl is her daughter, and she's wearing a threadbare Hannah Montana shirt, a pair of plaid shorts, and sandals. On a chilly morning.

Katie lifts her head. "Mom! Why aren't you at work?"

"I got off early." Kirsten glances toward the apartment, hoping to catch Hawkeye watching from the window. "Are you out here by yourself? Where's Hawk?"

"Inside."

"What's he doing?"

"Sleepin', I guess."

Kirsten presses her hand to her forehead and forces herself to count to three. "Okay, then. Let's go in. Did you get any breakfast?"

"I ate cereal."

"That's good." She takes her daughter's hand and leads her toward the apartment, fighting back a surge of fury as it roars in her ear. Bad enough that she overslept and left without seeing to her daughter, but obviously Hawkeye can't be trusted to care for a child. He should have taken Katie to school. He should have made sure she had a decent meal and dressed in decent clothes.

"Kate—" she strengthens her voice—"haven't I told you not to go outside alone?"

"There wasn't nothin' to do."

"You could have watched TV."

"Hawkeye said to keep the TV off so he could sleep."

Kirsten draws a strangled breath between her teeth. If not for Katie, she'd go in the bedroom and slap some sense into that man. What is he thinking, letting a nine-year-old girl go outside by herself? She could have been snatched up by any perv who happened to walk by. Who knows how many perverts there are per square foot in this neighborhood? Not to mention the fact that someone could have seen Katie sitting alone on a school day and called social services, who would come and take her away quicker than you could say *unfit mother*.

Kirsten quickens her step and looks up at the windows staring down like judgmental eyes. "Come on. Let's get in the house. I think you need to put on some warmer clothes."

"Are we goin' somewhere?"

"Not right now. Maybe later."

When the door has closed behind them, Kirsten moves toward the kitchen and drops her purse on the counter. As Katie climbs on the barstool, Kirsten pulls a carton of milk from the fridge, splashes some into a bowl, and pours cereal on top. There are no clean spoons in the drawer, so she takes one from the sink, runs hot water over it, and hands it to Katie.

"But I already ate cereal."

"Just *eat*, will you, while I think for a minute." She turns her back to her daughter and leans against the counter, her fingertips pressed to her temples. What is she going to do? If she stays here, she might end up killing Hawkeye. Maybe not literally, but at times like this she could happily strangle him with her bare hands.

So why not leave? Now that she's unemployed, there's no reason to stay in Alpharetta. She needs a fresh start; she needs a new home and a new man. But starting over takes money, and she hasn't much. Maybe five hundred dollars from her last commission check, if Hawkeye hasn't discovered her hiding place and drunk her savings away.

Leaving Katie in the kitchen, Kirsten goes into the small bathroom and locks the door. She runs water in the sink to cover the sound of her movements, stoops, and opens the vanity. The area inside the cabinet is crowded with a can of Comet cleanser, an old set of electric curlers, a supersize bottle of nail polish remover, a box of tampons, a carton of panty liners, a zippered pouch bulging with assorted cosmetics, a hair dryer, and her flat iron.

She shudders as she uses an old toothbrush to flick a dead roach toward the back wall; then she opens the carton of panty liners. There, nestled among the contents, are five one-hundred-dollar bills. Enough to get out of town but not nearly enough for a deposit on another apartment.

But what did that woman from Florida say? Something about Dad dying and changing his will. She hadn't been very clear, but money is money, no matter what its source. And Kirsten needs it. For herself and for Katie.

She studies the stern portrait of Franklin on the bill in her hand. *"I'll always love you,"* her father said.

Of course he would say that. Loving came easy to Gerald Huffman; *accepting* gave him trouble.

But he promised to love.

Kirsten breathes deep and makes a decision. Let Hawkeye have the apartment and their memories. She's leaving. No matter how much it hurts, she is going to be with her father. She'll brace herself for his disapproving glances, steel her nerves against his sermons, and gulp a few salt pills to counteract the sweetness that seems to ooze out of everyone around him. A much-loved man, her father. Probably more cherished now than ever.

But he is her ticket out of this hopeless rut. He is her ticket to a better life for Katie.

After snatching the money from the box and closing the vanity, she shuts off the water and unlocks the bathroom door. "Katie," she calls as she returns to the kitchen, "when you're finished, I need you to get dressed in something warm. Something clean. We're going somewhere."

"Where we goin'?"

Kirsten tilts her head and runs the back of her finger along her daughter's cheek. "We're going to see your grandpa."

I give Daniel a grateful smile as he unfolds his napkin. "You have no idea," I tell him, "how good it feels to get out of the house."

His eyes darken with concern. "Is Gerald failing faster than expected? Or are he and your mother squabbling?"

"Neither. Gerald and Mom are as thick as thieves lately. Mom has risen to the challenge of helping out around the house, and she's very attentive to Gerald. That leaves me free to look after the business and take care of the boys, but still—" I sigh and pick up the menu—"I'm always startled to realize Gerald won't be with us in a few months. I don't even want to *think* about him not being around."

Daniel lifts his menu, too, but clearly his thoughts are focused on Fairlawn. "How bad is Gerald these days?"

I shrug. "He tires easily. The doctor's put him on some kind of opiate for pain, so he's not supposed to drive. That's been one of the hardest things—Gerald isn't happy about giving up his freedom. Mom takes him on errands and we do pickups together, but I have to drive, and we usually have to ask for help with the body. This morning, for instance, we were out before sunrise picking up Francis Quick. We had to swing by and ask Ryan to help."

"Francis Quick?"

"You know him?"

"No, but I've heard his name around the courthouse. Apparently he found himself in legal trouble every now and again."

"He was in major trouble last night. Was running from a house—they think it was an attempted break-in—and he managed to impale himself on a fence. One of the pickets went through his femoral artery. He didn't call for help because he didn't want to get caught."

Daniel grimaces. "Not a good way to go."

"Not an easy embalming, either. We had to repair the artery before we could pump in the fluid."

Daniel shudders and shakes his head. "I still find it hard to believe that Gerald has decided to forgo treatment."

"I know, but I read some of the literature he brought home, and I *do* understand his reasoning. His condition is so advanced that nothing they can offer has any guarantee of success or even improvement. His options boiled down to one question: did he want to spend his last months undergoing chemo or living an ordinary life? Gerald wants his remaining time to be as normal as possible."

"I would probably feel the same way." Daniel glances at the menu; then his gaze catches and holds mine. "How are you holding up?"

"Me? I'm not sick."

"I'd like to keep it that way. So what are you doing to make sure you get through this in one piece?"

I lean back in my chair, pleased by his concern. Daniel has been a good friend ever since we came to Mt. Dora, but there's a fine line between demonstrating concern and showing pity. I appreciate concern, but I don't want anyone's pity. "I'm taking care of myself. I'm having lunch with you, aren't I?"

He laughs. "Like that's some kind of major treat. And the workload? Are you managing it okay?"

"We're not that busy right now. But when we do have a client, I'm at the point where I can pretty much handle everything but the heavy lifting by myself. We could use more clients to help with the budget, so that's why we're running a contest. Gerald still supervises me—legally he has to until I pass my board exam—but supervising doesn't tax him as much as the actual work."

We fall silent as a waiter approaches with two glasses of iced tea. "Your usual?" he asks, setting the drinks before us.

I smile and squeeze the lemon into my drink. Daniel and I try to find time for lunch together at least once a week, and the Beauclaire Dining Room is our favorite restaurant. I hadn't realized that other people were noticing our routine, but I suppose there's no harm in an observant waiter making note of friends who lunch together.

The waiter drapes a folded towel over his arm. "The chef asked me to tell you that we have a lovely homemade chicken potpie available for our luncheon guests. It's really quite exceptional."

"I've had it, and it is good." Daniel looks at me. "Potpie for you, too?"

"I'd better stick with my usual salad." I give the waiter a regretful smile as I return the menu. "If your potpie is that good, I doubt it's low calorie."

The waiter grins. "You have good instincts. One grilled chicken salad, one potpie. Anything else?"

Daniel gives the man his menu and assures him that we'll be fine.

Before we can get back to our conversation, a stout woman I've never seen before sidles up to our table. "Well, well, what do we have here?" She nods at my companion. "Daniel."

"Mrs. Meriwether." He stands. "So good to see you."

"Likewise." Her mouth curves in a smile as her sharp eyes rake me from head to toe. "I've heard about your friend. Jennifer Graham, isn't it? the Virginia woman from the funeral home?"

"Nice to meet you, Mrs. Meriwether." I offer the visitor a smile, then lift a questioning brow in Daniel's direction. Is this woman for real? There's something about the interloper—something so very Aunt Bee-ish—that I have to press my fingertips to my lips in order to keep from laughing out loud. Mt. Dora has always had what Mom calls "Mayberry potential," but this is the first time I've met a character who could have walked straight out of the old TV show.

"I've heard about you," Mrs. Meriwether says, clasping her hands as a beaded purse dangles from her wrist and threatens my iced tea. "And I've heard about the *two* of you."

Still standing, Daniel answers with forced politeness. "What have you heard, Mrs. Meriwether?"

I rescue my tea glass and hide a smile in my drink. Daniel is one of the most eligible bachelors in town—attractive, successful, and a genuinely good man. I suppose it's only natural that people should speculate about our friendship, but some folks in this town train for gossiping as if it were an Olympic event.

"I've heard—" Mrs. Meriwether peers down the length of her nose—"that you're in cahoots."

I blink at Daniel and play dumb. "Is Cahoots one of those little towns outside Orlando?"

Mrs. Meriwether glances at me with well-mannered disdain before nodding at Daniel. "People are saying that you use your remarkable gifts of persuasion to prey upon vulnerable folks while they are planning their estates. Then you send them to Fairlawn so *she* can sell them a high-priced funeral package."

This revelation is so startling I can't speak. I stare at Daniel, who appears every bit as surprised as I feel.

"Why, that's ludicrous," he says, giving the woman a bewildered smile. "We are most certainly not in cahoots, as you call it."

Mrs. Meriwether waves a bejeweled hand. "Surely you won't deny that you handled Marvin Renshaw's estate and *she* buried him three months later."

I resist the urge to snap at one of those fat fingers. "If I buried him, ma'am, it's because he needed burying."

The older woman sniffs. "All the same, you have to admit it looks suspicious. And you know what the Good Book says—avoid all appearance of evil."

"I don't think our having lunch together appears in any way diabolical," Daniel answers, his voice uncommonly icy. "And neither is our working hard to serve the citizens of Mt. Dora. But thank you for sharing the latest rumors with us. Now have a lovely day."

Mrs. Meriwether hesitates as if she wants to say something else, but having been dismissed, she tips her head in a sharp nod and sails off, trailing the strong scent of gardenia in her wake.

Speechless, I watch her go.

"Don't let her bother you," Daniel says, dumping the contents of a sugar packet into his tea. "She loves to stir up commotion. Things have been so quiet around here, I'd forgotten how much trouble she could stir up."

"Why would she make trouble for us? We're boring."

"Who knows? She's been up north for several months—a sick mother, I think. Anyway, maybe she's been displaced at the women's club or lost her standing in the Red Hat Society. Fanning a few flames may get her some attention with the old-timers who have nothing to do but gossip all day, but don't let her get under your skin."

I study the space where Mrs. Meriwether stood only a moment ago. It may be my imagination, but the air in that spot seems to tremble, still ruffled on some cosmic wavelength. "Could people really believe that?" I ask. "That you're purposely trying to send business my way?"

He snorts. "You make it sound as if I'm knocking people off."

"Be serious."

"I am. Listen, Jen, maybe I *have* mentioned your name a few times. My clients are already thinking about the end of their lives, so it seems only natural that they'd want to think about planning their funerals. I don't think it's unethical for me to recommend Fairlawn."

"Are you sure? People know we're . . . close friends."

"In a town this small, how could they not?"

"I don't want to get business because I'm your girlfriend."

"Are you really my girlfriend?" he asks.

"I'm forty. I'm too old to be anybody's girlfriend," I tell him, my face heating. "I was saying that I want people to come to Fairlawn because we do good work. Because they know they can trust us. I don't want either one of us to be accused of nepotism."

Daniel lifts his glass. "My clients trust you. Is that a crime?"

"How is that possible? Most of your clients don't even know me."

He shrugs. "Maybe I tell them you're a trustworthy person."

I gaze at him in dismay. "Why would you do that?"

"Would you rather I tell them you're a rank beginner and desperate for business?"

He's kidding—I think—but his words still shock me. When it's not dressed up in careful phrases, the truth sounds bald and ugly. "I'd rather you didn't say anything." My voice is as cool as the smoke off dry ice. "Or maybe you could simply give your clients a list of all the county mortuaries. Let them make their own choices."

Daniel's face changes—I see a slight squint of his eye and a sideways shift of his jaw—then he sips from his glass and lowers it. When he speaks again, his voice is quiet and intense. "I can't believe you're making such a big deal out of this. I am trying to help you."

"This is the kind of help I don't need," I hiss across the table. "People tend to have low opinions of funeral directors; we spent an entire week discussing the problem in one of my classes. It all stems from that woman Jessica Mitford, who wrote that book about death and dying in America. Ever since, people have had a tendency to believe that morticians are out to rip them off at a vulnerable time—"

"No one would think that about you. Especially not anyone who's worked with you or Gerald." Featherlike laugh lines crinkle around Daniel's eyes, and something in his voice slows my racing pulse.

But the idea that people might consider us a pair of scam artists bothers me. And as our meals arrive and we begin to eat, I find myself making perfunctory replies to Daniel's comments while my thoughts drift far from the conversation.

Two years ago, I left a perfectly good job on Capitol Hill because I didn't want to face people who were whispering about my ex-husband's affair with our nanny. I couldn't stand the pitying glances or the looks that silently inquired what I did to drive my husband away.

Since we've come to Mt. Dora, I've been grateful for a fresh beginning. I can see how the Lord orchestrated the events that led us to establish our new home, new friends, and new calling.

Surely God wouldn't lead me down another gossip-filled path. Thomas is gone, but rumors still surround me like shadows on the roadside, and lately they seem determined to dog my footsteps.

I don't like it. Not one bit.

While Katie watches the barely audible TV, Kirsten packs her daughter's clothes in plastic grocery bags and carries them out to the car. After coming back in, she surveys the kitchen—not much of value here, actual or sentimental. She purchased the ceramic cookie jar and most of the dishes and cookware at a local thrift store, and she'd make too much noise if she tried to carry any of the stuff out. Best to leave it all.

She hesitates outside the bedroom door. Hawkeye is sleeping inside, but he's likely to wake if she even tiptoes into the room. If she goes in for her clothes, he'll wake up, they'll argue, and things might get loud . . . or violent. Better to just walk away.

Kirsten stops in the bathroom and opens the lid of the hamper. Inside she finds two pairs of her jeans, underwear, a blouse, a sweater, a T-shirt, and a pair of pajama pants. Combined with the skirt, shirt, and jacket she's wearing, that's a functional wardrobe.

She tosses her dirty clothes into another grocery bag and rummages beneath the couch for her tennis shoes. Those go in a bag, too, along with a box of crackers and a package of chips from the pantry.

Kirsten stands in the middle of the living room and wipes her hands on her skirt. Not much to show for more than two years of living with Hawkeye, but for the last few months she's known this relationship isn't going anywhere. Now she's packed, so all she needs to do is get Katie and get moving.

As she grabs her purse from the kitchen table, she abruptly remembers an important detail. "Might be nice to have a phone number if we need it," she tells Katie. She clicks on the phone and scrolls through the caller ID information until the number for the Fairlawn Funeral Home appears in the display window. She scribbles the number on a page ripped from the phone book, then folds it and slides it into her purse. "Come on, baby."

Katie, sitting cross-legged in front of the TV, tips her head back, her eyes still glued to the screen. "I want to see the rest of this show."

Kirsten checks the clock. Hawkeye will be up soon. No matter how bad the hangover, he's never slept through two meals. "Get up. We need to go."

"No!"

"Kate!" Kirsten's patience evaporates in a blast of frustration. "Get your rear off the floor and move out!"

"I'm not ready!"

Kirsten clenches a fist. She ought to *make* Katie get up, but Katie will scream if she grabs her arm, and that'll wake Hawkeye. If he's still tired, he'll be furious, and that won't be good for any of them. "Katie Evelyn." She takes three steps toward the child and halts when the bedroom door creaks.

She glances over her shoulder. Hawkeye stands in the doorway, a pair of blue jeans hanging three inches below the waistband of his boxers. His hair is disheveled; his bangs curtain his eyes. Last year she might have found this sleepy look attractive. Now she knows that a lightning-quick temper lies beneath that drowsy demeanor, and her leaving might set him off.

"Hey." He rubs the stubble on his chin. "What are you doin' here? Thought you had to work."

"I came home early." Kirsten shifts her gaze to her daughter. "Katie, get up." Even she can hear the note of desperation in her voice.

Katie finally turns from the TV to stare at her mother.

Hawkeye slips one hand into his pocket and shuffles closer. "You goin' somewhere?"

"I have to run some errands."

"Okay. I'll watch Katie if you want."

"I want her to come with me. I was thinking of getting her some shoes."

Hawkeye's mouth flattens in a thin smile. "The girl has shoes."

"Good grief, do I have to explain everything to you?" Kirsten rakes her hand through her hair and moves toward her daughter. "Get up off the floor."

This time Katie obeys without arguing.

"Now go get in the car."

Again, Katie does as she's told but not before casting a questioning look at Hawkeye.

Why would she do that? He's not her father. He's not anything to her.

Kirsten yanks her purse to her shoulder, opens the front door, and enters the brilliant Georgia sunshine. Katie walks in front, her sandaled feet slapping against the sidewalk. Kirsten grimaces—she should have had Katie grab her sneakers; there's no time to go back now. But that's okay. Florida's warm.

When Kirsten steps from the sidewalk to the asphalt, for one fleeting second she's sure they've escaped, but then the front door opens with a complaining screech. Her nerves tense at the sound of Hawk's jeans dragging on the sidewalk. She strides forward, determined to leave no matter what. If he'll keep his distance, she can get away.

She opens the back door and practically pushes Katie inside. "Put on your seat belt." She doesn't wait to be sure Katie obeys but opens her door and slides into the driver's seat. A trickle of sweat glides down the track of her spine as she fumbles with the keys. Her seat belt can wait.

Hawkeye stops on the sidewalk, both hands in his jeans pockets, his sleepy eyes unfocused. He grins at Katie in the backseat and lifts his hand to twiddle his fingers in a wave.

Kirsten slides her key into the ignition and prays that the engine will turn over on the first try. A click to the right, a pump of the gas pedal, a roar. *Thank you, God.*

Hawk's still grinning at Kate, but then his smile evaporates. His eyes narrow at something he's seen in the car—the overstuffed grocery bags. "I thought," he says, his voice like chilled steel, "you were goin' *to* the store."

"I am."

"Then what's in all them bags?" Hawkeye looms over her window. "Where you really goin', Kirsten?"

"Nowhere."

"Don't lie to me." He props his hands on the top of the car as if he could hold it in place.

Kirsten drops her index finger to the button that operates the door locks, but the look in his eye paralyzes her muscles. He'll freak if he hears the click of the lock. "If you must know," she says, raising her voice to be heard through the window, "I'm going to see my father. He's dying."

Hawk's lashes flutter in a series of rapid blinks. "Why didn't you tell me?"

"Because I was upset and confused, okay? Because I wasn't sure I was going to go. But I am."

He frowns, staring, then slams a fist on the glass. "Will you put this stupid window down? How am I supposed to talk to you like this?"

Panic wells in her throat as she lowers the window, stopping it just below the level of her eyes.

The action seems to mollify Hawkeye, and he brushes the hair from his forehead. "What if I don't want ya to go?"

"I need to go. The man is dying."

"I might die, too, if you go away. I can't live without ya."

Kirsten gazes at the steering wheel in her grip. "Yes, you can."

"Don't tell me what I can and can't do. You know that makes me crazy."

She stares straight ahead, clinging to the steering wheel with damp palms. She knows far too much about this man—things she wishes she never knew. Trouble is, he knows all about her, too.

"Listen," Kirsten says, careful to keep her voice smooth. "My father is dying, and I have to go to him. He's never even seen Katie. Did you know that? So I'm going. Who knows? Maybe I'll come back with an inheritance."

Hawkeye studies her for a moment, calculation working in his eyes; then he shifts his weight and releases the car. "When ya comin' back?"

"I'm not sure."

"Are you sure you're coming back?"

She gathers her courage and slips the car into reverse. "Worried about your next meal? You might have to get a job while I'm gone."

"That's cold, woman. Let the old man be, and you come back in the house."

Kirsten takes her foot off the brake.

"Come on," he calls, raising his voice as she backs out of the space. "Aren't we good together?"

She shoves the car into drive, preparing to hit the gas, but here he is again, hunching over her window like a sharp-beaked vulture that won't let go of his prey.

"Hold up, Kirsten. You haven't answered me."

Kirsten glances in the rearview mirror to check on Katie. She's watching silently, her eyes big and round.

Kirsten peers up at Hawkeye. "You really want to know what I think? I think we stopped being good long before we met each other." She places a trembling finger on the window button and calls over her shoulder, "Tell Hawkeye good-bye, Kate. We have to go."

"Bye, Hawk," Katie says.

Hawkeye places his hands on the top of the window. "What'd I do to make you so mad?"

Kirsten lifts her foot from the brake, easing the vehicle forward a few inches. "You'd better let go."

"Come on, babe. You can't leave like this."

"Watch me." She presses the power window switch, grips the steering wheel, and presses hard on the gas.

As the car lurches forward, Hawkeye pounds the window again, making Kirsten flinch and Katie scream. The glass resists, however, and the pain makes Hawkeye yowl and hold his hand. Shouted curses spray from his lips as Kirsten speeds through the parking lot.

"Mommy?" Katie's voice is a high wail in the backseat. "Why is Hawk so mad at us?"

"It's okay." Kirsten blinks away nervous tears as she turns out of the apartment complex. "As long as we're together, we're going to be okay."

Beneath the glower of grumbling gray clouds, Kirsten slants in and out of traffic, working her way past a train of sluggish semis apparently intent on owning this stretch of I-75. Rain has been falling for the past hour. The rataplan of drops on the roof, coupled with the steady beat of the wipers, has lulled Katie to sleep.

Kirsten wriggles her shoulders to loosen her tight muscles, then leans forward and stares through the smeary arc made by the wipers. Back at the apartment, Hawkeye is probably sitting on the couch, a beer in one hand and the TV remote in the other. He's liable to sit there for two or three days or until the empty pantry drives him to the day labor office so he can afford to feed himself.

She exhales sharply and tosses her head. Hawkeye is no longer her problem. He's history, another piece of her past, a jettisoned heap of deadweight. With any luck, she and Katie will meet someone new on this trip, someone with enough taste to recognize a gem in the rough when he sees it.

She tips the rearview mirror. Katie has taken off her safety belt and is sprawled over the backseat, one hand pillowing her head. A sleeping angel.

Kirsten smiles as she returns the mirror to its proper position. Did her father ever see her as an angel? Maybe, when she was two or three. He certainly never saw her that way once she was old enough to think for herself. He certainly wasn't thinking of her as *angelic* when he asked her to leave home.

A shiver spreads over her as her brain serves up another round of painful memories. Still high on adrenaline and her peers' approval, she came home late from the theater one night and found her father waiting in the darkened kitchen.

"Where have you been?"

His voice sliced through the silence like a blade, nearly stopping her heart. Kirsten stood by the refrigerator, gasping with guilt and surprise, while he flipped the light switch.

That's when she saw the worry and anger in his eyes. Her father, who handled even the roughest church problems with gentle fatherly guidance, glared at her in a silent fury that spoke louder than a hellfire-and-brimstone sermon.

Kirsten wanted her mother in that instant, but Mom was gone forever. She was stuck with her father, who seemed an old man even then. "I was—" she hesitated, torn between defiant truth and a lie—"out with Monica."

His eyes narrowed. "What is that on your face?"

Her hand rose to her cheek, and that's when she remembered the stage makeup. He would never believe Monica had done this to her. These shades went far beyond slumber party experimentation. Kirsten dropped her hand and turned to face him. "I'm in a play," she said, lifting her chin. "I'm really good. I've always wanted to be an actress; you know that. But since you won't let me—"

"I've never said you can't be an actress," Dad answered, "but I have said that you can't sneak around without my permission. You were supposed to be spending the night at Monica's house."

She shrugged. "I was going to, but Monica went somewhere else after rehearsal. She and her boyfriend dropped me off here."

"So you lied to me about where you were going."

"I *was* going to Monica's house. I just never made it there. Would you want me to sleep on the street?"

He was in an Old Testament mood, unwilling to offer the other cheek, so she returned his hot gaze, knowing she could never be the kind of daughter he wanted her to be.

"This play," Dad said, his voice gruff. "What is it?"

Kirsten bit her lip. "You've never heard of it."

"Try me."

Again she considered lying. But if he checked around, he'd discover the truth and then he'd be *really* furious. "It's called *Hair*," she said. "It's a play about war and society."

"Are they," he asked, one brow arching, "doing it with the nude scenes?"

She stared at him, tongue-tied with amazement. How did he know about that?

"Kirsten," he said, his voice more broken than angry, "you are a smart girl, and you can do anything you set your mind to do. What I can't understand is why you would want to disobey me, why you would want to lie to me, and why you would want to stand on a public stage and take your clothes off in front of strangers."

She shook her head. "It's not what you think. It's a statement on society. It's art."

"I don't care about the play; I care about *you.* And I want you to drop out of this production."

Kirsten met his somber eyes without flinching. "I won't do it. I'm an actress, I'm talented, and the director said I have to take roles like this to prove myself."

"You're barely eighteen, you're naive, and you don't have to prove yourself to anyone. As long as you live in this house, however, you do have to obey and respect your father."

"Or what?"

A thin smile tightened his lips. "This isn't an either-or scenario. A parent deserves respect. But more than that, God deserves our love. That's what I can't understand—if you love God, you should *want* to obey him. How could you live in this family for so many years without realizing how simple and important it is to love God?"

Dad looked at her then, his lined face opening so she could see the hurt and agony she had caused. But couldn't he see *her* hurt? Couldn't he see that she needed her mother, and she could never measure up to what the world expected of her?

A horn blares, startling Kirsten back to reality. She jerks hard on the wheel, pulling the drifting car back into her lane, and checks the backseat to be sure Katie hasn't awakened.

More rattled than she wants to admit, Kirsten draws a deep breath and focuses on her driving. The past is past; it's trash in the garbage heap of life. She never did make it big as an actress, but she didn't crash and burn like her father expected, either. She left home and married the director who'd praised her efforts in *Hair*, then divorced him when she caught him fooling around with the star of his next production. One man led to another, one job led to the next, and now she's on her way back to her father, no richer than she was at eighteen and no more willing to grovel.

She is, however, far more experienced.

Joella drops a bottle of multivitamins into her shopping basket and pauses before the blood pressure machine discreetly positioned out of the pharmacist's view. *Free blood pressure reading,* the sign says. *In two minutes!*

She glances right and left to be sure no one is watching; then she strolls over to investigate the machine more closely. The procedure looks simple enough—sit down, insert right arm into the cuff, and press the red button to start. Within two minutes, the machine will provide both systolic and diastolic readings.

An older man is approaching from her right, so Joella pretends to study the selection of reading glasses. "Excuse me," he says, smiling as he moves down the aisle. She returns his nod and watches his retreating back until he rounds the corner.

Why should she care if anyone sees her checking her blood pressure? It's not like she's desperately ill; her hypertension is under control with daily medication. Gerald's the one who's sick. He needs the attention at Fairlawn. Still, if her hypertension were to get worse, how would she know it? She's so likely to get caught up in caring for Jen, Gerald, and the boys that if she does begin to feel bad, she'll attribute her malaise to exhaustion. After too many weeks of that, she's likely to drop in her tracks, without so much as a single warning from her overtaxed arteries.

Joella slides into the blood pressure booth and slips her arm into the mechanical cuff. She presses the start button and holds her breath.

The machine clicks and ticks off the seconds as the pressure on her right bicep steadily increases in intensity. Two digital boxes on the screen flicker with random numbers; then the cuff on her arm relaxes, the digital numbers settle, and with an audible whoosh, she's done.

She stares at the numbers in front of her. According to the machine, her blood pressure is 154 over 93.

Uh-oh, that doesn't sound good. Joella checks the chart on the machine as a tight feeling rises beneath her breastbone. Her top number should be below 120 and the bottom number below 80. "Untreated hypertension," warns a notice below the reading, "can lead to stroke, heart attack, kidney problems—"

She throws her hand up and looks away. She doesn't need to be reminded of her mortality. She knows about hypertension; her doctor is always reminding her not to skip her regular medication. But she's been in fine health since she started taking her pills. Every morning she swallows a handful of vitamins and herbal supplements, she eats fish twice a week, and she tries to have a salad at least once a day.

Joella stands and grabs her shopping basket, then moves to the magazine section. She'll pick up a copy of the latest *Prevention* and maybe a *Good Housekeeping*. She's probably feeling tense and overworked, and that's why her blood pressure has edged up a bit.

She hesitates at the magazine rack when a headline catches her eye: *Postmenopause and Blood Pressure: The Numbers You Need to Watch*.

Is the universe trying to tell her something?

Sighing, Joella goes in search of a home blood pressure monitor and tosses the package into her shopping basket. She's probably being silly, but better to be safe than sorry. She'll be no help at all if she doesn't stay well.

And helping Jen and the boys is why she came to Florida in the first place.

Four hundred forty-four miles later, Kirsten turns onto a gravel driveway and squints at the big pink house spotlighted by the rosy hues of sunset. The Fairlawn Funeral Home appears prosperous enough—the two-story Victorian is surrounded by wide porches and thick, green grass. A sign sits in the middle of the lawn, its lettering as tasteful and dignified as the calligraphy on the sign at Alpharetta's Park Towers.

"Your grandpa must be doing okay for himself," she tells Katie, putting the vehicle in park. She turns off the car and scouts out the area as the engine rattles and coughs before dying. Another driveway leads to a detached garage, where a shiny hearse sits in the shade. Hearses are expensive, and a house like this must cost a fortune to maintain.

Yep, the preacher must finally be doing all right.

She opens the door and steps out onto the gravel, then presses her hands to her sides and hunches forward, stretching the tense muscles in her back.

Katie clambers out of the backseat and spots the first sign of life. She points at the porch railing. "There's a kid."

Kirsten squints. A red-haired boy is standing behind the railing, his arms and one leg twined through the spindles as if he's grown in that spot like some kind of vine. How long has he been standing there? "Hello," she calls. "Do you know Gerald Huffman?"

The boy nods.

"Is he home?"

"No," the boy says, his voice high and reedy. He must be in first or second grade, a year or two behind Katie.

"Do you know where he is?"

The boy rests his chin on top of the railing. "He's at the cemetery, checking on a hole."

"Oh." Kirsten's not sure how to respond to that, so she gives the boy a smile. "Mr. Huffman owns this place, right?"

The boy releases the railing, disappears behind a column, and comes down the steps, taking them one by one. "You need to have a funeral?"

"No. I need to talk to the person in charge."

The boy marches over with his hands in his pockets, a little man. "Gerald and my mom run things here. If you need a funeral, you need to talk to them."

Kirsten gapes at the child. Could her father have married again? The woman who telephoned didn't say anything about being his wife, but perhaps she didn't want to break the news. After all, if Dad remarried, he ought to be the one to tell his daughter.

And who is this? She studies the boy, who is now close enough for a proper examination. He's thin, blue-eyed, and as cute as a puppy, but he looks nothing like her father. Not likely to be a half brother, but stranger things have happened.

Katie is staring at the kid like a chocoholic who has just discovered a box of Godiva.

Kirsten clears her throat. "Do you have a name?"

The boy nods. "Bugs."

"Really? And do you live here?" She gestures to the house.

"Yeah," Bugs answers. "Me and my brother and my mom and Gerald and Skeeter."

Katie finally finds her tongue. "Skeeter is a funny name."

"He's our dog." Bugs's smile widens as he looks at Kate. "He's around here somewhere."

Kirsten tamps down a rise of irritation. Okay, so Dad has apparently married a woman half his age. A woman with children. She'll be wanting a piece of the estate, too, and money for her kids.

It's a good thing the place appears prosperous. Otherwise, there'll never be enough to go around.

Gerald frowns as Jen pulls the van to a stop. An unfamiliar vehicle sits in the parking lot, and a little girl with blonde hair is standing by the driver's door. He looks at Jen. "You expecting someone?"

"No."

"Me, either." He turns to let himself out of the van, gritting his teeth against the pain in his joints. Lately, especially at the end of a long day, he feels as though he is moving through thickened air. People keep asking how he's feeling and he answers in a single word: *tired.* The smallest movements require a huge effort, and a trip up the stairs leaves him breathless and aching. Even when he tries to nap in the stillness of the afternoon, he can sense his energy flowing out of him, leaking from his fingertips, his toes, even from the corners of his eyes.

Gerald uses two hands to push the van door open, and then he lowers his right foot onto the gravel. He's still able to fulfill his responsibilities, but it takes longer to do routine tasks, and he has to ask for help more often than he'd like. Jen doesn't complain, though, and doesn't seem to mind that he takes forever to do something as simple as getting out of the car. Still, he's grateful that dying is something he'll only have to do once.

He draws a deep breath and lowers his left foot to the gravel, alongside the right. Only a few more movements and he'll be upright. A few steps and he'll be inside the house. He can catch his breath in the office and rest a spell before he tackles the stairs.

Then again, maybe it's time to ask Jen about setting up a cot in the prep room. It's not the coziest area in the house, but he won't have to climb stairs if she sets up a bed down there. He'll be able to work during the day, and he can sleep with the dead at night. They aren't likely to mind.

Through the accumulating shadows of approaching nightfall, he hears the sweet rise and fall of Jen's voice. She's talking to a woman, probably the driver of the car. Whoever came calling at this hour either has made a wrong turn or is desperate to get someone buried. Jen can send a traveler on her way in a mere minute, but it'll take longer to explain that burial consultations are best done after the body's been picked up.

He groans at the thought of another run in the old wagon because right now he's feeling as useless as a sucked-out orange. Maybe it's time to ask Ryan if he could help Jen handle all the pickup runs. Either that, or she needs to think about hiring an extra pair of hands—hands that come attached to a strong stomach and a sensible brain. Unfortunately, that combination is hard to find.

He turns in time to see Bugs and the little girl coming toward him. Bugs is jabbering a mile a minute, but he stops talking as they approach.

Gerald steadies himself against the side of the van. "Found yourself a new friend, Bugs?"

Bugs jerks his thumb at his companion. "I found this girl."

"Well, well. Do you live around here, sweetheart?"

The child, a pale slip of a girl, examines him with eyes that remind him of Kirsten's—at once willful and sweet. But she doesn't say a word. Maybe she's shy.

He tries again. "Did you come to visit someone here in town?"

"Yes." Her voice is soft and low. "My grandpa."

"Maybe I know where he lives. Who is your grandpa?"

The big eyes rise to meet his. "You are."

Gerald lets the van take his weight as her words echo in the quiet of early evening. He looks at Bugs, half expecting him to break out in a laugh or a cry of "April fool," but the boy is listening, expectant, and doesn't seem at all surprised that a flesh-and-blood miracle has appeared in this misty hour between daylight and dusk.

Gerald swivels, ignoring the red-hot pain in his shoulder and neck as he turns to see Jen and the driver of the car. The women have fallen silent, but in the fading light he can see that Jen has been talking to . . . Kirsten. She's older now, a little harder looking around the mouth and eyes, but she's definitely his daughter.

And the waiflike child before him is his granddaughter. Katie Evelyn.

"Katie?" The name cracks on his tongue. "Are you Katie?"

She nods.

"Then I am very glad to know you." Gerald wants to remain calm and dignified, but when he reaches out, something within him snaps and he tumbles to his knees.

As the women scramble over to him, Gerald finds himself with an arm around each youngster. "Bugs and Katie," he says, looking from one precious face to the other, "thank you for helping an old man pull himself together."

The sweetness of the moment evaporates when Kirsten's voice interrupts the quiet. "Are you all right, Dad?"

He releases the children and leans hard on the van, pulling himself up. "I'm fine."

Jen's face is a study in concern. "Do you need me to get the walker?" She turns to Kirsten. "The doctor sent him home with a walker, just in case we needed it. He's been managing okay so far, but—"

"I'm fine," Gerald interrupts, his voice frostier than he would have liked. Kirsten's been here less than five minutes, and already the women are talking about him as if he's a child who can't hear or comprehend. He shuffles to the sidewalk, where the going will be smoother and easier.

Jen takes the children into the house, and Kirsten falls into step beside him. "So, Dad—" she matches her pace to his—"how are you feeling these days?"

He wants to ignore the question just as she's ignored his cards and calls for so many years, but he can't let his hurt stand between them. She's driven a long way, by the look of things, and she has brought his granddaughter. He didn't expect so much.

"I'm tolerable." Gerald forces a smile. "Thank you for coming. I wasn't sure—I wasn't sure you could get away."

"I wanted to come." A quick smile reveals the dimple in her left cheek. "I only have one father. Since Mother's gone, you're all I have left in the world."

She links her arm through his, and he allows her to help him up the stairs.

After crossing the porch, he halts in the foyer and points to the sitting area in the south chapel. "If you don't mind, I'd like to take a breather. And that's a real comfy couch."

"Okay. I'll sit with you."

Gerald drops onto the sofa and lets his arms fall to his sides, not caring that he must look as frayed and worn-out as an ancient shroud.

Kirsten sinks to the end of the sofa, then pulls a pillow from behind her back. Sitting there, arms folded around the pillow, one leg tucked beneath her, he's reminded of the many nights she used to sit that way at home—except in those days she was usually scowling about something he'd asked her to do . . . or not do.

This night is as awkward as all the others.

"So . . ." He rubs his hand over his trouser leg. "Are you still living outside Atlanta?"

"Um, yeah . . . but I'm ready to make a change. Katie and I were living with this guy who's not so good for us, so we left."

"You were shacking up with a man?"

"Come on, Dad. Don't start preaching. I'm not one of your church members, and this isn't the twentieth century. Not anymore."

"You're my daughter. And I thought fathers were supposed to teach their daughters."

"Your teaching days are done. I learned it all the hard way, okay?"

Gerald holds up a hand in a gesture of surrender. "I'm not preaching. I'm . . . trying to understand."

Kirsten shrugs. "My situation's not that complicated. I'm a single mom, I've had to leave my job, and we're here with little more than the clothes on our backs. But we're here. With you."

He closes his eyes and moistens his dry lips. How does she always manage to tear out his heart? In the space of five minutes, she's made him feel glad, mad, and sad. At this stage of life, he ought to be able to lie down and die in peace, but now Kirsten has arrived. Like a tapeworm, she will wriggle her way into his guts and suck the life right out of him.

She gives him a bright smile and playfully punches his arm. "So, Dad, aren't you glad to see us?"

Half a dozen phrases jostle inside his brain, each competing for the right to be heard: *Yes, I'm overjoyed. No . . . I'm afraid. Why are you really here? Do you still hate me? You're too late. I'm so sorry . . . for failing you.*

Gerald loves his daughter, but he's wrangled with her before. And until she experiences a change of heart, he doesn't think she has a prayer of bringing him any sort of comfort or joy. But she has brought his granddaughter. Surely he can rejoice in that.

"I'm happy . . . and you can stay here tonight," he says, forcing words over his stammering tongue. "Jen will explain the sleeping arrangements, so why don't you go up and talk to her? I'm tired, Kirsten. I'd like to rest."

He can imagine the hurt that would fill any other daughter's eyes, but he can't bring himself to look at Kirsten. If Evelyn were here, she'd be shocked by his wariness and indifference, but Kirsten has always worn him out. She began trying his patience in her preteen years, and she hasn't stopped.

"I'll go upstairs, then," she says. He hears a soft whoosh as the sofa releases her weight. "If you don't want to talk—"

"What I want," Gerald says, "and what I can give you tonight are two different things. But thank you for coming . . . and thank you for bringing my granddaughter."

He rests his head against the back of the sofa and exhales in a heavy rush, too weary to listen for the sounds of her retreating footsteps.

In the bright overhead light of my kitchen, I get my first clear look at Gerald's daughter. My initial reaction is surprise—I imagined his daughter as much younger than me, but I'm pretty sure this woman graduated high school no more than three or four years after I did. Her blonde hair has been cut in a nice-looking pageboy, but dark roots clearly mark the part on the top of her head. She's wearing a beige blouse, a simple silver necklace, and a classic A-line skirt that has clearly suffered from several hours behind the wheel.

I don't know why I pictured Kirsten Phillips as a leather-clad, tobacco-chewing, tattooed crack addict, but this woman looks downright respectable. No matter what she looks like, I'm glad she came.

"Is this your first time to visit Mt. Dora?" I ask.

"Yeah. Yes."

"Did you have any trouble finding the place?" I grab two glasses from the cupboard. "I don't remember giving you directions when we spoke on the phone."

"I stopped at a gas station on the edge of town, and they sent me straight here." Kirsten sinks into one of the kitchen chairs. "Mt. Dora isn't that big, you know."

"True. But it has small-town charm." I fill the glasses with ice. "Would you like lemonade? tea? water?"

"Water, please." She glances out the doorway. "Is Katie with your son? Are they okay?"

"They're probably playing video games or something." I fill both glasses with water and set one in front of her, then sit next to her at the table. "Now I'm sure you're exhausted, so you can stay here tonight. I'll let the boys bunk together, and you and Katie can have Bugs's room. My mom's in the guest room, so—"

"I don't want to put anyone out."

"Nonsense. How long are you able to stay?"

Kirsten takes a sip of the water, then lowers her glass. "I was thinking I should stay . . . you know, until the end. I know that means I'll have to put Katie in school down here."

"Shouldn't be a problem. What grade is she in?"

"Fourth. She's a good student, so I don't worry about her. She'll do fine."

"I'll drive you over to the school tomorrow, and we can make the arrangements. Since you want to stay awhile, we can look for a place you can rent short-term."

She draws her lips into a tight smile. "I, uh, can't afford anything expensive. I had to quit my job, you see, and we left our place without packing much. I have to buy a few things, and . . . well, I guess you could say our funds are limited."

I study her face, searching for clues to explain her abrupt arrival, but her eyes remain blank and unreadable. How odd . . . nearly as odd as the way she reacted when I called her with the news of Gerald's illness. Perhaps she is one of those people who can absorb bad news only one bit at a time.

"Well . . ." I trace the pattern on the tablecloth, hoping to appear nonchalant and relaxed. "I happen to know of a vacant apartment that's available. It's in an old house owned by the Southern Sassies chapter of the Red Hatters—long story, but I think the ladies might welcome your company. The Hatters are fond of Gerald, so we might be able to convince them to forget about charging rent."

Kirsten lowers her jaw. "You're kidding."

"And you and Katie are welcome to join us for meals as often as you like. I'm sure you'll be spending a lot of time here, anyway, and that's a good thing. Your dad's one of those strong, silent types, entirely too stoic for his own good. He doesn't like to complain, but I'm ready to insist that he start taking more time to rest. Now maybe *you* can do the insisting."

Her mouth twists in a strange little smile. "Isn't that your job? After all, you're his wife."

"His *what*? Good grief, whatever gave you that idea? We're not married."

"But you both live here."

"Not in the same room!" I can't help laughing. Not even the most hyperactive town gossips ever buzzed about a relationship between Gerald and me. "We're *coworkers*. Gerald's my mentor, and we've been working together ever since the boys and I moved to Florida. We're good friends, of course, and we have become sort of a family. But *married*?"

I'm still laughing when I hear my mother's voice at the front door. "My mom," I explain, listening to the thump of her steps on the stairs. "She's been out at a meeting of the Southern Sassies."

My Red-Hatted parent sweeps into the kitchen and halts midstride when she spies Kirsten at the table.

"Mom—" I point to our guest—"meet Gerald's daughter, Kirsten. Her little girl, Katie, is around here someplace."

Mom shoots me an I-told-you-so smile as she extends her hand. "Welcome to Fairlawn. Any daughter of Gerald's is welcome in this family."

While Kirsten smiles and takes Mother's hand, I make a mental note to tell Mom about Kirsten assuming that Gerald and I were married.

I can't imagine any assumption being more wrong.

28

Ross pulls his blue Honda convertible into the gravel parking lot of the Fairlawn Funeral Home and wonders if the popping pebbles will hurt his metallic finish. He hops out of the car for a cursory examination of the wheel wells but decides no harm has been done.

He pushes his sunglasses back to the bridge of his nose and studies the hulking house before him. What a coup landing this place would be—great building, great location, great market. Florida is bubbling over with baby boomers zooming toward retirement today and eternity tomorrow.

And this place looks like it's in great shape, even though the building is old. The flat shingles indicate that the roof has been recently replaced, and the dignified sign on the lawn proves that the present owner cares about keeping up appearances. This annoying pebbly parking lot will have to be paved over, though, and the boxy hearse in the back driveway will have to be replaced. Today's customers want their loved ones to ride in sleek funeral coaches, not some rectangular relic.

Ross snags his folded jacket from the passenger seat and tosses it over his arm. With any luck, he'll catch the owner in a frustrated moment and they can close this deal within twenty-four hours. If Sean and Mary O'Donnell gave him reliable information, Fairlawn's present owner knows practically nothing about the death care industry. According to the online property records, the owner is a woman who'll probably be relieved to unload this white elephant and move on with her life.

He pauses to debate whether or not he should put his jacket on—should he be formal or deliberately casual?—then bends to check his reflection in the side mirror. A light swipe to smooth a few errant hairs over his ear and he's ready to begin his march up the long sidewalk.

Ross slows when he realizes he isn't alone—a blonde woman is sitting in one of the rocking chairs, and her knowing smile tells him she's been watching ever since he pulled onto the property.

So she saw him primping, big deal. It's not like she's never checked a mirror before stepping out to talk to a client. And he couldn't have asked for better timing—not only has he caught this woman in a quiet moment, but she obviously has nothing to do, which means no customers. No business.

No income.

A surge of adrenaline fires his blood. Time to rev up the Ross-a-motion sales machine. Time to churn out the charm like buttah.

"Good morning," he calls, flashing his brightest smile. "Are things always this quiet around here?"

"You read the sign," she calls back. "So you should know the dead don't make a lot of noise."

If he's reading that half smile correctly, he doesn't need permission to drop into the empty chair next to her. He sits, then tugs on his collar and leans toward the blonde, who, upon closer examination, proves to be quite attractive. "Is it always this hot down here?"

"Hmm. Seems to be."

"I'll bet you'd like to be somewhere a lot cooler . . . and more interesting."

She arches a brow. "I don't know who you are, but I like the way you think."

"I'm Ross Alexander, and that's nice to know."

"So . . . why are you here, Ross? Something tells me you didn't drop in to buy a casket."

"You're absolutely right." He runs his hand down the armrest of the old rocker. "As a matter of fact, I did drop in to buy something, but it's not a casket. I was wondering if you might be willing to sell this property."

Her full lips part slightly. "The funeral home?"

"Yes, ma'am. Unless you're dead set on being a mortician."

A deep, full-throated laugh flows from between those lips. "Honey, I can think of a thousand and one things I'd rather be."

"Then can we talk business?"

She smiles, revealing a dimple in her left cheek. "Tell you what—you buy me lunch, and I'll let you talk about buying anything you want. But I can't talk business when I'm hungry."

Ross grins, warmed by her forthrightness. Most people initially resist when he approaches with an offer; it's all part of the complicated dance between buyer and seller. Their list of reasons for not selling is usually as long as his arm: they can't sell because it's a family business, because the community depends on them, or because they can't afford to pay a capital gains tax in the current fiscal year. One man told Ross he couldn't sell because God had called him to be a funeral director, but he had no trouble hanging up on the holy hotline when Ross made him an offer spelled in seven figures.

But this woman . . . Something tells Ross she'd make quite a salesman herself. She's quick, she's charming, and those blue eyes could intrigue a customer as well as the promise of below-market pricing.

"I can talk over lunch." He stands. "I just got into town, so I hope you know a nice place."

She stands, too. "Don't worry. I have a nose for nice places."

Bugs crosses his arms and watches the girl examining his car. It's his favorite, the Matchbox Mitsubishi Spyder, and he's let her hold it for a full five minutes, something he wouldn't even let Clay do.

Mom told him to be nice to Katie, and he's doing his best. He let her and her mom have his room last night, and their stuff is still spread all over the bed.

Mom hasn't complained about the mess, though. She and Gerald are downstairs working on a dead guy, and Katie's mom is supposed to be finding out where Katie will go to school. She might have gone to Round Lake with him this morning, but it's a teacher workday with no school for kids.

"I like blue cars," Katie says, holding the Spyder on her palm. She brings it closer to her face as if she'd like to climb inside and drive away. "Do you want a car like this?"

"I have a car like that."

"I mean a *real* car. One you can drive."

Bugs takes the car from her hand and places it with the others on his nightstand. She doesn't understand that this *is* a real car and he can drive it fine—over the rug, through the hall, and into the living room. Once he revved it up and let it go down the stairs, where it flipped and flew all the way to the bottom before it landed right side up and rolled to the front door without a dent. What a crash! What a car!

But Katie doesn't get it.

He rises to his knees and stumps over to the big wooden chest against the wall. "This is my toy box. Wanna see inside?"

"Okay."

Bugs opens the lid and pulls out his Transformers, a couple of balls, some game cartridges, and a fistful of LEGOs. "See anything you want to play with?"

She peers inside, then tugs on her hair. "Do you have any Bratz?"

"What's that?"

"They're dolls. There's Cloe and Sasha and Jade—she's my favorite."

Bugs pulls out an action figure and drops it on the floor. "There's Spider-Man. I think I have Superman in here somewhere and a couple of wrestling guys." He leans into the big box and rummages through trucks, cars, and building blocks until he finds Superman.

When he straightens up, he sees Katie holding Spider-Man with a funny look on her face. "Don't you have the girl?"

"What girl?"

"The girl he kisses in the movie. His girlfriend."

Bugs thinks about diving into the toy box again just to make an effort, but he knows there are no girls inside. No way. "Wanna play with Superman?"

"Do you have Lois Lane?"

He draws a big breath. "I have a radio-controlled car. We could go outside and race it if you want. You can work the remote control."

She drops Spider-Man. "That might be fun."

"Race ya to the front door."

They leap up.

But just then Clay steps into the doorway and blocks their way. "Hey, kiddo." His mouth curves when he sees Katie. "Who's your girlfriend?"

"She's not my girlfriend," Bugs answers. "She's Katie."

Beside him, Katie nods, her eyes wider and bluer than ever.

Clay jerks his head toward the kitchen. "Grandma wanted me to tell you she made cookies. They're on the table if you want some."

After Clay walks off, Bugs runs into the hallway, then realizes he's alone. Katie isn't racing with him. Has she already forgotten about the car, or does she want a cookie? He turns. "You coming?"

Still in the bedroom, she blinks at him. "Huh?"

"Are you coming outside?"

Katie moves into the hall and looks at the closed door leading to Clay's room. "Who was that?"

"You mean Clay?"

She nods.

"He's my big brother. He goes to the high school."

Katie smiles. "Do you think he'll come out for a cookie? I'm a little hungry."

Bugs stares at her, but he's heard that girls are hard to understand. He ought to be mad, but the way she looks—big eyes, soft hair, pink smile—is so pretty he can't help thinking that if Spider-Man and Superman have girlfriends, maybe a girlfriend is a nice thing to have.

Maybe he shouldn't have been so quick to answer Clay the way he did.

"Katie—" he places his hands on his hips—"would you like to be my girlfriend?"

She pinches her lower lip with her teeth. "For how long?"

Bugs tilts his head. Is there a time limit? Superman has liked Lois Lane forever, but Dad didn't like Mom forever. "I dunno. A week?"

Katie takes a deep breath. "Okay."

At a table for two in the Windsor Rose Tea Room, Kirsten studies the handsome younger man who seems unaccountably eager to buy her lunch. He intrigued her from the moment he climbed out of his flashy sports car, and something about *her* obviously interests *him*.

The funeral home, he said. He wants to buy it—a wish she can certainly grant after she officially inherits the place.

She turns in her seat and searches for the waitress, pricked again by the hard truth that her father is dying. Even if she hadn't been forewarned, she would have realized it last night. The father of her memory was strong and implacable, but the man she saw in the chapel was pale and bent like a question mark. Deep violet rings circled his eyes, and he teetered as he made his way from the foyer to the sofa. She never imagined her father could falter.

When he goes, who will tell her she's ruining her life?

"So—" her companion glances around the restaurant—"do you come here often?"

Kirsten smiles at the waitress, who is approaching with an honest-to-goodness teapot. Hard to believe anyone would want to drink hot tea when it's eighty-five degrees outside, but maybe the air-conditioning will help her forget she's sipping tea in the subtropics.

"First things first," she says, unfolding her napkin. "I think we should begin with formal introductions. You told me your name, but I still have no idea who you are."

He waits until the waitress finishes pouring two cups of tea; then he extends his hand across the table. "Ross Alexander of Aldridge Elms, the nation's second-largest corporate player in the death care industry."

"That's a mouthful." She shakes his hand. "Kirsten Phillips."

"Phillips." His smile fades a notch. "That's not the name on the property records."

"I know. The owner is battling cancer and hasn't much longer to live. I expect to inherit the home within a matter of weeks."

His smile dims another notch. "I'm sorry to hear that."

"So was I. I have absolutely no use for a funeral home."

A flurry of emotions crosses his face—a token attempt at compassionate sorrow slips into a cunning smile that gives way to a grateful grin. So, this man *really* wants to buy the home. But why?

"Tell me, Mr. Alexander—"

"Call me Ross, please." His expression shifts to a look of sympathetic understanding.

"Tell me, Ross, why are you so interested in Fairlawn? The place isn't big, it's located in a sleepy little burg, and from what I hear, business isn't exactly booming."

He flashes her a salesman's smile. "Quite simply, Kirsten, my company aims to be number one, and I aim to be their number one salesman. I need—Aldridge Elms needs—a facility in this area, and we think Mt. Dora is the perfect place for us to set up another shop. The logistics are perfect, the property is great, and the surrounding population . . . well, let's face it, Kirsten, they're aging. With the dedicated service we can bring to the area, combined with the discounts our dealers are willing to provide, we believe Fairlawn could become a highly profitable little enterprise. In exchange for our high hopes, we're willing to make the official owner an extremely handsome offer."

The waitress stops to hand them menus, but Kirsten drops hers to the table, far more interested in the conversation than in food. "Listen, let's cut to the chase. The official owner is a little busy trying to stay alive right now, so I don't think this is a good time to be presenting any offers. I, however, am the only heir, and I've been involved with real estate. I'm a saleswoman, too, so you don't have to dazzle me and you don't have to repeat my name every two minutes. I know every trick in the book, so let's be honest with each other, okay?"

For an instant his expression remains fixed in a tight, polished smile. Then his face cracks in relief. "You're in the business?"

"I was."

"Where'd you sell?"

"Atlanta—Alpharetta, to be exact. Upscale condos."

Ross lifts his teacup. "I'm from Atlanta, too. And it's nice to meet someone who knows the lingo."

"Right, so let's start over. You want to buy the Fairlawn Funeral Home."

"Lock, stock, and barrel. We'll buy any existing preneed contracts, the property, and the complete inventory. We'll even buy that antiquated hearse I spied in the driveway."

"It *is* old-fashioned, isn't it?" She brings her fingertips together. "All right, what sort of an offer are you talking about? Assessed value, market price, or might you be *extremely* motivated?"

Ross's laughter turns into a cough. "Hold on. I haven't had a chance to evaluate the property or check the books."

"Come on. I'm asking for a ballpark estimate, not an official proposal—and you can even toss me a low ball. What's the least you're willing to offer on the property you saw today?"

Kirsten can almost see wheels turning in his head as he stares at her. "Um . . . if the building is in good shape—"

"It is."

"And the property large enough to support an extended parking lot—"

"No problem."

"Then I'd say—"

"Guesstimate?"

"Somewhere between one and one point two, plus whatever assets are in guaranteed accounts, minus any existing liabilities on the books."

She swallows hard. "That seems low. I'll bet I could find residential properties in the area selling for that much. Those historic houses like Fairlawn are popular . . . and pricey."

A smile quirks the corner of his mouth. "The price can go up, of course, once I examine the facilities. I'll need to do a full evaluation before I can make a binding offer."

Kirsten settles back in her chair. At least $1.2 million—and that's only the funeral home; surely her father has additional savings tucked away. Of course she'll have to pay taxes and cover his medical expenses, and he'll probably want to leave something to that assistant who's been helping him run the place. But still . . .

To a woman who owns a car and a few grocery bags stuffed with dirty clothes, $1.2 million is a lot of money.

She lifts her teacup, inhales the warm aroma, and sends a smile winging over the rim. "Thank you," she says simply. "It's nice to begin a business relationship with all our cards flat on the table."

"Katie, would you like some corn niblets?" I offer to pass the bowl, but the little girl recoils as if I were serving yellow poison pills.

"Kate doesn't eat corn," Kirsten answers, taking the bowl from me and setting it in the middle of the table. "We hardly ever eat like this."

I catch my mother's eye. What's so unusual about a family gathering around an entrée and a couple of veggies?

We're crowded into the kitchen, all seven of us gathered around a table that usually seats four. Mom cooked spaghetti and her special sauce. I know she pulled out the corn as a token vegetable, but my boys and I are the only ones eating it.

I give Kirsten a polite smile. "I looked around for you at lunch, but Bugs said you'd gone out."

Kirsten stops twirling spaghetti on her fork as a dusky red tide advances up her throat. "Yes, I went to lunch. I knew you had a funeral planned, so I thought I'd get out of your way."

Mom flashes a look at me, but Gerald voices the question uppermost in our minds: "You went to lunch by yourself?"

"Not by myself." Kirsten's voice is light, but now her cheeks are flushed. "I met someone, and he took me to lunch."

Mother abandons all subtlety and gapes at Gerald's daughter.

I have to admit I'm both perplexed and impressed. Kirsten Phillips is attractive, but I can't figure out how anyone could get asked out within twenty-four hours of arriving in town. This woman must have set a Mt. Dora speed record.

Gerald stops chewing and stares at his daughter, then goes back to cutting his spaghetti. He doesn't press for an explanation, so I follow his lead and keep my mouth shut. If Mom asks how Kirsten managed to find a man in record time, I'll have to kick her under the table.

What Kirsten *hasn't* mentioned is whether or not she contacted the elementary school or looked for an apartment. I'd ask, but I don't want her to think I'm pushing her out the door.

"You, missy," Gerald says, nodding in my direction, "can't forget about your exam on Saturday. Have you been studying?"

"In every spare minute," I assure him. "Which means I've studied a total of ten minutes this week."

"By the way," Mom says, drizzling melted butter on Bugs's corn, "how'd the funeral go today?"

"Quick," Gerald says, looking at me. We both laugh.

"Francis Quick," I remind Mother. "Not a very big crowd, I'm afraid. His parents, his parole officer, and a few people from his parents' church."

"I'll never get over the way you two joke around about funerals," Mom says.

"We're not being disrespectful," I tell her. "But sometimes you have to laugh or you'd spend all your time crying."

Bugs is grinning at Katie like a jack-o'-lantern. "Tomorrow after school," he says, bouncing in his chair, "I can take you down to the creek to look for tadpoles. Mr. Gerald showed me where they hide."

While he and Katie talk about worms and frogs, I can't help noticing that Kirsten and Gerald don't have much to say to one another. Kirsten picks at her dinner and occasionally chides her daughter about being so messy, apparently more concerned with the cleanliness of Katie's clothes than inquiring about her father's health.

Gerald picks at his food, too—a gesture that would hurt Mother's feelings if she didn't know about his illness—and finally asks about the weather in Georgia.

Kirsten replies that the weather's the same as always, and the pall of silence falls between them again.

"The weather here's been nice," I say, glancing at Mom and silently urging her to help me enliven the conversation. "Much warmer than last year."

"Much warmer than Virginia," Mom echoes. She leans toward Kirsten. "That's where I live, you see. When I'm not here, I'm up there."

Kirsten nods. "Good to know."

Gerald jerks his chin toward Katie. "How's her dad? Does she ever see him?"

Kirsten stabs a meatball with her knife and cleanly cuts it in two. "He left us. I don't know where he is and I don't care."

"The girl needs a father," Gerald insists. "Girls learn things from fathers—things they can't learn from mothers."

"Right." Kirsten's voice goes flat. "Like all the things I learned from you."

A sense of unease descends over the table like a fog, chilling me to the bone. Even Bugs and Clay have gone wide-eyed in the uncomfortable atmosphere. I see Gerald's Adam's apple bob as he swallows, and suddenly I want to leap up, wave my napkin, and declare a truce.

"Albertson's is having a sale," Mom says, her voice brittle and bright. "A good special on whole chickens. Do you still have that infomercial rotisserie?"

I shake my head. "I got rid of it when we moved."

"What about that man you were living with?" Gerald pins his daughter with his hot gaze. "Is he still in the picture?"

"I like a good rotisserie," Mom says. "And those George Foreman grills—have you tried those?"

Kirsten's knife clatters as it falls to her plate. "It wasn't working out, so Katie and I left." She glares at her father. "Would you rather we'd stayed in Georgia?"

Gerald clamps his lips together, imprisoning his response, probably for the sake of the children. I don't know much about the history between Gerald and Kirsten, but from what little I do know, I can imagine what he was going to say: *Nothing ever works out for you, Kirsten. What are you doing wrong?*

I turn to Mother. "George Foreman—isn't he the boxer with five boys named George?"

When the phone rings, I want to weep with relief. Someone is calling on the business line, offering me an opportunity to escape the tension at the table.

I excuse myself and answer the phone, make a note, and hang up. When I announce that we need to make a pickup, Gerald pushes away from the table with unusual force. "An adult?"

"Clovis Witherspoon."

"Big man. I'll get ready."

"Are you sure you should go?" Mom asks as Gerald braces himself to stand. "You're bound to be exhausted after such a long day."

"I need to go," Gerald answers. "Jen can't manage Clovis by herself. The man weighs three hundred pounds even without his huntin' boots."

I grimace at the thought of lifting so much weight. We *could* take Clay along, but though I'm sure he'd be willing to go, I'm not sure I'm ready to involve my child in the work of the funeral business. We could swing by the Biddle House and see if Ryan is available to lend us a hand.

"I'll get my jacket," Gerald says, lumbering toward his room. "Be back in a sec."

I turn to my mother and silently hand over control of the dinner table.

She accepts this responsibility with an almost imperceptible nod, then leans closer to Bugs. "If you eat all your meatballs, I have a surprise dessert in the fridge. You'll love it."

"For Katie, too?"

"Sure, if she eats all her dinner . . . and tries some of that corn."

"We should be back in an hour or so," I tell Mom. "Definitely before bedtime."

"Don't worry about a thing," she answers. "I'll clean up the kitchen."

Kirsten says nothing as I grab my purse and help Gerald down the stairs.

After sitting at the table for what she hopes is a decent interval, Kirsten carries her plate to the sink, leaves the kitchen, and moves toward the stairs. Katie doesn't seem to mind staying with the older woman and the boys, plus she's looking forward to dessert. But Kirsten couldn't stand another minute in that kitchen.

Reaching the foyer at the bottom of the stairs, she turns down the hallway that appears to bisect the first floor. She's not had a chance to explore this place, but she needs to have a firm grasp of the building's potential if she's going to continue discussions with Ross Alexander. There's no way she's going to let an attractive, smooth-talking salesman pull the wool over her eyes. She has no idea what a funeral home property sells for these days, but it's bound to be more than $1.2 million.

She peers into the large rooms opening to the left and right of the foyer. These are chapels, apparently. Both spaces are lit by wide windows that open onto the Victorian porch.

The scent of flowers still hangs over the smaller chapel, and someone has dropped a daisy and a program on the floor. Kirsten bends to pick up the paper and reads the name and dates printed at the top: *Francis Quick, January 6, 1973–April 16, 2008.*

She sets the program on a small table and peeks into the larger chapel, which features the sitting area where she talked with her father last night.

Kirsten steps into the room and gingerly lifts the cover of a leather-bound book on the coffee table. She had been afraid she'd see Polaroids of people in flower-strewn coffins, but the photos in this album are of empty caskets: the Preston Mahogany and the Marsellus Midnight Silver. A caption beneath each picture gives the model name and details about the construction.

She shudders and closes the book. What a business. Ross Alexander is welcome to it.

Kirsten leaves the chapel and tiptoes down the paneled hallway. A laundry room and a small bathroom lie to the left; to the right is an office cluttered with periodicals, notebooks, and filing cabinets. A computer sits on a desk, and though the desktop is reasonably tidy, a stack of correspondence rests in a basket on the corner. An open doorway stands at the back of the office, so she walks toward it, unsure of what she'll find. She grimaces at the threshold. The narrow room beyond is filled with caskets, some exposed, others still encased in cardboard. *Ick.*

She rushes out of the office and closes the door. The sooner this place is sold, the better. There's no way she's going to go through all the paperwork her father's leaving behind.

At the end of the hallway is a wide door labeled with a bold sign:

> **STOP**
> It is a violation of Florida law to enter
> this room without authorization.

Kirsten approaches and places one hand on the doorknob. This must be the room where they actually handle dead bodies. Unfortunately, she also needs to examine this area if she's going to counter Ross Alexander's pitiful offer.

She opens the door and thrusts her head into the opening. The room isn't as awful as she feared—just a large space with sinks and shelves along one side, two white tables in the center, and something like a walk-in freezer at the back. A door in one wall opens to the outside, and a single window overlooks the back porch. A lace curtain gives the area an almost homey touch.

Kirsten's seen enough. She closes the wide door and heads down the hallway, hesitating at the bottom of the stairs. She already scouted out the second floor, so she has a good idea of the building's layout. Before meeting Ross again, she ought to investigate the garage and count the vehicles, but for now she might as well go up and see what she can learn from Jennifer Graham's mother.

The sounds of running water, clacking dishes, and childish giggles meet her as she climbs the stairs. The children are laughing in one of the boys' rooms, but Joella is standing by the kitchen sink, her arms encased to the elbow in rubber gloves.

"Oh! Hi there," Joella says when Kirsten comes through the doorway. "Did you want some dessert? I made a pretzel Jell-O salad."

"No thanks." Kirsten takes a chair at the table. "I don't think I've ever had anything quite like that."

Joella shrugs. "The recipe was popular a few years ago. You use strawberries and cream cheese and gelatin. I used to make it all the time, but now I hardly ever cook unless I'm at Fairlawn. When you live alone, it's easier to eat frozen foods. Bad for the blood pressure, though. Too much sodium."

Kirsten folds her hands. "Your daughter certainly seems at home here."

"Oh, she is. It took a while, of course—at first she and the boys weren't wild about living in a funeral home. But your dad really took them under his wing. He showed Jen how the work could be a ministry as well as a business. She wouldn't be doing this if it weren't for him."

Kirsten exhales through her teeth. "Dad always did like to teach."

"He's a good teacher. I think Jen would say she's learned more from Gerald than from her teachers at mortuary school. Anyway, she'll soon take her national board exam, and after that she'll be fully licensed." The woman pauses, her voice softening. "We are grieving about your father's cancer . . . but we trust God to handle the timing of things."

Kirsten is tempted to ask how Joella can be so sure of what the Almighty is doing, but tonight it's probably better to keep quiet. She hopes this woman is right. Once Jennifer is licensed, she can take her boys, her dog, and her mother and go anywhere. Or maybe she can stay put—Ross Alexander's firm is going to need someone to run Fairlawn after the sale. Either way, it's not like Kirsten needs to worry about displacing the Graham family.

"When Jen passes her exams," Joella continues, her expression growing thoughtful, "I'm hoping your dad will be able to relax a little. He feels so responsible for her, and I worry about him. I don't want his last days to be filled with stress. It elevates the blood pressure, and that cuts your life short."

Was that some kind of hint? or maybe a warning? Kirsten runs her finger over the damp tabletop. "Will your daughter have trouble with her exams?"

"I shouldn't think so. She finished school not too long ago, so all those bones and blood vessels are bound to still be in her head. I know she'll be relieved to have the exam behind her, though—she wants to be able to focus on taking care of your father. Of course, she wants you to feel free to help, too."

As though Kirsten knows anything about taking care of the sick. What's she supposed to do, give her father pills? change his sheets? She brought his granddaughter and came to see him. Isn't that enough?

Suddenly uncomfortable in the overheated kitchen, Kirsten stands and pushes her chair under the table. "Thanks again for dinner, but Katie and I are still tired from the drive, and we have a big day tomorrow. I need to find a place to stay and see about enrolling her in school."

"Go get some rest, then," Joella answers, rinsing a glass. "We're so glad you came. Your dad is, too."

The words trail after Kirsten as she goes in search of her daughter. Her father may have told this woman that he's glad they came, but Kirsten hasn't exactly been overwhelmed with affection since her arrival.

She has barely seen him smile.

I'd rather embalm a dozen adult clients for free than prepare a child for burial. The boy on the table in front of me is no bigger than Bugs, and he died from leukemia.

After reaching the Witherspoon house last night, we discovered that our assumptions were wrong. The stout Clovis Witherspoon met us at the door, his gray hair askew and his eyes puffy from weeping. He led us into a back room, where two women sat beside a bed on which we found Clovis Witherspoon III, known to everyone in the family as Little Clove. Gerald and I had stopped by the Biddle House to pick up Ryan, but I leaned down and lifted the child easily, his body no heavier than a feather pillow.

Now I smooth wisps of wet blond hair from Little Clove's brow as the Porti-Boy pumps pink fluid through his arteries. On the other side of the table, Gerald sits on a stool, silently working the solution through the veins and capillaries in the boy's thin arm.

"I hate this part of the job." I lift the child's right hand, allowing his small palm to rest against my glove. "I'm not sure I'll ever get used to burying children."

Gerald swivels his tired gaze toward me. "I've buried far too many for my pleasure. But I take comfort in trusting that the little ones are with Jesus by the time they arrive here."

My throat fills with a potato-size lump as I bend lower over the boy's body. I can't think about heaven these days without remembering how close Gerald is to going there.

He hardly ever complains, but I can see him slipping away by degrees. His movements are slower than they were last week, and he no longer stands by the prep table but routinely sits on his stool. I know it's only a matter of time before he's unable to make it up and down the stairs.

This man's days are numbered and his daughter has come from Georgia, yet he and Kirsten appear no closer to reconciling than they were years ago. Though she has spent very little time with her father, I'm certain God brought her to Mt. Dora so she and Gerald can share in the healing power of forgiveness.

"Gerald—" I blink back unexpected tears—"can we talk about Kirsten?"

He slides from his stool and drags it toward the foot of the table, then perches on the edge and begins to massage the boy's legs. "Don't fret yourself about my girl," he says, his voice rough. "She seems to be fine."

"How can you say that?" The words clot in my throat. "How can your relationship be fine when you two barely speak? I think God brought her to us so you could—"

Gerald cuts me off with a sharp look. "Hold on. I learned long ago not to blame God for Kirsten's actions."

"I'm not blaming God for anything. I'm saying there must be a reason she came."

"Sure there is. You invited her," he says with a small smile. He picks up Little Clove's leg and exerts gentle pressure to break the rigor at the knee. "I know God is sovereign over his creation, but some folks are determined to go through life doin' what they want to do. Kirsten has repeatedly turned her back on everything Evelyn and I taught her. I've seen God set amazing opportunities in front of that girl, but she's too proud to do things his way."

I hesitate, not knowing how far I should continue this conversational thread. I hate to pry into painful memories, but sometimes a wound has to be lanced before it can heal. "Maybe—" I begin to massage the boy's opposite leg—"maybe she needs to be reminded of the things you and your wife taught her. Maybe she's lost her way, and she needs to know she can come back."

"She found her way here, didn't she? And it's easy to find your way back to God—it's as simple as admitting your need and forsaking your pride. Kirsten knows what she should do."

From beneath my bangs, I study Gerald as he works. I've never seen this side of him. I've never heard his voice this clipped and raw, but I don't think he's upset with me. This pain goes much deeper.

"Back when Kirsten was sixteen or seventeen," Gerald says, gently massaging the child's leg, "I used to preach a lot about the Prodigal Son. I know it wasn't very subtle, but I figured everyone needs to hear that story because we all tend to find ourselves rebelling like the younger son or feelin' resentful like the elder. Anyway, one day during the middle of my sermon, I got choked up and could barely finish. For the first time, I realized that the miracle didn't happen when the son came home; the real miracle happened when the father let the boy go. Loving his son, knowing what he would do, still the father gave him money and let him go. And that's when I knew that one day Kirsten and I would come to a point where I would have to release her into the hands of God."

He lifts his head, a look of intense pain pouring through his eyes. "So, when the time came, I let her go. I've been waiting for the prodigal to come home ever since."

"But she's here. Surely that counts for something."

"She's in the building. I'm not sure where her heart is." Gerald lowers the boy's leg, which has brightened from gray to a healthy pink. "I'm sorry," he says, his voice breaking. "I know I'm not exactly rational when it comes to Kirsten. I've tried to love her. I've given her time and money and support, yet all I seem to get in return is anger or indifference."

I step closer, bending Clovis's knee, then hugging it to my chest. "Don't you think . . . that maybe she's come here to make things right? Don't you think God can use everything that's happening to change her heart?"

"I think he'd have to break it first." Gerald closes his eyes, then shakes his head. "I appreciate what you're doing, how you've welcomed Kirsten and Katie. I'll meet her halfway if she wants to talk. But I haven't seen any signs of softening yet. As for myself—I don't know if you can understand this, but every time I look at her, I'm reminded that I failed at the most important job God ever gave me." His lids clamp tight to trap a rush of tears, but still they stream down his cheeks.

I stand on the other side of our young client, horrified and paralyzed by the sight of my friend's personal pain. What have I done by inviting Kirsten to Fairlawn? I hesitate, not knowing whether I should go around the table and hug him or simply stand and wait.

He uses his sleeve to wipe the tears from his cheeks. "It's all right. Like I said, don't fret yourself over my daughter."

"Don't you think she'll come around?"

"Only God knows. She might, but I don't think it'll happen in my lifetime."

Joella slips the blood pressure monitor onto her arm, presses the power button, and waits until the mechanism applies steady pressure to her wrist. After a minute, the pressure eases and the result flashes in the digital display: 165 over 93.

She presses her hand to her chest and swallows hard. What on earth is going on? She forgot to take her hypertension medicine last night, but would missing one dose shoot her pressure this high? Maybe it's the slice of pepperoni pizza she just ate for lunch. Pepperoni is loaded with sodium.

Joella tiptoes to her bedroom doorway and glances down the hallway, then closes the door and locks it. Jen and Gerald are working downstairs, so they shouldn't mind if she takes a little nap. Heaven knows she needs a break.

She reclines on the bed, props her feet on a pillow, and folds her hands across her stomach. Deep, slow breaths—that's the ticket for hypertension. Steady, even breathing in and out, in and out. Close your eyes and think of sunny beaches, swaying palm trees, handsome men serving lemonade on golden platters. . . .

She's about to settle into a sun-warmed imaginary beach chair when she remembers the squash. Gerald's nutritionist suggested lots of yellow vegetables, and she forgot to get squash at the grocery. That means she can't afford to lie here daydreaming; she needs to go out and pick up fresh vegetables.

She opens her eyes and focuses on the ceiling. So much pressure at Fairlawn now. Though Jen is doing her best to make sure life continues as normal, it's hard to relax with that woman and her daughter around. And as much as Gerald tries to downplay his illness, Joella can't avoid thinking about his special menus and the line of medicine bottles on the kitchen windowsill. Every time she sees them, she thinks of her own prescriptions and her own physical frailties.

One thing is certain—growing older is not for cowards. When the body begins to slow down, when years of unhealthy habits exact their toll, there's nothing you can do but pay the price and hope God is merciful.

Joella snaps the blood pressure monitor onto her wrist again. Maybe that last reading was a fluke. Because she simply can't slow down, not now, not here.

The people at Fairlawn need her.

By the time six o'clock rolls around, little Clovis Witherspoon has been casketed and I'm as grouchy as a millipede with sore feet. From my stool in the prep room I can hear the muted sounds of voices and clattering silverware, so I know Mom has managed to get dinner on the kitchen table.

I square my shoulders and draw a deep breath. I ought to go upstairs and ask my children about their day. I ought to ask Kirsten if she made it over to the Biddle House to look at the empty apartment, and I ought to ask Katie if she likes her new teacher at the elementary school. After we've eaten, I ought to help Mom with the dishes, and then I ought to insist that Gerald go to his room to rest instead of waiting up in case the phone should ring with news of a pickup. Finally, I ought to study for the national board exam, which I'm scheduled to take tomorrow.

So many *oughts*. They whirl around my head like whining mosquitoes, and all at once I can't make myself ascend those stairs. Instead I duck into the office, shove aside the latest batch of contest entries, and dial Daniel's cell phone. When he answers, I blurt out a question: "Have you eaten yet?"

I can almost see his startled face. "Has there been a breakout of food poisoning . . . or are you hungry?"

"I'm starving and my house is crowded. Can you come get me, or should I meet you somewhere?"

He doesn't hesitate. "I'll be there in five minutes."

"I'll be on the porch." Guilt surges through my veins like steaming lava as I grab my purse and tiptoe toward the front door, but I think Mom will understand. I'm not running away forever, only for an hour or two. Sometimes even a warrior needs time to relax and regroup.

Twenty minutes later, I discover that not even the sight of Daniel's smile across the table is enough to lighten my mood.

His brow crinkles with concern. "Rough day?"

Ignoring forty years of ingrained etiquette, I prop my elbow on the table and rest my head on my hand. "Very rough. Embalmed a little boy, made Gerald cry, and can't seem to reclaim Bugs's bedroom. Katie's no trouble; she spends most of her time playing with Bugs, but Kirsten sits all day on the sofa watching TV. I'm sure she can get the empty apartment at the Biddle House, but she hasn't made a move to check things out. I keep waiting for her to help or do something for Gerald, but she ignores him. I don't even know why she drove all the way down here."

"Maybe she's not ready to tell you why she came."

"Well, I'm ready to ask. I was happy to move her into Bugs's room, but it's been two days and she hasn't done anything but sit around and stare at us. I'm about *this close* to telling her what I think about the way she's ignored her father all these years—"

"Um, Jen? Did you want to tell the entire restaurant?"

I clamp my lips when I realize that other people, including our waitress, are staring. My diatribe is more entertainment than folks are used to at the Windsor Rose Tea Room. I sink lower in my chair and hide behind the menu. "What looks good tonight?"

"Even in a tirade, you do. And the roast beef is supposed to be excellent."

"Okay." I set the menu on the table, then press my hand to my forehead. "I have my national board exam tomorrow, and if I don't pass, I can't get my license. Tomorrow afternoon we have the Witherspoon boy's funeral. That will take a lot out of Gerald."

"Do you need help? I could come by."

"No." My reply sounds sharper than I intended. "Thanks, but I don't want you hanging around like an assistant. Bad enough that people are saying we're in cahoots. I don't want them thinking you're a silent partner."

Daniel chuckles. "No one thinks that."

"You know people in this town."

"Sure I do. I know they don't have any problem with one friend helping another out of a jam."

"I don't want a helping hand. I need to make Fairlawn a success on my own." Hot tears spring to my eyes, surprising me as much as Daniel.

He leans back in his chair. "Where's this coming from?"

"What?"

"This . . . stubbornness. This arrogant feminism."

I catch my breath. "You think I'm being arrogant?"

"Either that, or you're exceptionally hormonal today."

Something in me snaps. I look at him across the table as dozens of angry words leapfrog in my head. So Daniel Sladen is like so many other men I've known—men who have the audacity to blame a woman's most passionate emotions on the waxing and waning of her menstrual cycle. Thomas and one of my old college professors used to do that. I twist in my seat and yank my purse from the back of the chair. "You know, I've lost my appetite."

"Jen—" His voice is plaintive.

"I'll be going now."

"But I drove you here. Are you walking home?"

"I'll call a cab."

"You'll have to wait thirty minutes for a taxi. Why don't you stay, have some dinner, and cool off. I think you're exhausted. I *know* you're under pressure."

"And suffering from hormone-induced insanity; is that right? That's what my ex-husband said—right before he ran off with our nanny."

I fish my cell phone from my purse and snap it open. "I'll call my mother. She'll be here in five minutes." Leaving Daniel alone at the table, I sling my purse onto my shoulder, gather the tattered rags of my dignity, and stalk out of the restaurant.

❧ ❧ ❧

At 8:50 on Saturday morning, I cross the sidewalk in front of the Pearson Professional Center in Orlando and head toward suite 300. I've been on the road for the last thirty minutes, and my stomach feels jittery.

I probably should have had more for breakfast than a single cup of coffee and a handful of vitamins.

After entering the office, I show my confirmation letter to a bored-looking man behind a desk. He gestures to a closed door and I walk toward it, acutely aware of the creaking sound my loafers make with each step.

I enter the room and find it nearly deserted. I slide into a nearby desk and glance around the sterile space, then nod at the young man playing with his fancy phone across the aisle. He looks about twenty-two, probably fresh out of community college. His brain cells are quick and elastic, so he probably remembers everything he's ever heard about anatomy, business law, and microbiology.

I, on the other hand, can barely remember what I wore yesterday. Unfortunately, I *can* recall every sharp word that passed between Daniel and me last night, and I wince every time the memory surfaces. I know I'm often my own worst enemy, but why do I have to be everyone else's, too?

My young companion puts his phone away, then leans back and extends his long legs beneath the seat in front of him. He's wearing khakis and a polo shirt, which may be what young morticians wear on casual test days. What do I know?

He sets two sharpened pencils on the slanted desk and grins at me. "Not many people beating the door down to take this test."

I shake my head. "You can say that again."

"You working in Orlando?"

"Mt. Dora."

"Never heard of it."

Of course he hasn't. Mt. Dora is quaint and charming, not young and hip. "It's about thirty miles up the road. North."

He glances toward the door as it opens again. Two others enter, a blue-jeaned woman and a man who's probably in his midthirties. In that instant, a random fact slithers out of my brain cells to taunt me: 73 percent of all applicants who sit for the national board exam pass the test. That means 27 percent fail, so either Ms. Blue Jeans, Mr. Thirtysomething, Mr. Young Techie, or I will bomb big-time today. Odds are that one of us will waste the three-hundred-fifty-dollar application fee and two hours of a lovely Saturday morning.

I blow my bangs from my forehead and wish I'd stayed in bed.

At the stroke of nine, an older gentleman enters with a stack of printed booklets. He gazes at us over the top of his reading glasses and proceeds to give instructions. Politeness soaks his voice, but his way of looking down his nose assures me that he doesn't believe any of us are worthy to call ourselves morticians.

When the test booklet slaps the desk in front of me, I pick up my pencil and swallow hard. The test is divided into two parts, arts and sciences, and for a moment I'm certain I can't remember anything about anything.

Then I turn the page and read the first question under Funeral Service History:

Dr. Thomas Holmes is considered to be one of the founding fathers of the modern death care industry because of his work during which war?

Miracle of miracles, I know the answer. I darken the circle beside *The American Civil War* and skim the next question:

Who founded the first American school established exclusively for the training of students in the art of embalming?

Joseph H. Clarke, whose name I remember because his picture reminds me of a congressman I knew on Capitol Hill. I darken the circle beside his name as other mundane details come to mind: Mr. Clarke was a traveling casket salesman for a company in Indiana, and his school was called the Clarke School of Embalming.

Feeling more confident, I settle into my seat. I may find myself scratching my head in the pathology or chemistry sections, but I know dead people.

If only I understood the living half as well.

❦ ❦ ❦

Fortunately—or unfortunately, I can't decide which—the real world is waiting for me when I get back to Fairlawn. I thought I could relax after the exam, but the tension that tightened my neck and shoulders during the test returns when I walk through the front door and hear the children squabbling. Apparently they're all trying to watch TV, and though I can't see them from the foyer, their voices drift down to meet me.

"I want to watch cartoons," Bugs says.

"I want to watch whatever Clay wants," Katie answers.

"Good grief," Clay roars, slamming something—I'm guessing the remote—to the coffee table. "Why don't you leprechauns just leave me alone!" He stomps past the staircase, heading toward his room. An instant later, his bedroom door slams.

I exhale slowly and count to ten as I finish climbing the steps. When I reach the landing, I see Bugs sitting on the sofa, his arms folded across his chest, and Katie in the wing chair, her gaze focused on the hallway and Clay's closed door.

I move toward the kitchen. I need a Diet Coke.

I find Mom studying an open cookbook. "Have you made this skillet lasagna?" She taps the page. "You drew a star by it."

I lift the cover of the book. "That's not mine. It probably belonged to Evelyn or Uncle Ned's wife."

"Oh. Well, it looks easy. I think I'll make it for dinner." She blinks. "Oh! How did you do on the exam?"

I shrug. "I'll know in a couple of weeks. Some sections were easy; some were hard. I'm just glad it's over."

"I'm sure you did fine." Mom returns her gaze to the book and studies the list of ingredients. "I think we have everything I need."

I grab a diet soda from the refrigerator, pop the ring, and settle into a seat, not bothering to get a glass and some ice. I've had a rough morning and I deserve a break. I might even deserve a cookie or a Twinkie, if there's any left.

I'm about to raid the cupboard when Clay walks into the kitchen. He beats me to the pantry, opens the door, and stares at the contents. Since the younger ones have remained in the TV room, I figure this might be a teachable moment. "Clay—" I run my finger around the top of my soda can—"I heard what you said to Katie and Bugs. You shouldn't be so mean to them."

He turns, his face taut with anger. "Mean to *them*? I can't even go to the bathroom without them wanting to tag along. It was bad enough when it was just Bugs, but now there's a girl, too—"

"Shh!" I glance toward the living room, where Bugs and Katie are still watching television. "You're the older one. You should be nicer to them. Younger kids look up to older kids."

"They shouldn't. The dweebs should find someone else to follow around."

I cock my head. "I seem to remember you following an older kid a few months ago. When Brett's in town, you don't seem to mind tagging along in his shadow."

I hope my apt example will calm Clay down, but I should have known better. Instead of settling into a thoughtful expression of common sense, his brows darken with a thunderous scowl. "What would you know?" He spits the words at me. "You don't care about anything. You invite people to live here without asking us, and then you make Grandma take care of everything. You're a fat, lazy dweeb and I hate you."

My jaw drops. Before I can even gasp, he spins on the ball of his foot and sprints through the living room and down the staircase. A minute later, the front door slams.

I snap my jaw shut and look at Mother. I expect her to wear a horrified expression that mirrors mine, but her eyes are soft with compassion.

"He'll be back," she whispers. "He won't stay mad very long."

Still reeling in shock and hurt, I can barely catch my breath. "Did you hear what he said to me?"

Mom nods. "When they're upset, they lash out. And they hurt us the worst because they know we love them the best."

I drop my head onto my hand. "I don't know how to deal with this. Clay's been angry before, but I thought we'd moved past all that."

She sinks into the chair closest to me. "Teenagers are confused by a lot because they don't have the experience to understand. I suspect that Clay isn't really mad at you—he's upset with himself. But you're the available target. And you're the one who will always love him."

I blink back hot tears. "I would never—no matter how angry I was—say something like that to him."

Mom squeezes my arm. "That's because you're the mother. Though our kids love us, they'll never love us the way we love them. Accept that, honey. Being a mother in the teenage years is like being a guardrail on the highway. You're gonna get bumped and scraped and tested a lot. But it's your job to stand firm and keep your kid on the right road."

I sniff, grateful for her encouragement but a little discouraged by the advice. If the years ahead are going to bring more encounters like this one, I don't want to move ahead.

Why can't life settle into an even stretch and stay there?

On Sunday afternoon, right after church, Joella leads the way into the Palm Tree Grille and tells the maroon-haired hostess they need a table for eight.

"Seven," Jen says, walking up behind her.

Joella turns. "You've miscounted. There are four of us, three of Gerald's family, and Daniel."

"I don't think Daniel will be joining us today." Jen wears an inscrutable expression as she nods at the hostess. "A table for seven, please."

Joella purses her lips and studies her daughter. Come to think of it, she hasn't seen much of Daniel lately. He used to regularly drop in to check on Jen and the boys, and he always joined them for Saturday supper. But he didn't come last night, and this morning he sat with Jacqueline Prose on the other side of the church. Joella assumed he either noticed their crowded pew or arrived late, but not coming to dinner . . . this doesn't bode well.

Especially since he usually picks up the check.

She steps closer to her daughter. "What's going on with Daniel?"

Jen shakes her head. "Nothing."

"Why was he sitting with that librarian this morning? Jacqueline Prose is single, isn't she?"

"Yes. And I don't know. I can't read his mind, Mom."

"Jennifer Elizabeth, don't play games with me. Something's up."

"Nothing's up, so forget about it. And don't encourage Bugs to order lasagna today. I haven't gotten the stains out of his shirt from last week."

When the hostess motions them forward, Jen strides into the restaurant, followed by Clay—who *did* apologize to his mother last night during a bedtime heart-to-heart—and the younger children. Joella glances over her shoulder, about to ask Gerald if he knows why Daniel hasn't been around lately, but he is staring at the top of Bugs's head as if he expects a crop of lice to appear at any moment. Bugs and Katie are chattering away, and behind her father, Kirsten is standing in that chilly silence that frosts anyone who approaches within ten feet of the woman. She's been a pill this morning, first refusing to go to church, then changing her mind only when Jennifer remarked that if she didn't go, she'd be sitting alone at Fairlawn until well past two o'clock.

Joella drops her hands on Katie's and Bugs's shining heads and figures her blood pressure must be shooting through the roof. "Let's go to the table, shall we? Breathe deeply, children, and lead the way."

Bugs giggles. "You're funny, Grandma."

She sets her shoulders as she follows the younger ones. Obviously, something has come between Jennifer and Daniel. But misunderstandings can be explained and hurts can be forgiven.

And those two are going to be put back together if it's the last thing Joella ever does.

Bugs trails his Matchbox car through the soft dirt at the edge of the flower bed, then smashes it against a brick. He usually enjoys playing with his cars in this spot, but the Toyota Supra isn't any fun today.

Nothing is fun while Katie is in the house watching Clay. Clay's not even doing anything special. He's just hanging out in front of the TV with his Nintendo, but Katie is sitting beside him as if that stupid football game is the coolest thing in the world.

It's not fair. Clay doesn't even talk to the girl, but she follows him around like a goofy puppy. Clay doesn't care anything about Katie, but she stares at him all googly-eyed at every meal. Bugs has given her his favorite Mitsubishi Spyder, and after lunch today he let her have first pick of the cupcakes, but she barely even noticed.

He pushes the Supra away from the brick and drags it through the dirt again, trying hard to pretend he's driving through a desert occupied by enemy warrior aliens. One of the plastic army guys he lost last week is sticking a rifle up through the dirt, so Bugs pretends the guy has a bead on the Supra and is ready to blast it to smithereens. . . .

He looks up when a car pulls into the drive. It's Mr. Sladen's black BMW, and it kicks up dust when it slides to a stop in the gravel.

Mr. Sladen steps out with a bunch of flowers in his hand. He smiles. "Hey, Bugster. Lose something in the dirt?"

Bugs shakes his head.

"Okay. So you're just playing?"

"Not anymore." Bugs leaves the Supra in the flower bed and stands, wiping his hands on his shorts.

"Well, then . . ." Mr. Sladen tucks the flowers under his arm and slips his hands into his pockets. "Is your mom home?"

Bugs nods.

"Is she busy? Is she working, I mean?"

Bugs scratches his itchy nose. "She just picked up a new dead lady. I'm not a-posed to bother her when she's in the tomb room."

"I'd better not bother her either. It's too bad she has to work on Sunday afternoon."

Bugs sits on the front porch step and frowns, giving in to his bad mood.

Mr. Sladen bends to look at him. "You okay, bud?"

Bugs makes a face. "Why are girls so weird?"

Mr. Sladen sits on the step beside Bugs. "I don't know. But you're right—sometimes they do seem weird. But we probably think so because they're not like us."

"Why aren't they like us?"

"Because God made them different. If they were exactly like us, I don't think we'd find them nearly as interesting . . . and we wouldn't need them. But we *do* need them, and they need us, though sometimes neither one of us wants to admit it."

Bugs looks up at Mr. Sladen, whose voice has changed in the last couple of minutes. His eyes are wide and he's staring at the lawn. Bugs is pretty sure the guy is thinking about something else. Maybe the flowers.

"I only had a girlfriend three days," Bugs finally says. "She promised me a week."

Mr. Sladen grins. "As long as that?"

"Yeah. I asked Katie to be my girlfriend 'cause I thought she was pretty."

"She is," Mr. Sladen says. "Women are pretty . . . like butterflies. They're bright and colorful, and they seem to flit around a man. But if you try to catch one and you're rough with it, you'll hurt it. You have to be gentle with a butterfly. You have to let it float free until it learns it can trust you. Then, just maybe, it'll land on your finger." He smiles down at Bugs. "Just like a girl can land in your heart." He pulls the flowers from under his arm and hands them to Bugs. "Know what these are?"

Bugs peers at the white and yellow flowers inside the green tissue paper. "Daisies?"

"Right—but tell your mom they're a peace offering. I don't want to bother her, so I'll trust you to do that for me."

Bugs nods.

"And don't worry about girls. You've plenty of time for chasing butterflies."

Bugs sniffs at the flowers as Mr. Sladen walks back to his car. Sometimes grown-ups talk about stuff that makes no sense at all. But he said girls are like butterflies, and butterflies like daisies. . . .

He leaps up and grins, hiding the flowers behind his back. His mom will be working for a long time yet, but Katie should like the flowers.

Maybe enough to be Bugs's girlfriend for the rest of the week.

On a quest for a side dish to augment her sister-in-law's pot roast, Leticia Gansky yelps as she trips over an unexpected obstacle between the car and the neatly stacked canned goods in her brother's garage. "George," she calls, a cross note in her voice, "how am I supposed to reach the shelves with so much junk on the floor?"

Her brother steps out of the kitchen and tosses her a sheepish smile. "Sorry about that. Margot keeps telling me to get rid of that thing."

Leticia kicks at the boxy shape beneath the tarp. "I thought you'd have all your Christmas decorations up in the attic by now."

"You're not kickin' at decorations. You're kickin' a coffin."

Leticia forgets about the side dish and stares at the rectangular corner. "Did you say *coffin*?"

"Don't freak out. I had to bring it here after the kids staged that Fright Night event at the church last October."

Leticia bends and lifts the edge of the tarp. Sure enough, she can see the fabric-covered edge of a casket. "How in the world did you get a coffin?"

George moves a garbage can out of his way. "I bought one from the funeral home over on Woodward Avenue. It's dinged in one corner, so they couldn't sell it, you know, to regular people."

"Regular dead people, you mean."

"You don't have to be dead to buy a box." He shrugs. "I don't see why a dead person would mind a little nick, but the funeral director let me have it cheap so we could use it for Fright Night."

"Use it how?"

"Had a kid lie in it. When the other kids filed by, he sat up and gave 'em a scare."

Leticia pulls the tarp completely away from the coffin. The box certainly appears legitimate. "It's a regular casket, right? I mean, anybody could fit in it?"

"I guess. Unless they were extra large."

"And it's not really doing any good here."

George narrows his eyes. "Leticia . . ."

"Give me a hand with this, will you?" She lifts the top and discovers that the lid has two sections, upper and lower.

He steps to her side and glances uneasily out the garage. "Put that door down, will ya? I don't want the neighbors to see it. They'll think we're strange."

"George, you have a casket in your garage. That *is* strange."

"But I had a good reason. And trust me, I'd put it somewhere else if I had somewhere else to put it. You can't exactly stand a casket up in the corner of your living room."

"Why didn't you throw it out?"

"Come on—think. I'd *really* raise some eyebrows if I set it out with the trash."

Leticia bites her lip, scarcely listening. She's had an idea percolating at the back of her brain, but until this minute she never thought it might become reality. But here's her brother, a man who would do almost anything for her, and here's a casket. A real, certifiable, only slightly damaged casket.

She runs her hand over the thin inner mattress. The box is lined with a satiny fabric, and a small white pillow rests where the head should lie. She squats and fingers a gray smudge on the pillow. "Did you know this is stained?"

George rolls his eyes. "It's zombie makeup. The kid's face was still wet when he climbed in the box."

"Still, you could turn the pillow over."

"*Who* could turn the pillow over?"

"Anyone . . . who wanted to use this for a funeral."

George laughs. "You're frugal, but you're not cheap. When it's your time, I'll make sure Charley springs for a decent box."

"I'm not talking about when I die; I'm talking about now." Leticia casts him a loaded look. "I'm talking about my living funeral."

He crouches at the end of the coffin. "You're talking crazy."

"No, it'll work. I went to the funeral home and picked up all the paperwork. I would have put down a deposit if that woman hadn't looked at me like I was a lunatic."

"Maybe she had a point."

"I'm not crazy. I'm tired. Tired of being taken for granted, tired of being ignored by my own family." Not caring about her spotless jeans, she sits cross-legged on the dusty floor. "I could have the funeral this weekend. You could put me in this casket and call the Fairlawn Funeral Home. You could say I was embalmed here in Eustis, but you knew I'd want the funeral held in Mt. Dora. Maybe you found the paperwork in my desk."

"You have stripped your last gear." George straightens and stares at her. "I am *not* lying to your husband. What are you trying to do, give Charley a heart attack?"

"Well . . . no." Leticia thinks a minute, then waves her hand. "Okay, so we leave Charley out of it. He's off bear hunting for two weeks, anyway, so he won't know anything about this."

"You don't want your husband to know you *died*?"

"But I won't *really* be dead. I want my friends to know about the funeral. And the girls. And the ladies in my Sunday school class. I want them all to show up at the chapel to give me a grand send-off. When I can tell they're sincerely sorry I'm gone, I'll sit up and yell, 'Surprise.'"

"That's when they'll kill you for real," he says. "After that, you'll wish you really had expired."

"You've got it all wrong. My friends will be glad I'm alive, and they'll think twice before taking me for granted again."

"And your daughters? You want *them* to think you're dead?"

She considers his point. "Well . . . the other day, Emily asked if she could have my crocheted tablecloth when I'm gone. I'm guessing she'll start planning a dinner party once she hears that I've kicked the bucket."

George groans. "That's low, Tish."

"Maybe it is, but you don't know how I feel."

"Of all the ridiculous schemes you've had, this one takes the cake."

Leticia lifts her chin. "I think a living funeral is a fine idea."

"But you're playing a cruel trick on people who love you. I'm not going to lie for you. My conscience won't allow it."

"You won't have to lie . . . after that first call to the funeral home. Let them take care of everything else. After setting it up, all you'll have to do is deliver me a couple of hours before the service." She hesitates. "Better make that one hour before. My bladder's not as resilient as it used to be."

George's face contorts into a horrified expression of disapproval. "Come on. This is insane. You can't be serious."

"I've never been more serious. Let's see. . . . I suppose you're going to have to drill a hole in this casket—something small, nothing too obvious. But I have to be able to breathe."

"I'm not drilling any holes. Besides, it's not airtight. The kid who used it at Fright Night didn't have any trouble breathing."

"He's a kid. I'm fifty-five years old. And who knows? I might develop claustrophobia after spending a while in this box." Leticia stands, eyeing the narrow width and measuring her hips with her hands. "Gonna be a tight fit."

George swings his head from side to side. "It's a crazy idea, and I'm not having anything to do with it."

"Yes, you are. You're helping me and you're coming to my funeral."

"Nope."

"You are—" she holds up a warning finger—"or I'm telling your wife that you and Charley didn't *really* go hunting the last time you guys went away together. I'll tell her where you went—and how much money you lost in those Vegas slot machines."

She didn't know it was possible, but George's face goes pale beneath his tan. "You wouldn't."

"I would. Because this is important to me." Seeing the uncertainty in his eyes, Leticia steps closer and meets his gaze. "Have you ever felt invisible? Lately that's how I feel. I'm the ghost woman who cleans the house, makes the bed, washes the laundry, cooks the meals, and picks up the grandchildren when the girls are too busy to get away. No one *talks* to me anymore; instead they grunt in my direction. And my friends—they're nice enough, but to them I'm a fourth for bridge and the one who always brings the carrot cake to the ladies' social hour. I want them to *see* me. I want them to appreciate me . . . while I can still appreciate their appreciation."

George's eyes soften above an uncertain smile. "I guess I can see your point."

"Of course you can," she says, patting his arm. "You're clever—I know you can talk the lady at Fairlawn into letting you hold the funeral there. She's a nice young woman."

"But I won't lie."

"By then you won't have to. Just drive me over and drop me off."

He shakes her hand away. "What about the expense? Surely you don't expect to have a funeral for nothing."

"Charley and I have already agreed to buy a funeral plan and plots from Fairlawn. I have all the paperwork. I'll put it in an envelope, and you can give it to Ms. Graham when you drop me off. I'll write a check to pay for everything, but I won't *use* the cemetery plots and all the other stuff until I'm really ready to go."

George scratches his chin, his nails rasping over his weekend stubble. "You're askin' an awful lot, even from a brother."

"But you're a great brother. I've always known I could count on you."

"After this, I won't owe you any more favors, okay? And you can never, *ever* tell Margot about that weekend in Vegas."

"Hey—" Leticia holds up both hands—"after you do this for me, it's your secret to do with as you please."

"Okay, then." He sets his jaw. "If you're really aimin' to use this casket, I suppose we ought to get it cleaned up."

She draws a deep breath. "I'll go check the calendar. More people will be free to come on Friday or Saturday. If I want a weekend funeral, I ought to expire on Wednesday or Thursday."

A worry line creeps between George's brows. "You sure this is only pretend?"

Leticia laughs. "Trust me, I have no intention of quitting this earth until *after* my living funeral."

"Charley won't hear about this, right? I don't want my brother-in-law droppin' of a heart attack because he heard his wife's being buried back home. Too much like Romeo and Juliet."

She laughs again. "Don't worry. Charley won't have cell phone reception once they head into the wilderness. Besides, he wouldn't fret if I died this week—oh, he'd be a little sad, I guess, but he'd go out and sing depressing songs by the campfire with his guide. He wouldn't come home and miss his hunting trip."

George scratches his chin again, then turns his attention to the casket on the floor. "Wonder if a little furniture stain will disguise that nick in the corner."

After completing the arterial embalming on Hortense Hiller, I fit the trocar with a fresh tip and prepare to begin the cavity embalming. Gerald has gone upstairs to rest, and I'm glad. Cavity procedures are no big deal to him, but I'm still new enough at the work that they tend to unnerve me.

I place the sharp end of the trocar just to the left and slightly north of Hortense's navel, then push it through the soft flesh. The room fills with sucking and gurgling sounds as the narrow silver tube vacuums out whatever was inside the organs. I concentrate, imprinting a picture of the body's internal layout on my client's cool skin to be sure I puncture each organ and remove anything that might later break down and create a pocket of bacteria.

Mrs. Hiller arrived while we were eating lunch—fortunately, the Sunshine Hills Nursing Home delivers. As we pulled in from the restaurant, I spotted the white cargo van, so Mom herded the boys along the front sidewalk while Gerald and I walked up the driveway to meet the escort from Sunshine Hills.

Our client, the driver told me as he handed over the paperwork, died this morning from natural causes. Her closest relative, a grandson, lives in Michigan and has already been contacted.

"She was a ninety-eight-year-old Medicaid patient," he said, taking the gurney out of the back. "So unless the grandson steps up, there's no money for funeral expenses."

"That's okay," Gerald answered. "We'll take care of her."

I nodded in assent, but mentally I was running down a checklist of expenses: embalming, casket, hairdressing, burial, funeral plot, death certificate and permit, obituary. Not all of those things will take cash out of our business, but all of them will take time.

Gerald has a heart for people like Hortense Hiller. The State of Florida's Indigent Burial Program, administered through county offices, contracts with local funeral homes to provide direct burial of unclaimed bodies. Direct burial means no embalming, no service, no viewing. No muss, no fuss.

We could, of course, bathe Mrs. Hiller, put her back in her cotton nightgown, and quietly bury her, but doesn't her life deserve some kind of recognition? So we will embalm her and give her a funeral, covering the additional expenses out of our operating budget.

I withdraw the trocar and turn off the aspirator. I reach for a sixteen-ounce mixture of formaldehyde and phenol, pop the cap, and hold the plastic container at arm's reach. My eyes sting as fumes rise out of the narrow opening, but they subside when I slide a length of plastic hose into the bottle and connect the opposite end to the trocar. Now I flood the body cavity with this preservative solution.

When I have finished, I place a roll of cotton bandage into the small hole near the navel and wash the body, scrubbing away any splashes of fluid or blood.

I glance at the clock as I towel dry my client. I've been working for nearly two hours, and my shoulders are tight. I still have to do some cosmetic work, but I can take a break while Mrs. Hiller firms.

I pull off my gloves and apron, then stretch as I leave the prep room and go through the hallway. I halt on the landing, startled by the sight of white petals on the floor. They glimmer on the stairs like a trail of fairy feathers.

Perplexed, I climb the stairs. Bugs and Katie are sitting in the living room in front of the TV, their eyes glued to a Road Runner cartoon.

"Hey." I drop into a wing chair. "You guys having fun?"

Bugs nods. "Uh-huh."

That's when I notice the sheaf of daisies in the girl's lap. "Nice posies, Katie. Where'd you get those?"

"Bugs gave 'em to me."

"Really. Bugs, where'd you get the flowers?"

Bugs rolls his eyes. "Mr. Sladen."

"Mr. Sladen gave you *flowers*?"

"He said they were for the peas."

I shake my head. I should probably try to figure out this riddle, but I'm tired and my brain is addled from formaldehyde fumes. "Katie—" I look around—"where's your mother?"

"Outside," she says. "Sitting on the grass."

Great. The fresh air will do me good.

I know Gerald has told me not to fret about his daughter, but I am determined to sort out whatever stands between her and her father. If she came all the way from Georgia to be with him and can't find the willpower to leave our house, she must feel *something* beneath that diffident exterior.

I drag myself out of the wing chair and trudge down the stairs, then step outside and spot Kirsten in a folding chair on the side lawn. Apparently she'd been watching Katie and Bugs play with Gerald's old golf clubs, because the clubs are still scattered over the grass. She has a book on her lap and one of my straw hats pulled low over her forehead.

I try to ignore the fact that she had to go through my closet to find the hat—and she's borrowed it without permission.

"Hi, Kirsten." After checking the grass for anthills, I cross my legs and sit on the ground. I nod at the golf clubs. "Let me guess—Bugs and Katie?"

The brim of my hat dips in unenthusiastic acknowledgment.

"I thought so. They get along so well together." I wait, but when she says nothing, I plunge ahead. "I wonder if we might talk a minute about your dad."

Kirsten raises her chin, lifting the edge of the hat until I can see her eyes. "What's to talk about?"

"Well, when people approach the end of their lives, they usually feel it's important to mend broken relationships."

She turns her head and stares out over the lawn. "I'm here, aren't I?"

"And I'm glad you are. I know—and you *have* to know—that your father loves you very much. I know he wants to improve things between the two of you before it's too late. You're here and he's here, but I can't help noticing that things are still awkward between you. Is there anything I can do to help break the ice?"

Kirsten tosses me a disbelieving glance before looking away. "When did you become a miracle worker?"

I run my hand through my hair, more exasperated than I want to admit. I'm not used to running into brick walls. When I worked for Senator Franklin in Washington, I was known as the woman who never took no for an answer. I usually managed to get whatever the senator wanted with sincere persuasion and a smile. In the four days Kirsten and Katie have been at Fairlawn, I've been as pleasant and persuasive as I can be, but this ice princess doesn't want to thaw.

"I know it's difficult to start a conversation about bitter memories," I say, gentling my voice. "Maybe you could start off by simply saying you're sorry. I'm sure your father is ready to forgive anything."

"Sorry for what?" When the hat brim lifts this time, stony blue eyes glare out at me. "I'm not sorry for a thing I've ever done. I'm sure Dad would like me to apologize for being who I am, but I can't do that. I'll never be what he wants me to be, so there's no sense in pretending."

I flounder before the hot light in her eyes. "What has he asked you to be?"

She snorts softly. "You wouldn't understand. But don't hold your breath waiting for me to put on sackcloth and say I'm sorry for everything that's happened between us."

"Perhaps you could start fresh. Just sit with him and talk."

"About what?"

"About Katie. About his work. About your work."

Kirsten tugs the hat over her eyes again. "Obviously you haven't been paying attention. I can't say anything without my father judging me. I told him about leaving Hawkeye, and all he heard was that I was living with a man I never married. If I tell him I'm out of work, he'll think I'm lazy."

"Your father didn't say anything like that."

"I know what he's thinking. And if he really wants things to be all lovey-dovey between us, *he* could try apologizing to me."

Maybe I shouldn't rally to Gerald's defense, but I can't sit here and let her criticize a man I've known as consistently loving and gentle. "I don't know what your dad was like when you were growing up," I tell her, "but my boys and I love him. Everyone here loves him—"

"Would you *shut up* already?" There's no denying the venom in her voice or the sharp gleam in her glance. She looks away, her chin quivering, and the space between us fills with a hostile silence accompanied only by the distant warble of birdsong and the faint roar of a lawn mower.

Kirsten's lips curve in a smile, but she won't lift the hat to meet my gaze. "He's always wanted me to be something I'm not," she says, her voice rattling with a small quaver. "I know he finds it hard to believe he could have produced a daughter who can't attract a good man, earn a degree, or establish a career, but I'm doing okay. I have Katie and we're doing fine without him."

I wrap my arms around my bent knees, not knowing what else to say. Finally I voice the thought uppermost in my mind: "Why did you come to Mt. Dora?"

Her head turns slightly as she smiles. "Isn't it obvious?"

I want to answer no, the answer's not obvious at all, but she stands, drops her book into the chair, and strides across the lawn. When she's about fifteen steps away, my tongue slips and I vent the emotion I'm feeling: "You don't deserve a father like Gerald."

Her step falters, breaking the steady rhythm of the swishing grass, but then she resumes her walk toward the house.

I don't know if she heard me clearly, and at this point I don't really care. Though I know Gerald has enjoyed getting to know his granddaughter, he would have enjoyed Katie more if he'd had the opportunity to know her before he got sick. Kirsten's arrival has made things harder for all of us. I should be doing everything I can to make

Gerald's last days pleasant, but by inviting Kirsten to Fairlawn, I've opened old wounds.

I hate to admit it, but I'm beginning to think I should have minded my own business and let my friend go to his grave in peace.

To a man—and woman—we oversleep on Monday morning. Bugs is the first out of bed; he patters into my bedroom and tugs on my hair. "Mom? Don't we have school today?"

My eyes fly open as if they're on springs. "What day is it?"

Bugs grins. "Monday."

"Good night, nurse." I roll out of bed and hit the floor running. I dash into Clay's room, yank his comforter off the bed, and tap his leg like some kind of overwound Energizer Bunny. I knock frantically on Kirsten's and Mom's doors as I head toward the kitchen; then I plug in the coffeepot and check the clock. Already seven thirty, and I still have to get three children to school, arrange for a casket spray, and call the guys who operate the backhoe. Hortense Hiller needs to be in the ground by four or I'll have to pay overtime, and there's no room for overtime in our budget.

I rummage through the pantry for a box of Pop-Tarts and glance at Gerald's door. It's not like him to sleep late, but even from here I can see that he's circled today's date on the kitchen calendar. He has an appointment at the hospital this morning, and he may be worried about it. So for now, I'll let him sleep.

When Katie, Bugs, and Clay are dressed and munching on toaster pastries, I slap peanut butter and jelly on six slices of wheat bread and stuff the sandwiches into brown paper bags. Three packages of chips, three apples, three juice boxes, and all the kids are good to go.

"Put these in your book bags." I drop a lunch by each child. "Let me check on your grandmother."

Thankfully, Mom is coming out of her room by the time I sprint down the hallway. "What happened to us?" she says, finger-combing her hair.

"I think it was the rain." I gesture to the gray light seeping through the windows. "The sun didn't come up. That doesn't look like a morning sky."

She shakes her head. "I knew I should have set my alarm clock."

I look at Kirsten's door, but it's closed, and there are no sounds of movement coming from the room. Apparently she's still banking her beauty sleep.

While Mom takes the kids to school, I jump into the shower and dress. Because I know I have a funeral this afternoon, I slip into a white blouse and a dark blue skirt—I have a matching jacket I can put on before people begin to arrive. A quick application of foundation, a swipe of lipstick and mascara, and a touch of blush. Done.

Before going down to the office, I rap on Kirsten's door. "Kirsten," I call, opening the door a crack, "are you okay?"

A bleary face peeks out from beneath Bugs's comforter. "I think I'm sick."

"What kind of sick? Do you need an aspirin? Pepto-Bismol?"

She groans and covers her eyes. "It's a migraine. Just leave me alone."

My pleasure. I leave her to her headache and head down to the office.

An hour later, I sweet-talk the owner of the local florist into creating an economical spray for the top of Hortense's casket. He says I'll have to swing by and pick it up, though, because his delivery boy is out sick.

I sigh and add another item to my to-do list. "I'll be there."

I call the company that runs the backhoe and arrange to have the hole dug at the cemetery. "You can pick up the crate this morning," I remind them. "I'll have it waiting in the garage."

Next, I telephone Ruby Masters. When she doesn't answer, I call the Biddle House, where most of the Southern Sassies hang out. Sure enough, Ruby's there, and she says she'd be happy to play for a funeral at two thirty. "Anybody I know?"

"Did you know Hortense Hiller?"

"I don't know her. This town is getting so big. I used to know everybody who came through the funeral parlor."

After hanging up with Ruby, I pause and listen to the sounds from upstairs. Gerald is up and moving around, and Mom is back from taking the boys and Katie to school. Despite our disastrous start to the day, everything seems to be clicking along on schedule.

Let's see—backhoe, organist, florist . . . minister! I frown as I thumb through my address book. Since Sunday is a busy day for ministers, many of them take Mondays off. Gerald used to cover for us when clients didn't request a specific pastor, but I'm not going to saddle him with that responsibility today. Walter Parsons retired last year, and he's stepped in to pinch-preach for us on more than one occasion.

I dial the reverend's number and beg him to perform Hortense's funeral.

"I'd love to, Ms. Graham, but I promised to take my wife to the podiatrist this afternoon. Heel spurs are giving her all *kinds* of trouble."

"I'll give you cab fare for her if you can come. Please, Reverend Parsons, I'm desperate."

He laughs. "Tell you what. I'll see if I can't drop her off and swing by your place while she sees the doctor."

I nearly melt in relief. "Thank you, sir. See you soon."

I'm on my way to the chapel when I run into Mom and Gerald in the foyer. He takes one look at my flushed face and announces that he's not going to the hospital; he's staying behind to help out.

"No, you're not." I place my hands on his bony shoulders and push him toward the door. "You're keeping that appointment."

"But you need help."

"I'll get help. You need to check in with your doctors, and you need to be a model patient. No stalling, sir, so get moving." I look at Mom, who is trying her best to disguise a smile. "Keep a firm leash on him, will you? Don't let him leave until the doctors have done everything they need to do."

Mom nods, but she hesitates before leaving. "Are you sure you're going to be okay alone? We may be at the hospital for a while."

"I'll be fine. Just make sure Gerald doesn't try to skip out early for my sake."

I set up the folding chairs in the small chapel and wheel Hortense into the room, setting her in the position of honor down front. I stand on a chair to adjust the track fixtures so the bulbs shine on the casket with a soft glow—no woman over fifty should *ever* be lit in harsh white light—and then remember the floral spray.

After snatching my purse and keys, I drive over to the florist's, pick up the spray, pay the bill, and head back to Fairlawn. On the way, however, I realize that I've forgotten to ask Ryan if he'll be available to handle the hearse. He always stops by Fairlawn on his way to work to see if we have clients who need hair or makeup done, and I usually see him leaving the house. But this morning nothing has gone the way I expected.

I make a right turn toward Ryan's salon. His car is in the lot, so I park under the sign and run inside.

"Ryan!" I find him working on a young woman whose foiled head looks like it's being prepared for oven roasting.

"Hi, Jen." He waves a gloved hand. "What's up?"

"Everything." I roll my eyes and nod at the startled woman in the chair. "I meant to catch you this morning, but we overslept and I didn't see you leaving the house. Nice job on Hortense, though. She looks great."

Ryan smiles. "I thought so, too. She had amazing skin."

"Anyway, the funeral's at two thirty. Gerald's been at the doctor all morning, but he's not going to be able to drive even if he gets back in time. Would you be able—?"

A regretful look creeps onto his face before I even finish my sentence. "I'm sorry," he says, lifting a goop-filled squeeze bottle with one hand and gesturing at his client with the other. "But we're in the middle of a major procedure. We've got highlighting and coloring, a major cut, blowout, and brow stenciling. I'm going to be tied up for the next several hours."

I sag against the armrest of an empty chair. "Can you think of anyone else who might be available?"

Ryan bites his lip; then his face splits in a smile. "Spike could do it. She's a great driver, and she always dresses in black. She'd be a natural."

"Her name is *Spike*?"

"Hang on a minute." Ryan turns toward the back room, from which I can hear the whir of a washing machine and dryer. "Hey, Spike! Got a job for you this afternoon."

My heart thumps as a hulking shadow crosses the laundry room threshold. By the time a broad-shouldered woman steps out and looks at me with a deadpan expression, I can feel each separate heartbeat like a punch to my solar plexus.

"Spike, meet Jen," Ryan says, squirting more goop onto his client's head. "Jen, meet Spike. Tell her what Gerald usually does."

"He, um, drives the hearse," I say, taking in the woman's combat boots, tight black pants, sleeveless T-shirt, tattooed upper arms, and shaved head. Who would trust her head to a bald stylist? I look at Ryan, having forgotten what I'm supposed to be saying. "Did you ask me a question?"

"Tell her—" Ryan grins—"what Gerald does at the funeral."

"He helps me guide the pallbearers," I say, sounding like an automaton, "as they move the casket from the chapel and into the hearse. He stands there and looks dignified."

Spike cracks her gum and frowns. "You think I could do that?"

"I think you could, but if you don't *want* to—"

"Spike would be great," Ryan says, nodding at me. "And she has a slow afternoon, so I'll send her over at two."

Just like that, I have a chauffeur. One who will probably drive away all our future business.

❧ ❧ ❧

For a ninety-eight-year-old woman with no local survivors, Hortense Hiller draws quite a crowd. Though we barely got the obit into the Monday morning paper, we have to set up extra chairs in the small chapel for the funeral. Gerald sets a discreet contribution box near the back door, and the Mt. Dora community responds generously, helping us cover the expenses for the casket and burial.

Spike, much to my surprise, performs like a pro. She stands at the back of the room, her arms folded in such a way that her studded leather bracelets and arm tattoos are displayed to full advantage, yet no one seems to mind. Maybe they think she's one of Hortense's long-lost nieces.

With my hands folded in a somber pose, I stand on the front porch as Spike slides behind the wheel of the hearse and Gerald takes the passenger seat. I know he hates not driving our clients on this final journey, but he's not supposed to be driving while he's taking painkillers. And lately he's been taking painkillers just to get through the day.

After getting over the shock of Spike's unconventional appearance, I have to admit that she seems nice enough. At first glance, you wouldn't want to meet her in a darkened parking lot, but at one point during the funeral, I saw tears glistening in mascara-smudged wells of her eyes. Those tears made me wonder—is she afraid of death? Has she lost her hair because of chemotherapy? Is she struggling for her life just as Gerald is?

Maybe the Lord knew I needed another reminder not to judge people on first appearances.

The other cars crank their engines, filling the silence of late afternoon with the sounds of grinding motors and the gravel's pop and crackle. I remain on the porch, a silent sentinel, until the last car has rolled down the driveway toward the cemetery.

Now that Hortense is on the last leg of her mortal journey, I step back into the chapel and check to be sure the remaining flowers have been properly tagged. Before I inherited Fairlawn, I had no idea that people ever assigned funeral flowers for specific purposes, but Gerald says he's seen women come to blows over a potted philodendron. Apparently the practice of designating flowers is long established in some communities, and part of the funeral director's job is making sure that each bouquet, wreath, or spray ends up with the proper person.

Gerald put three undesignated wreaths into the car with Hortense, so her grave will be properly adorned after interment. Which means I'm left to distribute two sprays, a grapevine wreath, and a stuffed teddy bear bearing a card that says, "To go home with Lisa Stuckey after the funeral."

I have no idea who Lisa Stuckey is, but I'll speak to the nursing home administrator and ask if she knows Ms. Stuckey. If she wants the bear, she can pick it up.

I set the bear in the office and lean against the wall, exhaling in a long sigh. I wish someone would pick up Kirsten and Katie. While I'm glad they came to Florida, having two extra people in the house has begun to grate on our collective nerves. Bugs adores Katie, but since our fight the other day, Clay has been spending his afternoons locked in his room. Mom is happy to help us, but for nearly a week she's been cooking for seven instead of five, plus dealing with the special menus the nutritionist recommended for Gerald.

And Gerald—I can read the struggle on his face. Several times over the past few days I've told him to take a nap, but if he rests in his room, Kirsten might think he's trying to isolate himself from her. So what does the man do? He sits on the sofa in the living area, where the kids are always underfoot and the television always on. He keeps joking that he wants a cot in the prep room, and I'm about ready to order one so he can rest.

We might enjoy having Kirsten around if she was halfway hospitable, but the woman spends most of her day watching TV or—if Gerald enters the living room—smoking on the front porch. Every once in a while I catch her arguing with someone on her cell phone, but the moment I come near, she either ends the call or heads outside to argue in private.

How can you warm up to someone like that?

I flip the office light switch and turn at the sound of footsteps.

Mom is standing in the hallway, a frustrated expression on her face and a postcard in her hand.

I immediately focus on the postcard. "I hope that's not bad news."

"Another slogan," she says, glancing at the card. "'You're never really gone if you're embalmed at Fairlawn.'"

I grimace. "Put it with the others. And about dinner tonight . . ."

"How—" she folds her arms—"do you bring two stubborn people together when something has come between them?"

My gaze drifts toward the sidelights, through which I can see Kirsten smoking and pacing on the front porch. I don't think she's said two words to Gerald today, and our living in such close quarters only emphasizes the fact that they're not speaking.

"I don't know what to do." I sigh. "You'd think anybody would want to make things right. After all, peace is easier to maintain than hostility."

"I don't think *hostile* is the right word." Mom leans against the doorframe. "Seems to me that these two are only pretending to be mad at each other. But if they're not careful, they could spend the rest of their lives ignoring the right thing to do."

"I'm not going to let that happen, even when she moves out." I set my jaw. "Maybe we could tell Kirsten that Gerald needs her for something specific."

Mother blinks. "Who?"

"Miss Congeniality, who else?" I move away from the door on the off chance that Kirsten can hear through the windowpanes. "It's going to be tough, but I'm determined to restore that relationship before it's too late."

Mom rolls her eyes. "Honestly, Jen. Do you hear yourself?"

"What?"

"Here you are, talking about Gerald and Kirsten when something's come between you and Daniel. *That's* the relationship you ought to focus on. That's the relationship you can do something about."

For a moment I'm too surprised to respond; then I manage to force words through my tight throat. "Daniel and I are not officially related. There's no tie between us."

"You're friends, aren't you?"

"I hope we'll always be friends."

"So why are you ignoring each other? Why hasn't he come over in—well, how long has it been?"

I glance away, not willing to admit that I know *exactly* how long it's been since I've seen Daniel under this roof: two days, twenty-one hours, and about twenty minutes. But I don't miss him. Not at all. "If you don't mind—" I press past her—"I need to make a call about a designated wreath."

"If you want to get people together," Mom says, her mouth curving in a grim little grin, "they need to spend time together. Gerald and Kirsten are never going to reconcile if they never talk. If you ask her to move into the Biddle House, they may never see each other."

The thought stops me in my tracks. "Then how am I supposed to—?"

"Kirsten's unemployed," she points out, "and you could use some help around here."

"But she doesn't know a thing about the funeral business."

"She has a driver's license. And Gerald's not able to drive himself anymore."

"I don't mind driving for Gerald, and Spike's willing to drive the hearse at funerals."

"Spike is a public relations disaster. You're missing the point—those two need to be interacting; they need to get reacquainted. What better way than to put them together in a vehicle?"

Like a sparrow landing on a snow-laden branch, she causes an answer to rain down on me. I give her an appreciative smile. "Thanks."

Mom harrumphs and heads toward the stairs. "You're making my blood pressure rise, you know. I can't worry about you and Daniel and the boys and Gerald and Kirsten, too. My heart can't take the stress."

"Take your medicine, Mom. And stop worrying."

As I move into the office with the grapevine wreath, I realize that Mom's plan is almost perfect. Money might be tight for a while, but Kirsten will have a job, Gerald will have a driver, and I will no longer have to rush around like a headless chicken. Best of all, I can proceed with my plan of moving Kirsten and Katie into the Biddle House with a clear conscience.

Sometimes Mother knows best.

To Bugs, the news sounds like a clap of thunder: Katie and her mother are moving to the Biddle House.

Grandma makes this announcement when she picks Bugs and Katie up from school. Though she smiles when she says it, her voice is hard, with edges.

Katie doesn't say anything but looks out the window of the minivan. Bugs asks if they can stop for an ice cream cone, and Grandma says no, she has work to do at home.

When they reach the house, Grandma leaves Bugs and Katie by the door as she climbs the stairs. "Katie's mother will be back in a bit," Grandma calls, waving over her shoulder. "You kids play upstairs until she gets here, okay?"

Bugs looks up the staircase and drops his backpack. "Come on. Let me show you my pets."

Katie stands still. "Is Clay home?"

"Not yet. But you need to see my gerbils."

Katie drops her backpack, too. "I've seen 'em."

"Not like this, you haven't. Jack and Bob had babies."

Her eyes go all round; then she climbs the stairs after him.

Bugs grins, though part of him feels achy and sad. He'd give up his room forever if it meant he could see Katie every day. Katie's mother is at the Biddle House now, moving stuff in. So this might be the last afternoon Katie comes home from school with him.

She finally reaches the top of the stairs. "Will Clay be home soon?"

"I don't know."

"I want to tell him good-bye before I leave. Do you think he'll be home before three o'clock?"

Bugs glances down to the place where Katie's backpack is snuggled up against his. Clay usually comes home at three, but lately he's been staying out with his friends. "I don't know when he's coming. But my gerbils are in here. Miss Lydia gave them to me."

Katie looks at Clay's door before walking into Bugs's room.

Bugs blinks because the place looks empty without all the girl stuff scattered everywhere. The aquarium is back in its usual spot on the bookshelf, and the gerbils are scampering in their cedar shavings. But in one corner, in a round nest, four tiny pink things are squirming and pawing the air.

Katie presses her hand to the side of the glass and smiles. "When did they have babies?"

"Mom saw them this morning. She wasn't real happy."

"Why not?"

"Because Jack and Bob are a-posed to be boys. Mom says Jack is really Jackie. She tricked us."

"How can you tell which is the girl?"

"You have to pick them up by the tail. Like this." Bugs lifts the screened lid and sticks his hand in the aquarium. "Want to hold one?"

Katie backs away. "They look like rats."

"They're not. They're nice and clean."

"Do they bite?"

"Not unless you scare them. They just run around and poop." He lifts Bob by the base of the tail, exactly the way Miss Lydia showed him. As Bob rises into the air, he spreads his paws and peers around, his black eyes wide and curious. Bugs lowers the animal to his palm. "Put out your hand."

Katie thrusts her arms behind her back. "Are you *sure* he won't bite?"

"Just don't squeeze him."

Katie stares at Bugs for a long time, her lips twitching back and forth. She puts out her hand.

Bugs sets the gerbil on Katie's palm and releases Bob's tail.

Katie tenses, her mouth going tight, but as Bob stands and wiggles his nose, she grins. "He's so cute!"

"They both are." Bugs scoops Jackie out of the cage and sits on the floor, then releases the little rodent. Jackie scampers up to Katie's shoe and streaks away, running under the bed.

Katie sits and lets Bob hop down to play.

Bugs laughs as the gerbils race and hide under the bed. Soon he's lying on the rug, his chin propped in his hands, and Katie is beside him.

"They're adorable," Katie says, turning to Bugs. She rests her chin on her fist and looks at him with a smile in her eyes. "I wish I could have a gerbil."

"You could. Miss Lydia would give you one."

"I don't have anywhere to keep him. And Mom won't let me have a pet. She says we'll be moving on in a couple of months."

"You're moving . . . after the Biddle House?"

Katie nods. "I guess. Mom says this town is temporary; we're not going to stay here."

Bugs bites his lip. He doesn't want Katie to move away, but what can he do to stop a grown-up? "You can have Bob." He pushes himself upright. "And anytime you come over, you can play with him. He's yours . . . for as long as you want."

A dimple appears in Katie's cheek. "That's really nice of you, Bugsy."

He shrugs. "No big deal."

But he's glad she likes Bob. Because as long as she has a pet, she might still want to be his girlfriend.

I usually enjoy sifting through the afternoon mail, but today's batch holds far too many contest slogans, most of them awful:

"You pop 'em; we plant 'em."

"Life comes at you fast—and then it doesn't."

"Don't I look like myself?"

One entry, however, resonates with me: "We celebrate life." My thoughts fly toward Gerald, whose life is undeniably dear to me and so many others. Yes, life should be celebrated. No matter what its duration.

I smile at an airmail envelope addressed to Gerald in McLane's handwriting. Nice to know my sister is praying for Gerald and remembered to send a card.

I look up as Ryan comes out of the prep room with an empty cardboard box. "I brought some more of that shampoo you like." He hands me an invoice. "And I only charged you my cost."

"Thanks." I put the invoice with the other bills in my in-box.

"By the way, how did Spike work out?"

"Surprisingly well." I can't keep a grin from my face. "She's nice, and she handles the hearse beautifully."

"She's a unique lady. She's in beauty school most mornings, and she helps out around the salon in the afternoons."

"Is she—" I gentle my voice, not knowing how to broach the subject—"is she undergoing chemo?"

Ryan's forehead creases. "Does she have cancer?"

"I don't know . . . but she has no hair."

He laughs. "She's not bald because of chemo. She's bald because she burned her hair with a bad chemical straightener. She shaved it off and sorta liked the look."

"Okay, then." I give him a relieved smile and pick up the latest contest slogan. "What do you think about 'We celebrate life' as a motto for Fairlawn?"

"I like it." He nods. "And I'll see you later."

As he heads toward the door, I place that entry on top of my office calendar. I'll run it by Mom, Gerald, and Lydia, but that one seems to be a strong contender for the title. I ought to see what Daniel thinks of it, too . . . if he's still speaking to me.

The creak of the front door makes me pause in midmovement. Someone has come in, and it's not likely to be Clay because he usually makes a lot more noise. So it could be a potential client.

I stand, smooth the wrinkles from my dark slacks, and check my face in the small wall mirror. I still look presentable, a minor miracle this late in the afternoon, so I step into the hallway and see . . . Kirsten.

"Hi," I say, my tone guarded. "Everything okay?"

"Yeah." She points to the stairs. "Katie up there?"

"Yes, she's with Bugs."

I expect her to climb the stairs to fetch her daughter, but Kirsten rarely does what I expect. "Hey, Kate!" she yells, leaning on the banister. "Come on. We're going." She nudges Katie's pink backpack with her shoe. "Is that all she brought home from school?"

"I think so."

I want to ask how she's getting on at the Biddle House, if the ladies made her feel welcome, and if the apartment has everything she needs.

But Kirsten isn't even glancing in my direction."Katie! Get down here!"

A moment later, Katie and Bugs appear at the top of the staircase, both of them bright-eyed and effervescent. Katie is babbling about how Bugs gave her one of the gerbils, and she can play with it every time she comes over. Her gerbil is named Bob, the other gerbil had babies, and did Kirsten know that gerbils tickle if you drop them down your shirt?

"That's nice," Kirsten says, guiding her daughter toward the door. "Don't forget your stuff."

Katie picks up her backpack, then struggles to open the latch. Kirsten helps her.

Before she can follow her daughter onto the porch, I say, "Kirsten, I don't mean to pry, but how is your financial situation these days?"

She turns, pulling a hank of blonde hair from her eyes. "Well, the car needs some work and we don't have any groceries, but we have a roof over our heads."

"You're always welcome to eat with us," I say, my face warming with a flood of guilt. "And since you need a job, I think we might be able to help."

Kirsten gives me a look that's more skeptical than grateful. "How's that?"

"Fairlawn could hire you. Your dad can't drive when he's on his medications, so we thought maybe you could drive him."

Her brows lower. "Didn't you hear me? My car's in bad shape. The engine needs a new belt or something."

"You can use our vehicles. That way you won't have to worry about gas or . . . belts."

"What about Kate? How am I supposed to play chauffeur when she's not in school?"

"She can stay here at the house whenever you have to go out. Bugs would love the company, and there's nearly always someone here to supervise."

Kirsten studies the wallpaper behind my shoulder. "If the funeral home is going to employ me," she finally says, "I imagine I'd get paid something above free meals and babysitting?"

Mindful of our anemic budget, I give her a cautious nod. "I think we can manage a decent wage for the hours you're driving. That's better than earning nothing, isn't it?"

"What kind of driving are you talking about?" She crosses her arms. "Taking the hearse to the cemetery or picking up dead bodies?"

"You might have to do some of that," I tell her, "but I expect most of your driving will be helping your dad with errands around town."

The corner of her mouth quirks. "Maybe I could get a cute little chauffeur's cap?"

I shrug. "Maybe."

"Okay, I'll do it. After all, it's not like this is going to be long-term."

I grimace, chagrined by her choice of words, and give her a weary smile. "Drop by tomorrow after you get Katie off to school. We'll work out the details then."

Kirsten walks across the porch before I have a chance to tell Katie good-bye, but at least she has agreed to help us.

Gerald and his daughter may not yet be reconciled, but this is a start.

Leticia purses her lips and slowly inhales, reminding herself that the casket is not airtight. George keeps insisting she can't use up all the air in this box no matter how quickly she breathes, but it might be a good idea not to test her brother's theory.

She closes her eyes as the van comes to a stop. Too soon to have arrived at Fairlawn yet; they've been traveling only about ten minutes. She listens, straining to hear above the pounding of her heart and the dull roar of the van's engine. Somewhere in the distance an emergency vehicle is wailing, so George has probably pulled over to let an ambulance pass. This won't be a long pause on the journey—no time at all, really—and if she can't handle being shut in this box for a twenty-minute drive, how is she supposed to handle the hour or so she might have to wait before her funeral?

Leticia draws another slow breath as the van moves back into traffic. Good. They're on their way.

She sat right next to George as he handled all the details. On Wednesday afternoon he called Fairlawn with the sad news that Leticia Gansky, his sister, had expired during a visit to his home. Without knowing better, he'd called the funeral home in Eustis, and after the embalming he'd discovered papers from Fairlawn in Leticia's desk. So the funeral director at the Eustis home had agreed to allow Leticia to be transported to Fairlawn.

When the woman at Fairlawn asked if they should send someone to Eustis to pick Leticia up, George grimaced, so it was a good thing the woman on the other end of the line couldn't see his face. Leticia was terrified that he would break down and confess the entire scheme, but George said the Fairlawn woman didn't ask any questions and took down the details as if she were bored silly with the entire business.

"Well!" Leticia bristled at that. "So much for treating folks with dignity and compassion. If I weren't already committed, I might hold my funeral someplace else!"

Now she wriggles one arm free until it bumps the padded roof of the coffin. Not a lot of room in here, but it's really not too uncomfortable. Right above her forehead, a bright spot gleams against the underside of the satin lining, courtesy of a small hole she convinced George to drill in the casket lid. That bright spot is as comforting as a night-light.

If she can relax, she'll pull off this caper without any problem. She'll be able to lie back and listen to her family and friends as they realize how much she meant to them. After the shock of hearing she's gone for good, they'll finally learn to appreciate her.

The sound of singing tires slows as the van rumbles to a stop; then she feels the casket sway as the vehicle makes a right turn. The van lurches onto a bumpy road and finally slows to a stop.

"George?" Her frightened squeak fills the coffin.

"Quiet, now. We're here."

Leticia holds her breath as George gets out of the van. She hears the muffled sound of footsteps on gravel, followed by the metallic squeak of the van door.

"Okay," her brother says, his voice low. "After this, I don't owe you a blessed thing, you hear?"

She presses her lips together, unwilling to reply. She's at a disadvantage in this box—she has no idea who might be approaching outside the van. But if things go according to plan, in a couple of hours she'll be out of this casket and basking in the glow of new appreciation.

She strains to listen for the sounds of movement and hears what *could* be a screen door slamming.

"Mr. Josten," Jennifer Graham's voice calls, "it's so nice to meet you. But I'm afraid we have a problem."

Leticia catches her breath.

George clears his throat. "What sort of a problem?"

"The woman who took your call isn't a regular employee. In fact, I wish she had let you leave a message. She didn't know we already had a memorial service scheduled for this afternoon."

"But can't you—can't you have Leticia's service right after?"

"I'm afraid that isn't feasible. Mr. Huffman, my assistant, hasn't been feeling well, and he has a doctor's appointment this afternoon. We have an opening for tomorrow morning, so we could hold the service then."

"But what about—?" When George pauses, Leticia can almost see his befuddled face. "What about the funeral notice that went out in this morning's paper? Leticia specifically wanted that to go out so people would know when to show up."

"We'll call your family members with the correct time. And we can still place Leticia in the smaller chapel—we can open the casket and have a viewing tonight, so any folks who drive out won't feel disappointed. They'll still be able to spend some time with her."

A spasm of panic radiates down Leticia's spine. Spend the night in this casket? Lie motionless for hours while people walk by and gawk? Is this Fairlawn woman *nuts*?

She tries to send a silent message to George: *Please, pretty please tell her no, tell her it won't work, tell her it's impossible. I'm sorry for the time I called you zit face. I'm sorry for telling Emma Wiggins you peed the bed. I'm sorry for breaking your favorite model airplane by throwing it off the roof. . . .*

"Well," George says, "I'm only concerned about my sister, you understand. I want to do what she would have wanted."

"I can promise you she'll be in good hands."

"About that viewing . . . I'm not sure. That's an awful long time to be sitting out in the open."

Leticia tenses as a thread of laughter insinuates itself into her brother's voice. She's at his mercy, and he wants her to know it.

"If the body has been properly embalmed," Jennifer says, "it won't be harmed by a viewing."

"I suppose," George continues, "if she starts to wilt, you could stash her in your refrigerator—or do you have a deep freeze?"

"Mr. Josten—" Leticia hears confusion in Jennifer's voice—"we don't want to frost your sister. We'll keep her in the chapel overnight and hold her service tomorrow morning. How's ten o'clock?"

"That's good."

Leticia clenches her hands when he agrees.

"I think you'd better not hold a viewing tonight. I caught a glimpse of her before they shut the lid, and she wasn't a pretty sight."

Jennifer pauses. "I'll take a look at her makeup before the service tomorrow. If you'll wait here, I'll go get our gurney."

As the woman's footsteps recede, Leticia pushes on the lid of the casket and flings it open. "Are you *crazy*?" She raises her head to glare at her brother. "I can't spend all night in a coffin."

A smile tugs at the corner of George's mouth. "It's a box for sleepin', ain't it?"

"You don't know what it's like in here. It's tight. The lid presses on the end of my nose."

"It's cushioned. Just close your eyes and take a nap."

She stares at him. "I'm *afraid* to sleep. What if someone decides to drop me in a grave?"

"They wouldn't do that."

"You didn't think they'd postpone my funeral, but that's what they're doing. So now I have to either call the whole thing off—"

"Now there's an idea."

"I can't call it off after the obituary's been published! Everyone will know I chickened out."

George's face darkens with unreadable emotions. "Listen, Tish, you're the one who wanted this crazy funeral, so you're going to have to either get out of that casket and come clean or put your head down and shut your mouth. If you don't, you're going to have a lot of explainin' to do, starting with your daughters, who are quite torn up, by the way."

Leticia blows out a frustrated breath, ready to give him another piece of her mind, but the screech of the screen door cuts into the silent afternoon. She drops her head as something begins to rattle across the gravel parking lot.

"I heard you talking," Jennifer calls as the rattle grows louder. "Having a last word with your sister?"

"More like a last argument," George answers. "Until now, Leticia never let me have the last word."

Leticia feels her heart leap into her throat as the rattle stops.

"Oh!" Jennifer says, her voice close enough to lift the hairs on Leticia's arms. "I thought she wanted a blond resting vessel."

"Huh?"

"When I talked with your sister, she said she wanted a casket to match her hair color."

"Well, um—" George stumbles over his words—"the home in Eustis gave me a good deal on this one. It has a nick in the corner."

"I see that. I thought maybe you took a corner a little too sharply on the trip over here."

George laughs. "I drove real careful. Didn't want to get pulled over and have to explain my cargo."

Leticia rolls her eyes. Why is he yakking it up and laughing when his dear sister is lying dead in the back of his van? Jennifer Graham is going to know something's up.

"We could have picked her up for you," Jennifer says. "Saved you the trouble."

"It was no problem. Gave me one last chance to have a few words with Tish."

Jennifer chuckles. "I suppose I can understand that. Now, if you'll help me pull it onto the gurney . . ."

"On three?"

"Sure. One, two, slide!"

Leticia's mouth goes dry as the world seems to shift beneath her. The spot on the satin lining brightens and wavers as the casket rides on the gurney.

"Right up this ramp," Jennifer says, "through the doorway, and into the prep room—that's it."

The jarring movement eases as the casket glides forward on a smooth surface.

"Here is fine," Jennifer says. "Since you don't want a viewing, we'll leave her here until morning. Now, do you have the paperwork?"

Leticia stifles a groan as her brother answers: "What's that?"

"From the funeral home in Eustis. There's a form that must accompany all transfers. They should have given you a copy when you signed for the casket."

"Um, yeah . . ." Leticia hears a jingle, as if George is patting his pockets. "They did give me a paper, but I must have dropped it. Here are the other papers, though—the information you gave Leticia when she visited here. She's made a list of everything she wants at the funeral."

"Well, now—" Jennifer's voice slows—"you should bring the transport notice tomorrow morning. And . . . yes, I remember: she wanted six songs before the service begins. I see she wanted an open casket."

"Yeah, she was real firm on that. She wanted to be able to see—I mean, be seen. I think she had a touch of claustrophobia."

"That's no problem. But if you don't mind, I'd better take a peek and see if everything's in order. It's not that I don't trust other embalmers, but . . . well, I don't *completely* trust other embalmers."

"Okay, I guess."

Leticia holds her breath as a rush of air enters the casket. Unexpected light stings the back of her eyelids, but she struggles to keep her face frozen.

"Her hair." A note of disapproval enters Jennifer's voice. "Did she always wear it this way? I can't remember."

George coughs. "Looks like it always does."

Leticia curls her toes in an effort to distract herself from the punishing need to breathe.

"And her makeup?" Jennifer makes a tsking sound. "I hate to point out flaws in someone else's work, but see this line of demarcation around the jawbone? Our makeup artist does a much better job of making people look natural. Someone has made your sister look as if she's wearing a mask."

"You know, I'm the wrong guy to be askin' about such things."

"All right then. I'll clean her up later."

Leticia draws in a deep breath as someone closes the lid. Darkness has never felt so wonderful; air has never tasted so sweet.

"You're happy with the embalming?" Jennifer asks. "We could examine the work for you, making sure everything's been done properly."

"Please, ma'am, leave her as she is. If there's nothing else, I'll be going now."

"There's nothing else, but please remember to bring that paperwork in the morning. Tell Charley he can come by early—no, I'll call him myself."

A strangled sound escapes George's throat. "Charley won't be coming to the funeral."

"Not coming? Why?"

"He's off hunting in Alaska. And, uh, there's no cell phone reception up in those woods."

Something hard drops onto a table. "Then we need to postpone this funeral until he gets back," Jennifer says. "It's important for loved ones to say farewell, so we can slide Leticia into the cooler—"

"Ms. Graham." George's voice goes flat. "Truthfully, ma'am, I spoke to Charley myself a couple of days ago. I told him everything, and he said he didn't want to be bothered with Tisha's harebrained foolishness. He said he'd be mighty relieved to know it was all over by the time he got home."

Leticia struggles to swallow the lump in her throat. Is George kidding? Not likely. The sneak must have called Charley before he and his guide took off for the wilderness.

Jennifer Graham hems and haws, probably more confused than ever. "I know Leticia's requests are unusual," she says, sounding distracted. "Six songs *is* a lot of music, but I wouldn't call it harebrained foolishness. I would think Charley'd want to be here no matter what he thought of his wife's preferences."

"Please, let's just get it over with." George's plea is followed by a moment of silence in which Leticia imagines they are shaking hands.

"A pleasure to meet you, Mr. Josten. I'm very sorry for your loss."

George coughs again. "It's been hard on all of us, so I'd better get going."

"I'll see you out."

Leticia hears the soft squeak of rubber-soled shoes on tile and the sound of a closing door.

Followed by silence . . . as thick, they say, as the grave.

Joella steps out of the Instead of Flowers gourmet gift shop on Donnelly Street and nearly runs headlong into her favorite lawyer. "Daniel." She beams at him, unable to believe her good fortune. "Imagine meeting you here."

He points toward the southern end of the street. "My office is just a couple of blocks away, you know."

"I know, but here—at this store." She narrows her eyes and gives him a coy smile. "Are you in the market for a gift basket?"

Daniel slides his hands into his pockets and releases a short laugh touched with embarrassment. "Maybe."

"Would I happen to know the intended recipient of that basket?"

"It's a small town," he says, shrugging.

"Indeed it is. Well, if you're not going to volunteer any information, let me state for the record that Jennifer loves chocolate-covered cherries. And pecans. And she definitely prefers dark chocolate over light."

"Duly noted."

Joella smiles, letting the silence stretch as she studies Daniel's eyes. For some reason, he doesn't meet her gaze. "My blood pressure's been up," she says, searching his face for some sign of concern. "I worry all the time."

"About Gerald?"

"About everything—the boys, Gerald, and Jen."

"Jen is a strong woman."

"She's not as strong as she thinks she is. We miss you, you know. Haven't seen you in a while."

Daniel scuffs his shoe against the pavement. "I was out that way a few days ago. Didn't Bugs mention the flowers?"

She laughs. "It's a funeral home—flowers come and go all the time. But you should know you're always welcome at Fairlawn."

His gaze drops like a rock. "I'm not sure your daughter would agree."

"Since when does Jen know what's best for her? You stop by and see *me* sometime. I'll always be glad to see your handsome face at the door." Joella squeezes his arm. "Don't be a stranger, you hear?"

Daniel doesn't answer, but when she reaches the end of the block, she turns to make sure he has entered the gift shop.

Maybe he's buying chocolate-covered cherries and pecans.

Kirsten wipes the back of her neck with a damp tissue and gets out of the car. Nearly three thirty, and her father is still in the doctor's office. He asked if she wanted to go inside with him, but she refused, saying that the day was so nice she'd rather stay outdoors.

The day *is* nice, but after fifteen minutes in the Florida sunshine any car would begin to feel like an oven.

She pulls her purse from the car and walks to the bench someone has planted at the foot of a sprawling live oak. She settles on the seat and crosses her arms, then leans against the corrugated bark.

Back at that mausoleum of a house, Jennifer is holding a memorial service and Joella is probably baking cookies for Bugs and Katie. Katie is undoubtedly having a ball—ever since they came to Mt. Dora, Katie has had little to do with her mother, saving all her smiles for Jennifer, Joella, and Gerald. Kirsten doesn't think Katie is smart enough to deal in emotional blackmail, but she's intuitive enough to realize that she can drive her mother crazy by ignoring her.

Kirsten chews on the edge of her thumbnail and resolves to put the matter out of her mind. They'll be out of here soon, and the Graham family will fade into irrelevant history. They aren't even blood relations, so why should Kirsten worry about Jennifer and her clan?

You don't need an MBA to realize that the funeral home is a couple of caskets away from going under. The company is paying Kirsten fifteen bucks an hour to play chauffeur, and she has the feeling that even the paltry sixty or so bucks she earns each day is about to break the budget.

She hopes Jennifer Graham has her résumé up-to-date. Because as soon as Fairlawn is hers, Kirsten is selling the place to Aldridge Elms, Inc. Good riddance.

Kirsten startles when her cell phone rings. She grabs it from her purse and scans the caller ID. This time it's not Hawkeye calling to whine, thank goodness. It's Ross Alexander. She flips the phone open. "Hello?"

"Kirsten? Ross here. Hope everything's fine at your end."

"It is. Thanks."

"Listen, if you have a minute, I have a favor to ask. We've been able to access the online tax assessment for the Fairlawn property, but all we have is total square footage. Do you think you could get a tape measure and map out the premises for us? Doesn't have to be to the inch, but we'd really appreciate a proper floor plan."

Kirsten stares across the parking lot as a breeze stirs a carpet of fallen oak leaves into a miniature cyclone. "Um . . . when do you need it?"

"As soon as possible. We're particularly interested in the preparation rooms."

"As soon—" She clenches her teeth, finding herself inexplicably irritated. "I'll do it," she says, "when I get around to it. The owner *is* dying, you know."

"I know." Ross's voice takes on a sympathetic tone. "And I'm sorry if this seems insensitive. I'm simply trying to keep this deal on the fast track because I thought that's what you wanted."

"I do. It's just . . ." Kirsten stops, at a loss for words.

"It's what?"

"Never mind. I'll get you the measurements as soon as I can."

"By the way, how is the patient?"

She glances toward the door to the doctor's office. "Hanging in there."

"If there's anything I can do, you know who to call."

"Yeah, right. Thanks." Kirsten hangs up and drops the phone back in her purse, then sits with her hands limp in her lap. Why do people always say that? What are they supposed to *do*? Wave a magic wand and make things better? Heal the sick, pay the bills, erase the mortgage?

She closes her eyes, repulsed by the idea that Ross Alexander and his cronies are sitting in some corporate office rubbing their hands together and waiting for her father to die. She's no great fan of Gerald Huffman's, but she's not ready to bury him yet, either. The old man means a lot to a lot of people . . . including Katie.

Last night, when Kirsten finished helping Joella clean up the kitchen, she went to get Katie and lingered in the hallway outside Bugs's room. A quick peek revealed her dad sitting on the floor with Bugs on one side and Katie on the other, both children resting their heads against Gerald's chest as he read a chapter from *The Incredible Journey*. His voice cracked as he read about the joyful reunion of Luath, the Labrador; Tao, the Siamese cat; and Bodger, the bull terrier, with their beloved humans.

Something—maybe it was the story or the rasp in her father's voice—tore at Kirsten's heart and sent her into a hasty retreat around the corner. She stood in the hallway for a moment, rubbing the lump in her throat and struggling to steady her breath. People were always crying around her dad, telling him their problems, asking him for advice. She wasn't going to be one of those people.

When Kirsten finally walked into the room, Katie was palming tears from her cheeks.

No doubt about it, her father has a gift. Too bad she won't inherit it along with the funeral home.

* * *

Joella steps through the door of Walgreens and glances right and left. If the newspaper ads are to be believed, this drugstore has just opened a Take Care Health Clinic, where a patient can visit with a nurse practitioner and be diagnosed in a matter of minutes and without a lot of fuss.

Time to see if their advertising is reliable.

She strides to the pharmacy, where a young man in a white coat stands behind the counter. "Excuse me," Joella says, glad to find herself alone. "I'm looking for the walk-in clinic."

The young man nods and points to his right. "Over there. Sign in and have a seat."

Joella draws a deep breath and enters the small space—a cubicle, really, but how much room does a nurse practitioner need? She fills out a form on a clipboard and drops it into a chute, trusting that someone will retrieve it on the other side of the wall.

Sighing, she takes a seat and picks up a ruffled magazine. She could be dying out here, suffering from a heart attack, and what would anyone do to help her? She'll be lucky if they send someone out before she has a stroke or a seizure. She's still having those strange stabbing pains in her side, though she can't predict when they're going to come or go.

A young woman opens the door. "Mrs. Norris?"

Joella grips her purse. "Yes?"

"This way, please."

The petite nurse practitioner—a cute brunette who doesn't look older than twenty-five—leads the way into a small room and gestures to a chair. "While I'm doing this," she says, pulling a blood pressure cuff from a basket on the wall, "why don't you tell me why you're here?"

"You got all day?"

"I've got a little while."

As the young woman straps the Velcro fastener onto her arm, Joella tells her about the high blood pressure and her pills. About the stabbing pains, the heartburn after meals, and the suffocating sensation that descends on her at night. About how she worries for her daughter and her grandsons and how hard it is to keep Jen from ruining her life while she's also making sure Gerald eats enough leafy greens and yellow vegetables.

"And there's that ridiculous contest." She rolls her eyes. "Jen's convinced it's going to save the mortuary, but I don't think 'A tisket, a tasket, let us bury you in our casket' is going to bring in much business."

The nurse nods, clucks in understanding, and makes a couple of notes on her clipboard. She pulls a stethoscope from around her neck and listens to Joella's heart and lungs, interrupting every now and then with commands to breathe deep and exhale.

When Joella has finished, the nurse sits on a stool and clasps her hands. "Your blood pressure is 115 over 83," she says, smiling, "and that's very good. Your heart is strong and your pulse steady. I think, Mrs. Norris, that your other symptoms are caused by stress."

Joella harrumphs. "Tell me something I don't know."

"There's not much we can do about the responsibilities you're facing," the young woman says, "but we can consider why you're facing them. Tell me—why did you come to Florida?"

Joella frowns. "Isn't it obvious? To help my daughter, of course."

"Why do you want to help your daughter?"

"She needs help. And it's what a mother ought to do."

The nurse lifts a brow. "Is that all?"

"I want to help my grandsons and even the old man."

"Why do you want to help?"

"Because . . ." Joella tilts her head. "Because I love them?"

The young woman smiles. "Exactly. The next time you're feeling stressed, I want you to stop what you're doing, breathe deeply, and remind yourself of why you're down here. Think about that love and let your body's endorphins rev up and sweep your stress away."

Joella blinks. "Is this some kind of new age medicine?"

"Not at all. Endorphins are powerful hormonal transmitters, and they're produced when we love. They dull our pain, help us relax, and banish stress." The nurse sets her clipboard on the table. "I want you to keep taking your medication and monitoring your blood pressure, but I don't think you have anything to worry about. Next time you're feeling tightness in your chest, relax and think about why you're here. If the situation doesn't improve after a few minutes, come see me again."

Joella takes a deep breath and smiles when she inhales easily and without pain. "What do you know? I feel better already."

"You've been worried—not only about your family but about your own health. When you learn to put that worry aside, you're going to feel a lot better."

"You know," Joella says, standing, "I wasn't expecting much when I came in here, but I think you're the best doctor I've ever seen."

The young woman smiles as she stands and opens the door. "Don't let yourself get discouraged. I'm sure your family appreciates you more than they say."

"They do," Joella answers, slipping her purse onto her arm. "I truly believe they do."

When silence has fallen like a cloak around her and the airhole has faded to black, Leticia gathers her courage and presses on the cushioned lid of the casket. The top rises without a sound, then settles back on its hinge with a slight squeak. Darkness fills this space Jennifer Graham called the prep room, and the air carries the bone-rattling chill of a winter morning. Despite what she told her brother, Leticia probably could close her eyes and sleep in this cozy box except for one problem—she desperately needs a bathroom.

Moving as cautiously as a cat, she sits up and looks around. In the stream of gray light from a lace-curtained window, she can see two long white tables, each edged with a gutter that leads to a sink—for reasons Leticia doesn't want to imagine. Her casket is resting on a wheeled gurney that seems sturdy enough, and it's not too far from the floor. Climbing out of this box, though, might be easier said than done.

With exaggerated care, Leticia lifts the lower half of the casket lid and props it open. She wriggles her feet, grateful for the opportunity to stretch her muscles, and swings one leg over the side of the casket. This would be so much easier if she didn't have to climb out of a box *and* lower herself to the floor.

With both knees bent over the edge of the casket, she scoots toward the center of her narrow bed and considers her options. If she lifts her weight up and over the edge of the gurney, she should clear the side, but the momentum might tip the box and bring it down on top of her. George said the coffin is fabric-covered particleboard, probably the cheapest model ever made, but it's heavy enough to do serious damage if it lands on her arm, leg, or head.

Come to think of it, *she's* heavy enough to do damage if she lands on a vital organ.

Leticia braces herself on her arms and peers past her toes. The tile floor might as well be a mile away. Is the attempt worth the risk? If she dozed off, would her kidneys sleep, too? Closing her eyes, she imagines the scenario but feels a warning twinge from her over-pressured bladder.

No doubt about it, she has to take this leap.

If she were twenty years younger, this might not be such a big deal. If she were twenty pounds lighter, she might be able to leap like a gazelle. But there's no sense in moaning about impossibilities now.

After Leticia rocks from side to side, she leans forward and imagines herself poised like the space shuttle on the launch pad. Ten, nine, eight . . .

Her bladder sends another warning twinge.

. . . seven, six, five . . .

She holds her breath as footsteps echo overhead. Coming down the stairs? No.

. . . four, three, two . . .

Leticia exhales quickly, then slowly inhales through her teeth.

Ignition . . . Blastoff! She presses on her hands, waiting to feel her body rise, but nothing happens. Has she grown that weak? Is she that heavy? She curls forward, pushes on her palms, and tosses her head, *willing* her body to rise, but the casket only groans in complaint.

She doesn't have the strength to jump out of this box. When did she become an overstuffed weakling?

Again her bladder protests, this time shooting darts that travel from her spine to her toes, and now her body *has* to obey her urging. She leans forward once more, resting her weight on the side of the casket, and gulps a frantic breath. She is about to heave herself over the edge, risking any and all consequences, but the side of the casket abruptly gives way with a loud crack.

Leticia crumples forward, barely managing to save herself from a head-on collision with the base of an embalming table. Her feet hit the floor first, followed by her knees and chest, and by some miracle her hands catch the steel support of the table and prevent a denture-shattering smashup. As her heart dances in a calypso rhythm, she holds her breath, certain that the noise will bring someone rushing into the room with a gun or the Mt. Dora police, but no footsteps thump on the stairs and no voice calls from the hallway beyond.

An odd snatch of song begins to play in her head: *"When the bough breaks, the cradle will fall . . ."*

Trembling in every limb, Leticia picks herself up and covers her mouth with her hand, stifling the relieved cry that threatens to escape at any moment. *My goodness, what a thing to happen!* She gazes at the injured casket, sees one side hanging limply by a few threads, and realizes that the particleboard was glued at the corners. The old glue, the worn fabric, the unusual pressure she applied . . . No wonder the casket cracked.

"And down will come baby, casket and all."

Mercy! What is she going to do now?

First things first. If memory serves, a small powder room lies off the hallway that leads to the foyer and the chapels.

She pads forward in her bare feet, opens the wide door, and peeks through the crack. Nothing moves in the gray darkness, though the sound of children's voices echoes from the second story. The guests from the other memorial are long gone, and apparently Jennifer Graham has concluded her business for the day. The coast is clear.

Leticia slips through the doorway, then remembers to check the knob to be sure the door doesn't lock automatically. The sign on the door is intimidating, but she can't be accused of violating state law if someone carried her into the forbidden room, can she?

She tiptoes down the hall and slips into the little bathroom. After locking the door, she turns on the light and takes care of business, practically melting in relief as her kidneys rise up and call her blessed.

Though it goes against every instinct in her nature, when she is finished, she can't bring herself to flush the toilet. In a building this old, how can she know the pipes won't sing out and announce her presence?

So she squirts her hands with liquid soap, massages the lotion over her fingers, and wipes the residue away with a paper towel. She tosses the towel in the trash and studies her reflection in the oval mirror above the sink. Why would anyone think she was wearing a mask? And what did Jennifer Graham mean by that comment about a "line of demarcation" on her jaw?

Leticia lifts her chin, then runs her finger over her jawbone. Funeral directors should have better manners. If one shouldn't speak ill of the dead, morticians shouldn't criticize the deceased as they lie helpless in their caskets.

But it's useless to fret now. And though she'd rather spend the night in this cozy little bathroom than in the casket, she can't risk being discovered.

As the foyer clock strikes the hour, Leticia creeps back to the prep room. Night has fallen outside the window, so there's no way she can repair the damaged casket without turning on the light. But once the Graham family has gone to bed, maybe she can find a bottle of glue and repair the damage before sunrise.

For now, though, she can do nothing but sit in the darkness . . . and wait.

I'm tucking Bugs into bed when I hear a crack and clatter from downstairs.

My son's eyes widen as he grips my arm. "What's that?"

"I don't know." Automatically, I look around for Skeeter, who is usually to blame whenever something shakes, rattles, or rolls. But the dog is curled at the foot of Bugs's bed, so this time he's not guilty.

"Grandma or Clay probably dropped something," I tell Bugs, pulling the covers to his chin. "Don't worry about it."

"The noise didn't come from up here," he insists. "It came from the tomb room."

"Maybe Gerald dropped something. He's been tired, you know? Something probably slipped out of his hand."

"You sure?"

"I promise I'll check it out. Now close your eyes and go to sleep."

After making sure to leave a light burning, I step into the hallway. My mother is propped up on her bed in the guest room, a book in her hands, and Clay is doing homework on the coffee table in front of the TV. I smile, certain that I'll find Gerald downstairs, but my smile fades when I glance through the arched doorway and see him sitting at the kitchen table, dutifully counting out his nighttime medications.

He looks up. "Something wrong?"

"Why would you ask?"

"Because I haven't seen that look in your eye since the time you forgot to pack Mr. Floyd's nose and embalming fluid leaked out during the funeral."

"Don't remind me. If you hadn't covered for me, our reputation would have been blackened forever." I steady myself with the back of a chair. "Did you hear a strange sound a minute ago?"

He shakes another pill into his palm. "Like what?"

"I don't know. A crash, maybe."

Gerald tosses the pill into his mouth, chases it with a sip of water, and shakes his head. "Didn't hear a thing."

That's only natural, since the kitchen sits over the chapel. Bugs's room, on the other hand, is located right over the preparation area.

"Don't worry about it." I give him a quick smile. "You doing okay?"

"Fine." Gerald lifts another bottle, squints at the label through his reading glasses, then sighs and unscrews the lid.

I move toward the prep room and hesitate at the top of the stairs. What if someone has broken in? Mt. Dora is a sleepy town, but no town is immune to crime. Furthermore, a recent article in *Mortuary Management* reported that funeral homes are often targeted by teenagers who smoke pot. Apparently they've discovered that joints soaked in formaldehyde deliver an unusually dense stupor, and many mortuaries have been raided by teens on a search for the chemical.

The skin on my arms contracts into gooseflesh when a shadow looms behind me. Ready to scream, I whirl around and come face-to-face with my mother.

"I heard it." She nods toward the stairs. "And I've already called for help."

"Why didn't you say anything?" I whisper.

"For the same reason you didn't. I don't want to frighten the boys."

I run my hand through my hair, not sure if I should feel nervous, exasperated, or irritated. "What if it's a false alarm? I'll feel silly if the cops show up for no reason."

"I didn't call the cops," Mom answers. "I called Daniel."

No contest, irritation wins. "You didn't tell him I *wanted* you to call, did you?"

"When someone's breaking into the house, you don't take time to give details."

"I'm sure no one's breaking in." I force a smile to prove my point. "I'm going to check things out, and then you'll see. Something fell over; that's all."

"Things don't fall over unless they have help."

"Not true. There's a scientific law that says things *must* wear out and fall over—the second law of thermo-hydraulics or something."

"Jen, don't go. Wait for Daniel."

"I don't need Daniel Sladen."

"Then ask Gerald to go with you."

"I'm not bothering Gerald." I lower my voice. "He's too weak for this kind of silliness."

"If-if you *insist* on going," Mom sputters, "don't go empty-handed. You need protection."

"We don't keep guns in the house."

"Then take a flashlight."

"You think I'm going to walk over to a burglar and hit him with a flashlight?"

"You don't *hit* him with it—you shine it in his eyes and blind him until you can attack. It's called defensive flashlighting."

I stare at her. "You made that up."

"Did not. I read it in a magazine."

"Doesn't matter. Even if it works, I can't attack anyone."

"Then use the time to get away."

"Do you even *have* a flashlight?"

Mom holds up a finger. "Give me a minute."

I sag against the wall while she scurries into the guest room, her slippers slapping the floor. I hear her rummaging through drawers; then she reappears, a flashlight in her hand. A flashlight no bigger than a pencil.

"I carry it in my purse," she says. "You never know when you're going to run into an emergency situation."

With two fingers, I pluck the flashlight from her palm and click it on. I don't know what I was expecting—maybe some variation of Luke

Skywalker's light saber—but the instrument glows with an anorexic beam that barely lights my skin when I hold my hand in front of the bulb. "This is useless."

"Take it. If all else fails, you can poke him in the eye with it."

I give her a black look and point the flashlight down the stairs. "Okay, I'm going."

"Wait!" Mom skitters into the darkness of Clay's room and returns with his baseball bat.

I'm determined not to accept it, but in that instant I hear the unmistakable click of the latch on the prep room door. I don't think the law of thermo-hydraulics pertains to latched doors that open and close by themselves. I grip the bat with my right hand and lower my left to the banister.

"Mom?" Clay's head appears in my peripheral vision. "Where ya goin' with my bat?"

Mother wraps an arm around his shoulders. "Your mother heard a noise. Instead of waiting for help, she's going downstairs to fight off an intruder."

Clay's eyes widen. "Sweet. Can I come?"

Now she's done it. I'm not sure if Clay wants to fight off the intruder or cheer me on, but I don't want my son involved in whatever sort of encounter waits on the ground floor.

"I'm sure it's nothing." I tighten my grip on the bat. "Gerald must have left the window open, and the wind has blown something off a shelf. And closed the door."

"Gerald hasn't opened that window in ten years," Mom says, making a particularly unhelpful observation. "I think it's painted shut."

"It's not," Clay says, his eyes bright. "I've opened it before, from the outside. It's not that hard to break in there, Grandma."

Not exactly what I wanted to hear.

Mom studies Clay. "Do you have something your mother could use for self-defense? Like a BB gun?"

"Mom won't let me have one."

She squeezes his shoulder. "You wouldn't happen to have a Taser, would you? or a slingshot?"

I glance at Clay, half-afraid he's going to admit that he has an arsenal hidden in his backpack, but he shakes his head. "Sorry."

Mom folds her arms. "I know—let's send the dog."

I gape at her. "Skeeter? He'd lick any intruder to death."

"But they wouldn't *know* he's friendly. He'd go down the stairs barking, and maybe that'd scare them off before you even get to the prep room. I say we wake the dog and toss him downstairs."

"We're not *tossing* Skeeter anywhere."

"Then wake him up and throw his ball down the stairs. He'll go after it."

"Right. And then he'd carry it to the burglar and beg him to play fetch."

"Mom?" A thin wail seeps out of Bugs's bedroom. "Is there a burglar in the house?"

I give Mother a now-you've-done-it look. "Don't worry, honey," I call. "Everything's fine."

I repress a groan when Gerald staggers toward us, his bushy brows furrowed. "What's going on? Is there trouble downstairs?"

I smile and try to hide the baseball bat behind my back. "Nothing's going on. I heard a noise and Mother's overreacting. I was on my way to check things out when—"

"I should go." Gerald pushes past Mom and Clay. "I'm the man of the house."

"No." I step in front of him, silently implying that he'll have to push past me to make it down the stairs. Gently, I place my hand on his chest. "It's nothing. You go on and get ready for bed. I can handle this."

"It's nothing," Mom echoes, now more concerned about Gerald than the bogeyman. "Probably just the creaks and groans of an old house."

"The law of thermo-hydraulics," I add, smiling. "You know—that bit about how everything eventually breaks down."

"That's the law of entropy," Clay says, his voice dry. "Also called the second law of thermodynamics."

I roll my eyes at my son. "When did you get so smart?"

Gerald looks from me to Mother to Clay, and then we hear pounding on the front door.

"Thank goodness," Mom says, fanning herself with her hand. "Daniel's finally here."

"If you all are concerned about nothing, why is Daniel here?" Gerald growls.

"Because he's my friend," I say, skipping down the stairs. "He's coming for a visit, so everyone else can stay right here and relax."

I fling the door open and find Daniel alarmed . . . and armed. His hair is dripping wet, he's wearing pajama bottoms and a trench coat, and he's carrying a gun.

I peer past Daniel into the darkness. "Is it *raining*?"

He ignores the question. "Are you all right?" His eyes strafe my face and register the baseball bat in my hand; then he glances up the stairs as if taking a head count. "Everybody okay up there?"

"We're fine," I say, ashamed to hear a tremor in my voice. "But we haven't searched the downstairs. The noise came from the prep room, I think."

"Then let's go." There's a grim look in Daniel's eye, a fierce protectiveness I've never seen . . . and one I'm not sure I want to see again. He turns on the hall light and hurries forward.

I linger to wave at my family. "Back to what you were doing, all of you. Everything's going to be fine." I speak with far more confidence than I feel, but something about Daniel's attitude—and his gun—has reassured me. I'm also stunned that he would drop everything and rush over here.

"What are you wearing?" I ask, hurrying after him. "Did Mom get you out of the shower?"

He ignores me again and halts outside the prep room door, his head cocked as he listens for sounds of movement in the room beyond.

I stand back and let him listen, taking in the sight of his battered loafers, his trench coat, his plaid pajama bottoms, the hint of bare chest beneath his coat. Was the man getting ready for bed at eight o'clock?

He glances over his shoulder at me, brings his finger to his lips, and places his hand on the doorknob.

I nod, grip my baseball bat, and the door slowly swings open.

When we enter the area, my gaze darts first to the bottles of formaldehyde. They remain upright on the shelf, apparently unmolested. The window and exterior door are closed and locked. No one else is in the room—no one living, that is.

I approach the wall of cabinets and check each one, searching for anything out of place. The scalpels are still neatly arranged, along with the cotton, tubes, trocar plugs, and eye caps—nothing is missing. In fact, I don't see anything out of the ordinary.

"I guess it was a false alarm." I relax and give Daniel a grateful smile. He has, thankfully, put the gun in his pocket and pulled the edges of his coat together, covering his bare chest. "I don't see anything out of the ordinary. . . ." My voice trails away as I notice the casket against the wall. "Wait—that's definitely odd."

More confident now that I know we haven't been burglarized, I stride toward Leticia Gansky's casket, where one side hangs like a useless flap of skin. The lid remains closed, though, and no marks mar the surface.

"Wow." Daniel comes over and fingers the dangling slab of particleboard. "I had no idea caskets could be this flimsy."

"Most of them are better constructed than this one." I fit the loose edge back into position. "I've never seen anything this cheaply made. It's too late to send the casket back; we're supposed to bury this woman tomorrow."

"May I ask who?"

"Leticia Gansky. Charley's wife."

A sad look settles on Daniel's face. "Oh, that's too bad. I'll bet Charley's broken up."

"I wouldn't know. Her brother handled all the arrangements."

Daniel's frown deepens. "Come to think of it, isn't Charley off hunting in Alaska?"

"That's what I hear. Apparently he can't be bothered to come home for his wife's funeral service."

"Don't you think that's unusual?"

"Of course I do. But Leticia was odd—a real eccentric. Maybe Charley is, too."

"Seems to me that a husband should be the one who looks after his wife, even in death." An odd note fills Daniel's voice—a note that seems to imply that he's talking about far more than Charley and Leticia Gansky. But I'm not about to get into a discussion over the proper roles of men and women, not now and not here.

I run my hand over the top of the casket. "If there's one thing I've learned in this business, it's that there is no such thing as typical. Maybe Charley is so grief-stricken that he wants to mourn in the woods."

"If you say so." Daniel pushes his wet hair from his forehead and leans against the embalming table. "About this problem—could you put her in another casket? Like a display model?"

I consider the idea, then shake my head. "I'm going to have to call her brother. Since we didn't handle the embalming or the casket purchase, I don't think I can switch boxes without permission from a family member. And there's the financial loss—since we didn't furnish this casket, we'll take a hit if we give her a replacement."

"You could bill the estate."

"But they shouldn't have to pay twice for one casket."

"Yet you're thinking about giving her one." Daniel rests an elbow on the coffin and gives me the slow smile that always turns my knees to jelly. In moments like this, when he recognizes glimmers of my more noble nature, I'm so amazed that I want to throw myself into his arms.

But this certainly isn't the time or place for *that.*

"I have an ivory casket that might do," I admit. "That's closer to the color she wanted. But I can't do anything until I talk to a family member."

"Anything would be better than this."

"You're absolutely right." I grip the broken piece with both hands and wonder if it could be repaired with glue and a vise. "I didn't know the woman very well, but she did come by to inquire about a funeral plan. She seemed a little sad to me. Pitiful, really." I press the broken piece back into place and gesture for Daniel to hold the other end. "Do you think a little Gorilla Glue could do the trick?"

"Maybe."

After lowering the board slowly, I touch the lid. "Want to see her?"

Daniel waves my offer away. "No thanks."

"Then turn around, because I want to make sure everything's okay."

He turns his head while I lift the upper and lower lids. Leticia Gansky is resting just as I last saw her, her hands folded at her waist, a half smile on her lips, her makeup tinted an unflattering shade of orange . . . but the makeup line at her jaw has faded. I bend closer, convinced the light is playing tricks on me. "That's odd."

Despite his refusal, Daniel peeks over his shoulder and glances at the casket. "What's wrong?"

"Give me a minute." I scan the rest of the body. Leticia is wearing a simple flowered dress and no stockings. The mortician in Eustis didn't include her shoes, but that's not unusual, since it's hard to fit shoes on feet that are too stiff to flex.

A chill runs up my spine when I notice that Leticia's knees are smudged, as if she's fallen onto a dirty surface or been dragged across the floor.

I glance at the tile on this side of the room. Because this area is used mainly for storage, I don't regularly mop this space. If I didn't know better, I'd think Leticia climbed out and fell on this dusty floor.

Humming quietly, I step to the end of the casket, pretending nonchalance until I am able to see the soles of her feet. Brown, both of them.

I swiftly close the lower lid, resisting the urge to run a fingernail down the ticklish insole of one of those feet.

"Everything seems fine," I tell Daniel, my mind racing. I move to the head of the casket and lower the upper lid, then examine the dimpled surface of the box. There, barely discernible in the fabric, I see a small hole, a bright spot of raw wood gleaming beneath the dark cloth.

"So, are you satisfied? Feel safer now?"

"Yes." I slip my hands into the pockets of my jeans. "Thanks for coming. I'm sorry Mom dragged you out here for nothing."

"It wasn't for nothing . . . I don't think." Daniel smiles into my eyes, but I'm so distracted by the thought that I have a living woman in my prep room that I can only press my fingertip to my lips and lead him away.

Now that I know my loved ones are safe, the night outside seems warm and comforting. I walk Daniel to his car, lean against it, and break into a relaxed smile. "You never answered me." I point at his wet hair, shining now in the porch light. "Did Mom get you out of the shower, or were you swimming laps?"

"If you must know—" he pulls the trench coat over his chest in a display of exaggerated modesty—"I showered early because I thought I'd settle in for a night of reading. And I think I look rather dashing, to tell you the truth. Not every man would grab the first available pieces of clothing and run out of the house to investigate a creaking coffin."

"There's a little more to the story," I assure him. "I don't know why she's doing this, but Leticia Gansky is alive."

"Is this when you tell me she has a long-lost twin? Because that woman in the casket certainly looked like Leticia."

"You're absolutely right—Leticia *is* in the casket, and she broke it herself, probably when she tried to climb out."

Surprise blossoms on Daniel's face. "Why would a mentally stable, adult woman want to be buried alive?"

"I don't know how mentally stable she is, and I don't think she wants to be buried. But a couple of weeks ago she came by to tell me she wanted a living funeral."

"Was she joking?"

"She described it as a funeral for a living person. I told her we didn't do such things and sent her home with an application for a preneed package. Bottom line, I think she only wants to know that her family cares about her."

"She can't *tell* them what she needs?"

"Apparently not."

"Well, I don't think she's the only woman in town who can't seem to say what's in her heart."

I'm not sure what he means by that comment, but I'm not going to ask for further clarification. I adore Daniel—I really do—but my life is so filled with emotional situations that I'm about to burst at the seams.

Daniel nudges my arm. "So what are you going to do about Ms. Gansky?"

I tap my finger against my chin. "I need to march in there and tell her the jig's up. I don't think she has any idea how cruel this scheme is. But most of the damage has already been done. Her daughters and her friends—they've already heard the news."

"And Charley?"

I snort as George's comment suddenly makes sense. "Charley's smart; he stayed in Alaska."

Daniel's eyes narrow as he gives me a sly grin. "Would serve her right, you know."

"What?"

He jerks his thumb toward the house. "Isn't your guest room occupied?"

I smile as understanding dawns. "Ooooh. If I tell Leticia her funeral's off, where's she supposed to sleep tonight?"

Daniel nods. "Might as well wait until morning."

"You're right. I can speak to her before people start arriving for the funeral."

We stand together in companionable quiet; then Daniel slips his arm around my shoulder. "You cold?"

"Not really." But I slide closer, nestling in the space under his arm, because I feel like I belong there.

"I've been meaning to ask," he says, his breath warming my ear, "how Gerald and his daughter are getting along."

I shake my head. "Like a sunburned hairless dog and a cat with blistered feet."

"That well?"

"Bringing them together wasn't one of my brighter ideas."

Daniel squeezes my shoulder. "I thought you'd learned that lesson."

"What lesson?"

"You can bring people together, but you can't make them reconcile. I thought you learned that with McLane and her father."

I groan as the memory comes rushing back. No wonder the Gerald-Kirsten situation feels like a bad case of déjà vu. I have inherited my mother's penchant for meddling, and just like Mom, I can't seem to learn that meddling doesn't work.

As the crickets chirp a chorus in the pines, a dozen unspoken questions wedge into the silence between us—questions that have nothing to do with Gerald, Kirsten, or Leticia Gansky. We have been apart, we have been separated by our stubbornness, and this would be the perfect opportunity to confess our foolish mistakes and restore our relationship.

But I have a breathing corpse in my prep room, a terminally ill partner, and a family of unexpected gerbils upstairs. My business is a few weeks away from a last gasp, and my brilliant idea for a slogan contest has resulted in a slew of useless sayings, including "Let us pickle the skin you're in."

I have problems enough; my life doesn't need more drama.

Before Daniel can broach the subject of our relationship, I pull myself from his embrace and take a step toward the house. "By the way—" I turn—"Bugs said you gave him flowers."

Daniel straightens. "That's right."

"You gave him daisies . . . for the peas?" I crinkle my nose. "Sorry, but I don't get it."

"They were a peace offering. For you."

"Oh. Well, thanks. And thanks again for coming."

Daniel opens his car door and pauses. "Are you *sure* Leticia's not dead?"

I cross my arms and take another step forward. "I'll be sure tomorrow."

Once Mom has cleared the breakfast table, I tell Gerald what I suspect about Leticia Gansky. He gawks at me in disbelief, then erupts into laughter. After a couple of crowing whoops that delight my boys and alarm my mother, he wipes tears of mirth from his face and settles back into seriousness.

"In all my years as a mortician," he says, wheezing, "I have wanted to play a practical joke on someone. Looks like the Lord has finally sent the perfect opportunity."

I'm not so sure that comedy is the best tactic a struggling business could employ, so I shoot him a worried glance. "What do you have in mind?"

"Follow my lead," he tells me, pushing up from the kitchen table. "Feel free to improvise—in fact, why don't you begin by examining our client."

So we go downstairs to the prep room, where everything looks just as Daniel and I left it last night. I walk over to the casket, loudly complaining about the poor quality of particleboard boxes. When I lift the casket lid, I see that Leticia appears intent upon maintaining her charade. The side is still broken and her knees are still smudged, but the lipstick that tinted her mouth last night has definitely been worn away.

I cluck in disapproval and call to Gerald over my shoulder. "Do we have any of that Forever Last lipstick? The mortuary in Eustis must have used the cheap stuff. It's completely evaporated."

He comes over to inspect our faking corpse. "Don't have that lipstick, but we could use some red varnish I have under the sink. Her bones will turn to rubble before that stuff wears off."

"But doesn't that chemical eat away at the skin?"

Gerald chuckles. "Under all that varnish, who can tell?"

I peer more closely at our client. Is it my imagination or is her lower lip trembling?

"Forget the lips. I'm more worried about her hands," I say. "They seem to have shifted during the night. I'll either need a pair of those Velcro bands to hold them in place, or I'm going to have to stitch them together."

"A cross-stitch by the wrists," Gerald advises. "Use the heavy-duty thread."

We wait for a reaction—a flutter, an involuntary twinge, anything—but Leticia Gansky must have nerves of steel. Either that, or she's fainted dead away.

I can't help but admire the woman's fortitude as I snag a pair of Velcro bands from the cabinet. When I pick up her arm, any lingering doubts as to her viability vanish completely.

Most people think of the dead as limp—tell a kid to play dead, and he usually melts into a heap, as loose as a marionette with sliced strings. Some people know about rigor mortis, of course, but people who know about rigor also know that the condition passes in a few hours. After that, a dead body *is* limp; within a few days, in fact, it's a slippery mess.

What few people realize is that an embalmed body is about as flexible as carved wood. When we dress someone for the casket, we can't work with people as if they were jointed dolls. They are as unyielding as the proverbial board, so we usually end up slitting their dresses and suits down the back. Even then, dressing a corpse is far from easy.

With a bendable wrist and warm skin, Leticia Gansky is as alive as my mother's tendency to meddle.

"These bands will work fine," I say, fastening one around our client's left wrist. "But what are we going to do about this casket? We can't wheel her out there in a box held together by duct tape."

"We could use the Preston Bronze we have in storage. It'd give this lady a little extra hip room."

I fasten the second strap around Leticia's right hand. "It's airtight, isn't it?"

"Yeah." His mouth quirks with humor. "They're sealed so well several of those models have exploded in mausoleums. Gases build up from the decaying body, and if there's not a release valve—*kaboom*! Not a pretty sight for anyone who comes to visit the family crypt."

I tilt my head to see if we've evoked a reaction. Yes, Leticia's eyeballs are twitching behind her closed eyelids, but apparently she's still unwilling to call off this sham. I suppress a smile and position her hands so one strip locks upon the other.

"Then again," Gerald says, winking at me, "you have to think of the family's wishes. If they picked out this casket, they must have wanted it. So I vote for piecing it back together and leaving her in it."

"But how?"

"A little Gorilla Glue, a little spit. It'll hold long enough for us to get her in the ground."

Gerald and I study Leticia's face for a reaction—nothing else is visible, though I'd be willing to bet her pulse is rattling like a snare drum.

I glance at my partner's sparkling eyes and stifle a laugh. I don't think I've ever seen Gerald have this much fun at work. In that instant, I change my mind. I'm not going to tell Leticia that her living funeral has been canceled. She paid for it, so I'm going to give it to her. The idea is completely crazy, but this experience will be a fitting gift for Gerald, who has spent so many years wearing a somber face in the chapel. *This* funeral he can enjoy.

I turn to him. "Will we have to de-casket her while you do the repairs? I could prop her up against the wall."

Gerald heaves a dramatic sigh. "She can lie there while I work. It's not like I have to glue anything on *her*. Unless her lips or eyelids begin to open."

I can't be sure, but I think the woman's mouth compresses as he speaks. I squeeze Gerald's arm as I turn toward the door. "You repair the casket; I'm going to go print the programs. People will begin to arrive before we know it."

Behind her closed eyelids, Leticia keeps repeating a desperate mantra: *Lord, help me get through this. Help me. Help me. Help me. . . .*

Somehow she managed to endure the night, slipping out only twice more in order to visit the powder room. Somehow she managed to fool Jennifer Graham and the geezer who's probably as old as the funeral home. By some miracle, no one called Charley. And by some fortunate quirk of fate, the old man decided not to drag her out of the casket in order to repair the damaged wall. She would have screamed for sure if he'd tried to prop her up like some kind of department store mannequin.

Leticia can hear him now, shuffling and fussing with some kind of clamp at the side of the casket. But he hasn't laid a hand on her, and he hasn't spoken since Jennifer left the room. Mostly he hums, breathes heavily, and coughs occasionally, now and then clearing his throat as if some great gob of sorrow has lodged there.

Despite his careless comment about her needing extra hip room, she finds herself pitying the old man. Could he be feeling sorrow for *her*? Maybe he mourns over every body that passes through this room. Maybe he only does this work because he feels guilty about some deeply hidden secret sin. Maybe that's why he's stayed so long in the mortuary business—he considers his work a kind of penance.

At least he's performing a useful service. Heaven knows she

wouldn't want to clean up someone else's dead relatives and make them look presentable for their last public appearance. She loves her husband and her brother, but she wouldn't want to dress them for their funerals. It'll be hard enough choosing what clothes Charley should wear in his casket.

At the thought of Charley's funeral—hopefully not imminent but certainly inevitable—a lump rises in her throat. She will miss her husband when he goes. She'll have the funeral at Fairlawn and she'll sit in the front row, as faithful in death as she has been in life. She'll make sure they play "How Great Thou Art," his favorite hymn, and she'll bring that good picture from the den so Jennifer can display it on an easel. Charley would never go to a photographer's studio, but he had that picture taken the last time they agreed to sit for the church directory.

Should she bury him in his church suit or his work uniform? Probably in the uniform—not many people would recognize him in a suit. But everyone knows Charley Gansky of Gansky's Get Great Air. Nearly everyone in town has called him at one time or another, and everyone loves him because he makes their lives comfortable . . . for a reasonable price.

Charley, Charley, Charley . . . No doubt people will pack this place when it's time to send him off. She, on the other hand, will be lucky if her funeral draws more than a dozen people on a Saturday morning.

Her chin quivers in a spasm of self-pity. She tries hard to think about something else, but now her nose is tingling and her sinuses develop that spongy feeling that accompanies tears. Sure enough, water is leaking from beneath her closed eyelids, but maybe the old man won't notice if the tears run off into her hair.

Leticia finds herself wishing that the old man would close the lid so she won't have to worry about revealing her swirling emotions on her face.

"There," he finally says. "That should hold."

Is he talking to himself? She hears the scrape of his stool and senses looming darkness.

"Hate to do this to you," he says, speaking as if she were still among the living, "but you'll have the lid up soon enough. For now, you've got to take a ride into the chapel."

Leticia remains perfectly still as the lid lowers. If she has to ride in this thing one more time, she'd rather take a spin with the top down.

51

By nine thirty, the flowers are in place and the chapel has begun to fill with mourners who've come for Leticia Gansky's service. Several wear the shell-shocked expression of those who have experienced an unexpected death, and my irritation with Leticia grows by the minute. The compassion I felt for our client is being eroded by the heartfelt weeping of her friends and loved ones.

After uncovering Leticia's deception, Gerald and I added a notice to her funeral program. I couldn't be so bold as to proclaim that our client is a big fat liar, so at the top, right under her name and dates of birth and alleged death, I printed a pertinent Bible passage. I only hope people read it.

As the mourners file in and the soloist begins the first of Leticia's requested songs, I hand out copies of the program and greet our guests with a brittle smile. I'm tempted to spill the beans, but Leticia is a paying client, and something in me insists that I ought to honor her wishes. Gerald says it's the right thing to do, but I also know that he's having way too much fun with the woman in the battered box.

I only hope no one holds this hoax against Fairlawn when Leticia reveals her secret.

At 9:50, mourners continue to stream into the chapel—Leticia's friends from church, her fellow Red Hatters, and her neighbors. Her two daughters show up, red-eyed and bewildered, supported by

Leticia's grandsons. Both women are clinging to Jason, Stephanie's husband, and wailing about being unable to reach their father.

"But I don't understand," Stephanie cries as she moves past me. "Why wouldn't Uncle George let us postpone the funeral until Dad gets here?"

Because your mother is more than a little crazy?

Thankfully, I see no sign of Charley Gansky, so George and Daniel must have been right about the man's hunting trip. For Charley's sake, I hope he stays far away from all this foolishness.

Kirsten shows up in her black pants, black jacket, and chauffeur's cap, a formal touch she insisted on adding. After she nods at me and sends Katie upstairs to play with Bugs, she walks down the hallway and enters the office. I'm surprised because she's never evidenced any interest in the office before, but maybe she wants to use the phone or the computer.

Finally, George Josten, Leticia's brother, crosses the threshold. I let his wife pass before shoving a program into George's big hand and pinning him with a sharp look and an uplifted brow.

For a moment he appears confused; then his expression melts into pure contrition. "Do you want to kill me?" he whispers, his shoulders slumping.

"That would be bad for business," I tell him, "as we seem to be overrun with inappropriate bodies right now."

He glances around. "So where is she?"

"Down front." I pull George into the hallway and look him dead in the eye. "Things have been interesting around here. Your sister *broke* the casket last night—I think she had to get out to use the facilities."

His eyes go as wide as saucers. "Did you catch her in the act?"

"I figured it out. Trouble is, she's still playing possum. She's paid for a funeral, so we're giving her one, but if she doesn't resurrect by the time the pastor says the final amen, I'm calling her bluff."

George groans and pinches the bridge of his nose. "Don't worry; I'll do it for you." He shakes his head. "I told her it was a stupid idea. I warned her it might backfire."

"Well—" I soften my voice—"it's a pretty drastic thing to do, so she must have good reasons. I only hope she accomplishes her goals."

"Does she ever?" George sighs, then looks at the program in his hand. His broad face curves in a smile as he reads the Scripture verse. "Heh, heh, that's a good one. You think of that?"

I glance at the page.

> *When Jesus arrived . . . he saw the noisy crowd and heard the funeral music. "Get out!" he told them. "The girl isn't dead; she's only asleep."*
>
> *—Matthew 9:23-24*

"Gerald recommended that verse." I grin back at George. "Now you'd better wipe that smile off your face and go find your wife. You're family, so you have to sit in the front row."

George sidles into the chapel as the music finally fades into silence. I tug on the bottom of my blouse and brace myself for the coming storm, but I'm distracted by the sound of the office door. Kirsten steps into the hall, but she startles when she sees me—and attempts to hide something in her hand.

I gesture to the chapel. "Did you need something? Want me to get your father?"

"No, no." She smiles. "I, uh, just wanted to use the phone."

I nod and move into the chapel, but not before I glimpse the silver object in her right hand. At first I assume it's a cell phone—and yes, she has one, so why does she need ours?—but then I see the telltale yellow tab and realize that she's carrying a tape measure.

What in the world is Kirsten up to?

Ruby has stopped playing the organ, but since there are still mourners beside the casket, I give her the signal to keep the music coming. Since we had no viewing last night, most of the mourners are taking advantage of this time to file by the coffin and pay their last respects. Nearly every woman clutches a tissue, and some of them drop roses into the open casket.

I hope Leticia isn't allergic to flowers.

I stand next to Gerald, close enough to hear comments from the passersby. I hear several cries of "You just never know, do you?" and "I had lunch with her only last week," but no one questions the inexplicable randomness of death. They are far more interested in critiquing the work of the mortician.

"Doesn't she look good?" Gertie Whitehead says, dabbing at the corners of her eyes. "Like she just lay down for a nap."

"I think she looks a little tangerine," Carol Conrad answers. "What happened to her lipstick?" She glances over at me. "Did you do her face, Jen, or did Ryan?"

"Leticia came to us from a funeral home in Eustis," I explain, pitching my voice so it travels down the viewing line. "We didn't have anything to do with the preparation of the body, but Leticia wanted to have her service here."

"Thoughtful of her," Ginger Sue Wilkerson agrees. "Not making us drive over to Eustis."

"Downright inconsiderate, her dying in April." Annie Watson sniffs into her tissue. "I wanted her pound cake recipe for the bake sale next month. And where's Charley? He ought to be here."

"I heard he was hunting bear up in Alaska," someone down the line calls.

"I heard he was too distraught to leave the house," someone else answers.

Sharon Gilbert steps out of the line to speak to George, who is sitting like a chastened lump in the front row. "Wasn't Leticia at your house this past week?"

George's complexion flushes to the color of the roses on the casket. "Don't look at me. I didn't plan any of this."

"Well, it's not like you *could*," Sharon answers, nonplussed. "But maybe you should have made her stay home and take it easy. I mean, for a healthy woman to drop in her tracks, she must have been under some serious stress."

"She *was* carrying those extra pounds." Annie tips her chin in a sober nod. "I told her to lay off the pancake breakfasts, but she wouldn't listen."

"Cholesterol," Ginger Sue says. "Too many eggs."

Lydia halts beside the casket, her program in hand. "What an odd Scripture verse," she says to me. "What's the application to a funeral?"

Sharon lifts her program. "I think it's lovely. A perfect picture of how our bodies enter a temporary rest until we're resurrected to be with the Lord."

"That's right." I step forward to move the ladies along. "If you'll find your seats, I believe the minister is ready to begin."

The minister, a tall, blond associate pastor from First Baptist Church, confesses that he didn't know Leticia Gansky well, but he's heard good things about her life and character. He smiles at Leticia's daughters, Stephanie and Emily, and pauses to pat each of her grandsons on the shoulder.

Without much ceremony, he reads the traditional Scriptures about the many mansions in heaven, and then he closes his Bible. I find myself wondering how long he's been in the pastorate. I've heard more experienced preachers ad-lib for twenty minutes without even knowing the decedent's name.

"I'm sure some of you would like to add a few words about Leticia," the minister says. "Who would like to come forward?"

Leticia's daughters sob into their tissues, but a middle-aged man comes forward from the back of the chapel and faces the crowd. "I had Mrs. Gansky as my driver's ed teacher at the high school," he says, gripping the microphone stand, "and I'm here to tell you, she saved my life. The other day I would have been kilt for sure if I hadn't been hanging back at least a car length for every ten miles per hour on the speedometer. So when I heard that Mrs. Gansky had passed on, I had to come testify. She was a good—no, a *great*—driver's ed teacher."

I take pains to keep my face composed in neutral lines as the man makes his way back to his seat. I didn't know Leticia had been a high school teacher until I read her obituary, but I'm still having trouble picturing her behind the wheel of a driver's ed car. Shouldn't driving instructors be unflappable and *stable*?

The crowd murmurs in appreciation as the man sits down. I glance at the casket, wondering if this is affirmation enough to inspire an awakening in my client, but she slumbers on in artificial oblivion.

I nudge Gerald as several of the Red Hatters glance around, probably daring each other to go next. Before any of them stand, however, Stephanie, Leticia's younger daughter, rises from her place in the front row. She moves to the center aisle, deliberately wiping her eyes and nose before she speaks.

"Some folks," she says, a quaver in her voice, "thought of my mother as a ditzy blonde. To be honest, there were times in my teenage years when I thought the same thing. Sometimes our house was like a three-ring circus, with church socials, school projects, and band rehearsals all packed into one night. We were always running here and there, and Mama acted like she'd never even heard the word *schedule*."

Several audience members twitter at this, and I can easily imagine the whirlwind Leticia's household must have been. What I can't imagine, however, is what Leticia must be thinking. Is this what she wanted to hear from her daughter?

"I'll be honest." Stephanie looks up, her brown eyes sweeping the room. "For a kid who craves routine, she wasn't the easiest mom in the world. She was always saying that no one took her seriously, but since she had trouble settling down to *be* serious . . . well, you get my point. Mama was none of the things I needed and all the things my friends wanted their moms to be: funny, zany, and willing to do almost anything. She always said you go around only once in life, so you might as well give it all you've got."

She brings her hand up to cover her mouth, and the other mourners wait in an expectant hush. "The thing is," Stephanie finally says, her voice breaking, "I spent most of my teenage years wishing for a different kind of mother. Since I heard the news about Mom's passing, I've been numb—but not so numb that I haven't regretted all those feelings. I've spent so much time shutting her out of my life, I'd give anything if I could go back and do things differently. Now that I'm a mother myself, I wish I were more like her. I'm going to miss her more than anything."

A quiet murmur of sympathy ripples through the crowd as Stephanie blows her nose; then the silence shatters with a heartrending cry. "Baby, I am so sorry!"

Every head in the room swivels toward the casket. Leticia has pushed herself up, spilling roses onto the floor in her eagerness to comfort her daughter. Tears have dampened the hair above her ears, and her eyes are red above trembling lips.

Stephanie jumps back and collides with the minister, who catches her in an awkward embrace. Emily, Leticia's older daughter, utters a frightened squeak and gapes at her mother, her eyes hardening as reality hits home. The Hatters are stunned into a momentary silence. A buzzing begins in the back row, growing in volume and intensity until it threatens to burst into a dangerous explosion.

"Mama," Emily cries, standing, "how *could* you?"

"I—I . . ." Leticia pulls a handkerchief from her sleeve and swipes at her wet face. "I only wanted you to miss me."

Stephanie's husband, Jason, pries his wife away from the minister and escorts Stephanie to her seat. If the stern set of his shoulders is any indication of his mood, I'm sure he'd like to escort his wife out of the chapel, but like a bystander who can't tear his gaze from an impending train wreck, he can't leave. No one can walk out while there's so much tension in the room.

"I only wanted to feel appreciated." Leticia gazes over the crowd with wide, sorrow-filled eyes. "I thought maybe people would stop taking me for granted if I weren't around anymore."

Edna Nance, one of the leading Hatters in the Southern Sassies chapter, stands and hooks her purse over her bony shoulder. "Tisha Gansky, you ought to be ashamed of yourself."

Myra O'Hara leaps to Edna's side. "I second that motion."

Alyce Baker joins the others. "All in favor?"

"Aye."

Leticia's lower lip trembles when the vote is nearly unanimous. When she says, "Forgive me," I'm sure no false corpse ever sounded more plaintive. She turns to gaze at her daughters. "Forgive me, Steph and Emily, for not being the mother you needed while you were growing up."

"Mom—" Stephanie's eyes well with fresh tears—"you are the mother God sent us. You are the mother we needed . . . because even with your faults, you made us into the mothers we are today."

Leticia opens her arms, her chin wobbling. "Girls, can you forgive me?"

To a round of applause from the onlookers, Stephanie and Emily rush toward the casket to hug their mother. I'm about to help Leticia climb out of the box, but as she leans forward, the fresh repair gives way, tumbling Leticia Gansky straight into the waiting arms of her daughters.

The Southern Sassies break into laughter as the three women embrace, and the hasty funeral dissolves into a love fest.

I sidle over to Gerald and link my arm through his. "Did you ever imagine this would turn out so well?"

He chuckles softly. "I had a feeling the Lord wouldn't disappoint us."

I consider his answer as the Hatters retrieve roses from the casket spray and distribute them around the room. Leticia is welcomed back to the land of the living with kisses, hugs, and firm warnings that she never pull a stunt like that again.

At one point, she catches my eye. When I nod at her, she mouths a question: *You knew?* I nod again, and she blows me a kiss.

As the funeral party disperses, my thoughts return to Gerald's offhand comment. He knew we had a living corpse in the prep room, and he trusted the Lord to work everything out. And everything *has* worked out, at least for now.

But what will happen when word of this fiasco gets spread around town? The rumor mill works overtime here, and it's not known for accuracy. By next week, people could be whispering that our funerals are a joke or that we almost buried someone alive.

As Stephanie and Emily wrap their arms around their very-much-alive mother, I wonder what they'll say about Fairlawn next week. I wouldn't be surprised if they sue us for causing severe emotional distress.

"No good deed goes unpunished," I murmur.

"Hmm?" Gerald lifts a silvered brow. "What was that?"

I squeeze his arm, not wanting to bother him with my worries. "Never mind, G-man. Never mind."

As the balmy days of April slide into the warmer days of May, our household adjusts to a new pattern. Kirsten shows up at eight thirty every morning with a cup of coffee in her hand and our newspaper under her arm. She drives Bugs and Katie to Round Lake Elementary and vanishes unless Gerald rings her cell phone. Then she usually arrives within five or ten minutes and off they go to run an errand or make a pickup. Each time, as I see them drive away in the old station wagon we use as a call car, I wonder if this might be the day they'll begin to whittle away at the wall between them.

I can't forget that each page on my daily calendar marks one less opportunity for them to make things right.

With Kirsten available to help with some of the carpool duties, Mom jumps back into her Red Hatter meetings, frequently spending most of the day at the Biddle House. She brings me whispered reports from the other ladies, who keep a close watch on Kirsten, their newest tenant. "She's quiet," Mom tells me, "but she goes outside to smoke and talk on her cell phone. They think she has a new man friend."

This news does not excite me. I don't want Kirsten distracted by thoughts of a new relationship when she should be thinking about her relationship with her dying father.

Despite coming to our rescue on the Night of the Noisy Corpse,

Daniel has not resumed regular visits to Fairlawn. I am often nagged by the conviction that he's waiting for me to invite him, but I have too much on my mind to risk another emotional entanglement. I like Daniel a lot—I might even love him—but this is not the time for me to think about giving my heart away. This is the time for me to practice standing on my own two feet.

On May 8, our postal carrier brings the official announcement—I passed the national board exam, so I'm now eligible to be a licensed funeral director and embalmer in the state of Florida.

When I show Gerald my letter, he kisses me on both cheeks and insists that we celebrate with a pair of steaks he's been hiding at the bottom of the freezer.

"Steaks—for lunch?"

"Why not?" He grins. "You defrost 'em in the microwave while I fire up the grill."

While Gerald and I eat our steaks on the back porch, he reminds me that the National Funeral Directors Association convention will be held in Orlando this weekend.

I struggle to swallow an overcooked bit of meat. "Surely you aren't thinking about going."

"I think we ought to go," he says. "I want to show you the ropes. It'll be important for you to make some connections and learn about the industry's big picture."

I don't answer as I slice another bite of the filet mignon. Gerald doesn't complain, but his step has slowed and he's been going to bed a little earlier every night. In unguarded moments I frequently catch him grimacing, and I've noticed that his breathing is more labored each time he climbs the stairs or struggles to maneuver a corpse. He ought to be taking it easy, but if going to this convention will make him happy, who am I to deny him?

I lower my knife and reach for Gerald's hand. "I'll go with you," I tell him, looking directly into his eyes. "But if you start to feel bad, I want you to tell me right away."

His forehead creases. "Don't you want to go?"

"Sure. But not as much as I want you to be okay."

⁂

Fortunately, Orlando is only a half hour's drive from Fairlawn. Gerald and I arrive at the convention center early Saturday morning, park amid dozens of midsize rental sedans, and take our time entering the building.

Ruby Masters, who usually plays the organ for Fairlawn funerals, offered to loan us her late mother's wheelchair, so I insist Gerald use it while we navigate the convention floor. He protests, of course, but after one particularly arduous climb he relents.

The carpeted convention center lobby teems with booths advertising trade journals and other industry organizations. I handle the wheelchair as best I can, but it's not easy to thread our way through the boisterous crowd of morticians. I'm a little surprised at *how* rowdy the crowd is—not at all what I expected from an organization of funeral directors. At one point Gerald has to tap my hand and point me through a hokey pokey–dancing line of conventioneers in Hawaiian shirts and Mickey Mouse ears, but we finally make our way to the registration desk.

Our badges, hanging around our necks like giant toe tags, allow us official entry onto the exhibitors' floor, where the crowds are more controlled and business far more in evidence. We stroll past displays of merchants offering every conceivable item that might be useful in the mortuary trade—caskets and urns, clothing and makeup, disinfectants and deodorants. Salesmen for the death care industry have spread their wares over a floor the size of two football fields, hawking plugs, needles, scalpels, lotions, glues, vaults, blankets, quilts, programs, guest books, flowers, monuments, funeral coaches, sound systems, stained glass window designs, organs, freezers, and ovens.

At one booth Gerald studies a machine that looks like a garage door opener with dangling straps. "Jen." He gestures to the device. "You need this."

"What is it?"

"What it is—" the plastered-hair salesman homes in on us like a kid spying free candy—"is the Body Shovel by Lift-A-Lot. With this machine suspended from the ceiling, one employee can easily manage dressing, casketing, and shipping. You'll never have another backache if you install the Body Shovel."

Ignoring the man's sales patter, Gerald smiles at me. "It wouldn't take up floor space because it hangs from the ceiling. You run the straps under the client in three spots and let the machine do the lifting."

"I'm sure I don't have to tell you that Americans are getting heavier," the salesman continues, smiling like a Cheshire cat. "Did you know that medical examiners' offices are now ordering extra large carts and autopsy trays? The number of obese Americans has jumped to 33 percent, and not even a woman as fit as yourself can lift an obese body without help."

I bite my lower lip and pretend to examine the machine. Gerald is recommending this, of course, because he's thinking he won't be around to give me a hand, but Mr. Salesman doesn't know that. And Gerald's not likely to talk about our reality—not here.

When I am sure my emotions are steady, I reach for a brochure. "I'll keep one of these. Your contact information is on it?"

"But don't you want to take advantage of our convention special?" Mr. Salesman gushes. "Free shipping and a 10 percent discount on all orders placed this weekend."

I give him a careful smile. "I'd like to read the information later and think about it."

"Are you sure?" He winks at Gerald. "I'm sure your father will assure you that this is a great deal."

"He's not my father." I tuck the brochure into my purse. "If I'm interested, I'll call you later."

Three booths later, we find another ceiling-mounted machine, this one called the BackSaver X1000 Lift. It sells for quite a bit less than the Body Shovel.

"I didn't think that guy had cornered the market," Gerald says, grinning.

I squeeze his shoulder, grateful that he has taught me not to make rash purchases. The BackSaver X1000 will be a useful addition to our prep room no matter who's working at the embalming table. And fortunately, the manufacturer is offering a payment plan that's interest-free for one full year.

We place our order, both of us feeling that the purchase is a wise investment. I'm so thrilled that I'd be content to head home, but Gerald insists that we need to stick around to see what's new in the business.

So after grabbing a burger and a Coke at a convention center snack shop, we sit through a seminar on the changing face of the industry. We learn about the huge corporations that are buying up independent funeral homes and forcing others out of business. We hear about the dangers of prepaid funeral plans and why it's important to make sure that at least 70 percent of prepaid income is reserved in a safe, interest-bearing investment account. We see mug shots of funeral home operators who are now in prison because they absconded with preneed payments and later canceled thousands of prepaid funeral plans.

I make a mental note to talk to Daniel about the financial structure of Fairlawn's preneed plans. I don't want to disappoint our clients, nor do I want to end up behind bars. One thing is clear: no matter how tight our budget becomes, I cannot dip into the account holding other people's money.

Moving on, the keynote speaker explains that cremation now accounts for nearly a third of all body disposals. Since Fairlawn does not offer cremation, this is not good news for us.

"On the other hand," the speaker says, flashing a wide smile, "the baby boomers will soon begin to die off. The U.S. death rate is projected to rise to nearly 9 per 1,000 in 2010 and 9.3 in 2020. Many of those decedents will opt for cremation, but many more will choose traditional burial for religious and personal reasons. A funeral is something you can do only once, so people want their last service to be meaningful."

I glance at Gerald, who's breathing deeply and evenly as his head hangs forward. He's asleep.

I lean back in my chair and wonder what he's requested to make his funeral service meaningful. I know he's already picked out his casket and written out his wishes, but I haven't been able to bring myself to read his written contract. The longer I can put it off, the longer I can pretend that my mentor and good friend won't soon be in need of my professional services.

The BackSaver X1000 Lift arrives during the third week of May. Since no one in the Gansky family has elected to sue us, we call Charley and ask if he can install the machine. Fortunately, the man loves a challenge . . . which is probably why he married Leticia.

Gerald watches from his stool as Charley and his helper mount the machine on the ceiling brackets. When the installation is complete, we attempt to test it on Clay, who proves to be an unfit subject.

"Hey," he says, wiggling as the motor groans and the harness tightens around him. "This thing tickles!"

"Don't move," I warn, afraid he'll damage something before we have a chance to use it. "Just hang there, please."

"Like a stiff?"

"Exactly."

Charley peers at me over the top of his reading glasses. "It says here that you can adjust the height. You want the body to go higher?"

I turn to Gerald. "What do you think? He's about two feet up. Will we ever need anyone to be higher than that?"

Gerald's brow crinkles. "The widest casket I've ever seen was thirty-six inches across. You'll need to be able to clear that distance to lift the lid."

I look at Charley, who's climbed back onto his ladder. "We're going to need thirty-six inches of clearance from the tabletop."

"You're going to have the cadavers as high as the lightbulbs," Charley jokes, looking into the mechanical box on the ceiling. "But I'll make the adjustment."

Fortunately, the BackSaver X1000 works like a dream when the plus-size Jose Fernandez arrives from Eustis. We bring him in on the gurney and strap him into the X1000. I hold my breath when Gerald presses the button to lift him, but the motor hums and Jose rises without a hitch.

He dangles in midair while we push the gurney away and position the prep table beneath him.

"This is almost *too* easy," I tell Gerald, lowering the body to the table. "I'm going to have to start lifting weights to keep my muscles toned."

❦ ❦ ❦

At the Fernandez funeral the next morning, I take my usual place in the back and wait for the minister to approach the platform. When he does, I shift my attention to Gerald, who's standing by the casket. He seems hunched, as if he's unable to stand up straight.

Ripples of alarm spiral up my spine. When we're working, I can almost pretend that Gerald isn't sick. Aside from the fact that he goes to bed earlier, sleeps a little later, and takes an occasional nap, I could forget that he's not well.

But today I can't deny the pallor on Gerald's face. I've worked on healthier-looking corpses.

When Jose Fernandez has been safely interred at the cemetery, I return to the house and find Gerald sitting in one of the chapel chairs, his face as pale as paper. Beads of perspiration dot his forehead and upper lip, and when I call his name, he doesn't immediately try to stand and assure me that he's fine.

His silence alarms me more than anything. I snatch my cell phone from my pocket and punch in his doctor's number. I expect—I *hope*—Gerald will say I'm making a mountain out of a molehill, but like an overtired child he leans sideways until he's lying across the row of chairs, his head resting on his folded arm.

I'm so panicked I can barely hold a thought in my head. Why doesn't the doctor answer?

Finally, a female voice comes on the line.

"Hello? This is Jennifer Graham, calling about Gerald Huffman. I don't know what the doctor is giving him for pain, but whatever it is, it's not working. He looks awful, and he can't—he can't even sit up."

My frustration rises when the nurse calmly promises to have the doctor call me. Shouldn't she rush to wherever the doctor is?

I snap the phone closed and walk over to Gerald, then kneel beside him until my face is only inches from his. His eyes are closed, his breathing rapid and shallow. I don't know if he's even conscious, but this much is certain: death is bearing down on us with a definite and deliberate step, and I am powerless to stop it.

"Hey, G-man." I push a fringe of gray hair from his forehead. "Want me to help you upstairs?"

His eyelids flutter without opening. "So tired. I never dreamed . . . getting out of bed . . . could wear a body out."

"You've done a lot more than get out of bed today. Let me help you upstairs so you can rest."

I help him sit up, slip an arm under his shoulders, and urge him to stand. Like a couple in a slow-motion three-legged race, we take the steps one at a time. With each movement I find myself praying that God will give Gerald the strength to rise to the next tread.

The journey from the top of the stairs to the kitchen has never seemed so long. We pause in front of the sink, where Gerald steadies himself on the counter as I get a glass of water and a pain pill from the row of prescription bottles on the windowsill.

"The doctor warned . . . the cancer would soon . . . be in my bones," Gerald says as I drop the pill into his trembling hand. "I guess that's why it hurts . . . to be."

My eyes fill with tears as he places the pill on his tongue and slowly raises the glass. "I'm so sorry," I whisper. "I wish this weren't happening."

"I shouldn't complain about . . . somethin' as natural as . . . the law of thermo-hydraulics." He grins as he sets the glass on the counter and angles himself toward his bedroom. "Things break down, and lots of folks . . . have it worse."

I watch him go, my heart rising in my throat. "You need any help? I could help you get ready for bed—"

He flaps his hand at me in a vague underarm motion. "I can manage. I know you have things to do."

I wait until I hear the click of the door; then I blink away tears and trudge down the stairs. Why hasn't the doctor called? If Gerald needs to be in a hospital, I'll take him myself. If he needs more drugs, I'll get them. I'll do whatever it takes to keep him comfortable and content.

In the foyer, I nearly run into Kirsten, who is coming through the front door, a McDonald's bag in her hand.

"Where have you been?" I demand, not really wanting an answer. "Your father needs you."

She blinks. "He didn't call me."

"Why should he call you? He doesn't need a *ride.* He needs his daughter. He needs you to help him get up the stairs, get into bed, and get . . . through this. The man is dying, Kirsten, or haven't you noticed?"

A steely look enters her eyes. "Who are you to speak to me like that? You weren't there when my father told me to shape up or ship out. You don't know anything about us."

"I know your father. I know the sort of man he is."

"Well, so do I. I know he's not the sort to enjoy having a woman like me around." Kirsten spins on the ball of her foot and leaves as suddenly as she appeared.

I follow her out the door and stop on the front lawn. "Where are you going?"

"What do you care?"

"Your father needs you here."

"You hired me to drive him. Apparently he's not going anywhere."

When my hand tingles with the urge to slap the smirk off her face, I realize that my anger is getting in my way. I look across the lawn, then swallow hard and try to assume a more reasonable tone.

"Kirsten—" I face her—"why don't you come inside and see if your dad would like you to sit with him. Maybe you could read to him."

She makes a face. "Why? He's not blind."

"Then go and *talk* to him. Talk about the past and see if you can do something to make things right. Ask him to forgive you and put his mind at ease."

"Why do you assume it's me who needs forgiving?"

Because I know you. The words dance on the tip of my tongue, but they're not the words that will convince Kirsten to climb those stairs. I hold up both hands and back away. "Forget what I said. Just go and tell your dad how you feel. Open the doors of communication and get things straightened out. We're losing him, and I hate to see you two at odds—"

"You don't have to see me at all," Kirsten answers, stalking toward her car. "I'll be at the Biddle House if the boss decides to go out. You have my cell number."

Every bit of restraint falls away as I storm after her. "If you don't want to see your dad, why did you even come here? Can you help me understand why you showed up?"

She yanks the car door open, tosses her McDonald's bag inside, and glares at me. "Why do you think?" she says, her words clipped. "I was broke and you told me Dad was about to change his will. So I came down here to make sure he didn't forget me and Katie."

I stand on the grass, blank and shaken, as she gets in the car and roars out of the parking lot. For a while I can't move; then I press my hands over my face and release a noisy sob.

What have I done? I invited Kirsten here. I dangled the will in front of her like bait.

So why am I so furious with her for snapping at it?

Kirsten glances at the clock on the dashboard, then mutters an oath and points the car toward state road 46. Time to pick up Katie and Bugs from school, which means she'll have to go back to Fairlawn again. She could probably drop Bugs and leave, but Katie will start whining about seeing that blasted gerbil.

Well, this time she'll just have to whine. They are not going into that house, not with Jennifer prowling around and ready to take off someone's head.

Kirsten pulls onto Round Lake Road and turns into the school entrance. A line of sedans and minivans has already formed, moms and dads waiting to reclaim their little darlings and take them home.

At the end of the line, she shoves the car in park and kills the engine. A breeze whispers through the open windows and ruffles her hair, so Kirsten leans back, trying to enjoy it. In another month it'll be impossible to sit out here without the AC blowing, but now the weather is almost pleasant.

It's really too bad Jennifer Graham has turned out to be such a nag. In another world, she and Jennifer might have been friends. They're nearly the same age, they have children who go to the same school, and they're both single.

Then again, Jennifer is as much a prude as her father. The way she pulls her hair back . . . and those somber clothes. She's got a nice shape, but she doesn't seem to care about showcasing her attributes. She doesn't seem to care about anything but her kids and working at that dreary funeral home.

Why in the world did her father hire a woman like Jennifer Graham? He must have been desperate if the best applicant he could find was an inexperienced single mother with two kids. Either that, or he had a secret crush on her.

Kirsten rejects that idea. No way her straitlaced father would allow himself to feel anything as silly as an infatuation with a younger woman. Gerald Huffman does not allow himself to feel anything inappropriate. He doesn't lust, cuss, drink, or smoke. All he does is preach and teach, marry and bury. And be adored by everyone who knows him.

After glancing at the clock on the dash again, she digs in her purse for a cigarette. She doesn't like to smoke in front of the little boy, but she has at least five minutes before the bell rings. And heaven knows she needs something to do with her hands. She shakes a cigarette out of the pack, brings the filtered end to her lips, and searches for the lighter. One click and the Zippo flares.

Kirsten inhales, then exhales slowly and rests her elbow on the car door. Jennifer Graham can be obnoxious, but she has more than her fair share of courage. Not every woman could pick up a scalpel and slice into a dead body. Not every woman could sit and listen to weeping people go on about how much the dearly departed loved Elvis and standard poodles. For all her annoying characteristics, Jennifer has her strengths.

Obviously. Dad dotes on her.

She tastes the end of her cigarette again and wonders if her father has ever doted on *her*. When she was little, maybe. When she was still naive enough to believe that fathers knew best and the preacher's word was gospel.

But that was before her mom died and she learned that God doesn't always answer prayer the way she wants him to. That was before she realized that she could never measure up to what people expected of the preacher's daughter. And that was before she wanted to audition for a local production of *Jesus Christ Superstar* and her father wouldn't allow it.

From those days forward, Kirsten and her father have been at loggerheads. They disagreed over the clothes she wanted to wear, the music she wanted to play, and the friends she wanted to have. That's when she began to hide her true self. She lived a sullen life at home and a spirited life with her friends until she left home at eighteen and vowed never to go back.

Kirsten purses her lips around the end of the cigarette and drifts back to the moment when she took her first curtain call. At seventeen, she played a working girl in an indie production of an original play—not her favorite role but her first. That night, with her face still streaked in fake blood from the murder scene, she stood in the blinding footlights and heard applause and approval from the audience.

And in that moment, she counted every sacrifice worth it.

55

Saturday, May 24, 10 a.m.

I am writing this for you, Kirsten, because I want you to know how your father spent his last days. Someday perhaps you or Katie will appreciate this journal. I hope so.

Gerald is failing faster than we anticipated. I am sitting with him in his room, and he is much weaker today but not in as much pain. Clay, Bugs, and Katie have just spent a half hour with him, and though he enjoyed the kids' company, I know the simple act of staying awake while they sat on his bed and watched TV has left him drained and weary.

"I'm glad Katie came to Mt. Dora," Gerald says, pulling my attention from my diary. "Now I'll know what she looks like when I find myself watching for her at heaven's gate." His eyes catch and hold mine. "You'll keep tabs on her, won't you? I'm not sure Kirsten is going to take the time to make sure Katie learns about Jesus . . . and I really want my granddaughter to know the Savior."

I drop my hand to his arm. "I'll do my best."

"Please. Do whatever you can." His eyelids close, and beneath the thin skin I can see his eyes roving in their sockets. "That little girl shouldn't have to suffer from the problems between her mother and me. That wouldn't be fair."

Gerald's voice is calm, his expression clear, so I summon the courage to venture into territory far beyond the boundaries of home and business. "What happened between you and Kirsten? Neither of you ever talks about it."

His breathing quickens. "It's the old story, I think—preacher's daughter rebels against everything her parents represent. Her mother and I tried not to pressure her—we never said she ought to do or not do things because her daddy was the preacher. Our philosophy was much simpler. We lived a certain way because we loved Jesus and wanted to obey him. To my way of thinking, that means living honestly, modestly, and patiently."

I snort softly. "Let me guess—as a teenager, Kirsten didn't want to be honest, modest, and patient."

Gerald grins at me. "She didn't want to be anything but angry. She was as headstrong as any child I've ever met, and though a strong will can be a good thing, she was always exercising it against us. She could have stood against her foolish friends, but she lied to us. Stole from us. Finally, she ran away."

"She told me you kicked her out of the house."

"That would be how she saw it. But I'd never cast off a child who was willing to be part of the family. We had house rules, but Kirsten wanted no part of them. Evelyn and I had pledged to serve the Lord, and Kirsten wanted to serve herself. When she was eighteen, a couple of years after Evelyn died, I told Kirsten she couldn't use our home only as a place to shower and sleep between her nighttime prowls, so she took off."

"Were you . . . Did you ever regret that decision?"

His tender gaze melts into mine. "When it comes to parenting, I've second-guessed every decision I've ever made. Like most parents, Evelyn and I operated on trial and error, but by the time Kirsten was eighteen, I realized something: the best parental model I had was God himself. He's a perfect parent—he loves us, disciplines us, and welcomes us home when we repent. But he doesn't bless us when we sin, because he knows we need to feel the pain of our poor choices. If only we were perfect children . . ."

When Gerald closes his eyes, I'm sure he's drifted into a doze. But then he speaks again, his voice slow and drowsy. "I know Kirsten has suffered, and I'm sorry I wasn't around to help her through the pain. But I have never stopped praying for my girl . . . and I have never stopped loving her."

❦ ❦ ❦

On Sunday afternoon, we meet Allison Crawford, the tall, able-bodied woman who'll be our hospice nurse. With a firm hand she takes over Gerald's care, insisting that Mom and I get some rest and leave most of the caregiving to her. She brings in a folded cot, which she props in the corner of Gerald's room. "Only when necessary," she tells me when she sees me eyeing the cot. "We want life to continue as normally as possible."

Mom and I creep out of the room, not wanting to get in Allison's way. Though I go to my bedroom and lie down for a nap, I can't sleep. My brain hums with a thousand thoughts, and nine hundred ninety-nine of them involve Gerald, Kirsten, or Daniel.

Daniel hasn't dropped by for a visit in over four weeks. I keep telling myself that Gerald needs me more than Daniel, but maybe . . . maybe I need Daniel. I find myself wanting to talk to him, to get his opinion, to see his smile. And if the rumors are true and he's begun to visit the town librarian . . .

I resolutely push the thought from my mind. Mom came home upset the other day because of something she saw at the library. I tried to ask what was wrong, but all I got was a teary declaration that she'd seen Jacqueline Prose eating chocolate-covered pecans behind the reference desk.

I didn't bother to ask. Mother has her quirks, and she's welcome to keep them.

At five o'clock I head into the kitchen to fix soup and sandwiches for Mom and the boys.

Nurse Allison meets me at the doorway leading to Gerald's room. "He'd like to see you," she says, moving to the sink with an empty glass.

I hurry to Gerald's bedside, expecting the worst, but he seems rested and content. "I'd like to see Daniel," he says, his cheek twitching with a small smile. "Would you ask him . . . to come over?"

"Tonight?"

"As soon as it's . . . convenient for him."

So I rush into the kitchen and dial Daniel's home number. Not because I'm trying to patch things up between us, but because Gerald asked me to call.

As the phone rings, I think of the other visitors who've dropped by to check on Gerald's condition. Visitors to his sickroom tend to take one of two approaches. Either they enter the room with a falsely bright smile and behave as if Gerald's been stricken with something as trivial as a passing cold, or they enter with the intention of letting him know how much they love him and have appreciated his life.

Unfortunately, far too many people operate in the first category. They promise that they're praying for a quick healing, pat Gerald on the shoulder, and assure him that he'll be up and around soon, refusing to acknowledge what anyone can clearly see. They'll be the ones who weep loudest at the funeral, feeling desperately sorry because they never took the opportunity to express their deepest feelings.

Through their denial, they are cheating themselves . . . and Gerald.

Few people fall into the latter category, but those are the guests who do the most good. I have stood in the back of the room with tears streaming down my face as they placed their hands upon my friend and told him he'll be missed. Instead of ignoring the impending specter of death, they hold Gerald close and offer their strength and love.

They ask if he's afraid, if he's in pain. And when he answers no, I know the presence of friends has relieved him in a way no pain pill ever could. Their gentle hands are the best palliative a dying man could receive.

My voice clots with emotion when Daniel comes on the line. "Hi," I say, forcing words through my tight throat. "It's me."

"Hi." His voice sends a ripple down my backbone.

"Gerald asked me to call you. Hospice is here." I would have said more, but a lump rises in my throat and prevents further speech.

A drop of silence, then Daniel asks, "How much longer?"

I clear my throat. "A couple of days, maybe."

"I'll be over tonight. Does he need anything? Do *you* need anything?"

I need you. I fight a sudden rush of tears as the truth hits me like a renegade wave. I ignore it, however, because this night isn't about me—it's about my sick friend. "You got a couple of extra years in your back pocket? Gerald could use those." I wait for a flippant answer, but Daniel doesn't even attempt one.

"I'll be over by six. And don't cook; I'll bring dinner for the family."

I open my mouth, about to tell him he doesn't have to put himself out on our account, but he clicks off the line before I have a chance.

Daniel arrives, as promised, bearing boxes of kung pao chicken, cartons of fried rice, bags of egg rolls, and chopsticks. The boys are thrilled with the chopsticks, and Mom gushes her gratitude as she spreads the feast over the kitchen table.

I lean against the arched doorway as Daniel walks into Gerald's room and closes the door. Allison Crawford comes out, leaving the two men alone.

Mom and I exchange a glance. Did Gerald and Daniel have some kind of unfinished business? After a few minutes, Daniel asks for Allison. I'm instantly alarmed, but he assures me that Gerald is fine and he'll need the nurse for only a moment.

The rest of us are munching on rice and chicken by the time Daniel emerges, tucking a folded sheet of paper into his pocket.

Mom stands and offers her seat. "We saved you some," she says, reaching for a glass in the cupboard. "Sit down and eat."

Daniel smiles around the table, and his gaze comes to rest on mine. "I'd love to, but I need to run by the office." He pats the pocket with the paper. "I'll stop by tomorrow to see how he's getting on."

I'm about to tell him good-bye when I hear the front door open.

Bugs springs from his chair and darts out of the kitchen to see who's come in. "It's Katie!" he calls from the landing.

Daniel moves toward the stairs. "I'll get out of your way."

I barely have time to thank him for dinner before Kirsten and Katie troop into the kitchen. Katie's eyes widen when she sees the food, so Mom sits the child in a chair and sets an empty plate on the table.

I pull Kirsten into the living room. "The hospice nurse is in there with your father," I say, studying her face.

"Why's she here?"

"The doctor thinks it's only a matter of days."

Watching her, I see something that looks almost like bewilderment enter her expression. "He's actually dying?"

"The nurse is right inside his room; you can go talk to her."

"No."

"Don't you want to do *anything* for him?" A wave of frustrated anger rises inside me, threatening to drown every good intention, but some still-functioning part of my brain remembers the impressionable children only a few feet away. "Kirsten—" I grip her arm and draw her behind the wall so the kids can't see us—"there's nothing sadder in the world than a missed opportunity."

Kirsten stares at me, her eyes glassy. "What are you talking about?"

"I'm talking about your dad. About the things you should say to one another before he leaves us."

Before I can say anything else, Allison comes up beside us. "Mr. Huffman would like to speak to his daughter," she says, her gaze darting from my face to Kirsten's.

Kirsten looks at Allison for a moment, then strides past the nurse, through the kitchen, and slams her fist against Gerald's bedroom door.

From a few feet behind her, I hear Gerald rasp, "Kirsten?"

"What do you want with me?" Her words are as sharp as rough stones. "I could never be the daughter you wanted. I have to be who I am, not some perfect Goody Two-shoes."

I peer over Kirsten's shoulder and see that Gerald's eyes are leaking tears. "I didn't want you to be perfect," he says, wheezing. "I only wanted you . . . to be willing."

Kirsten turns and walks away, glaring at me as she goes. "Thanks for bringing me here," she snaps. "Thanks for nothing."

Silence settles over the kitchen after Kirsten and Katie leave, an odd absence of sound that reminds me of the hush after a booming thunderstorm. The boys stare at their plates, all signs of joy wiped from their faces, and Mom's lower lip quivers. Nurse Allison, who must be used to all sorts of histrionics, scrubs out a mug at the sink. I watch, amazed by her staid calmness.

I used to think that morticians had one of the most emotional jobs in the world. Now I'm beginning to understand that dying is far more difficult than being dead.

I tiptoe into Gerald's room, half-afraid of what I'll find. He is lying on his back, his hands folded across his blanket, his eyes closed. I assume he's sleeping, but then I spy the telltale tracks of wetness running from the corners of his eyes. If I didn't know the man, I might think he was weeping from physical pain. But I *do* know him, so I know these tears are the overflow from a pool of sorrow buried deep within his heart.

I creep to the chair beside the bed and sit down. He may not realize I'm nearby, and that's okay. If he needs me, I'll be here. If he doesn't need me, maybe I need to be here for my sake.

Sometimes I think Gerald is one of the godliest men I've ever had the privilege to know. I used to think him reserved, even aloof, but these tears demonstrate that he's a more sensitive man than I realized.

Gerald once told me that God is immutable—he never changes—and even though he possesses emotions, he is not driven by them as humans are. In his steadfast constancy, God always hates what he hates and always loves what he loves.

Just as Gerald will always hate what rebellion has done to his relationship with Kirsten . . . even as he constantly loves his daughter. Kirsten may not understand that. I'm just beginning to understand it myself.

One thing I do know: I have failed. I tried to bring two people together, and I have accomplished nothing.

Despite my efforts to be quiet, the chair creaks when I curl up in it.

Gerald opens one eye and directs its beam at me. "Are you . . . all right?"

Why is he worried about *me*? "I don't know how to make things right," I confess. "I'm sorry, but I don't know how to reach Kirsten."

His hand inches across the covers and clasps mine. "I don't think . . . that's your job. She's responsible . . . for her own choices." He runs his tongue over his cracked lips. "I keep thinking . . . about Cain and Abel. Cain must have known he needed to offer a blood sacrifice . . . but he insisted on offering . . . plants. When God disapproved, Cain got mad enough . . . to murder his brother." Another tear rolls down that lined cheek and trickles into his ear. "Kirsten has always known . . . that God wants a repentant spirit. But she keeps . . . doing her own thing, offering up everything else."

I try to answer but can't find the words. My best friend is dying, and all I can think about is how deeply I have failed him.

"But God . . . didn't give up on Cain," Gerald continues, each word an effort. "Even after God . . . banished him from his home, he placed a mark on Cain . . . for protection. God never stopped loving Cain . . . and he'll never stop loving my girl. Don't give up on her, missy. Hold on . . . to your faith." He sighs and closes his eyes, retreating once again into that shallow doze that provides an escape from pain.

I fall back in my chair, letting him go. Even now, he looks for the best in people. Even now, his faith is stronger than mine. Yes, Kirsten might come around, but I don't see a change coming anytime soon.

I lower my head onto my folded arms because I don't want Gerald to awaken and see the discouragement in my eyes. I've tried so hard to bring those two together, and what have I accomplished? I've filled a dying man's days with strife. I've reminded him of past hurts and failures I'm sure he'd rather forget.

I should have learned the lesson from my mother—meddling always results in mayhem.

Nurse Allison unfolds her cot on Sunday night. She sends Mother and me to bed and tells us not to worry, but I can't help worrying now that I know the end is near. I withdraw into a fitful sleep and dream of chopsticks and flying bodies and angels that bend low to confer the mark of Cain upon my forehead.

I wake with the sun on Monday morning. I am trudging toward the coffeepot when I hear a clatter from Gerald's room. Adrenaline floods my bloodstream as I race forward, and when I arrive, I find Allison bent over Gerald, who is lying on the floor of his bathroom.

"You should have called me," she says, looping his arm around her strong shoulders. "I'll get you a bedpan."

As she puts him back to bed, I stand in the bathroom, the tiles cold beneath my bare feet. What in the world was he doing?

That's when I notice the small appliance on the floor. At first glance, I assume it's an electric toothbrush, but on closer examination I realize it's a battery-operated nose hair trimmer.

What on earth? I glance toward the bed, where one of Gerald's bare feet extends beyond the edge of the sheet.

That's when the truth hits me with the force of a blow. Gerald came in here to trim his nose hairs. Not because he is delirious or vain, but because he wanted to spare me the small detail of having to put Nair in his nostrils. Even now, he is trying to make things easier for me.

I press my hand over my mouth, imprisoning a sob, and rush out of the room.

Much to my surprise, Daniel shows up at ten and remains at Gerald's side for the next several hours. Mom and I take turns sitting at the foot of the bed, and while Gerald drifts in and out of consciousness, we read his favorite Scripture passages or flip through old photograph albums and describe family pictures as best we can.

"He can hear you," Allison keeps assuring us. "You may think he's far away, but it's only his body that's shutting down. His mind is still with us and still active."

Maybe not his mind but surely his soul.

When Gerald's breathing becomes so labored it's obvious the end is imminent, I step into the kitchen and dial Kirsten's cell phone. She doesn't answer, so I leave a voice mail. I can't believe she's angry enough to miss her father's final hours, so I continue to call throughout the afternoon. She drops Bugs off from school at the usual time, but she doesn't come in and she won't answer her phone.

At eight thirty, just after the sun has gone to bed, Mom brings Bugs and Clay in to say good-bye. I was a little worried about my sons witnessing a deathbed scene, but now I think this might be one of their most valuable life experiences. They have seen Gerald handle dying with the same grace and dignity with which he lived.

I watch in stunned amazement as Gerald's eyes flutter open at the sound of the boys' voices. He rests his hand on Bugs's cheek, then tells both boys to be good and mind their mother.

"Gerald?" Bugs stares at Gerald with wide blue eyes that seem to occupy most of his face. "Are you scared?"

Gerald snorts and flutters his fingers. "Not a bit. Only people who don't know . . . where they're going get scared before they set out . . . on *this* trip."

Bugs nods. "So you're goin' to heaven?"

"I'll see ya again," Gerald answers, a faint smile hovering about his lips. "And we'll go fishin' . . . in the Jordan River."

A good man is teaching future good men how life ends. Not with a whimper but with steadfast faith.

When all our good-byes have been said, Mom takes the boys to bed, Daniel goes home to sleep, and Allison unfolds her cot. She glances at her watch as she takes Gerald's pulse. "I'm going to snatch a wee catnap," she says, her voice low and soothing. "Call me if you need me, but it won't be long now. He should simply drift off."

Drift off—how many times have I used those words to describe sleep? After she lies down, I open my Bible and begin to read a psalm:

> *You keep track of all my sorrows.*
> *You have collected all my tears in your bottle.*
> *You have recorded each one in your book.*

"Jen?" The voice is so faint I think I'm imagining it. But Gerald is speaking, his hand lightly tapping the blanket over his chest.

I lean toward him. "You need something?"

"You should . . . get some rest."

"I can rest later." I smooth his blanket. "I'd rather stay with you."

"I'm good. Good . . . to go."

"I'll wait. You didn't leave me when I came to Fairlawn, so I'm not leaving you now. I'll stay right by your side, just like you've always been by mine."

The suggestion of a smile lifts a corner of his mouth. "You . . . have been . . ."

I strain to hear. "What?"

"Dearer than a daughter."

I press my hand over my lips as my throat closes with guilt. What have I done to this man? In trying to make his last weeks perfect, I have reintroduced him to old arguments and pain . . . yet here he is, trying to ease my grief.

"I'm so, so sorry," I say, the words tumbling over each other in an effort to escape my constricted throat. "I should never have tried to meddle in your relationship with Kirsten. I should have left things alone."

"You have given—" Gerald pauses to draw a quavering breath—

"exactly what we needed." He lifts his hand and gestures to the desk beside me; then his arm falls as if that simple movement required a supreme concentration of effort.

I make sure he's resting comfortably before examining the items on the desk. A calendar. A Bible. A box of tissues and a legal pad. On the legal pad, I see a folded sheet of lined paper marked by a single word: *Jen.*

I glance at Gerald, but his eyes are closed. If he's sleeping, I don't want to disturb him. I unfold the sheet and discover a letter, probably written last night while I slept.

Dearest Jen—

Forgive me for writing this, but talking seems to require more breath than I have these days. I want you to know that you did a good thing by inviting Kirsten to Fairlawn, and I'm grateful you were brave enough to take that step.

I want you to know that no matter what happens, I am at peace about that girl. Her mother and I dedicated her to the Lord right after she was born, and I believe God still has a plan for her. The story isn't over yet.

We were never supposed to have children, you see. In those days, men didn't want to know much about women's internal plumbing, but doctors told Evelyn we would never have kids. Evelyn suffered through three miscarriages before she got pregnant with Kirsten, and one day early on in that pregnancy she started bleeding. I took her to the hospital, and as I was driving, I heard the Spirit speak to me through the words of Proverbs 13:12. "Hope deferred makes the heart sick, but a dream fulfilled is a tree of life."

You know I'm not one for plucking verses out of the Bible willy-nilly, but I believe that verse was given to us as a promise. I told Evelyn that she was going to be okay, and this baby would be our tree of life.

The Lord kept his promise, and Kirsten was as healthy a baby as you'd ever want to see. A sweet little girl and the apple of our eyes, even after she decided to go her own way.

When Evelyn died, I thought all hope was lost; Kirsten would never come back to the Lord now that her mother was gone. For years after she left home I allowed myself to be discouraged whenever I thought about her.

But gradually I began to realize that God's promises have no expiration date. Kirsten is still our tree of life, and the Lord's still working on her. So I don't have to worry, and neither should you. All we have to do is pray and trust. Don't give up on my girl. Keep praying.

Thank you, my dear friend, for walking with me at the end of my journey. May the Lord bless you for your kindness and your love.

By the time I finish reading Gerald's letter, I am weeping so hard the words blur on the page. I reach across the blanket and take his hand, which has grown cool. I find myself breathing in the slow rhythm of his exhalations, and for several minutes I do nothing but sit and breathe in and out with him, until he exhales . . . and I wait for an inhalation that never comes.

I watch a glistening tear run from the corner of his eye to his cheek, to the base of his ear, to the pillowcase . . . and I realize he's gone.

I lower my face to the blanket and swallow a sob. A truly good man has departed the earth, and at this moment, I alone am bearing the loss.

Clay and Bugs are asleep, Mom is chuckling over a rerun on television, and at the Biddle House, the Southern Sassies have gathered for their weekly bridge club meeting. None of them know that Gerald is rejoicing in the presence of God.

A heavy quiet fills the room; even the steady tick of the clock on the dresser seems muffled by the reverberating silence. The hush is so thick, the atmosphere so changed, that I fully expect the nurse to wake and gasp in alarm.

But still she sleeps. I lift my head and look around the room, realizing that though I own this house, I have crossed this threshold no more than ten or eleven times. This will always be Gerald's space and the heart of our home. From this room he emerged each morning, adjusting his suspenders or his string tie, to carry the responsibility for Fairlawn and its clients. Legally, I have owned and operated the business for over two years, but Gerald actually carried the burden.

Now it rests on my shoulders, and I groan beneath the weight.

As my gaze falls to the book on the desk, my eyes light on another verse: "The Lord cares deeply when his loved ones die."

I close my eyes as my sinuses tingle with the onset of fresh tears. If God, who holds eternity in his grip, can grieve the death of a good man, then I can, too. Though I know Gerald is in heaven and I will see him again, I am keenly aware of his absence.

And smarting with disappointment. Why didn't God answer my prayers? Gerald may have resigned himself to waiting for God to work, but I was expecting a timely answer. After all, I didn't ask for a miracle. I didn't even ask for a physical healing. On a cosmic scale, my request was simple—one reconciliation, including a couple of *I'm sorry*s and maybe a whispered exchange of *I love you*s. I wanted Gerald to leave this life at peace with his loved ones, yet the person who should have been closest to him at death wasn't even around.

I press my hands over my face. Did I do something wrong? Did I not pray hard enough or long enough? Should I have kept my mouth shut and let Kirsten stay in Georgia? Or maybe I was right to do what I did, and all of this is *her* fault. . . .

I wipe away tears and look toward the window, where the filigreed curtain has been lit by the glow of a silver moon. God does not speak to me in the silence; no words magically appear on the wall or reverberate through my heart.

But then I consider Gerald's letter. "God's promises have no expiration date," he wrote, so I need to keep praying. And because Gerald loved Kirsten and I love Gerald, I need to love her, too.

I swallow hard as an unpleasant truth hits home. That prickly, confused, hardened woman isn't much different from me. We may have grown up in different circumstances, but we have both known disappointment and loss. She has hardened her heart toward Gerald, but how is that different from how I've been treating Daniel?

Because I've suffered loss, I've been afraid to get too close. So has Kirsten.

I raise my head and study Gerald's face, paler now that death is marking his features. I lift his right hand, cup it in my left, and run two fingers over his eyelids, closing them forever. "I will offer Kirsten a job," I whisper, "and be whatever she needs. I'll love her for you, G-man. And I'll keep praying.

"I promise."

An Emily Dickinson poem keeps drifting through my mind as Allison and I tidy up Gerald's room:

The bustle in a house
The morning after death
Is solemnest of industries
Enacted upon earth,—

The sweeping up the heart,
And putting love away
We shall not want to use again
Until eternity.

Daniel comes to the house to help me get Gerald on the stretcher; we carry him downstairs while Allison fills out the death certificate and Mom strips the bed.

When Gerald is lying on the embalming table, I cut off his worn pajamas and pull out the sprayer, testing the water temperature on my wrist. Daniel stands nearby, a silent witness, as I bathe Gerald's skin and shampoo his silver hair. I shave his face and throat, then smile when I glance inside the nose to be certain I will not have to apply a depilatory. If Gerald could have managed a bath and a shave today, I'm sure he would have spared me this effort, too.

But caring for his body is a labor of love.

At eleven o'clock I send Daniel home and check on Mom and my sons. The boys are asleep. Mom is sitting upright in bed, her eyes red and a tissue in her hand as she pretends to read. I give her a wavering smile, go downstairs, put on my apron and gloves, and begin the arterial embalming.

I'm glad the motions have become automatic, because none of this feels real. Though Gerald's body lies before me, I can almost feel his presence emanating from the stool on the other side of the table.

"Probe gently with the scalpel; find the artery. Good work. Now insert the arterial tube, steady. . . . You really have a knack for this, you know."

I don't believe in ghosts, but I do believe in souls. I also know that the body does not die the instant the heart stops beating. Individual cells can remain alive for several minutes after death, depending upon the external environment. Though my Bible tells me that to be absent from the body is to be present with the Lord, I'm not sure anyone can say exactly when a soul exits the body.

Though Gerald may be dancing in a heavenly dimension, the Lord is definitely with me. I can move and breathe and work without weeping, comforted by knowing that the same Spirit who lived in Gerald will enable me to complete this difficult task.

I finish my work at 2 a.m. I wrap the straps of the BackSaver X1000 Lift around Gerald, raise his body above the table, and head into the hallway to get the Preston Bronze, one of the many fine caskets we keep in storage.

When I enter the office, I see that someone has slipped an envelope beneath the door. I open it and discover a handwritten statement with three signatures: Gerald's, Daniel's, and Allison Crawford's.

Jen—

Don't put me in the Preston Bronze. Leticia Gansky's casket is out in the garage, and it'll suit me fine. Bury me in that, and no arguing.

I stare at the signed statement. Leticia's particleboard casket should have been taken to the dump; I had no idea Gerald saved it. The Preston Bronze is part of Gerald's prepaid package, but how like him to insist I keep the expensive casket and bury him in a particleboard shell. I'm tempted to refuse this request—if anyone deserves a decent resting vessel, he does—but how can I deny his wish when he's gone to the trouble of having it verified by two witnesses?

I go outside and find the cheap coffin, repaired and waiting under a tarp, exactly where Gerald said it would be.

As usual, Ryan swings by the house at daybreak to see if we have any new arrivals in the prep room. I meet him at the door, bleary-eyed and exhausted, and his smile fades when I tell him Gerald is waiting.

"I've already casketed him," I explain, tightening the belt of my robe after I close the front door. "I know that makes things harder for you, but I thought we might have people dropping by early."

"I'll be careful—" Ryan promises, his voice expressionless as he moves toward the prep room—"not to drip anything on the lining."

After I take a quick shower, I wake Clay and Bugs, give them the sad news, and sit with them while they adjust to their latest loss. They have said their farewells and they knew death was near, but both boys shed a few tears before I hug them and send them to my mother, who's waiting in the kitchen.

When I return to the prep room, Ryan is washing his hands and Gerald looks perfectly natural. His silver hair is combed back and trimmed, his silver brows are smooth, and neither his cheeks nor his lips are pink.

"I know how he hates pink lips," Ryan says, his voice wavering as he dries his hands on a paper towel. "I think that flesh-colored lip gloss does the trick."

I give Ryan a grateful smile. "He would be so pleased."

We stand by the side of the casket for a long moment, and only when I see movement from the corner of my eye do I realize that Ryan is sobbing. I slip my arm around his waist. "I understand," I whisper, not knowing what else to say. "I'm going to miss him, too."

"He never judged me." Ryan fans his face as if he could cool the sudden emotional surge. "A lot of people in this town don't have much use for me outside the salon, but Gerald saw me as a regular person. I think he understood—you know, the things I struggle with—but he never condemned me. He just kept urging me to follow Jesus."

My gaze drifts over Gerald's lined face, which has retained a gentle aspect even in death. "He was an encouragement to me, too. In so many ways." I adjust the knot on Gerald's tie. "He was so smart and talented, but all he wanted to do was serve. Not many people are willing to do that."

I give Ryan a hug and release him when I hear the sound of someone coming through the front door. "Oh, brother," I say, swiping a tear from my cheek. "I knew the word would start to spread, but I was hoping people would wait until midmorning before coming by."

I stiffen when I recognize the voice calling my name. Our early morning visitor is Kirsten Phillips.

By the time I reach the foyer, Kirsten is already halfway up the stairs. Mom is peering over the balcony railing, her eyes wide, and Kirsten halts midstep, a suspicious expression on her face.

I glance out the open door and see Katie in the front seat of the car, her backpack on her lap. Kirsten is wearing sweatpants and house slippers, which means she's come by to pick up Bugs for school.

She doesn't know.

"Kirsten." When she turns, I give her what I hope is my most compassionate look. "We tried to reach you yesterday afternoon. I called several times and left messages. I even called the Biddle House and left a message on that machine."

She glares down her nose at me. "What does he want now?"

"He's gone, Kirsten. He passed last night about nine thirty."

"No." Her tone is flat and firm. "That's impossible because I had my phone with me all day."

I bite my lip, not willing to argue. Some people react to bad news in unexpected ways, and in the short time I've known her, Kirsten has been anything but predictable.

"See?" Kirsten pulls her phone from her purse and pushes it toward me. "No messages."

The phone's screen is blank.

"That phone isn't powered on. Did you charge the battery?"

She regards me with a stony expression, marked only by a twitch of her eye.

I move slowly up the steps, drape my arm around her shoulders, and lead her back down to the landing. "My mother will take the kids to school," I say, telegraphing my intention to Mom, who's hovering at the top of the stairs, "while you spend some time with your dad."

As I lead her into the prep room, I'm grateful that the embalming is done and my equipment put away. Gerald rests in his coffin, looking as though he has just fallen asleep so his soul could fly straight into the throne room of heaven.

Kirsten may not have come in time to reconcile with her father, but at least she has come.

That has to count for something.

"Well, Dad, looks like I missed the boat again."

Kirsten's voice trembles in the stillness of the room as she stands beside the open casket and gazes at her dead father's face.

His lips, which formed so many words in her hearing, will not speak again. Death has silenced the voice that hounded her throughout adolescence and beyond.

Kirsten. She claps her hands over her ears as the sound of it echoes in her mind. *Why are you always hardening your heart?*

She closes her eyes against the battering memories and wills them to go away. Her father is dead, her mother, too, and they cannot influence her anymore. They cannot criticize; they cannot leave her feeling as though she will never measure up to their standards. . . .

What standards, Kirsten? What did we ask you to do?

"To be perfect," she hisses through clenched teeth. "To give up my dreams."

We asked you to obey. To obey us and God.

"Well, okay. Obeying the Almighty is a pretty tall order—don't you think? Not everyone can dot every i and cross every t. Not everyone wants to be a saint. Some people want normal lives."

We weren't perfect, and we never expected you to be. We only wanted you to love God. Everything else would have fallen into place.

"Where *you* wanted it to be."

Where God wanted you *to be.*

Kirsten opens her eyes and stares at her father's face, half-expecting his eyelids to flutter open so those brown eyes can sear her with an intensity from beyond the grave. But the lids remain closed and the lips stay curved in a gentle smile.

Except for the accusations of a guilty conscience, she is alone. Her father, the generational link that always stood between her and death, is gone. She is officially an orphan, the only living person sheltering Katie from the vast emptiness of an uncaring world.

She squares her shoulders beneath the heavy mantle of responsibility. She hasn't been the best mother—small wonder, considering her own confused childhood—but she needs to do better. She's seen distance in Katie's eyes far too many times, and she can't allow Katie to withdraw the way she did.

When it's her time to die, she doesn't want Katie to feel this awful sorrow.

"I didn't mean to stay away," she says, her voice echoing in the sterile room. "I would have come if I'd known the end was so close. I meant to come."

Only her pounding heart responds.

"I wanted to love you, Dad," she says, her voice cracking. "I wanted your approval more than anything."

But on your own terms.

Her eyes fill with tears. Of course on her own terms. How else could she be happy?

Kirsten grips the side of the casket, then covers her father's folded hands with her own. The skin is cold beneath her palm and as inflexible as marble. She'll find no warmth or forgiveness here.

Maybe she'll never find it anywhere.

I sit in Gerald's favorite rocker and wait for Kirsten. After about twenty minutes, she comes out of the house, closes the door, and stands on the porch, her gaze fixed on some point of the distant horizon.

I gently clear my throat. "I'm so sorry, Kirsten."

She closes her eyes. "It's not like we didn't know he was dying."

"Still . . . death is hard. And the loss of a parent is especially tough."

I expect her to brush me off and move down the steps, so I'm a little surprised when she walks over and sits in the chair next to me. "I didn't expect him to go so quickly."

"None of us did. In fact . . ." I rock in silence for a moment, then glance at her. "You know, I keep a five-year journal. I'm not always faithful, but I scribble a few thoughts for every day. And last February, I noticed something about your dad."

Kirsten grunts softly without looking at me. "So?"

"I noticed that he seemed really down in the dumps one day. When I wrote about it on the page for February 5, I saw that I'd written the exact same thing for the year before. Now I think I know why he was sad."

She chuffs softly. "Who are you, Sherlock Holmes?"

"February 5—that's your birthday, isn't it?"

Her eyes squinch tight and her lips compress into a thin line, as if she's determined to stop a rush of emotion. She stops rocking and I wait, but a full minute passes before her face relaxes and she begins rocking again.

"He called every year," Kirsten says, keeping her eyes closed. "I never answered, so he always ended up leaving a voice mail. He'd sing 'Happy Birthday,' every blasted note of that stupid song."

I want to say so many things—I want to chide her for not picking up, I want to explain that he loved her, and I want her to see that those calls were evidence of his faithfulness as a father. But I'm not going to. This time, I'm going to let Kirsten learn for herself.

"I never answered," she says again, her lashes batting as she opens her eyes and looks at me. "But every year, I always listened." She gulps hard as tears slip down her cheeks.

I say nothing until she sniffs and wipes her face with her fingertips; then I run my hand over the journal on my lap. "The other day I started this diary for you. I was going to keep a record of everyone who came to see him, but I didn't write more than a couple of paragraphs before—well, the end came real fast. A lot faster than anyone expected."

Kirsten shrugs. "I wouldn't have known any of those people, anyway."

"Maybe not. But if you stay here, you might get to know them."

She casts me a sharp look. "Why should I stay here?"

"You have someplace else to go?" When she doesn't answer, I shift to face her. "This is a nice town. The people are friendly, the cost of living is reasonable, and you can't beat the weather. Plus, Katie's settled in her new school and you have a job—"

Kirsten snorts. "Right. Like I plan to drive a hearse for the rest of my life."

"I thought you said you were in real estate sales." I wait until she looks at me before I continue. "I hate sales and would be thrilled to turn that part of the business over to someone who's actually good at it. I don't think there's really much difference between selling condos and selling cemetery plots. After all, they're both residences."

A flash of humor crosses her face as she studies the front lawn.

"Cute idea, but I'm not interested in this funeral home. Besides, I've already made arrangements to move on."

"Still—" My tattered voice breaks, but I press on, determined to be nice to this woman because Gerald loved her. "You can change your plans. The ladies at the Biddle House adore you and Katie, so you could stay there indefinitely."

"The ladies at the Biddle House also adore the UPS guy and the woman who brings the mail. They love anyone who'll stop and talk."

"Isn't that what community is all about?"

Kirsten exhales heavily through her nose. "I suppose you'll have the funeral tomorrow?"

"That's right. One o'clock, I think . . . if that's all right with you."

She glances at me. "Whatever is fine."

"Then one o'clock it is. That'll give people time to drive over after lunch."

We sit without speaking, the silence broken only by the steady creak of our rocking chairs. When Kirsten stops moving, I wait, expecting her to get up or say something, but she remains motionless.

And then I know what I have to say.

"I'm sorry." The words tumble out of my mouth. "I've been pretty hard on you over the last few weeks. I thought you didn't care about your dad . . . and I was wrong." I lean forward to examine her face. Tears have gathered in the corners of her eyes and are spilling from the ends of her lashes.

"Don't you see—" her chin wobbles as she blinks at me—"that people will never love me like they loved him?"

The statement catches me by surprise. "Why would you—?"

"All my life, all I've ever heard about my parents is how much people love them. Mom and Dad were so good, so spiritual, so almost perfect. How was I supposed to measure up to that? How could I ever make them proud?"

As I fumble for words, Kirsten waves me away and palms tears from her eyes. "Never mind. It's all water under the bridge now, isn't it?" She sniffs and frowns at the shimmer of wetness on her hand. "You wouldn't happen to have a tissue, would you?"

I take a small package from my pocket. "A tool of the trade," I say, handing it to her. "I try never to be caught without one."

She pulls a tissue from the package and blows her nose. "Thanks."

I catch her wrist and look directly into the wide eyes that are so much like Gerald's. "You are not your father, and you are already deeply loved. God loves you. Your father adored you. And this town will welcome you, if only you'll let us."

Kirsten narrows her eyes, regarding me with a speculative gaze, then yanks free of my grip and stands. "Tomorrow," she says, moving to the top of the steps. "One o'clock?"

I nod. "There's a viewing tonight, if you want to come."

"I saw him already. I'll come tomorrow."

As she walks toward her car, I sit in silence and hear my heart break. Kirsten is not ready to soften, but no amount of words from me is going to bring her to that point. Yet I can't forget that buried within her memories, like a hidden treasure, are all the wise words Gerald ever shared in her youth. She has heard his sermons and his prayers, she has watched him minister, and she has lived with his selfless example.

Gerald and Evelyn poured their lives and hearts into this woman, and I have to believe that their efforts were not in vain. I don't know what God has in store for Kirsten, but I know he is faithful and the story isn't finished.

One day, when she is ready, Kirsten will open her box of memories and sort through her rich inheritance. When she does, she will discover that her parents were selfless people who loved her with a genuine and sacrificial love.

That kind of love cannot touch a life without changing it.

The casseroles begin arriving at 10 a.m. Mom keeps busy running from the door to the kitchen, and soon the table is groaning under the weight of dishes ranging from sweet potato casserole to brown sugar pecan cake. Several of the Southern Sassies bring their Crock-Pots, each filled with an aromatic soup or stew, and our counters fill with more food than our family could eat in a month.

We share this bounty, of course, with those who come to offer their condolences and reminisce about what Gerald meant to them. He spent more than twenty years in Mt. Dora, and to many people he was the heart and soul of Fairlawn.

"Don't get me wrong," Ruby Masters explains. "Your uncle Ned was a fine funeral director, but he was more business oriented. After Gerald came, things began to take on a more personal touch. When he talked people through the arrangement of a funeral, you got the feeling he was doing a lot more than selling folks a slab and a service. He *listened* to them . . . and he comforted folks better than anyone I've ever met."

I sip from my coffee mug and feel a stab of memory, a fragment as sharp as a stiletto: Gerald explaining why he became an embalmer. "We show Jesus we love him by loving his people," he once told me. "I show Jesus I love him by performing a service nobody else around here wants to do."

Gerald loved people by taking care of the living *and* the dead. He tried to teach me how to do the same thing. Now, if only God will give me a portion of Gerald's wisdom.

At the funeral, I pull myself off the back wall and walk to the microphone, ready to offer the last eulogy. Gerald has already been praised by his pastor, many friends, and several relatives of former clients, but I know everyone is waiting to hear what I will say. Apart from Kirsten, I suppose I knew him better than anyone in this room.

I turn in the center aisle and look over the chapel, crowded with Gerald's friends and neighbors. Lydia sits with Mom, Clay, and Bugs in the front row, right beside Kirsten and Katie. Daniel sits in the second row, and his gaze catches and holds mine. Even from six feet away, I feel encouraged.

I give him a smile and lift my voice. "Gerald Huffman was everything a friend should be," I begin, "and the heart behind the Fairlawn Funeral Home. Many of you sitting here have been touched by his kindness, but no one has been more influenced—or more undeserving—than me. When my boys and I came to Mt. Dora two years ago, we thought we'd be heading back to Virginia after a few weeks, but Gerald helped me see that the Lord had other plans. Without Gerald, I would never have realized the potential of a career in mortuary ministry, and I would never have had the patience to go back to school. I am a mortician today because Gerald opened my eyes to the needs of others."

I take a slip of paper from my pocket. "This may seem unorthodox, but I thought this would be a fitting occasion to announce the winner of our slogan contest. We received many submissions, but one really sums up the purpose and guiding principle of the Fairlawn Funeral Home. Gerald liked this slogan, and I do, too: 'Because life is precious.'"

I wave the winning entry as the crowd responds with murmurs of agreement. "Because all life is precious," I conclude, "I'd like to continue the work that Gerald pursued here. So I'd like to thank you for coming and thank you for supporting us. I know Gerald would join me in saying God bless you all."

An after-hours quiet envelops Fairlawn when the last funeral guest has departed. Kirsten and Katie go back to the Biddle House, my mother takes Clay and Bugs to McDonald's for a snack, and Spike parks the hearse in the garage and slips away.

For the first time in two years, I am completely alone with my inheritance. I walk through the foyer, oddly aware of the sound of my heels against the tiled floor, and lean against the doorframe that opens into the chapel. Most of the flowers are gone, either taken to the cemetery or sent home with Kirsten, but the scent of roses still lingers on the air.

I've kept one bouquet at the house—a charming basket of daisies and yellow mums, decorated with two black-and-white checkered flags and a card that says, "Congratulations, you finished the race!" McLane and Jeff sent the bouquet. My sister must have chosen the design—she knows how cheesy floral expressions always make me smile. I set the basket on the table, then step back to admire it.

How time changes things! Two years ago I walked into this place desperately determined to rid myself of what I considered a pink monstrosity. The chapels looked spooky to me then. The house seemed like a broken-down relic that would be better off beneath a bulldozer. I remember climbing the staircase with Daniel and struggling to breathe the overheated air. The sight of dead flies on the windowsills and the thought of bodies in the basement nearly sent me running back to Virginia.

But now this place is home. The air is cool and sweet, the windows sparkle with sunlight, and my sons' shoes litter the upstairs landing. The chapels have become sanctuaries of warmth and respect, and entering the prep room subdues my heart with a reverent stillness.

That's been Gerald's gift to me. He has given me a new job and a new ministry. One that fills me with hope.

Someone dropped a program on the floor near the last row of seats. I pick it up and smooth a dog-eared corner.

> *Gerald Milburn Huffman*
> *January 4, 1935–May 26, 2008*
>
> *For the Lord delights in his people;*
> *he crowns the humble with victory.*
> *Let the faithful rejoice that he honors them.*
> *Let them sing for joy as they lie on their beds.*
> *—Psalm 149:4-5*

I chose the Scripture verse without asking for Gerald's input. Though he could have easily written out his own funeral program, I knew he wouldn't include anything that might draw praise to himself. But if anyone deserved a tribute, he did. I have never known a man who better exemplified what a humble servant of Christ should be.

I ought to stack a few chairs and bring in the vacuum, but I can't seem to find the energy. Grief has wrapped this place in a shroud every bit as restrictive as the Velcro bands I applied to Gerald's wrists to hold them in place.

I rest my hands on the back of a chair and hang my head as tears flow down my cheeks, as warm and cleansing as spring rain. I'm not sure how long I stand there, but after a moment I'm aware of the touch of a breeze on the back of my neck, followed by the citrusy scent of men's cologne.

Daniel.

His hand falls on my shoulder. "I thought I might find you alone," he says, his voice gentle. "How are you holding up? You looked a little tired at the funeral."

I swipe at my cheeks. "I look tired because I'm wearing only half my mascara."

His brows lower. "Mind explaining that one?"

"When I think I might cry during a service, I put mascara only on my upper lashes. It helps prevent smearing, but it makes me look half-asleep."

He pulls a folded handkerchief from his pocket and dabs at my cheek. "I'd offer you a shoulder to cry on, but it doesn't look like you need one."

How can he say that? I've never pretended to be Superwoman, never portrayed myself as one of those tough-as-nails women who doesn't need help from anyone.

Or have I?

In that instant, my scattered thoughts leap into line. I study Daniel's dear face and realize exactly what I've been resisting.

"I could use one." I take his hand. "And I'm sorry I've been so dense. When Gerald got sick, all I could think of was how I had to hold the line and remain strong. The men in my life are always leaving—my father, Thomas, Gerald—so I thought it was important to prove that I can run my life by myself."

Daniel smiles, his dark eyes creasing in an admiring expression. "I've never had any doubts about your ability, Jen. You've brought this place to life."

I shrug away the compliment. "I've acted like an idiot with you and I'm so sorry. I can understand why you've begun to see Jacqueline Prose—"

"*See* her?" His mouth twists in a barely discernible grimace. "I'm not dating her. No matter what the Biddle biddies say."

"Oh." I look away to digest this news. "If you're not seeing her . . ."

"I've been waiting," he says, slipping his fingers beneath my chin. He tips my head to meet his gaze, and again I catch the aroma of his cologne. "I know you've had your hands full, so I thought I'd wait and let things settle down. I'd wait forever. But I hope I won't have to."

My hand rises to clasp his. "Lately it's just been so . . . hard. My life has had so much change. I was hoping for a few months of stability."

"Stability is just another word for stagnation," Daniel says, the whisper of his breath caressing my cheek. "Life *is* change, and it's much easier when we face it together." He bends and presses his lips to mine.

I blink, stunned by a single thought—*finally!*—and then I am aware of the softness of his mouth, the slight scratch of his afternoon stubble, and a nearly overwhelming urge to giggle like a schoolgirl. The urge vanishes, however, when his arms draw me closer and I feel the power in his embrace. I've always known about Daniel's intelligence and goodness. Now I'm ready to learn about his strength.

Four hours after Gerald's funeral—which, Ruby Masters assures me, was so dignified and beautiful that no one in Mt. Dora will ever think again about using a mortuary in Eustis or Tavares—Daniel calls a meeting in his office for the reading of the will. I find myself sitting at a conference table across from Kirsten. A young man in a business suit sits with her. Though he looks vaguely familiar, I'm not sure I've ever met him.

"As you may have heard, Gerald left a will," Daniel says, removing a document from an envelope, "and he appointed me to be the executor. As executor, it's my job to see that any debts are paid and the remaining proceeds of his estate are distributed as he wished."

I glance at Kirsten, who has refused to meet my gaze since entering the room. *What could I have done to offend her this time?*

Daniel clears his throat and begins to read. "'I, Gerald Huffman, being of sound mind and body, do declare that this is my will. First, I revoke all wills and codicils that I have previously made. Second, I have one child now living, whose name is Kirsten Huffman Phillips. Third, I make the following bequest of personal property: I give all my personal possessions to Jennifer Graham, certain that she will be a good steward of the few items with which I've been entrusted.'"

Across the table, Kirsten straightens her spine. "That doesn't include the funeral home, does it?"

"No," Daniel says. "It doesn't." He continues to read. "'Fourth, to my daughter, Kirsten Huffman Phillips, I give the contents of my checking account at the First National Bank of Mt. Dora.'"

Kirsten lifts her hand. "How much is that?"

"As of today—" Daniel consults a bank statement—"$2,030.18. But keep in mind that the proceeds will not be disbursed until after the estate has gone through probate and any outstanding debts are paid."

Kirsten bites the edge of her thumbnail and settles back in her chair.

"'Fifth,'" Daniel goes on, "'the balance of my savings account at the First National Bank of Mt. Dora is to be divided evenly among Katie Phillips, Clay Graham, and Bradley "Bugs" Graham, to be held in trust until said minors enroll in college, at which time the funds may be applied to tuition expenses.'" He lifts a brow. "The present amount is fifteen thousand, so this is at least a five-thousand-dollar contribution to each child's college fund."

He runs his hand over the rest of the will. "The remainder of the document pertains to my appointment as executor, provisions for the paying of debts and inheritance taxes, and the prompt handling of probate. The document is signed, witnessed, and dated April 12 of this year."

The frown line between Kirsten's brows deepens. "Wait. What about the business?"

Daniel lowers the document. "Excuse me?"

"He can't leave the funeral home to this woman—she's only an assistant. She's not even a relative."

I blink. "You thought—?"

"Ms. Phillips—" the corners of Daniel's mouth deepen into a smile—"your father has never owned Fairlawn. He was an employee of the mortuary."

Kirsten's complexion goes pale beneath her tan. "He didn't *what*?"

The young man next to her releases a brief grunt of surprise, then taps the table in front of me. "*You're* the owner of Fairlawn?"

I nod. "For the past two years."

He flashes a smile. "Pleased to meet you. I represent Aldridge Elms, the second-largest funeral home conglomerate in the United States, and we're actively acquiring new facilities. We've had our eye on your place for some time—"

"Not interested," I tell him, crossing my arms. "First, because I've heard about what usually happens when you big conglomerates take over—you rip off the people who have placed their trust in a funeral home. Second, I'm not interested because my family and I aren't going anywhere. We've put down roots in Mt. Dora."

"Let's get out of here, Ross." Kirsten stands, reaches over, and plucks the bank statement from the table.

Daniel smiles at me as Kirsten stalks out of the room. "I'm glad to hear about those roots."

I'm so distracted by Kirsten's huffy exit that his comment doesn't register. "What's that?"

"The roots you're putting down in Mt. Dora. And now that Gerald's gone, I was wondering if you might be interested in another pair of helping hands. I know the work can be hard, and it'd be nice to have someone to relieve that round-the-clock pressure."

"I think I'll be able to manage," I begin, "now that we have the X1000—"

"Jennifer," my mother says, "would you shut up for once?"

I gasp, startled by her brash comment until I catch the twinkle in Daniel's eye.

"I think," Mom says, "that I could find something to do outside."

"Maybe take the car for a wash," Daniel calls after her. "Take my car, if you like."

When she has gone and we are alone, I walk toward Daniel, sit on the table, and bend until my face is only inches from his.

"I might be interested in taking on some extra help," I tell him, crossing my legs, "but there's that pesky problem of the townspeople thinking we're in cahoots."

"No longer a concern," he says, standing. He grips the edge of the table and leans over me. "I think I've found a legal solution to that complication."

"And that is?"

"If you can't fight 'em, join 'em. Let's create a formal partnership and make it official. Then the biddies can cackle all they like . . . over a bowl of punch and a slice of wedding cake."

I'm about to make another quip about the cackling biddies, but I don't get a word out before Daniel pulls me into his arms and kisses every quip away.

I'd love to report that everything at Fairlawn has been sunshine and daisies since Daniel's proposal, but my conscience won't allow me to be less than completely honest. We miss Gerald something awful—his smile, his wisdom, and the creak of his rocking chair. But as May faded into June and June melted into July, our memories of him began to center more on the good times we shared than the sad. We will always have our memories, so he will live in our hearts until we meet him again in heaven.

Immediately after the reading of the will, Ross Alexander took his briefcase and went back to Atlanta, but I'm sure the loss of one prospect won't upset him for long. The death care industry is like any other—some folks are primarily preoccupied with profit, while others are mostly focused on people. As long as I'm around, Fairlawn will always be a mortuary more concerned with ministry than money. That's what Gerald would have wanted.

To my surprise, Kirsten and Katie have remained in Mt. Dora. When Kirsten's not driving the hearse, she has taken over our preneed sales, and I've been impressed by her manner and her results. She is practical without being pushy, and she can make a Preston Bronze sound like a late model Cadillac. She seems more relaxed these days, and I think her crusty exterior is beginning to soften. We'll just keep loving her until it crumbles.

I'm hoping that she'll get to know her father by remaining in Mt. Dora. People often talk about Gerald, and if she learns to see him as other people saw him, maybe she'll realize why people loved him so.

Maybe she'll learn that being a Christian isn't a matter of doing or not doing but *being* a person in love with Jesus.

Katie and Bugs continued to ride to school together, and Bob the gerbil now lives at the Biddle House apartment, along with a couple of his offspring. I hope Katie keeps them in their cage—wouldn't want one of the wily rodents to escape and scare one of the Southern Sassies into an early grave.

Bugs still likes Katie as a friend, but a new girl at school caught his eye. I think Lucy Byestrowski now owns three of his Matchbox cars.

Clay went to summer camp with a group of kids from church in early June. He came back with a deep tan and a new enthusiasm for spiritual things. A girl has entered his life, too, a sweet young lady who wears her hair in matching barrettes and sings in the church choir. Who knows where this will lead?

Mother has remained with us. As summer drew down like a suffocating blanket, she threatened to go back to Virginia, where at least the nights are cool. But there was the wedding to plan and the boys to look after, so she stayed in the guest room.

On Saturday, the fifth of July, I step out of a rented black limo and walk toward the gate at the Pine Forest Cemetery. I'm wearing a white suit that once belonged to Mother (something old), carrying a bouquet of calla lilies (something new), wobbling on a pair of Lydia's heels (something borrowed), and praying that my mascara doesn't melt and run into my eyes (something blue).

The cemetery's picket fence has been festooned with swags of roses and daisies, a white satin runner has been laid over the grassy path, and Brett Windsor and Clay have decorated the sprawling live oak canopies with toilet paper streamers.

I didn't approve that last bit of decoration, but I have to admit the effect is charming. I just hope the guys get all that paper out of the trees before we have our next thunderstorm.

My bridal party—Lydia as matron of honor, Bugs as ring bearer, and Katie as flower girl—parades before me as Charley Gansky plays "Here Comes the Bride" on his accordion. Leticia stands beside him, dabbing at her eyes with a tissue.

My groom waits just inside the gate with our minister, several of the Southern Sassies, Daniel's three brothers and their wives, and my mother. Mom balked when I told her we wanted to be married in the cemetery—she kept complaining that a graveyard was no place for a wedding, no matter what the bride's occupation. After all, she insisted, the people I wanted to include—Gerald, my niece Mia, Uncle Ned, and even Thomas—weren't really *there*.

"But their memorials are," I countered, "and I want to acknowledge their significance in my life. What's the point in having a memorial if no one ever looks at it?"

With no answer for that, Mom threw her hands up and went off to check her blood pressure.

My groom—tall, handsome, and blessed with an abundance of silver hair—has never looked better. His dark eyes twinkle above a warm and spontaneous smile as I approach; then he pulls me into his arms for an ad-libbed hug.

"Hey," the minister interrupts, "don't jump ahead of the program."

While our pastor reads the traditional prologue about marriage being a symbol of the union between Christ and his church, I look into Daniel's eyes and see everything I need in a husband and friend.

I was so frightened by the thought of being alone, and no wonder. I had barely begun to heal from the trauma of being divorced when Thomas died, leaving me as the only parent to two boys. And when Gerald was diagnosed, I feared losing the new life I had worked so hard to establish. Better to cut off my relationship with Daniel than come to depend upon it and lose it.

But love does not exist in a vacuum. It depends on others and it takes risks. Most of all, it exercises faith.

"Do you," the minister says to my groom, "Daniel Joseph Sladen, take this woman to be your lawfully wedded wife, to have and to hold from this day forward, for better or for worse, for richer or for poorer, in sickness and in health, to love and to cherish till death do you part?"

Daniel's smile is alive with affection and delight. "I do."

"Jennifer Elizabeth Graham, do you take this man to be your lawfully wedded husband, to have and to hold from this day forward, for better or for worse, for richer or for poorer, in sickness and in health, to love and to cherish, till death do you part?"

I look into Daniel's precious eyes and see myself reflected there . . . along with my hopes and dreams for my children, the future, and our new family. "I do."

The minister takes our hands and holds them between his own. "Forasmuch as Daniel and Jennifer have consented together and professed their desire before God and this company, and by the power vested in me by the State of Florida, I pronounce that they are man and wife. What God has joined together, let no man put asunder." He releases our hands and grins at us. "Daniel, you may kiss your bride."

And he does.

From far away I hear applause, raucous shouts of approval, and the sound of my mother's elated laughter, but the sensation I'm most aware of is the feel of Daniel's arms around me. How could I have ever thought I might want to stand alone?

When Daniel releases me, we join hands and face the crowd before running through a shower of birdseed toward the car. Just before sliding into the backseat of the rented Lincoln, I stop in my tracks.

"Almost forgot," I tell Daniel. I turn my back to the crowd, close my eyes, and toss my daisy bouquet over my shoulder. I hear several excited squeals and turn in time to see Kirsten catch my flowers by a dangling ribbon.

She peers at me, her eyes searching mine from beneath the brim of her chauffeur's cap.

"Congratulations," I call. "Now . . . are you going to stand there and gawk or drive us to the airport?"

She touches the brim of her cap in a snappy salute. "Be right there, Mrs. Sladen. My pleasure."

About the Author

Christy Award winner Angela Hunt writes books for readers who have learned to expect the unexpected. With over three million copies of her books sold worldwide, she is the best-selling author of *The Tale of Three Trees*, *The Note*, *Magdalene*, and more than 100 other titles.

She and her youth pastor husband make their home in Florida with mastiffs. One of their dogs was featured on *Live with Regis and Kelly* as the second-largest canine in America.

Readers may visit her Web site at www.angelahuntbooks.com.

Discussion Questions

1. Have you read the first two Fairlawn books, *Doesn't She Look Natural?* and *She Always Wore Red*? If so, how has Jennifer changed since the day she first heard that she'd inherited the Fairlawn Funeral Home?

2. What do you think the author intended as a theme in *She's in a Better Place*? Who's in a better place at the end of the story?

3. Do you have a favorite recurring character in these books? Who is it, and why do you like this character? Which character reminds you most of yourself?

4. Has reading books set in a funeral home changed your view of death or mortuaries in any way?

5. Leticia Gansky planned a fake funeral because she felt invisible and ignored. Have you ever felt this way? Have you found a "cure" for this condition?

6. If you had to write a slogan for a funeral home, what would you suggest?

7. Gerald thought of Kirsten as his prodigal daughter. Do you have a prodigal in your life? Did this story affect your feelings about that person?

8. Why do you think Kirsten rebelled in her teenage years? Could Gerald and Evelyn have prevented this?

9. What did you think of Jen's decision to hold her wedding in such an unusual setting?

10. What do you think Kirsten will do with the rest of her life?

11. Would you recommend this series to other readers? Why or why not?

12. Have you given any thought to what sort of funeral you would like? What would you request to make sure the experience was memorable? What sort of memorial message would you want shared with your guests?

Brown Sugar Pecan Cake

. . . one of Fairlawn's most comforting funeral foods

Ingredients for cake:

- 3 cups flour
- ½ teaspoon baking powder
- ¼ teaspoon salt
- 1 cup milk
- 1 teaspoon vanilla
- 3 sticks butter (1 ½ cups), softened, plus extra for greasing the pan
- 1 pound dark brown sugar
- ½ cup white sugar
- 5 eggs

Ingredients for glaze:

- 1 stick butter
- 1 cup light brown sugar
- ½ cup evaporated (not condensed) milk
- 4 cups sifted powdered sugar

1 teaspoon vanilla

½ cup chopped pecans

Preheat oven to 325 degrees. Grease and flour a ten-inch tube pan.

In a large mixing bowl, with a large fork, combine flour, baking powder, and salt. Set aside. In a smaller bowl, with a spoon, combine milk and vanilla; set aside.

With a mixer, beat butter at high speed until light and fluffy. Add brown sugar a little at a time, then add all of the white sugar, beating well after each addition. Add eggs one by one, beating well.

Reduce mixer speed to low and add half of the dry flour mixture and then half of the milk mixture. Add the rest of the flour and the remaining milk in the same way. Immediately scrape the batter into the tube pan and bake until the cake is brown at the edge, springs back when touched at the center, and a wooden skewer inserted into the center comes out clean—about seventy minutes.

Remove the pan from the oven and leave it on a wire rack for up to a half hour. Loosen the cake from the pan with a knife and turn it onto the wire rack, then leave it to cool completely. After cooling, glaze with caramel glaze.

To make glaze: in a large saucepan, place butter and brown sugar over medium heat. Stir until the butter melts and blends with the brown sugar into a smooth sauce, two to three minutes.

Add milk and let the icing come to a gentle boil. Stir well, remove from heat, and add powdered sugar and vanilla. Beat well with a mixer, whisk, or spoon until the glaze thickens and loses a little of its shine, one or two minutes. Add chopped pecans and stir until coated. Use immediately, or glaze will harden. Pour over the top of the cake and let it drizzle down the sides.

References

No novelist writes alone, and I owe a debt of gratitude to the following people and sources:

Halpern, Ashlea. "Merchants of Death." *Detroit Metro Times*, December 6, 2006.

Harris, Mark. 2007. *Grave Matters: A Journey Through the Modern Funeral Industry*. New York: Scribner.

Laderman, Gary. 2003. *Rest in Peace*. New York: Oxford University Press.

Stair, Nancy L. 2002. *Choosing a Career in Mortuary Science and the Funeral Industry*. New York: The Rosen Publishing Group, Inc.

A special thanks to Randy Alcorn, whose book *Heaven* (Tyndale House, 2004) turned my thoughts toward things eternal; Stephanie Grace Whitson, who taught me about defensive flashlight techniques; Brandilyn Collins and Robin Gunn, both of whom gave me great lines for Joella to utter; and my excellent editors Karen Watson, Becky Nesbitt, and Lorie Popp.

One final note: Mt. Dora is a real city in Lake County, Florida. If you have an opportunity to visit that charming town, you will discover that many of the buildings, landmarks, and streets described in this novel actually exist . . . but not the Fairlawn Funeral Home. To visit that establishment, you will have to rely on your imagination.

Other Novels by

Angela Hunt

Contemporary

Doesn't She Look Natural?
She Always Wore Red
She's in a Better Place
The Face
Uncharted
The Elevator
The Novelist
A Time to Mend
Unspoken
The Truth Teller
The Awakening
The Debt
The Canopy
The Pearl
The Justice
The Note
The Immortal

Historical

The Nativity Story
Magdalene
The Shadow Women
The Silver Sword
The Golden Cross
The Velvet Shadow
The Emerald Isle
Dreamers
Brothers
Journey

For a complete listing,
visit www.angelahuntbooks.com

CP0158